KISSING TJ

At the Morning Glory, TJ accompanied her up the stairs and waited while she fumbled through her purse to find her house keys. She thought about inviting him in for a drink but couldn't remember if she had any wine or beer. When she finally found the keys, he took them from her hand. He let out a breath, as if he'd been contemplating something, and a cloud of condensation formed in the air like smoke puffs.

Then he bent down and kissed her, gently pressing her back against the door. It was a bit of a shock, almost surreal. She was kissing TJ Garner.

He went slow at first, testing the waters. But as she arched into him, he took the kiss deeper, licking into her mouth, sliding his hands down her sides, and pulling her closer until she felt more than just his lips and tongue. The man was no novice. He made her want to lose her clothes—and her inhibitions . . .

Books by Stacy Finz

The Nugget Series
GOING HOME
FINDING HOPE
SECOND CHANCES
STARTING OVER
GETTING LUCKY
BORROWING TROUBLE
HEATING UP
RIDING HIGH
FALLING HARD
HOPE FOR CHRISTMAS

The Garner Brothers
NEED YOU
WANT YOU

Collections
THE MOST WONDERFUL TIME
(with Fern Michaels, Shirlee McCoy, and Sarah Title)

Published by Kensington Publishing Corporation

Want You

STACY FINZ

ZEBRA BOOKS
KENSINGTON PUBLISHING CORP.
http://www.kensingtonbooks.com

ZEBRA BOOKS are published by

Kensington Publishing Corp.
119 West 40th Street
New York, NY 10018

All Kensington titles, imprints, and distributed lines are available at special quantity discounts for bulk purchases for sales promotion, premiums, fund-raising, educational, or institutional use.

Special book excerpts or customized printings can also be created to fit specific needs. For details, write or phone the office of the Kensington Sales Manager: Attn.: Sales Department. Kensington Publishing Corp., 119 West 40th Street, New York, NY 10018. Phone: 1-800-221-2647.

Zebra and the Z logo Reg. U.S. Pat. & TM Off.

First Printing: March 2018
ISBN-13: 978-1-4201-4192-4
ISBN-10: 1-4201-4192-9

eISBN-13: 978-1-4201-4193-1
eISBN-10: 1-4201-4193-7

10 9 8 7 6 5 4 3 2 1

Printed in the United States of America

To Rebecca Hunter. There are no words.

ACKNOWLEDGMENTS

An enormous thank you to everyone involved in the making of this book, and to my family, who puts up with me. A special shout out to Wendy Miller, who kept me on course.

Chapter One

TJ Garner looked at the stack of time cards on his desk and gave them the finger. It was nine in the morning, he was bleary-eyed from doing paperwork the night before, and right now he'd sell his soul for a doughnut. Hell, he'd settle for a cheese Danish. But that would require him to leave the office and walk a block to the Morning Glory Diner when he was up to his ass in work.

In two hours, he had to make payroll, a chore that had been put on the back burner because he was too busy putting out fires. A website that continued to crash, tour guides who were no-shows, and a new retail operation that couldn't seem to achieve liftoff.

That was the irony of his life; he ran Garner Adventure, his family's extreme-sports tour company, but never went outside. He'd taken over as CEO from his dad five years ago so he and his three brothers could start running the business and his parents, who'd founded the company in the 1970s, could semiretire. This wasn't exactly the life he had envisioned all those years ago when he'd been trying out for the U.S. Olympic team.

The phone beeped with a call from the front desk. "Hey, Darcy, what's up?"

"We've got a situation."

When didn't they? "What's it this time?"

"One of the members of Win's mountain biking tour took a tumble into a thirty-foot ravine on Glory Mountain."

Damn. "Is he okay?"

"They're trying to get him out, but he may have broken his collarbone."

Ah, Jesus. "Win called 9-1-1, right?" TJ's oldest brother, Colt, was Glory Junction's police chief. He was clutch in a disaster. Win, his youngest brother, not so much.

"Yes. But the cyclist is a lawyer."

Not good. "Is he threatening to sue?" He reached for his cell phone to check for texts from Win, hoping that by now he had everything under control and TJ could go back to the exciting world of payroll. But there was nothing.

"Yep," Darcy replied.

He let out a sigh. "All right, I'll go up there to see what I can do."

"That might be good," Darcy said and signed off.

He grabbed his down jacket and gloves, texted Win for his GPS coordinates, and loaded his bike into the back of his Range Rover.

"Hello, friend," he said, gripping the handlebars. "It's been a while." And now he was talking to inanimate objects. Boy, did he need a vacation.

Halfway to Glory Mountain, his phone pinged with a text. It was Win with his latitude and longitude. He tried to call him for an update, but boy wonder wasn't answering, so he sent an emoji of a phone and texted, Call me, hose bag.

Two minutes later, he got No can do.

Things must be pretty bad if Win couldn't talk. But who knows, he could've been superbusy updating his Tinder account.

TJ shot off another one. Accessible by vehicle?

Y was the only reply, which TJ took for a yes.

He turned on his GPS and let it lead the way. Upon reaching his destination, he shook his head. *WTF, Win, you couldn't have just told me it was the trailhead?* He parked in a clearing by a large pine tree next to his eldest brother's police cruiser. A fire truck and an ambulance sat closer to the edge of the cliff, where a crowd of cyclists peered down at the gorge below.

TJ got out of his truck and Colt, who was huddled with the fire chief at the skirt of the mountain, waved him over.

"Where is he?"

Colt and the chief both pointed over the ledge. TJ moved closer and looked down, where a blue porta-potty lay on its side, wedged between two trees, the plastic door smashed to hell.

"Ah, jeez." TJ scrubbed his hand over his face. "Don't tell me."

"Yep," Colt said and perched over the edge for a closer look.

"Dude." Win came over from where he was standing with the crowd, holding his phone in the air. "He's threatening to own us by tomorrow."

TJ blew out a breath. The morning had just jumped five points on the Richter scale of suck. "I thought he wiped out on his bike." At least that was what he'd assumed. "And Darcy said he fell thirty feet down." By his estimation, it was no more than twelve.

"I don't know where she got that," Colt said. "But he's all yours."

TJ crouched in the dirt to get a better visual. "He's still down there?"

"Yep. Inside the john. We can all say a prayer of thanks that the thing was empty."

TJ got up and looked at Win. "How did this happen?"

"I have no idea. He went off to take a leak before we started the ride and the next thing I knew, the porta-potty was rolling down the mountain."

The fire chief picked a piece of yellow Danger tape off the ground near where the porta-potty once sat and waved it at them. TJ and Colt exchanged glances.

"Now why on earth would someone use something that's been red-tagged?" The chief kicked the dirt where part of the mountainside had crumbled.

It was early February and they'd already gotten a truck-load of snow, which was normal for California's Sierra Nevada. But after five years of punishing drought and a spate of wildfires, they were experiencing mudslides and erosion. In Malibu, five hundred miles away, houses slid into the ocean. Here, it was porta-potties into ravines.

TJ watched the firefighters make their way down the craggy mountainside with a stretcher and a brace. "His collarbone is busted?"

"I doubt it." Colt rolled his eyes. "He's been screaming at Win on his phone for the last twenty minutes about how he's going to sue us fifty ways from Sunday. Either he has a high threshold for pain or he's full of crap."

"Really? Toilet jokes?" TJ shook his head. "Why would anyone leave an empty porta-potty on an eroded mountain-side?" The trailhead was maintained by the county.

"I suspect it wasn't eroded when they left it; then they discovered it was a hazard after the last storm and red-tagged it. They were probably just waiting for the sanitation company to pick it up." Colt toed a mound of snow that had turned to slush. "Until a couple of days ago, the road to the park was impassable."

TJ turned to Win. "What's his name?"

"Stanley Royce."

He began to hike down the same trail the firefighters had used, trying to avoid patches of ice and snow.

"What are you doing?" the fire chief called.

"I want to talk to him, make sure he's okay." This was what he did now, fix problems. Fifteen years ago, he'd had different plans, ones that involved whooshing down a pristine, snow-covered mountain, not following the trail of a fallen porta-potty. Thank God it was empty.

"Let my guys handle it, TJ."

"Nah," Colt said and stifled a laugh. "You should absolutely go down there. Work your magic, little brother. I'll go ahead and stay up here. Just whistle if you need police assistance."

TJ flipped his brother the bird and continued to make his way down the hill. Someone had to deal with this and Colt probably wasn't the right guy for the job. Even though he owned an equal share of Garner Adventure and was their go-to guy in an emergency, Colt wasn't what you would call a diplomat. Josh, two years younger than TJ, was a little more tactful than Colt but had physical therapy this morning. And Win . . . well, if their client had been a woman, their baby brother would've been their guy.

By the time TJ made it to the porta-potty, the firefighters had already managed to get Stanley on a stretcher and were checking his vitals. Someone needed to zip Stan's fly.

"Mr. Royce"—TJ stood to the side so as not to get in the way—"TJ Garner. You okay?" *Yeah, stupid question.*

"It took you people long enough to get here. I could be dead right now."

"We're doing everything we can, sir." TJ sat on the ground while Shane, one of the firefighters and a buddy from high school, checked Royce for fractures, cuts, and bruises. "Anyone you want me to call, Mr. Royce?"

Stanley whipped his head around and shot TJ a dirty

look. At least his neck was okay. "What kind of operation are you people running here?"

TJ examined the overturned outhouse, which still had large pieces of yellow tape stuck to it, and was tempted to say an operation where 99.9 percent of their clients were smart enough not to use a portable john with the word *danger* posted all over it. In the end, he figured Stanley had been humiliated enough without TJ telling him he was a moron.

"Hang tight, Mr. Royce. I know it's . . . uh . . . uncomfortable." *Sometimes bad things happen to good people?* There really were no words for this sort of thing. "Whatever we can do—"

"Oh, you'll do plenty. When I'm through with you people you won't have a pot to piss in." *Interesting choice of words given the situation,* TJ thought to himself.

"How's your collarbone?" It wasn't swollen, which was a good sign. And by the way Shane and the other firefighter were jostling him around, they probably didn't think it was broken.

"I'm in agony," he said. "I may have spinal injuries."

Shane gave an imperceptible shake of his head. Stan was milking this for all it was worth. TJ looked up at Colt, still standing at the top of the embankment, giving him a big, thumbs-up sign. In return, and out of Royce's line of vision, TJ made a gun with his fingers and pretended to shoot himself in the head.

"We're going to get you some excellent medical care, sir."

"Here? I doubt it. I'll be using my own physicians." Royce kept yelling about how they were all idiots and how he was going to die from norovirus.

TJ got a text from Colt. A smiley face emoji and **Keep up the good work.**

He fired back, **Not helping, asshole,** and slid his phone into his jacket pocket.

Usually, he was very adept at finessing disgruntled clients—not that they had many—but Stanley continued to berate TJ, Garner Adventure, the firefighters, and anyone else he could think of.

TJ threw out, "How about I reserve you a suite at the Four Seasons?" Maybe a night in a luxury hotel would calm Royce down.

"You think you can buy me off with a hotel room?" Stanley barked. "Ha. That's just the beginning of what you'll get me."

"So, I'll take that as a yes." TJ tried to sound conciliatory.

Stan continued to make threats and TJ figured he may as well be productive rather than sit around listening to Royce bitch and moan. So he climbed back up the mountain and started making arrangements, leaving the firefighters to finish dealing with Stan.

Win pulled TJ aside. "Is he okay?"

"According to him, he's dying from norovirus as we speak."

Win shook his head. "He couldn't have just gone behind a freaking tree?"

TJ shrugged and glanced at the members of Win's group, many of whom were taking pictures of Stanley on the stretcher with their cell phones. "Why don't you get the ride started? No reason to ruin the tour."

"Sure, but is he still going to sue us?"

"He says he is, but who knows?" It's not like the guy had a legal leg to stand on, but if he was really an attorney, he could tie them up in court long enough to cost GA a pretty penny. "For now, let's just focus on getting him to a doctor."

Over the next ten minutes, TJ made calls, including to the Four Seasons for a reservation.

"Hey, TJ." Shane came up alongside him. "Royce doesn't appear to have any significant injuries. But we're taking him to Sierra General just in case."

That was good because TJ wanted a full medical work-up. Garner Adventure was all about safety and having its clients leave in the same shape they came. "I appreciate that, Shane. Someone will meet him at the hospital to take him to the hotel after his checkup. I'll get his bike."

"All right," Shane said and grinned. People would be talking about this for weeks to come. That's the way it was in a small town.

Colt wandered over and TJ said, "Don't you have anything better to do?"

"Slow crime day." Colt's mouth tipped up because, as usual, he was full of it. Glory Junction might not be San Francisco or Los Angeles, but there was plenty to keep him busy. "He's got nothing to sue over. By tomorrow he'll be apologizing for ignoring the Danger tape."

TJ hoped so because he had enough to deal with, including GA's new retail division, his brainchild despite resistance from his three brothers. Selling adventure clothes wasn't exactly in their wheelhouse, but Colt's fiancée was a world-famous fashion designer who was doing a sports line specially for GA. And Josh's wife owned Glorious Gifts on Main Street and had a ton of retail experience. And Win . . . if he wore the clothes, women would line up to buy them for their husbands or boyfriends. With those kinds of resources, he figured they should diversify, even if it was a calculated risk. And if it failed . . . he'd have a lot of explaining to do.

"At least it's a nice day," TJ said. Even though it was forty degrees out, the sun had slipped past the clouds and beamed through the canopy of branches. With all the snow they'd gotten—always a boon for business—it was nice to have a break from it.

The area was an adventurer's paradise, so even when the snowpack was low, there were rocks to climb, rivers to raft, lakes to kayak, mountains to hike, and acres of unparalleled trails to ride. People from all over the world flocked to the small town to get their extreme sports on.

"It is that," Colt said, looking up at the sky.

TJ glanced over at his truck and considered pulling out his bike. He'd already missed the payroll deadline. Sorely tempted as he was, responsibility won out as it always did these days. He'd left his skis and the dreams that went with them on these slopes a long time ago. Better to move forward because he sure as hell couldn't go back.

The next morning, Darcy called in sick and texted TJ that she'd already put in a doughnut order at the Morning Glory Diner. Because he was the first one in, picking them up for the meeting would now fall to him. His family's love of doughnuts was epic. Sometimes he thought it was the only reason they came to the meetings.

At least he'd missed the breakfast rush at the diner. The tables were mostly empty except for the back, where Deb Bennett was hunched over a sheet of paper. He usually tried to avoid her. But in a town this small and with her being best friends with his sister-in-law Hannah, it was near impossible; Deb was everywhere he was.

The thing was, he was head over heels for her and probably had been since the beginning of time. Or when her parents had first started cleaning Garner Adventure's offices twenty years ago. But Deb had chosen Win. The two had been inseparable since the ninth grade, and while they were split up now, it was widely understood that was temporary and that they would eventually wind up together. That was why he stayed away.

But today, curiosity won out over good sense.

He strolled over to catch a glimpse of what Deb was looking at so intently.

"Not my shift," she said without glancing up. "Talk to Ricki."

"What're you working on?"

She lifted her head, big brown eyes taking him in and a spot of pink in her cheeks. And he felt that familiar ache.

"Oh, hey, I didn't know it was you."

He pointed at what he could now see was a spreadsheet. "What've you got there?"

"My screwed-up life." Flustered, she gathered up the paper and shoved it in her purse.

"Why's it screwed up?"

"I just have a lot of bills," she said and looked away.

Against his better judgment, he grabbed a chair at her table. "Want me to take a look at it?"

"Uh-uh. It's embarrassing."

His eyes locked on hers. "Nah, come on."

She shook her head. "It's just . . . someone like you wouldn't understand."

"Someone like me?" he repeated. They hardly talked anymore, and when they did it was about how many inches of snow Royal Slope got or which kayak was better for racing. So what did she know about him?

Deb let out a breath, blowing a strand of dark hair out of her eyes. "Someone who's Mr. Responsible. Someone who has it together and looks down his nose at us mere mortals."

Way to make him sound like he had an iron rod up his ass. A guy could have his finances together and still not be judgmental. She sounded like his brothers.

"Come on, Deb, when have I ever looked down my nose at anyone?" He leaned across the table and pointed at her bag. "You do know what I do for a living, right? I could probably help you."

"No, thanks."

"Your choice." He got up and focused his attention on the counter to see if his doughnuts were ready.

Felix, the owner, waved him over and started filling a white bakery box with crullers.

"If you change your mind, you know where to find me," he said, got his box, and paid at the cash register, sneaking one last look at Deb, who was digging in her purse and didn't seem to notice that he'd walked away.

As he left the diner, he wondered for the millionth time why he even bothered.

Chapter Two

Deb pulled the spreadsheet back out of her purse the moment TJ left. Her shift started in fifteen minutes and she still hadn't figured out how she was going to pay for a new car transmission and at the same time make all her bills and next month's rent. She had no savings and was one paycheck away from being homeless. At least her heap of a car could second as shelter.

Felix leased her the one-bedroom apartment above the diner. It was the size of a garage, perpetually smelled like french fries, and had a view of a Dumpster. Besides being all she could afford, there'd been a time when it had served its purpose—just a place to lay her head at night.

But in two weeks she was turning the big 3-0 and was finally taking stock of her life, which to the casual observer could be described as a derailed train. Or just a train to nowhere. Because while everyone else she knew spent adulthood focusing on things like careers, starting families, and buying real estate, she'd worked at a dead-end job, drowning in debt to help her parents tread water.

They'd worn their fingers to the bone to save a floundering janitorial company, only to wind up broke.

And though she gave them everything she could, it

wasn't enough. She couldn't get enough traction to make a difference. She'd attended the local community college but, instead of transferring to a four-year university, ended up waiting tables to keep a roof over all their heads. But now it was time to get serious—or about time. Last spring, she'd applied and been accepted to the University of Nevada, Reno, where she'd hoped to get a degree in community health sciences and specialize in kinesiology. The one true talent she had, one even she had confidence in, was athleticism. But after finding out the cost, she'd had to put the idea on hold until she figured out how to afford it.

Though it was nice of TJ to offer to help, having him sort through her messy finances would be the final mortification in her already loser life. It was bad enough that her parents used to clean the Garners' toilets. And, unlike her, TJ was the great American success story.

He'd gone to the prestigious Haas School of Business at UC Berkeley and had returned to their hometown to turn his parents' small enterprise into one of the top adventure companies in the western United States. He was smart, entrepreneurial, and ambitious. And once upon a time, he had been her everything. The boy she'd dreamed of someday marrying. And while she was prone to being impractical, she wasn't stupid. It hadn't taken her long to figure out that TJ was way above her station.

And he proved it every time he saw her: by walking in the opposite direction.

She focused on the spreadsheet and pondered her options. She could try to sell the car and buy a newer one. But who in their right mind would purchase a fourteen-year-old Honda Accord with more than two hundred thousand miles on the odometer and a slipping transmission? No one, that's who.

She could charge the repair if not for the fact that her

credit cards were maxed out and no legitimate bank in the world would lend to her, not even for a student loan. That ship had sailed along with her FICO scores years ago. Her only solution was to leave the car in its present condition until she could come up with cash. At least work was only a flight of stairs away from her home.

"Bennett," Felix bellowed. "You're up."

She glanced at the clock as she shoved the spreadsheet in her bag. Time to sling hash for the lunch crowd.

The week's snowfall had brought busloads of skiers to the mountains, which meant the restaurant would be busy. Until recently, the Morning Glory had mostly attracted locals. Tourists tended to eat their meals at the resorts. But more and more of them had discovered the fifties-style diner—complete with black-and-white-check floors and red-vinyl upholstery—with its down-home menu, kid-friendly atmosphere, and moderate prices. The restaurant's popularity had also grown with the population. Lots of well-heeled folks from the city were now buying or building weekend homes in Glory Junction.

It was great for tips, but still not enough to dig herself and her parents out of debt and properly support all of them.

The next hour passed in a blur. One of the servers had called in sick, leaving Deb half the restaurant to serve. Around one, Win and a couple of his buddies came in and grabbed a booth in her section.

"Ricki, will you take Win's table?"

Deb just wasn't up to seeing him today. Win ignored her half the time anyway. He was always friendly, generous with his smiles, and if he really wanted to throw her a bone, he'd generically compliment her: "*Looking good, Bennett.*" The attention he gave her was on par with what you would give your neighbor's Irish setter. Lately, instead of feeling hurt by his indifference, she was okay with it. This was disconcerting because he was supposed to be The One.

While TJ had been completely out of reach—captain of the varsity ski team, president of the student council, valedictorian, and an Olympic hopeful—Win, an underachiever like her, had seemed like a more realistic fit. They'd been hot and heavy in high school. Her first boyfriend. But when Win went off to college, their different paths killed the relationship. When he came back full time, they'd started up again only to break up a year later. Ever since then, it had been on and off so many times Deb had lost count. Nowadays it was off, even though everyone believed they were destined to be together.

Unfortunately, she'd also convinced herself that they were the perfect match for way too long. But not anymore. Now, he just felt like another debt on her books and a constant reminder of how much she'd settled in life.

Ricki grabbed four menus. "Take my table on ten." She hitched her head at a group of nice-looking men. "You're welcome."

They were up from the city. Deb could tell because they had that Financial District thing going on. Clean-shaven, expensive skiwear, and one of them was reading the *Wall Street Journal* on his iPad. Guys like them were usually good tippers.

"What can I get you?" Deb grabbed her order pad from the pocket of her apron.

One of the men brazenly looked her up and down. "What's good?" he asked, continuing to leer at her like she was a juicy piece of prime rib.

"Everything," she said, antsy to move on. She didn't like the vibe he was sending off.

"Well, that's not very helpful. Why don't you take a load

off and tell us about what you like best?" The one giving her the once-over scooted down on the bench to make room.

Ugh. Deb would've been better off waiting on Win's table after all.

She pasted on a smile. "Sorry, can't. See all these tables of people?" She waved her hand at the rest of the dining room. "They're waiting for me to take their orders."

"But we got you first." He patted the space next to him. "Come on, you can sit for a minute."

"Steve," one of the others said, his eyes imploring.

Yeah, Steve, bugger off. She held the gaze of Steve's friend. "You know what you want?"

"I'll take the tuna melt and a side of fries."

"To drink?"

"I'll stick with water."

She went around the table until she came back to Steve. "What'll it be?"

"I thought I made myself clear on what I want." This time, he rested his hand on her thigh.

The guy had to be kidding. It was the middle of the day, the place was packed with families, the restaurant could double for the freaking set of *Happy Days,* and Steve here wanted to play grab-ass with the waitress. Not wanting to make a scene, she inched enough to the left that his hand fell away.

She stared him down.

"I'll have the double cheeseburger and the steak fries," he finally said. "What are you doing after work?" he asked, flashing an unctuous smile that said, *I've got twenty-five roofies in my pocket.*

Nothing with you. "I'm busy." She started to walk away when she felt that hand on her leg again. She whirled around. "You don't want to do that."

"Why? You a master in Krav Maga?" He laughed and his hands inched higher.

"Come on, Steve," his buddy said, but Steve was too much of a dickwad to listen.

He was strong and he pulled her against the bench seat until the corner of it dug into her leg. "Just give me a chance. I'm a nice guy."

Her eyes dropped to where his hand still rested. "Nice guys don't put their grubby hands on a woman's thigh. Get it off. Now!" To punctuate her demand, she jabbed his arm hard with the sharp end of her pencil.

He yelped and quickly pulled his hand away, putting up his palms in a surrender motion. "All right, all right. Bitchy, aren't you?"

"You need to leave." Suddenly, the restaurant went silent, and Deb could feel the gaze of every diner on her back. Felix, always worried about his profit margin, would surely fire her, but she wasn't putting up with Steve's crap. No matter how bad she needed the money. "You heard me. Out!"

The guy who'd called Steve on his attitude started to slink out of the booth, his face stained bright red.

"Now wait a minute," Steve said. "You're overreacting. I was just being funny."

"Take your sense of humor out the door and don't come back or I'll file a sexual assault charge against you."

Steve started to raise a fuss, but his compadres were smart enough to take her threat seriously and managed to convince him of the wisdom of leaving. They sheepishly filed out of the diner while everyone watched. Everyone but Win, who was flailing his hands, telling a story, completely oblivious. All she could do was laugh to herself, finding it hard to believe this was the guy she'd set her sights on for over the last decade.

"You okay?" Felix came up beside her. When she nodded, he said, "You did good. You're a tough cookie, Bennett."

That surprised her. Everyone knew Felix was a stickler about the customer-always-being-right thing. Apparently, he set the limit at pervy customers groping his waitresses. "No big deal. I'd better get back to work." She started to walk away and then stopped. "Thanks, Felix."

"For what?"

"For not firing me." Lord knew she needed the job . . . and the apartment, such as it was.

"Hey, no one messes with my employees."

After the lunch service, she and Ricki divvied up the tips. Her cut was two hundred bucks, phenomenal for a Wednesday afternoon. People were probably trying to make up for creepy Steve, which helped restore her faith in the human race. Unfortunately, the haul wasn't going to get her out of her black hole. She grabbed her purse and walked to Sweet Stems to hang out with Foster, who she'd known since high school and would've been the love of her life if not for the fact that he played for the other team. So instead, he and Hannah were her besties.

When she got to the florist shop, he was in the middle of a consultation with two women. From the conversation, Deb deduced that the younger woman was getting married in the spring. Weddings and big floral arrangements for the resorts were Foster's bread and butter. She snooped around the shop to kill time, found a couple of porcelain figurines of a bride and groom, and posed them in a provocative position to see how long it would take Foster to notice.

He pulled the statues apart two minutes after the women left and shook his head.

"Aren't they for cakes? Why do you even have them in the store?"

"You'd be surprised at some of the centerpieces people want me to make. I work a lot with fake swans." He shuddered. "Scary."

"When I get married I want a ski theme." They'd been

playing this game since they were sixteen. Each one trying to outdo the other in absurdity. Foster wanted an all-you-can-eat crème brûlée bar.

"Which reminds me, what are we doing for your birthday?" he asked.

"Getting drunk and then setting my car on fire."

"I'll bring the gin and marshmallows." Foster pushed a green bin to his workstation and began tossing cut flower stems into the can. "I told you I'd lend you the money for the transmission."

"And I told you how much I appreciate it, but no, thanks."

Although Sweet Stems was killing it, Foster still owed a large chunk of change on the floral shop. Between that and the new cottage he'd recently purchased on the south side of town that needed updated electrical and plumbing, he wasn't doing much better than she was. Well, not exactly as bad. He had a career he loved and owned his own home, while she stood on her feet all day, serving the likes of Steve and his ilk. And the only thing she owned was a piece-of-crap automobile.

"What about Hannah? Would you let her lend you the money? Because I know she would."

"Nope. Then Josh would have to know and that would be weird."

"Why?" Foster wiped down the table and put his tools in neatly arranged compartments. "There's nothing wrong with needing a little help. Normally, that's what parents are for." But Foster knew Deb's weren't in a financial position to help her.

"I'd rather not have people up in my personal business. It's bad enough that TJ came in the diner while I was studying that list you told me to make and offered to help me figure it out." It was sufficiently embarrassing that he'd catch her staring at him like a starstruck teenager from time to time. The last thing she needed was him having a bird's-eye view of how little she'd accomplished in life. At least Win was just a regular guy whose apartment wasn't much better than hers.

"I don't know, Deb. It seems sort of stupid not to take his advice. He's a financial wiz. All due respect to Gray and Mary Garner, but it's TJ who grew that company. The guy's pretty savvy."

"I don't need someone savvy. My problems are simple. I don't make enough money. I hardly need him to tell me that."

"No, but he can play with the numbers, figure out what you should pay down first. Maybe he has some consolidation tricks."

She hopped up on the counter. "Why don't you counsel me? You own a thriving business."

Deb watched him pull a bucket of roses from the refrigerator and use a thorn stripper so he wouldn't get stuck.

"Here's my dirty little secret," Foster said. "I suck at business. I'm way too liberal with my spending." He glanced at the shelves stacked with high-end vases and fancy containers. "And I'm a terrible bookkeeper. But I'm twenty times more creative and more reliable than the competition and don't charge that much more. That's why I do well, not because I'm Richard Branson.

"You'd be better off taking advice from TJ," he continued. "He's a business genius. I mean, he got Delaney Scott, one of the biggest names in high fashion, to design adventure wear for his company when they didn't even have a retail line! And if he judges you a little, who cares? It's not like his opinion of you matters, even if he is the hottest single guy in Glory Junction."

It mattered more than she'd let on. The rest of their friends had enjoyed huge successes. Besides Foster, Hannah owned Glorious Gifts, a great house, and a car that ran. Two of her high-school buddies had made it to the Olympics and another one was a high-paid engineer for Google.

"I'll think about it," she said. "Want to take a break and grab a coffee at Tart Me Up?"

"I've got a big order I have to finish and deliver. And not to sound like a nag"—he gave her a hard look—"but you shouldn't be spending money on coffees at Tart Me Up."

He was right, of course.

"I should let you get back to work," she said and got down from the counter.

Foster walked her to the door. "Think about what you want to do for your birthday. Hannah and I will plan it." Which was Foster's way of saying they'd pay for it. She wished they wouldn't—she'd never been good at accepting gifts like that—but they were stubborn that way.

If nothing else, Deb had excellent friends.

"See you around," she said, and endured the cold on her way to the bank to deposit her tip money.

"Hi, Deb," Cheryl, the teller, greeted her. The thing about living in a small town was, everyone knew everyone.

She filled out a deposit slip and plunked her wad of cash on the counter. Cheryl straightened the bills and counted them, her long, acrylic nails tapping on the keyboard.

"You know you're overdrawn, right?"

"No." Deb leaned over the counter to get a look at the computer monitor.

Cheryl turned the screen so Deb could see better. "Two checks came in and your account had insufficient funds."

Great. This was going to cost her sixty bucks in overdraft fees, more than a quarter of her tips.

On her way home, she passed Hannah's gift shop, considered going in, and decided she didn't need to sprinkle downer dust on her best friend. When Deb reached the

Morning Glory, she climbed the stairs on the side of the building and went inside her apartment. Today, it smelled like a combination of onion rings and patty melts.

Her answering machine blinked with messages. The first one was from her mother, who asked if Deb could lend them money for a cord of firewood. There went the rest of her tips. It was cold this winter and she didn't want them to freeze.

During the recession, her parents' janitorial company had taken a big hit and never fully recovered. Then her father had injured his back falling off a ladder. Two years ago, they'd sold the company at a fraction of its worth. Dad went on disability and Mom got a job as a cashier at the local supermarket.

The next two calls were from collection agencies. One, an outstanding bill from an emergency room visit when Deb had come down with pneumonia last winter—she didn't have health insurance—and the other for a late payment on a credit card.

She plopped down on the sofa, a hand-me-down from Hannah's first marriage, and buried her face in the pillows. The University of Nevada catalog had somehow gotten wedged under the seat cushion and stared back at her mockingly.

Man, she needed a new life. The one she had was seriously broken. She pulled out the spreadsheet from her purse and studied it for the umpteenth time, looking for ways to trim the fat. The premium cable channels had been cut months ago and she'd already gotten the cheapest phone plan known to mankind. Short of turning off her utilities, she didn't know what else she could cancel.

She let out a long breath and, with desperation outweighing pride, reached for the phone and dialed. "For the record,

I'm not happy about making this call. You still willing to help me?"

"Sure." She could almost see TJ's told-you-so smile beaming through the phone. "Come over now if you want to."

No way was she going to GA. The whole Garner clan didn't need to know her situation. They were like a second family to her and she wanted to make them proud, not feel sorry for her.

"Want to come here instead?" The offer was out of her mouth before she thought to look around her apartment. There was a stack of dishes in the sink, mail scattered across the kitchen table, and a layer of dust as thick as the snow on the surrounding mountains. Besides, having him here would be a distraction. A big, sexy distraction.

There was a pause on the other end of the line. Then he finally said, "Let's get coffee."

She cringed, Foster's words coming back to haunt her. But what could she do, tell him she couldn't afford a measly cup of coffee? "Okay, but not at the Morning Glory." She'd seen enough of the diner for one day.

"We could go to Tart Me Up, Old Glory, or Starbucks."

"Tart Me Up," she said. Old Glory would be too loud, and at nearly four bucks a latte, she'd rather give her money to Rachel Johnson than Starbucks.

"Meet you there. Bring your spreadsheet and any other financial information you have."

Deb laughed to herself. Yes, she'd bring her whole portfolio, which would fit in her change purse.

It took her less than six minutes to get to the bakery on foot. She beat TJ, stripped off her layers, and grabbed them a small table near the back. Tart Me Up only sat about twelve comfortably. In the mornings, it was packed with patrons waiting in line for Rachel's mouthwatering pastries, croissants, breads, and breakfast sandwiches. Customers literally had to take a number. The crowds usually died down after lunchtime and started up again at five, when Rachel sold what was left in the bakery cases for half price.

TJ came in and acknowledged Deb with a nod. Then he went to the counter, where he proceeded to chat with the barista for five minutes. He looked good. Tall, broad, and successful. But unlike the well-to-do polish of douchebag Steve and his friends, TJ had the ruggedness of a man who hailed from these mountains.

"What do you want?" he called to her.

"A latte."

He brought the latte, a regular coffee, and a plate of biscotti to the table. When she handed him a five-dollar bill, he pushed it back at her.

"I can afford my own coffee, TJ."

He raised his brows, snapped one of the biscotti in half for himself, and slid the plate at her. "Let me see that spreadsheet."

She tugged it out of the bottom of her purse and tried to flatten it the best she could. He took it from her and stared at it for a few seconds.

"This your first time using Excel?" There was no mistaking the sarcasm in his voice.

"No," she lied. "I did it fast."

He glanced up. "What's the interest rates on these cards?"

Too embarrassed to admit ignorance, she didn't say anything, just took a bite of one of the cookies.

He looked up from the spreadsheet. "You have them with you?"

She pulled out her wallet and flipped it open. One glance at the rows of plastic and he let out a whistle. Then he got up, walked to the bakery counter, and returned a few minutes later with a scissor.

"What's that for?"

"Take a wild guess." His eyes gleamed, and for a minute, a burst of nostalgia washed over her. This was the playful way he used to be with her, before she'd hooked up with Win, before her life went to hell.

Deb made a protective circle around the wallet with her arms. "No way. It's not like I can use them anyway."

"Then it won't matter if I cut them up." He had the nerve to wink. "You can keep two. We'll choose the ones with the lowest interest rates. Definitely no department-store credit cards. They're the worst."

"I realize you're supposed to be a financial wizard, but I'm pretty sure cutting them up isn't going to magically pay what I owe on them," she said.

"Nope. But it'll keep you from getting into this predicament again." TJ took off his jacket and draped it over the back of his chair. Foster was right; TJ was unequivocally the hottest single guy in town. And the most unavailable . . . at least to her. "You got a pen?"

Trying to appear unaffected, she fumbled through her bag until she found a pencil from the diner and handed it to him. He did a few quick calculations with his phone and took notes in the margins of the spreadsheet.

"How much you take home a week?"

Hell no, she wasn't telling him that.

He glanced up at her and pierced her with those blue eyes of his. "Deb, I can't help you without having basic information."

She had a sudden flashback of a fifteen-year-old TJ talking to her father about the Nasdaq and how he was rounding out his portfolio with a certain tech stock. Her father had been mopping Garner Adventure's lobby at the time. Even at twelve, she'd felt a hot flush of humiliation creep up her neck and face.

"Deb?" His voice was impatient.

She thought about it for a few seconds, then warned him, "So help me, if you laugh, I'll put laxatives in your Morning Glory doughnuts," and reluctantly told him.

"That with tips or before?"

God, this was mortifying. "With, give or take some."

He jotted down the number and, to his credit, showed no facial expression whatsoever. Not shock, nor pity. Pure poker face. "You have any other income besides the diner?"

"You mean from my trust fund and angel investments?"

He didn't appear to find her attempt at humor funny, ignoring her question and pointing to the spreadsheet. "Then according to this, your expenses are roughly twice as much as your earnings."

That sounded about right, and she certainly didn't need him to tell her that. "Yes. Now, how do I fix it?"

"It's simple economics—you have to make more money."

But how? In Glory Junction, there weren't a lot of career options for someone like her. Residents of the resort town either owned their own businesses, provided professional services, or worked at one of the resorts for minimum wage. That was why she needed to go back to school.

"You can pick up hours at Garner Adventure," he said. "We're desperate for good guides."

"No offense, but I could make more taking extra shifts at the diner." Guide work was seasonal and the excursions were all-inclusive, meaning no tips.

She huffed out a breath; it was an impossible situation. It was above and beyond of TJ to take the time to help her, but even someone as smart as he couldn't pull money out of thin air.

"How far behind are you on your bills?" he asked, and she didn't answer, letting the silence speak for itself. "Some of your creditors might be willing to consolidate your debt. I could make some calls for you, see what your options are."

"Why? Why would you do that for me? Ever since high

school, you've been doing your best to avoid me at all costs." Deb had gotten the impression that she was a major annoyance to him. In all honesty, it had been easier that way. So long as he was absent from her everyday life, she couldn't regret choosing the other brother.

His eyes locked on her. "Some might say you've done the same." He leaned back in his chair as if to say, *touché*.

She didn't reply, not willing to confess the truth. She'd known the Garner family her whole life. Win might be fickle as the Sierra Nevada weather, but she understood him. Josh Garner was married to her best friend and Colt Garner was like a big brother. TJ, on the other hand, had always seemed to be so out of reach, so . . . flawless. And here he was, offering to get involved in the mess that was her life.

It was weird, especially because she never would've expected him to do anything that didn't revolve around Garner Adventure or professional advancement. There was absolutely nothing in it for him. Nothing at all.

"You really think it would make that much of a difference?" she asked, because from where she was sitting, it seemed like consolidation was a Band-Aid when what she needed was a tourniquet.

He reached across the table and wiped a biscotti crumb off her chin, the simple action feeling more intimate than it should've. "The way I see it, you don't have a lot of other choices. At least if we could get the payments down to something you could manage, it might save your credit. But the bottom line is, you have to figure out how to increase your income."

"The only skill I have other than waitressing is athleticism," she said and took the other half of the biscotti and washed it down with her latte. "But I'm not good enough to turn it into a profession, at least not one that will pay me a decent wage. I was thinking of going back to school and becoming a phys-ed teacher. But I still have to pay my bills, put a roof over my head, and fix my car."

"What's wrong with your car?"

"I need a new transmission. Mine is slipping."

"You sure you don't have a fluid leak?"

"Burl over at the Shell station checked. He says it's going."

"That sucks." He sipped his coffee, watching her over the rim of the mug. "My dad knows a guy who sells rebuilt ones for a fraction of what they go for. I can get you a deal."

She let out a sigh. "Thanks, but I'm putting that on hold for a while."

He nodded. "Whenever. Just let me know."

There he went, being helpful again.

"You okay, TJ? You're being so . . . considerate."

His lips kicked up in the corners. "Something wrong with that?"

She took a minute to examine him. Same gorgeous guy he'd always been. He had Win's eyes, Colt's cleft chin, and Josh's determination etched across his face. But there was something else there, that same indefinable character Deb remembered from their childhood. Empathy? Whatever it was, she thought it had disappeared as he'd morphed into a ruthless businessman. Or maybe it hadn't, but it was convenient to see him that way.

"Nope," she said. "I really appreciate your help, TJ."

He hitched his shoulders. "I'm afraid I haven't done much."

"Well, I'll take you up on your offer to help me with my creditors." She offered a wan smile. "It's a start, right?"

"Definitely. You want to save your credit. In the meantime, give me your cards. I'll take them back to the office and make some calls."

"You have time?" One thing she knew about Garner

Adventure was that they had more business than they had staff. Colt was always grousing about how they were calling him in to guide a tour when he already had a full-time job as police chief.

"I'll fit it in." He winked, and damned if she didn't feel a flutter in her chest and a gush of warmth. It was exactly what she didn't want to feel. Not from him anyway. Too reckless.

"Thank you," she said. "I'm not good at that kind of thing."

He leaned across the table and in a soft voice said, "Deb, you have to start thinking about changing your situation. Maybe you should talk to a career counselor."

"Sure." She let out a wry chuckle. "I can tell them how I want to turn recreation into a full-time profession."

"Why not? That's how Garner Adventure got its start." He flashed a grin that did crazy things to her insides.

"Are you telling me to open my own adventure tour company?"

"Nope." He rubbed that square jaw of his, and again she felt a zing. "I'm telling you to make your passion work for you. Hannah's done it, Foster's done it; you can do it too."

"I'll think about it." That's what the kinesiology degree had been all about; then her dad's back. . . . Life didn't always go as planned. She stood up and shrugged into her jacket, having taken up enough of his time.

He watched her while he drained the rest of his coffee. "That one of Delaney's?"

"Uh-huh. She gave it to me." She didn't want TJ to think she was so irresponsible that she'd drop four hundred bucks on a designer jacket, especially after he'd just offered to help with consolidating her debt.

"We're selling those same jackets, or at least trying to. I'm working on our online store."

"That's what I hear. They'll do well. I love mine." She flipped her hair from inside the collar.

He continued to watch her closely. "It looks great on you."

She stopped in midzip, wondering why Win's compliments had never sounded that sincere.

Chapter Three

Ah, hell, what had he gotten himself into? It was the spreadsheet, he told himself all the way back to the office. He hadn't realized how much Deb had been supporting her parents until he'd pored through her finances. Nearly half her paltry waitressing salary went to helping Sid and Geri pay their mortgage and incidentals. Family was everything and he respected her dedication to her parents, but it was too much for a person in her financial bracket to take on.

He wished someone would've told him. Win was in the best position to know but was too busy playing and having a good time to pay attention to anyone but himself.

TJ loved his brother. He really did. And most of the time, he even liked him. But it didn't take a particularly astute person to see that Win was emotionally stunted. He'd always lived in his own private Idaho, where life was a perpetual beach party full of women who threw themselves at him.

Everyone expected Win would eventually grow up. And when that day came, he would come to his senses about Deb and they'd live happily ever after. That's why TJ needed to stay away from her as much as possible. Except sometimes he couldn't help himself. Like this thing with her financial problems . . . He kept telling himself he was a money guy,

and it was what he would do for any of their circle of
friends. Only he didn't want to kiss his other friends or see
them naked, or do any number of other things that could
technically be classified as X-rated.

When he got to Garner Adventure, the button on the
phone at the reception desk flashed red. With Darcy out,
he was responsible for dealing with the messages. After
eating up an hour with Deb, it was another thing he didn't
have time for.

He went to his office, rang up Darcy, and looped her in
on the morning's meeting.

"Drink lots of liquids," he said, echoing his mother's
advice whenever one of them got sick, and ended the call.

"What are you, the staff doctor?" Colt wandered in wearing his police uniform.

"May as well be, because I'm everything else around
here."

Colt sat down on the sofa TJ had stolen from his dad's
office. Gray barely spent time at headquarters anymore,
preferring to work as a part-time guide. TJ could certainly
appreciate his dad's shift in priorities. Until recently, he
hadn't realized how tough it was for a Garner to be a desk
jockey.

"I can lead the speed-riding tour next weekend," Colt
said. Six guys from the city wanted to strap parachutes onto
their backs and ski and paraglide down the face of Glory
Mountain. Good times.

TJ had hoped Colt couldn't do it, providing him with an
excuse to lose his CEO title for the day and guide the tour
himself. "You don't have wedding planning to do?"

"Probably." Colt's lips curved up. "Why do you think I'm
volunteering?"

"That bad, huh?" TJ turned his chair around so he could
face Colt.

"Let's just say Delaney and I have differing opinions on

how to throw a party. I thought it would be cool to climb to the top of Sawtooth, pop a couple of bottles of champagne, and pitch a tent for the night. She wasn't into it. Not even a little."

TJ whacked him upside the head. "Hey, moron, you're marrying a fashion designer, not the president of the Sierra Club."

Colt got a lovesick grin on his face, then changed gears. "You hear anything from Stanley Royce?"

"Not yet." But TJ wasn't banking on him going away. "At least Operation Porta-potty gave me an excuse to get out of this place for a few hours." He looked up at the white ceiling.

"Operation Porta-potty? Is that what we're calling it? And I thought you loved being the boss and lording it over the rest of us."

"Yeah, right. Herding cats. Or in the case of you, Josh, and Win, idiots." TJ waved his hand at the window. "I like to see the sun every once in a while, you know?"

Colt looked him over. "You have gotten a bit vampirish, but I hear chicks dig the look."

"Chicks dig me. Period." The phone rang. TJ checked to see what line it was and let it go to voice mail. "You missed the meeting, asshole."

"For your information, I was busy protecting and serving. Anything good happen?"

"I announced that we're hiring Lauren Fisher for the retail position." TJ glanced at her résumé laying on his desk. Her credentials were impeccable. She'd worked five years at Patagonia and had moved to San Francisco three years ago to head up the sportswear department at North Face. "Just need to make her the offer."

For a few crazy moments at Tart Me Up, the idea of Deb doing the job had crossed his mind. It was stupid on a dozen levels, the top one being that she had zero experience and this was too important to screw up. Yet he knew the salary and benefit package they were offering for the position would solve her financial problems.

Uh, when had he risked the future of his family's company to help a friend? Never, that's when.

"You think she'll take it?"

"Pretty sure. She's hot to live here and has already studied the local real estate market." TJ got the feeling Lauren had bucks, maybe stock options from one of the companies she'd worked.

"No offense, but it'll be good to have someone dedicated full-time to Delaney's adventure wear. Someone who knows what she's doing." Colt checked his watch and got to his feet. "I need to get back to the station. We doing our regular hump night at Old Glory?"

"I'll try to meet you there later." He stared at the pile of paperwork on his desk.

But instead of tending to his own work after Colt left, TJ spread Deb's credit cards on his desk. He tried to tell himself it was for Sid and Geri's sake.

He started calling the customer service numbers on the back of the cards. If he couldn't work something out, Deb's only option was to file for personal bankruptcy, which would destroy her credit for the next ten years. He didn't want to see her do that if it could be helped and continued making calls until it was dark outside.

A light tapping noise made him look up to find Hannah standing in his doorway. "Hey."

"Hey back." She came in, kissed him on the cheek, sat in Colt's vacated spot, and bobbed her head at the clutter of cards. "Deb called and told me about that. It's nice of you to try to help."

"So far, I'm not having much luck." Only a few department stores and one bank had been willing to make minor concessions, but he'd keep trying.

"Deb thought it was a long shot. I think she was just happy to have an advocate. Did she tell you what happened at the Morning Glory?"

"No." He combed his hand through his hair. "What happened?"

"Some perv assaulted her."

TJ jerked his head in surprise. "What?" This was a town where someone's wart made front-page news. How was it he didn't know this?

"A guy who was with a group of male tourists hit on her, and when she rejected him, he got all handsy. She booted him and his friends out of the restaurant."

"You're kidding me. She never said a word. Colt was here earlier and didn't mention it either. Didn't Felix call Glory Junction PD?"

"I'm probably making it sound more dramatic than it was. Still . . ."

"Damned right. I wish I would've been there to coldcock the prick."

"Win was," Hannah said. "But from what Deb said, it doesn't sound like he even knew what was going on. She handled it . . . Jabbed the guy with her pencil."

TJ chuckled because that was so Deb. Ballsy. Self-sufficient. "Maybe she should spend the night with you guys . . . you know, in case she's shaken up." Though she hadn't seemed remotely traumatized when he'd seen her earlier.

"She's always welcome to stay with Josh and me," Hannah said. "But you know Deb . . . she won't."

"Won't what?" Josh came in, sat down next to his wife, and kissed her.

"Deb won't stay with us." Hannah started to tell him what had happened at the Morning Glory.

"Yeah, I heard," Josh said. "I saw Felix at the physical

therapist. I miss the old days, when only nice people came to Glory Junction."

"Yeah, when was that?" TJ asked. For the most part, Glory Junction was the picture of small town USA, embodying all the Mayberry clichés. But the town's five ski resorts had also attracted its share of self-entitled dickheads who could be real pains-in-the-ass when they didn't get their way.

"I guess before I left." After high school, Josh had blown out of Glory Junction faster than a bullet train, first to go to college, then to join the army and become a ranger, nearly losing his leg in a roadside bombing in Afghanistan. Even after a string of surgeries, he'd never be 100 percent.

"You're reinventing history, dude. But whatever."

"When did you get so cynical?" Josh put his hand on Hannah's knee.

"I'm not cynical. Just realistic." TJ glanced at the clock. He needed to call Lauren. "You two going to Old Glory?"

Josh's hand moved a little higher. "Nah, we've got uh . . . a thing."

Whatever that thing was, it looked like news to Hannah. But she nodded, and the two made gooey faces at each other like a pair of loons.

TJ rolled his eyes. "You want me to leave?"

Josh got up and socked him in the arm, then held his hand out for Hannah. Married nearly a year and they were still nauseating. Colt and Delaney too. That left him and Win, the second and fourth sons, as the last Garner men standing. TJ was more than ready to kiss bachelorhood good-bye. Win, not anytime soon.

"See you tomorrow," Josh said and tugged his wife by her hand.

Once they were gone, he found Lauren's number at the top of her résumé and dialed. Only to get voice mail.

"Hey, Lauren, it's TJ Garner from Garner Adventure. It's six o'clock and I'll be in the office another hour or so. I'm calling to offer you the job . . . look forward to hearing from you." He left the number to his direct line but not his cell phone. If she called while he was at Old Glory, he didn't want to talk salary and benefits from a bar with music blaring and pool balls crashing in the background. Unprofessional.

He grabbed his jacket and walked a few doors down Main Street to Old Glory.

The gastro pub, done up in an American flag theme, was always crowded on Wednesday nights. Boden Farmer, the owner, ran a craft beer special and served small plates at happy-hour prices until midnight. The Garners had their own spot near the pool tables and dartboards. TJ filled a bowl with peanuts from one of the big oak barrels on the floor and made his way back. Colt, Delaney, and Win were already there. A couple of pitchers and a basket of pub fries sat on the table. TJ put the peanuts down and poured himself a glass of beer. In the corner, he noticed Deb and Carrie Jo, Colt's receptionist, playing a game of darts with two men TJ had never seen before.

Deb saw him and waved. She'd changed out of her jeans from earlier into a tight little black skirt that hugged her perfectly round ass. And suddenly he was eighteen again, wanting to cover her up at the lake so Duffy Manzenelli and Rodney Strong would stop drooling over her.

It was a long time ago, he told himself, and rubbed his hand over his face. He had to start dating. Tonight, he promised to make it his mission to find at least one woman he hadn't grown up with to talk to.

"Yo." Win shoulder-checked him, making his beer slosh over the rim of his glass.

TJ snatched one of Win's sliders and popped it into his mouth. "How was your afternoon tour?"

"Dude, you ever talk about anything other than Garner Adventure? We're in a bar, TJ; have a good time. Come on, I'll play you a game of eight ball."

TJ followed Win to an empty table, racked the balls, and grabbed a pool stick off the wall.

Win won the coin toss to break, sinking two stripes. Colt and Delaney came over to watch while Win called his second shot and pocketed his object ball in the corner. On his next try, the shot went wide.

TJ turned to Colt. "Stick around; this shouldn't take long." Less than ten minutes, to be precise.

"You suck." Win refilled his beer.

Colt, a much better player than Win, took the next game. TJ won that one too, while surreptitiously watching Deb and the guys she was with out of the corner of his eye. After the game, she and Carrie Jo wandered over without their dart partners. TJ saw the two men move onto a group of women standing at the bar.

He waited until Carrie Jo walked away to say hi to someone she knew and pulled Deb out of earshot of the others. "I'm still working on your stuff."

"I didn't expect you to get it done today." She smiled, and the pure radiance of it reminded him why helping her or even standing with her in a bar was a bad idea. Slash that. It was worse than bad. It was hopeless. "I know how much you've got on your plate, TJ.

"We'll get you situated." It was overpromising, but he wanted so badly to fix her problems that the words just burst out. "I heard you got harassed at the diner this morning. Why didn't you tell me about it at Tart Me Up?"

"It was nothing." She waved it off, but a spot of red crept up her neck.

"You call Colt . . . ask him to level charges?"

Before she could respond, Win appeared and hooked his arm around Deb's waist. She looked at TJ uncertainly and rolled her eyes at Win. They started talking, and instead of TJ standing there, watching her with his brother, he went to get another pitcher of beer. Patrons were shoulder deep to order drinks, so he leaned against the bar, waiting his turn.

"You want more of the Blind Pig IPA?" Boden asked from the taps.

Colt was the expert on craft beer, not TJ. He'd happily drink Budweiser.

"Whatever Colt got before," he responded. "Looks like business is good."

"Never better, man. In fact, if you know anyone looking to bartend, I'm hiring."

TJ gazed over at Deb again. The tips at Old Glory had to be better than the Morning Glory. "Deborah Bennett might be. I don't know if she has bartending experience, though."

Boden followed his line of vision. "Normally, I make it a requirement. But for Deb, I'd make an exception."

"Yeah, how come?"

"She's hot, and as much as I hate to say it, she'd be good for my bottom line, regardless of whether she knows how to make a Sazerac. Plus, I like Deb. Wouldn't mind hanging out with her." Boden watched Win give Deb a squeeze and move on to the next pretty face. "What's the deal with her and your brother?"

TJ's stomach knotted. "You'd have to ask them."

Boden nodded, filled the pitcher, and put it on the Garner tab. "I'll come over to say hi as soon as things slow down back here."

TJ didn't see that happening anytime soon. "All right."

Elbowing his way through the crowd, TJ wondered if Deb would be interested in picking up shifts at the bar. On a night like this, she could take in a good haul. Yet, the prospect of her working here didn't sit well with him. It wasn't the atmosphere that disturbed him. It was Boden, who was a great guy. And a chick magnet. And the fact that he was jealous of Boden making a move on Deb, a woman he'd long ago ceded having any designs on . . . well, it was pathetic. TJ told himself that he was just protecting his brother's interest.

"Hi, TJ."

TJ turned to find Mandy Forsyth standing there and switched the pitcher of beer to his other hand so he could shake hers. Probably too formal, given the fact that they were in a bar and the Railbenders were on the jukebox singing "Let's All Get Stoned." But she was a business acquaintance: an event planner at the Four Seasons at Winter Bowl. Garner Adventure and the Four Seasons had a partnership of sorts. GA put many of their high-paying clients up at the hotel and used the ski resort for a lot of winter activities. In exchange, the hotel and resort referred Garner Adventure like crazy.

"How's it going, Mandy? You trek down the mountain to hang out with us proletariat?"

She laughed, and he took a moment to appreciate how pretty she was. Petite, blond hair, blue eyes, very put together. She ran the entire event and banquet division of the hotel, a big deal because the Glory Junction Four Seasons was a huge destination wedding venue, hosted two golf tournaments a year, and had a busy concert schedule in summer. That didn't include its top-notch ski program. Suffice it to say, a lot of people wanted Mandy's job. And on paper, she was the perfect woman for him.

Yet he continued to search the bar to see what Deb was doing and caught her by the stage staring at him. He snapped his gaze away and went back to focusing on Mandy.

"Sometimes working and playing in the same place can give you cabin fever. A group of us came." She pointed to a table at the other side of the room, away from the pool tables. TJ recognized a few faces. "We love the live music."

He scanned his table to see if they were waiting for the beer and decided a few more minutes wouldn't kill anyone. "My brother's band plays occasionally."

"I know. His is one of our favorites."

Huh; he'd never seen her at one of Colt's shows. Then again, the concerts were crowded and he hadn't been look-ing. He wondered if *our* meant she had a significant other. She didn't wear a ring, so not married. "You and your boy-friend's?" How was that for subtlety?

"No." Her face lit up at his obvious attempt to see if she was single. "The gang from the Four Seasons. We all hang out because we apparently don't see enough of each other at work."

"Ah." Out of the side of his eye, he caught a glimpse of Boden heading over to Deb. "Hey, I've gotta go deliver this." He held up the pitcher. "It was great seeing you."

"Oh. Yeah, you too." She looked disappointed, but TJ didn't want the beer to get warm. That and he was a freaking loser.

He dropped off the brew and inconspicuously tried to listen in on Boden and Deb's conversation. It was too loud to hear anything. But having seen Boden in action many times, TJ knew how smooth he was. Though he sent off that bad-boy vibe—the tattoos, biker boots, and two hundred pounds of muscle—he was always quick to donate beer for charity events, volunteer his bar for community meetings, and put his back into any town project that required a little elbow grease. Deb could certainly do worse.

TJ searched the bar to see if Win saw Boden. Nope; his little brother had moved on to a redhead, who was teaching him how to line dance. From the looks of things, she was the one he'd be taking home tonight.

TJ checked his watch. Ten o'clock. Tired of watching men vie for Deb's attention, he found his jacket by the pool table and headed out. He was halfway to the door when he heard Colt say, "Where you going?"

TJ turned around and nearly collided with him. "I've got an early morning."

"I thought you'd hang out with Mandy for a while. She's cute, man."

"Yeah, I'm gonna call her." TJ didn't know where that had come from, but maybe he would. She seemed interested.

"Good." Colt scrutinized him for a second. "You okay?"

"Of course; why wouldn't I be?"

Colt punched him. They did that instead of hugging. It drove their mother crazy. "See you tomorrow."

TJ started walking toward Garner Adventure, where his car was parked, and heard someone shout his name. Deb came chasing after him in her short skirt. It had to be twenty degrees outside.

"What's up?"

"I had an idea for you . . . about your store."

"Yeah?" His lips quirked because why now? Why outside of a bar in the freezing cold? He cocked his head in the direction of GA. "Should we go inside?"

"Okay." Her teeth began to chatter and he hustled her along.

They got inside, and he disabled the security system and motioned for her to take a seat in the foyer on one of the sofas near the big river-rock fireplace.

He went to turn up the thermostat and wondered at the advisability of being alone with her. All these years he'd

managed to keep his distance and suddenly he'd done a
one-eighty by offering to help with her finances. He tried
to tell himself it was just one of those things, happen-
stance. But he knew better. Then he told himself to grow a
set, but it was too late because he was already staring at her
bare legs.

Get a grip.

He sat on the opposite sofa and leaned forward.
"Whaddya got?"

She cleared her throat. "It's probably a dumb idea. I got
it this morning when you mentioned my jacket."

He bobbed his head for her to go on.

"What if Delaney could design these jackets to also be
tents?" She watched him, gauging his reaction. "You're
laughing, aren't you? But think about it. It would be one less
thing to carry when you're bouldering or skiing in the backcountry and want to camp out."

"I'm not laughing." No, he was trying to keep it together
and not make a move he would later regret. "It's a good
idea." Sure, it was a little wacky, but backpackers were forever trying to lighten their load. And a warm, lightweight
jacket that had multiple functions was smart. If it was done
right. "I don't know if it would be something Delaney is
interested in creating." She was a high-fashion designer, not
a tent maker.

"But you don't think it's crazy?" She met his gaze and
played with her lower lip. It was driving him crazy.

"Nope, not necessarily. What made you think of it?" It
seemed so out of the blue.

"I don't know. Sometimes I think of weird things like
that. Maybe I should've been an inventor, except I wouldn't
know how to execute the idea or even draw it. I'm better at
coming up with stuff and telling people like you about it."

"It's the idea that counts. Look at Steve Jobs. He was the face of Apple because he was the company's visionary. But it was Steve Wozniak who actually engineered the computer." Jeez, he sounded as if he was delivering a college dissertation.

"I didn't know that." Her brown eyes sparkled and she looked at him like he was the smartest guy on the face of the earth. He wasn't, but . . . damn.

"You ever think of going into marketing?" She'd told him she wanted to be a PE teacher, which was great. No doubt kids would love her. But there were other options, better-paying ones.

"I don't have a degree or any experience. Who would hire me?"

Me.

No, it was nuts and his family would kill him; besides, he'd offered the job to Lauren, someone with serious retail chops. "When you go back to school, you should take some marketing classes and try to get an internship."

She cocked a brow. "A thirty-year-old intern. Yeah, right."

"You have to start somewhere. If you want, we could talk about it some more." What had happened to his plan to maintain distance? Clearly, he'd thrown that out the window.

"Thank you, TJ. But you don't have to do any of this." She reached for his hand and held it. It was a small gesture, yet he felt the heat of her touch travel south of his belt with the speed of lightning.

They just sat there like that, his eyes locked on her brown ones until he came to his senses.

"I have to go . . . early morning." He hastily got to his feet.

"Oh . . . okay."

He turned on the alarm and they walked out together.

The forecast had said more snow, but there were still no sign of flurries. Soon, though. TJ could feel it in his bones.

"I'll walk you home," he said.

"Nah. I'm going back to Old Glory."

He watched her until she disappeared inside the bar and fished his keys out of his pocket.

The next morning, he got to work by eight after a stop at Starbucks, which was late for him. The snow had come hard and fast sometime between midnight and four. And even though his Range Rover was all-wheel drive, the roads were slippery.

He dragged his ass through the front door to GA's lobby and was surprised to find Darcy at the counter.

"Whoa. Don't take this the wrong way, but you look awful." Her nose was red, her eyes glassy, and there was a mound of used tissues on her desk.

"I didn't want to get behind." She stared at his cup of coffee. A grande, a venti, or whatever the hell they called it.

"I bought, sorry," he said sheepishly. Darcy took a lot of pride in the fact that she was the only one in the office who could make a decent pot of coffee. "I didn't think you'd be here. You should go home, Darce."

"It's okay. I'll be fine."

"This was a helluva morning to go out sick in." He watched the snow continue to fall outside the window. The town and ski lifts would be jammed this weekend. "If you change your mind, I can give you a lift back home. Just say the word."

He started for his office when Darcy said, "Lauren called. I left her number on your desk."

By the end of the day, GA would have itself a retail expert. It should've been good news, but he was still thinking of

Deb for the position. Nope, he told himself, Lauren was the best person for the job. "Thanks."

He passed Win's office, which was empty. He couldn't remember whether his brother was scheduled for a tour that morning. Depending on what they had going, they might have to cancel because of the weather. A hassle, because clients usually wanted to reschedule, which took considerable juggling. They were booked through most of the year. Not that TJ was complaining.

He'd had just enough time to strip out of his jacket before Darcy buzzed.

"We got three new orders for Delaney's jackets, but we only have two."

"Okay, I'll call her," he said and started to hang up.

"Wait. Campbell is running late for the toboggan tour because of the snow," she continued. "What should I do?"

TJ tapped his keyboard until he found the paperwork for the toboggan trip and relayed a name and number to Darcy. "That's our contact for the group. Call to let them know Campbell is on his way."

As soon as he got off with Darcy, he rang up Campbell. "What's your ETA?"

"Five minutes."

"They're waiting. Stay safe, but move your ass."

Josh stuck his head in. "What up?"

"Just got here. What do you have going?"

"Dad asked me to look at some bobsleds with him."

"Over at Davenport's?"

Josh sat on the arm of TJ's couch. "Yeah, though I don't feel like driving in this weather."

"You want to take my Range Rover?"

Josh contemplated it. "Maybe. Let me talk to Dad. It won't be so bad once we get over the pass." He glanced at his watch. "But we better get moving if we don't want to hit

Sacramento traffic on the way home." It was a three-hour drive each way.

"There's an extra set of keys at the front desk."

"Thanks."

When Josh left, TJ picked up the phone and dialed Lauren's number. She answered on the third ring and TJ heard traffic in the background.

"Hi, Lauren, it's TJ Garner. Is this an okay time to talk?"

"Yes, yes, just let me get inside." On the other end of the line, someone greeted her, maybe a doorman. "Sorry. I'm here now." There was a long pause, then, "I have to decline the offer, TJ. Something else . . . another opportunity . . . came along and, well, I can't pass it up."

He hadn't seen that coming. When he'd interviewed her a week ago, she'd sounded hungry for the job. "Any chance we could persuade you to take our position instead?" He could up her salary, even though it would put a dent in their operating costs.

"I'm really flattered, TJ, but I've made my decision. I hope we can keep in touch, though."

"Absolutely. Anytime you're in Glory Junction, stop by, we'll take you to lunch," he said and hung up.

Leaning back in his chair, he aimed a NERF ball at the hoop over his door. *He shoots, he scores, the crowd roars.* And his family was going to kill him.

Chapter Four

"I'm never doing this again," Delaney said, dripping sweat and panting.

Deb ignored her and powered forward. She squatted, grabbed rubber, and flipped the 250-pound tire until it clattered on the gym floor. Two more until she made it to the end of the row. Then she'd work her way back.

While the woman next to her looked about ready to drop dead, Deb was just getting her second wind. Her heart rate had reached 190 according to her Fitbit, an incredibly generous Christmas gift from Hannah. Her life might be in the toilet, but at least when she turned thirty she'd be in tiptop shape. She'd always been a fitness freak, but for some reason it seemed more important than ever. Maybe because it was the one thing she could control.

She repeated the exercise again and again. Squat. Rubber. Flip. Squat. Rubber. Flip.

"Remember to use your hips," the instructor shouted over the music.

The fast, thumping music changed to something slower, signaling that it was time to cool down. She grabbed her towel, wiped her face, and did a few stretches. Her heart rate started dropping and she got that euphoric feeling that came after an invigorating run or a fast ski down the slopes.

"There's something wrong with you," Delaney said as they headed to the women's locker room together.

Deb laughed, stripping as she ducked into one of the showers and pulled the torn plastic curtain closed. The gym wasn't fancy, but it was cheap and didn't require an annual membership fee, just a monthly charge for unlimited use. A big plus for someone in her financial situation.

"What time do you have to be at the diner?" Delaney asked from the stall next to her. "I thought we could grab something to eat. God knows we earned it."

"Today's my day off," though Deb could've used the extra shift. "Where do you want to go?" Deb prayed Delaney didn't pick one of the expensive resort restaurants. She was a famous fashion designer and eating forty-dollar pancakes meant nothing to her.

"I'm assuming the last place you want to spend your day off is the diner."

Actually, Deb got an employee discount at the Morning Glory. "We can do the diner. The new cook makes a killer Belgian waffle."

"Great," Delaney said, and Deb heard her turn off the water.

She did the same and got dressed. After a while, Delaney joined her at the vanity and applied moisturizer and a little makeup. Delaney was who Deb wanted to be when she grew up. Poised, gorgeous, smart, and successful. Oddly enough, the celebrity designer had become part of their motley crew. When she'd moved to the mountains full time, Deb had assumed she'd be a snob or at the very least intimidating. But when Hannah began selling Delaney's designs at Glorious Gifts, she'd started hanging out with them.

Foster liked to say Delaney had their same dark sense of humor, she just wore it better.

"Ready to go?" Delaney asked after she finished blowing out her hair.

Delaney had driven them in her Tesla. The car barely made any noise and ran a hell of a lot smoother than Deb's Honda, which barely ran at all. At some point, when she had the money, she'd have TJ introduce her to his transmission guy.

When they got to the diner, Karen, Delaney's fashion house manager, was there with a few colleagues. While Delaney went over to their table to say hello, Deb checked her phone. TJ had left a message to call him. After breakfast, she'd stroll over to Garner Adventure.

"What you looking at?" Delaney scooted into their booth.

"I was just checking my voice mail." She slipped her phone back into her purse.

Ricki came right over and took their orders. Deb got the waffle with extra whipped cream. She'd earned it flipping tires.

"How's Karen adjusting to life in Glory Junction? After living here two months, I'd imagine she'd be jonesing for the big city." Deb loved everything about her hometown—the majestic mountains, the fresh smell of the pine trees, and knowing all her neighbors—but it had to be a culture shock for someone who wasn't from a rural area.

"It's different from Los Angeles, that's for sure. But she seems to like it. Thank God, because I don't know what I'd do without her. Since moving the business here, she's been my rock. What do you think of me setting her up with TJ?"

"Uh . . . well . . . you think?" Deb gazed across the dining room at Karen and felt a pang of envy. She was absolutely the kind of woman TJ would be interested in. Sophisticated and accomplished. She single-handedly kept the trains running at Delaney's company, Colt and Delaney, the same way TJ did at Garner Adventure. And then there was the fact that Karen was gorgeous. Pretty hard to compete with all that when the best she had to offer was a proposal to turn a down jacket into a pup tent.

"He may be seeing someone." Deb had noticed him talking with a blonde at the bar. Watching him with the woman had in part prompted her to chase after him, using her cockamamy tent scheme as an excuse.

Which by the way, she had no intention of mentioning to Delaney.

"Colt didn't say TJ was seeing anyone," Delaney said. "I think they'd be perfect together. They're both ambitious businesspeople, incredibly good-looking, and close to the same age. She enjoys skiing and kayaking, though I don't think she's as fanatical about it as TJ."

Deb didn't know anyone was as obsessive about adventure sports as the Garners, except maybe her.

"Is Karen also a workaholic?" she asked. It was a catty thing to say, but TJ spent so many hours at Garner Adventure that everyone joked that the company was his wife.

"Leave TJ alone. He's a sweetheart and may just be the best of the Garner men."

"Better than Colt?" she asked, surprised.

"Okay, not better than Colt, but I'm biased. And Colt's taken, which leaves TJ and Win."

"And you wouldn't set Win up with Karen because of me." The whole town thought she was still obsessed with Win, which was not only mortifying, it wasn't true.

"Yes, but also because I think Win has a lot of growing up to do." Delaney was clearly trying to deliver Deb a message. "We all love him to pieces, but I don't think he's the one for you. And that's all I'm going to say about it."

Deb sat back against the red vinyl bench, quietly surprised, and a bit relieved, to hear that maybe not everyone in her orbit believed she and Win were meant to be.

Ricki brought their meals and Deb drenched her waffle in syrup. Planning to ski later, she needed carbs. Lots of them.

After breakfast, Delaney went to work and Deb headed to Garner Adventure. As she passed Glorious Gifts, Hannah was redoing her Valentine's Day display. The holiday always made Deb melancholy, but she popped in anyway.

"You off today?" Deb nodded and Hannah passed her a bowl of chocolate Kisses. "Eat a bunch so they're not lying around—too much temptation."

"I just had breakfast." But she unwrapped one and popped it in her mouth just the same. She took a handful more and shoved them in the pocket of her ski jacket.

"Foster wants us to get together soon to plan your birthday," Hannah said. "He's thinking a big party."

"Oh, I assumed it would just be the four of us and Carrie Jo, if she wanted to come."

Hannah added a heart-shaped basket to her display and stepped back to appraise her handiwork. "We can do better than that. Thirty is a milestone. You need a party."

"I'd love a party, but I can't afford one right now and I don't want you guys paying for it. Foster's got a house to refurbish and you have a business to run."

Hannah rolled her eyes. "Whatever. You can't stop us. If you try, we'll make it a surprise." Deb hated surprise parties and Hannah knew it. "Don't worry. It's not like we'll be renting out the grand ballroom at the Four Seasons. It'll just be something casual, but better than one of our usual nights at Old Glory. Can you live with that?"

"I might be able to," Deb said and wrapped Hannah in a hug. She didn't know what she'd do without her friends. They were the one constant in her life. "You guys are the best."

"Can you meet tonight? My house?"

"Sure. You want me to bring anything?"

"Nah. I'll make a big salad."

Hannah continued to tinker with her display. She always got a little OCD around the holidays, but Deb figured Valentine's Day had to be a big revenue generator for a gift shop, especially if it was the only one in town.

"Take that other wicker thing out. It's too busy."

Hannah stood back to see what Deb was talking about and then moved the basket. "You're right. Maybe I should hire you to merchandise my store. You're good at it."

"People go to school for that kind of thing, don't they?"

Hannah shrugged. "Or they just have an eye for it, like you. Where you off to now? Maybe I could rope you into doing more displays with me."

Deb thought for a second. "Why not?"

Darcy was at the reception desk at GA when Deb arrived. She didn't know the receptionist well, but she'd always seemed nice. According to town scuttlebutt, she'd moved from Reno to live with her grandmother, a sweet lady who resided on the edge of town in a quaint cottage that had the most amazing flower boxes. That was the only 4-1-1 Deb had on Darcy. Maybe she'd invite her to her birthday party so Darcy could meet more people.

"Hey, Darcy; is TJ in?"

Darcy nodded, then held up a finger while she called TJ on the phone to announce Deb's arrival.

Deb walked back to his office and found TJ sitting in a

desk chair, hunkered over a pile of papers. He had on a blue Henley shirt that matched his eyes and stretched across his chest like a second skin, a pair of faded jeans, and Vasque hiking boots. He dressed more casually than most CEOs. Then again, he ran an adventure company, not a bank.

She reached into her jacket pocket, scooped up a few Kisses, and put them on his desk.

He stared down at them. "You brought me Kisses?" He looked back up and grinned.

"Yep." And suddenly she felt silly.

"Thanks, Deb." He winked, popped one in his mouth, and let his eyes dance over her. "I love Kisses."

Flustered, she looked around. "Nice office."

Though she'd practically grown up in GA, coming with her parents when they used to clean, she'd never been inside TJ's office since he'd been promoted to the boss. It was twice the size of Win's and neat as could be. But there were still touches of him everywhere. Poster-sized pictures of various Garners skiing, kayaking, parasailing, and bobsledding. A collection of ridiculous plastic action figures. And a miniature basketball hoop.

Everything else—the brown leather love seat, the Navajo rug, the tan walls—felt more perfunctory than heartfelt, almost as if a decorator had picked them out. It was like the old, fun TJ was battling it out with the new, corporate TJ. She wanted the old one to win.

And . . . yeah . . . she was thinking way more about him than she ought to be.

He looked around the space as if he were seeing it for the first time. "It's not bad." Then his eyes quickly scanned her fitted jacket and yoga pants and she felt herself blush.

"So, anyone go for it?" She pointed at the pile of her credit cards on his desk.

"Not all, but some were willing to lower your monthly

payment." He showed her a yellow pad where he'd scrawled a few figures.

It was more or less what she'd expected, but a part of her had held out hope that consolidation would save her. That was her problem; she was unrealistic about everything. Thinking she could support herself and her parents on her waitressing wages. Thinking if she just ignored her mounting debt it would go away. Thinking Win would eventually come around and commit to her and that would somehow make her happy.

And there it was hitting her at once—the utter hopelessness of the situation. On the verge of losing it, she wanted to get out before TJ saw her cry. "Thank you. I really appreciate everything you've done," she said in a shaky voice and started to leave.

"Sit down for a second."

Ah jeez, now came the lecture. But after TJ had been so nice to her, she didn't want to be rude and found a spot on the couch. He got up to shut the door and she thought, *here it comes*. Couldn't he see she was a breath away from breaking down?

Before he could start the sermon, she blurted out, "Boden offered me a job."

"Bartending." He sat back down in his chair and wheeled closer to the sofa.

"Yeah. How'd you know?" It was more likely Boden would've hired her to waitress, because that was her vocation. Serving people tuna melts. Bartending wasn't much better, but at least the tips were. She'd heard some of his people pocketed as much as three hundred bucks on a good night.

"I suggested you when he told me he was looking."

"Why? I have no bartending experience."

He tilted his head and looked at her with blue eyes that

seemed to see everything. Her desperation and despair. It should've been humiliating, but it made her heart move in her chest. "Because you need the money," he said. "That's what I wanted to talk to you about."

She just nodded, the lump in her throat making it difficult to speak.

He rested his hands on his knees. "You can't continue this way or you'll go further in the hole. You're only covering interest on most of those cards." He nudged his head at the stack of plastic on his desk. "At that rate, you'll never make a dent on the principle, and I think it's pretty safe to assume you can't afford more than the minimum payment."

The sad truth was, she barely made the minimums.

He let out a sigh. "There's an opening here if you want it."

"Ah, TJ, that's so nice. But we talked about it yesterday . . . bartending might be more lucrative, don't you think?"

"I'm not talking about working here as a guide. We have a new position for someone to run the retail division of GA. It's salaried with health benefits, paid vacations, and a 401(k) match. It'll get you out of your hole."

Wait, she was confused. "You're offering this to me?"

"Yes. You."

Stunned, she was at a loss for words. Of course, she wasn't going to accept the offer, as generous as it was. The Garners had done enough for the Bennetts. When the recession happened and most businesses, including GA, could no longer afford the luxury of having a cleaning service, the Garners had stuck by Deb's parents.

"I can't, TJ." There were a million reasons why it would be a terrible idea. One of those reasons was sitting right in front of her. Old crushes were only dormant so long as you didn't revive them. Win had hurt her. She suspected TJ had the power to destroy her.

"You don't even know what the job entails and you're

already turning it down? Not a good way to impress your new boss, Bennett."

She smiled because he'd always had that take-charge tone. Back when they were kids, he was forever keeping her out of mischief. The dumbbells on the weight trees that were too heavy for her to lift. The kayaks stacked against the wall that would wobble dangerously when she tried to scale them. The climbing ropes she loved to play with but would ultimately get tangled in.

Her cries of frustration always brought him running to her rescue. Her own personal hero.

"The job would require you to decide what items we want to sell and to buy and merchandise them," he pushed on. "You'd be responsible for the retail section of the website, filling orders, and, at some point, a brick-and-mortar store here."

"But . . . why me?" Besides the fact that she desperately needed a better-paying job and he so obviously felt sorry for her. "Oh God." She covered her mouth. "Last night, when I told you my ridiculous tent idea . . . you didn't think I was angling for a job, did you?"

"It wasn't ridiculous and no, I didn't think you were angling for a job. The fact is, you're our target consumer. You wear the clothes." Again, he eyed her wardrobe. "You buy the equipment. You know what appeals to a sportsman or sportswoman."

"I don't know anything about retail, though."

"Then I suggest you learn if you want to do well at the job. Because, Deb, make no mistake about it, if you suck, I'll fire you."

That she knew was true. Business always came first with TJ. He wasn't a dick about it, but his family's livelihood rode on his decisions, which made it all that much stranger that he would offer her the job.

"Why are you really doing this, TJ?" She needed to hear the real reason because the temptation to jump at it was so great.

"Because you need the job"—she knew it!—"and I believe in investing locally. And truthfully, I believe in you, Deb."

Well, shit. It had been a long time since she'd heard anyone tell her they believed in her. And as much as it sounded sincere, Deb couldn't help but feel like TJ was only blowing smoke up her behind. "I can't, TJ. It's a really generous offer, but I just can't."

He studied her closely. "You afraid of failing, Bennett?"

"No, I'm afraid of using family friendship to take a job I don't deserve." And she was afraid of her complicated feelings for him.

"The diner or Boden offer health insurance?"

He knew damned well neither of them did. She started to get up.

"The entire business world operates under the premise that it's who you know, not what you know. No one passes on an opportunity because they have too much dignity to take a hand up. But if you want to live over a diner, drive a busted car, and eat ramen the rest of your life, suit yourself. The rest of us will happily use our connections to get ahead and prove ourselves." He slid his chair back.

They weren't the most flowery words, but they were honest.

He reached around his desk for a manila folder. "That's the official offer with your salary, benefits, and GA's employee handbook."

She opened the file and gasped at the salary. It wasn't six figures, but it was a hell of a lot more than she made at the diner.

TJ watched her take it all in, then leaned over and pointed to a paragraph in the contract.

"What's that?" she asked.

"It's the benefits we offer." Holy shit, dental. She was still paying for the crown she'd gotten the previous year. "When can you start?"

She hadn't said yes yet and silently contemplated what he was offering. A way out of her financial problems, that was for sure. But at what price?

"Think about how you could help your parents." He held her gaze and wouldn't let it go.

"Wow, you know how to go for the jugular, don't you?" Few people knew the extent of her parents' reliance on her, but he'd seen her list of expenditures right down to the penny. Her head spun. What would everyone think? Would she even be able to do the job? She let out a long breath. "I know I seem adrift, but I'm a hard worker. But this . . . I have no training whatsoever."

"You'll have to learn and you'll have to learn fast, because I needed someone to do this job yesterday."

Could she really do this . . . work with TJ? See him every day, maybe watch him fall for someone like Karen? Did she have a choice? "I have to give Felix two weeks' notice." Despite being the world's biggest pain in the ass, he was a good employer, giving her the best shifts and always having her back. "But I can come in here a few hours a day and get up to speed. You wouldn't have to pay me."

"I don't expect anyone to work for free. We'll figure something out." He turned to the calendar on his wall. "Let's make your official start date on the eighteenth."

The day after her birthday. It would be like turning a new page. She liked it. "Okay."

He got up, and for some reason it struck her how very tall he was. "Come on; I'll show you your office."

No way. She got her own office? He led her down the hallway to a room about half the size of TJ's. It had a window that faced the courtyard and let plenty of light in and a basic computer setup.

"You can do whatever you want with it," he said. "As soon as you're ready, we can meet and go over things. In the meantime, write down some ideas. Remember, you're our type of consumer. Think about what appeals to you, what makes you buy something."

"Uh . . . sure." She already felt overwhelmed and she hadn't even started yet. But she had Hannah and Delaney. They did this stuff in their sleep and could give her a crash course on retail.

She filled out paperwork and was given tax forms to take home. Caught up in the moment, she hugged him. "Thank you, TJ." He felt so solid and smelled so good that she held on a little longer than she should've.

He rebounded from the hug a little shell-shocked but gave an imperceptible nod. On her way out, she nearly collided in the lobby with Win.

"Hey, hot stuff. You looking for me?"

The song "You're So Vain" flitted through her head. "Nope. TJ."

He raised his brows. "What's going on with TJ?"

It hit her that he didn't know, which was odd. All four brothers had an equal share of the company, even Colt, who wasn't a full-time employee. A job this important . . . well, she would've thought it'd been a group decision.

"I'm working here now."

"Really? Cool," he said and headed for his office. "Catch you later, Bennett."

She shook her head, wondering how Win could be that clueless. It hit her that she'd be working closely with him now. Not so long ago, that would've filled her with anticipation. Today . . . well, nothing.

She zipped up her jacket and headed to the Morning Glory to give notice.

Chapter Five

"You did what?" Colt kept shaking his head.

TJ still had to tell Josh, but he wouldn't be home from Sacramento until late. He probably should've consulted with them first, but he was pulling rank.

"I saw an opportunity I thought would work," he told Colt, but even to his own ears it sounded absurd and so out of character for him that his family must think he'd lost his mind.

Colt got up and paced TJ's office. "I love Deb. I really do. But this is a new venture and we're totally out of our depth here. The whole point was to bring in someone who actually knows what they're doing, someone with experience selling adventure wear, someone who's done it before. Delaney's got a lot on the line, letting us have the exclusive deal on her clothes. And now we're going to hand it off to Deb, who, with all due respect, isn't exactly a go-getter."

"That's bullshit, Colt," Win said and had the good grace to sound affronted. TJ should've been grateful for Win's backing, but all he felt was jealousy, which in turn made him feel like a jerk. "She's no different from us. She likes to play hard and she's damned good at it."

"Then make her a guide. I have no problem with that.

But running a retail division takes a business head. There's no evidence whatsoever that she's got one."

TJ held his tongue because everything Colt was saying was true. But he believed in her. "She's our customer. She lives, eats, and breathes outdoor sports. She spends any extra money she makes—which isn't a lot—on gear. And because of that, she knows what like-minded people want. That's what I'm banking on."

Colt eyed him dubiously.

"And Deb already lives here," TJ continued. "You think it's that easy to get someone with marketing experience from the city, where jobs pay twice as much? Why do you think Lauren didn't wind up taking the position, huh?"

Win spread out on the couch. "My money is on Deb. I'm good with TJ's choice."

Colt shoved Win's legs out of the way and sat next to him. "You made her the offer already, right?"

"As soon as Lauren said she didn't want the job, I gave it to Deb. She's excited about it." She'd hugged him and for one stunned moment he'd nearly kissed her. "By now, she's given her two weeks at the diner."

"Great." Colt leaned his head against the top of the sofa. "We're stuck with it."

Win kicked him. "Be nice to her."

"I'm always nice to her. You're the one who leads her on. Hot one day, cold the next. Make your move already, asshole."

TJ tried to tune them out. Because Deb was Hannah's best friend, he suspected Josh would be more circumspect about TJ's decision to hire her. His parents would take some convincing, but they'd always had a soft spot where Deb was concerned. Hell, his mom had been planning her and Win's wedding since the two of them were sixteen.

"Are we done here? I've got work to do." Win was the first to leave, when usually he was the one to loiter.

Colt, on the other hand, took his time. "You know I'm not just trying to be a dick about this, right?"

"I do?"

"Come on, man. I just don't want my fiancée to get screwed. She could've gone with the biggest sports retailers in the market, but she went with us."

"I know, Colt. Have a little faith, wouldya?"

He leaned forward. "I just don't get it. Of all of us, you're the rational one. You're the one who puts business before friendship. So what's the deal?"

Way to make him sound like Ebenezer Scrooge. "I think she can do the job, it's as simple as that." Ha; nothing about it was simple.

"I hope you're right. Nothing would make me happier for this to be a win for Deb and a win for us." Colt got to his feet. "You call Mandy?"

"Why? Something going on with the Four Seasons?"

Colt gave him an exasperated look. "To ask her out, idiot."

"Uh, not yet. But I'll get around to it." As soon as Deb started, he'd take Mandy on a date. Maybe they'd like each other, get married, and have a million kids. And maybe he'd win a billion-dollar jackpot playing Powerball.

"I don't know what the hell you're waiting for." This from the guy who'd fought for a year with Delaney over a stupid parking space before making a move. "You need to have some fun, TJ . . . stop making this place your whole life."

Ya think? "Thanks for the advice, Oprah. Could you go now?"

Colt looked at the time. "Crap, I have a meeting with Rita at city hall."

"Send my regards to the mayor," TJ called after him as he left and spent the next thirty minutes returning emails.

When he finally came up for air, it was well past lunch and he was hungry. Usually, he brought something and ate at his desk. Today, all he had were a few protein bars shoved in the back of his drawer. On his way out, he stopped by the reception desk to see if Darcy wanted anything, then walked over to Old Glory and ordered a cheeseburger and fries.

"Coming right up," Boden said as he wiped down the bar. "You want a beer?"

"Nah, I'm working."

"Deb tells me you hired her at GA . . . big job with a good salary."

"Yup." He probably should've told her to keep her lips sealed until he'd told his entire family. "Sorry. I know you were hoping to recruit her."

Boden put a glass of ice water in front of TJ. "Probably for the best."

"Why's that?"

"Dating in the workplace, not a good idea."

Nope. It sure the hell wasn't. But that wasn't going to be a problem for him and Deb.

"So, you're dating now?"

"Not yet, but planning on it."

TJ suddenly felt like he'd swallowed lead. Unlike TJ, Boden didn't live with the Win legacy. "Good luck with that."

Boden laughed. "I know she's hung up on your brother. But I'll unhang her."

TJ just looked at him because as far as he knew, no one had ever captured her attention the way Win had. And even he didn't seem to get her attention as much these days. Or maybe that was just wishful thinking on TJ's part. "Like I said, good luck with that."

When his food was ready he asked to take it to go and ate in his office.

Later that day, he called Josh to tell him about Deb before Hannah did. By now, all of Glory Junction likely knew. Why not? Deb should be able to share her new job with anyone she wanted to.

Because his dad was with Josh, TJ killed two birds with one stone. They reacted with skepticism the way he'd expected them to but took it better than Colt had. His mom had gone to Reno with a couple of friends, but Gray promised to fill her in.

About four, Darcy tapped lightly on his open door.

"Hey, Darce, you want to go home early?"

"No." She crept over the threshold two steps, then stopped as if she was trespassing.

"Come in; have a seat."

She smoothed her skirt and sat on the sofa. He waited for her to say what she wanted, but she continued to just sit there and stare.

"What's up?"

"You hired Deb for the retail position?"

Ah hell, he'd forgotten to fill her in. "Yeah. Lauren didn't take the job, so I gave it to Deb. You like Deb, right?"

"She seems nice." She picked a piece of lint off her skirt and refused to look him in the eye.

Okay, then what's the problem? Because she was obviously unhappy about something. "Talk to me, Darce. What's going on?"

She stuck out her lower lip, started to say something, stopped, and looked down at her lap.

"I feel like I'm getting passed over."

Passed over? What on earth was she talking about? "You wanted the retail job?" he asked, confused. She'd never said anything about it. With all his other responsibilities, was he supposed to be a mind reader too? "If you want something, Darcy, you have to speak up."

"I didn't want the retail job per se, but I don't want to be a receptionist forever."

TJ rubbed his hand down his face. "I didn't realize you were unhappy." He didn't want to lose her. She was a fantastic receptionist. Responsible, smart, always on time. "It's a really important job. You're the first person the public sees and talks to; you're their first impression of GA."

"I'm not unhappy," she said, continuing to gaze into her lap. "I'm . . . uh . . . impressed with the company and hope that there's room for me to grow in the organization." It sounded like something she'd memorized from a self-help book on how to talk to your boss.

"Of course there's room for you to grow here. You're awesome, Darce. Seriously, you've been a total lifesaver. And if you want a promotion, I'll give you one. But first we have to find a job that suits you." And money in the budget. Right now, all their extra was going toward the new website and the retail venture.

"Okay," she said. "It's just . . . uh . . . I don't want to be invisible or get passed by."

"I get it." Probably more than she knew. There were days when he still wondered what his life would be like if he'd made the Olympic team, if he still competed. "What you and I need to do in the next few months is to look around GA, figure out what's missing to make things work better, and what skill sets you have to make that happen. Does that sound good to you?"

She nodded enthusiastically and rose to her feet. "Thanks, TJ. I won't bother you anymore."

"Darcy, you're not bothering me. I'm sorry I didn't know how you felt. But you've got to communicate these things to me, okay?"

"I'm trying to . . . be more assertive."

"Good." With the Garners, if you weren't you went hungry.

He put in three more hours. Before leaving, he stopped in Win's office. Strangely, his brother was there. Win used the space as a second closet and little else. His clothes and gear were everywhere. A patchwork quilt their mom had made lay rumpled on top of the sofa and leftover cups from the Juicery dotted his otherwise unused desk. His brother was a slob.

"Why you here so late and what're you doing?"

Win glanced up from his computer. "Stuff."

"Looking at PornHub again?" TJ found a place to sit among the clutter. "Thanks for supporting me on Deb."

Win hitched his shoulders. "She's a good hire. Mom and Dad love her and she'll fit in around here."

What about you; do you love her? "It won't be weird, right?"

"Nah. Deb and I, we've always been good. And Colt's right, I need to get my act together where she's concerned."

TJ's heart sank, though he'd always known they'd be together. That was the thing about Win; he never had to work hard for anything. Things just came to him. And with little effort at all, Deb would forgive him for running around all these years and ignoring her.

"Then I'll see you tomorrow," he said.

Win didn't respond, just returned to staring at his computer.

He seemed a little off today. Maybe he'd whacked that dim bulb of his on a chairlift.

Win scanned the website page over and over again. It had a lot of useless information. Things like: "pregnant and vegan," "what to put on your registry," and "when will I get my baby bump?" There was nothing on what a guy was supposed to do when he'd knocked up a woman he hardly knew. Nothing at all.

God, he was so screwed.

Three days ago, Britney had come out of the bathroom, pale as a ghost, waving a pregnancy stick in the air. Positive. It said positive. Just to be sure, she took three more tests. Two lines, still positive.

He wanted her to go to the doctor, but she wanted to wait, as if one of those lines would magically disappear. Even Win, who steered away from anything difficult unless it was a black diamond trail or a sheer-rock mountain, knew that wasn't gonna happen.

So here he was, trying to sort this out for both of them because Britney seemed to have a serious case of denial.

He'd met her over the summer in Tahoe, where she worked as a blackjack dealer at one of the casinos. Brown hair, green eyes, legs up to her chin, and an ass like you wouldn't believe. But she was flighty. Up until now, it was part of her charm and easy, because the last thing Win wanted was a serious relationship. He liked her, she liked him, they had some laughs, and headboard-banging sex. Other than that, they didn't have too much in common.

She liked flashy cars, flashy clothes, and seemed taken with the fact that he was part owner of a successful business. But she didn't show any interest in what the business was or how he spent his days working there. When they were together, she liked to go to expensive restaurants where the food was too rich for his taste and the atmosphere too stuffy. She also expected him to buy her gifts, which he didn't mind because he liked being generous. But her self-entitlement rubbed him the wrong way.

The truth was, the relationship had just about run its

course until she'd waved that stick in the air. Pregnancy was definitely a game changer. No baby of his would go without a father. And Britney . . . he wasn't sure what kind of a mother she'd make.

He picked up the phone and for the fifth time that day tried to call her. Still no answer. She was avoiding him; he got that loud and clear. Win thought about driving to Tahoe. It would only take him thirty minutes, but no telling where she was. Maybe on one of her spur-of-the-moment trips to Los Angeles or Scottsdale. He used to like that she constantly took off to go here or there. It made her seem interesting, though a little secretive. Most of the women he'd dated had been clingy and the opposite of mysterious. But Britney had this whole life going outside of him.

Now it was just plain inconvenient. They had things to work out, a life to talk about.

He rummaged through his pile of ski stuff to find his jacket and pulled it on. Screw it. He'd go to Old Glory, drink a pint, and lose his head in a game of darts.

The bar was less crowded than it had been the previous night. At one of the tables he spied his sister-in-law, his soon-to-be sister-in-law, and Deb. They were probably celebrating her new job. He strolled over and gave Hannah and Delaney pecks on the cheek.

"You," he said to Deb and crooked his finger. "Give me a hug." He pulled her out of the chair and swung her around. "Congrats, Bennett! Welcome aboard."

"Thanks. I'm superexcited."

"Hey, barkeep," he yelled to Boden, "bring these ladies a drink on me."

"What do you guys want?" Boden asked.

They went around the table, calling out drinks. Win went over to say hi to Boden, order himself a beer, and leave the women to do their thing. Rita Tucker came in and sat next to him.

"Hello, Mayor." He bobbed his head at her. The old broad gave him the once-over.

"Getting your drink on?"

"I'm having a beer, if that's what you mean." Although getting plastered wasn't a bad idea.

He slipped his phone out of his pocket and checked to see if Britney had called. Still nothing.

"I put you down for December again," she said and ordered a bourbon neat. "We'll be meeting soon to talk about locations and wardrobe."

"It's only February. The next calendar doesn't come out for another year."

"You know how much planning goes into something of this magnitude?"

This magnitude? It was a poorly printed calendar of amateurishly shot pictures of local dudes wearing next to nothing. One for each month. Every year it got more and more pornographic. If it didn't raise a buttload of money for the volunteer fire department, it would've been banned by the city. Though, now that Rita was the mayor, who knew?

"You ever think about how this exploits men, turns them into sex objects?" he asked her.

"Yep." She smirked over the rim of her glass, "Payback's a bitch."

Boden delivered Win's beer and he took it with him to find an open dartboard and a worthy opponent. He was in the mood for hitting something. Hard. When he got to the area with the pool tables and dartboards, he found Chip nursing a soda with a group of guys from the Department of Fish and Wildlife. At least Win hoped it was soda. Chip was a recovering alcoholic who used to be married to Hannah. Ancient history.

"Chip, you up for a game of darts?"

"Sure." Chip met him at one of the boards. "I hear you guys hired Deb for some big position at GA." That was the way of a small town; word traveled fast.

"Yup. She'll be heading up our new retail division."

"Huh. I never would've pegged her for something like that. A tour guide, sure, but an executive? I'm assuming you got her the gig." He waggled his brows, and Win wanted to deck him.

He'd always liked Chip, even when he was an obnoxious falling-down drunk. Hell, the guy used to be Josh's best friend. But what a crappy thing to say.

Win threw him some shade. "Nope, it was TJ's idea." Everyone knew TJ was all business. No special favors for friends, not if it would hurt GA's earnings. It's why they were as successful as they were. "Chip, do you even know Deb anymore? When was the last time you had a conversation with her?"

"The truth"—Chip had the decency to look contrite—"she doesn't talk to me, not since Hannah. Pretty sure she hates my guts."

"If you want to repair that, don't be talking smack about her."

They played a few games and Win continued to check his phone compulsively. It was a switch for him. Usually he was the unavailable one. But the pregnancy was weighing on him, and he wanted to get their future sorted out. He thought about telling TJ, who would know exactly how to handle the situation. Of all his brothers, TJ was the problem solver. Funny, because Colt was the cop and Josh the former army ranger. But they were about busting down the fortress and taking prisoners. TJ was more analytical, more thoughtful, and smarter in a lot of ways. He was also judgmental as hell, and the last thing Win needed right now was being told what a fuckup he was.

Win took his empty glass back to the bar. The girls were still at their table, gabbing. Even Boden had pulled up a chair. Rita had left and there were a few new people sitting at the bar. Win didn't recognize them. Tourists. There wasn't a whole lot to do after dark in Glory Junction. He used to stop over at Colt's a few nights a week to eat his brother's cereal, drink his beer, and watch his TV. But Colt had moved in with Delaney, and although Win was always welcome, it wasn't the same.

He thought about going to his parents', where he could get a hot meal, but Britney might call and he'd rather have that conversation without his mom's big ears around. Same with going to TJ's. And Josh was in Sacramento.

He supposed it wouldn't kill him to go home, clean his apartment, and do a load of laundry. When he got outside, the snow had stopped falling and nothing but stars dotted the inky sky. Hell with it. He got in his Jeep and headed for Tahoe. Worse came to worse, he'd skip the nine a.m. meeting at GA if he wound up staying overnight at Britney's.

It wasn't as if he'd get any sleep if they didn't figure this out. The whole drive there, he weighed his options. The one that made the most sense was getting married. Yet the thought of it made it difficult for him to breathe. He hardly knew her.

Hang on, brah. You're getting ahead of yourself.

Before anything, Britney needed to go to the doctor for a prenatal visit. She probably should be taking vitamins, laying off the caffeine and booze, and avoiding the cigarette smoke at the casino where she worked. That couldn't be good for a baby.

It was past nine when he pulled up in front of her swanky condo. The place had views of the mountains, a big open floor plan, and the same modern architecture that was taking over Glory Junction. To this day, he didn't know how she afforded the lease on her blackjack salary. She'd told him she knew the developer and had gotten a good deal.

Her lights were out and Win wondered if she was sleeping. She worked odd hours at the casino, but not usually on Thursdays.

No one answered the door. It'd been a fifty-fifty shot finding her home, but it beat checking his phone every five minutes. He knocked and rang the bell again, just in case she was in bed.

Her girlfriend, Cami, came out of the condo next door. "You looking for Britney?"

"Yeah. You know where she is?"

"No, but she's not home. You want to come in and wait?" Cami looked him up and down like a hungry wolf.

She worked with Britney at Harrah's. Guys thought she was hot. But Win wasn't attracted to her thirsty, bleached-blond hair and fake tits. She and Britney seemed to get off on competing for the same men. Another thing he didn't find attractive. And either she was independently wealthy or knew the same developer as Britney.

"Nah. You think she's working?"

"Could be." Cami shrugged, then flipped her hair. "You sure you don't want to wait? I've got a fire going and could fix you a drink."

"I'm gonna cruise by Harrah's, see if she's there."

"Suit yourself," Cami said and went back inside, letting the door close with a thud.

He drove to the casino and left his truck with the valet. The unnatural lighting, the noise from the slot machines, the cloud of tobacco smoke: Win hated it all. Why gamble when there were so many other ways to get a rush? He scanned the crowded ten- and twenty-dollar blackjack tables where

Britney dealt cards and came up empty. One of the floor managers waved. Win knew him from skiing and made his way through the crush of people to say hello.

"Britney here tonight?"

"Nope, night off. How you doing?"

"Good." Win absently continued to search the floor.

"You want me to hook you up?"

"To play?" Win shook his head. "I'm just looking for Britney."

They shot the breeze for a few seconds, talking about Alpine Meadows versus Winter Bowl and all the snow they'd gotten this year. Afterward, Win left. He considered going back to her place but didn't want to run into Cami again.

Halfway home, his phone pinged with a text from Britney. Finally.

Went to Palm Springs for the weekend. Talk to you when I get back.

Palm Springs? He was glad to see she was taking the future of their baby so seriously.

Chapter Six

Darcy wasn't at the front desk on Friday and Deb didn't quite know what to do. Go to her new office? Check in with TJ? Or wait in the lobby until someone escorted her back?

Josh came through the door as she deliberated. "Hey, you." He wrapped her in a hug. "Congratulations."

She stepped back and tugged on her bottom lip. "You think it's crazy?"

"Uh . . . a little bit . . . yeah. But in the immortal words of General George Patton: 'If a man does his best, what else is there?'"

She lifted her shoulders. "Getting fired?"

Josh chuckled and chucked her on the chin. "You'll do fine. TJ know you're here?"

"Uh-uh."

"Follow me back."

She went with him through the hall and it dawned on her that he barely limped anymore. If she hadn't known about the bombing, his leg, the surgeries, and the long recovery, she wouldn't have noticed the slight hobble at all.

Josh stopped at TJ's door. "Your new hire is here." He mussed her hair and headed for his own office, calling behind him, "Good luck."

TJ got to his feet and . . . wow! Today he had on a crisp pair of khakis, a sports coat, and a tie, looking every bit the CEO of a prosperous company. She preferred the jeans and hiking boots, but he wore a tie and jacket well. Like *hell yeah* well.

"We've got to go," he said.

"Where?" Shoot, maybe she was supposed to have dressed up. She had on black pants, a red turtleneck, and a pair of pumps. At least it wasn't exercise clothes, but she certainly didn't look as professional as TJ.

"A meeting with a website designer in Reno. She's revamping our entire site and has been working on the online store. I want her to meet you so you can handle it from now on."

Deb didn't have the first clue about web design but figured it was sink-or-swim time. "Let's go."

He put his hand at the small of her back and a tingle went up her spine and then everything else began to tingle and she felt her face flame. They got inside TJ's Range Rover and he immediately cranked up the heat, which didn't help matters. He leaned over the center console and pressed a button.

"What's that?" she asked.

"Seat warmer." A few seconds later, she wiggled her butt and he asked, "Too much?"

"Are you kidding? It's amazing." Except now she was on fire.

But that was TJ for you. Everything had to be top of the line. She considered herself fortunate when the defroster in her Honda worked.

He grinned, the corners of his mouth creasing into almost dimples and, again, she felt a streak of heat rush through her and it sure as hell wasn't the seat warmers.

Working for him was going to be a constant temptation.
And an extra dose of humility.

"You read your employee handbook?" he asked.

"Yep." She didn't know why she did it, but she recited the
section on the office-romance policy. Sex with a coworker
wasn't forbidden, but there were rules.

He slowly nodded. "We've had a lot of drama with
guides dating and fighting on the job."

"I remember how it was when I worked for you guys the
summer after high school." Every day had been like a soap
opera, with guides hopping from one bed to another. She
and Win had been as guilty as the others. TJ had spent that
summer in San Francisco, working for a financial institution.
She suspected he wouldn't have tolerated all the histrionics.
He was too mature and professional.

His smile faded. "While we're on the topic, don't let
whatever is going on between you and Win get in the way
of work, okay?"

"TJ, I don't know if you've noticed, but there's nothing
going on with me and your brother."

"Hey, it's not my business," he said, then, a little while
later, contradicted himself by adding, "But you want something to be going on, right?"

She didn't say anything at first because it was weird talking about her love life with him. "I don't think so." She left
it at that. For a while now, she'd come to the realization that
Win had become a convenient excuse for not moving on ro-
mantically when the real reason might be fear of failure. But
she wasn't about to share that with TJ, who never failed at
anything.

"I suspect he'll come around."

She shifted in her chair. "Why do you say that?" The
statement bothered her. It was as if TJ had suddenly become
attentive to her for Win's sake.

He cleared his throat. "I don't know. Isn't that what you guys do?"

She shook her head. It was what Win did, not her. The minute she showed an iota of disinterest in him, he came sniffing around. It was beyond old. "Let's not talk about it." No need parading her rejection in front of TJ.

She turned and took in his profile. His square jaw, his sharp cheekbones, his blue eyes. He could have any woman he wanted.

"What? Do I have something on me?"

She could feel her cheeks burn. "Nope, you're good."

He slanted her a look from the corner of his eye. "Then what are you staring at?"

"Nothing. How do you know this web designer?"

"I met her a few months ago, had her look at our existing site, and she came up with a bunch of ways to improve it, including adding an online store. Until now, we haven't had one. I just stuck a few of Delaney's pieces on the homepage. You know anything about SEO?" When she shook her head, he continued. "It stands for search engine optimization. Basically, it's creating a big presence on the internet so that when someone plugs specific words—adventure, climbing, skiing, mountain biking, stuff like that—into a search engine, Garner Adventure is one of the first websites to pop up."

"Do you have to pay for it?"

"Nope. That's the beauty of it. By using certain techniques and strategies, you can get a load of free marketing on the World Wide Web."

It sounded interesting to Deb, like something that would not only help the online store but could get GA more business in general.

"Do you shop online?" he asked her.

"Doesn't everyone in Glory Junction?" They didn't have a big shopping center with a lot of department and chain stores. The closest ones were in Reno.

"Say you're searching for shoes." He glanced down at her pumps. "What are the first sites that come up?"

"Zappos and Amazon."

"Yep. That's what we want to do with Garner Adventure. Someone is looking for rock climbing pants, bam, they get GA."

She poked him in the shoulder with her finger. "You're kind of a genius, aren't you?"

He laughed. "Not even close. What did Felix say about you quitting?"

"He was mixed. Happy for me but sad for him. I'm a good waitress."

"And you'll be good at this, too." He reached over and brushed her leg, leaving a warm imprint on her thigh, then slid her a look. "Did you tell Boden you're not taking his bartending job?"

She was actually considering taking a few shifts a week to get a jump on paying off her debt but didn't want TJ to think she was spreading herself too thin. "I just assumed he knew when I told him about getting the job at Garner Adventure."

"I'm sure there are no shortage of people who'll bartend." He drummed his fingers on the steering wheel.

"Probably not."

TJ exited when he got to downtown Reno and navigated the city streets like he knew where he was going. He pulled into a pay lot.

"We're across the street." He pointed at a modern four-story building.

Deb had met a few web designers in her time. They'd worked from their homes, making her think this person must be a big deal.

The office had that ultramodern loft-thing going. Exposed brick and railroad tie beams. A guy in black skinny jeans and a hipster beard asked them if they wanted coffee and proceeded to make them espressos in a sleek machine, nicer than anything at the diner or even Tart Me Up. A few minutes later, a dead ringer for Amanda Seyfried floated into the room. She had on a mesh top and a black bra and a teeny, tiny black skirt.

"TJ," she trilled and pushed her boobs against him for a hug while he held his minuscule espresso cup above her head, careful not to spill it.

"Good to see you, Jillian. This is Deborah Bennett, our new retail manager."

"Hi, Deborah." Jillian extended her hand but kept her eyes on TJ. It could've been Deb's imagination, but she would've sworn Jillian licked her lips. "Come inside my office."

They followed her into a room equally as modern as the rest of the space. TJ picked up a framed picture of Jillian in a bikini with her dog at the beach.

"Nice Lab."

It was all Deb could do not to roll her eyes. *Nice Lab, my ass*.

"Thanks," she said and flashed her Amanda Seyfried smile.

This must've been the reason for the jacket and tie, because from the look of the staff, TJ could've worn jeans and a sweatshirt. Or his underwear, like Jillian.

"I've got all kinds of good ideas for the site I want to show you," she continued.

"Great." TJ pulled out a chair for Deb and waited for Jillian to sit down before taking his own seat. "Show us what you got."

She hit a remote control and a screen inched up from a metal console that looked like it came from one of those modern furniture stores like Design Within Reach. Then she tapped on her keyboard until GA's homepage appeared on the screen. Deb attempted to pay attention, but she was distracted by trying to figure out if there was something going on between Jillian and TJ.

She assumed Jillian was exactly the kind of woman TJ was attracted to. From the looks of this place, Jillian was supersuccessful. Not to mention gorgeous, self-assured, and outgoing.

"I thought something like this," Jillian said, showing GA's homepage on the big screen. It looked amazing, with a video montage of the Garners in action. Gray parasailing, Win bombing down a slope on a snowboard, Colt riding white-water rapids with a boat full of people, and Josh conducting a cave tour at night.

Where was TJ? she wanted to ask. She'd seen him ski, mountain bike, and kayak and had always admired his skills. Athletically speaking, he was the most well-rounded of the Garner brothers. Pretty much outstanding at whatever he did.

"I like it," TJ said, and turned to Deb.

"It's fantastic."

Jillian clicked on the About page. "I had one of our writers tune up your story a bit. People love family-owned businesses and I didn't think your old site played that up enough. I do it here on the bio page, too." She clicked over, and there were headshots of the whole Garner family with blurbs about each one of them. It didn't hurt that they were an extremely good-looking family. "We'll add Deb as soon as you get her photo taken."

She continued to navigate through the site. Deb tried to remember what the old site looked like and couldn't, which meant it wasn't memorable. This one, however, she'd be loath to forget. It was one of the slickest, prettiest websites she'd ever seen. Jillian had used a lot of shots of the Sierra

Nevada, including the ski resorts, Lake Paiute, and the Glory Junction River. You couldn't get more picturesque than that.

"I thought we'd have a 'fun stuff' page where you could post pictures of your clients during their tours," Jillian said. "You could change them out every month, which would keep customers and their friends and family returning to your site. Somewhere on the page we could post a list of upcoming deals or promotions."

It was smart. Deb didn't have to be a marketing genius to see how a crop of pictures of people having a wonderful time would act as an incentive.

"Yep, I like it." TJ said.

"I'm so glad." Jillian practically vaulted herself over the glass desk to touch TJ's shoulder.

"Let's see the retail store." He seemed to be blind to her obvious crush. Either that or he was maintaining his professionalism for Deb's sake. Or he wasn't the ho his brother was.

"I think you're going to love it." Jillian went back to the homepage and clicked on the Store button.

The page looked like a vintage J. Peterman catalog, which was cool for J. Peterman but not for an athletic wear store. At least in Deb's humble opinion. Instead of saying anything, she waited to hear TJ's feedback.

"Isn't it great?" Jillian said, her voice orgasmic.

"I like it." TJ turned around and smiled at her.

"Uh, I don't know," Deb said, not able to curb her concern. To her, it looked incredibly dated and didn't fit the image of Garner Adventure, which was . . . well, in your face. Extreme sports for the bold and adventurous. The sketches of Delaney's clothes didn't do them justice and looked kind of wimpy. "It doesn't seem like GA's image."

"Why not?" TJ asked.

"You're selling performance wear. GA's consumers will

want to see the gear in action." She felt presumptuous saying it, but TJ was listening, looking at her intently, so she pushed on. "Maybe more videos or at least pictures of the guides wearing the clothes, instead of sketches. It just doesn't work for the brand."

"It absolutely does," Jillian cut in. "Each garment, each piece of equipment tells a story. Put together, it's an entire narrative."

Deb started to disagree, but Jillian was adamant. "I've been doing this a long time and wouldn't steer you wrong if I thought it wasn't the best possible way to sell your merchandise."

Deb couldn't be certain, but TJ looked torn. She knew he wouldn't have been if they were talking about ice climbing or parasailing or freestyle skiing. He was one of the best athletes in the extreme sports world . . . or at least he used to be.

"It's different than anything else out there, that's for sure," he said, examining the page closer. "Hopefully, it'll set Garner Adventure apart."

Deb didn't know diddley about marketing or selling adventure wear, so maybe she was wrong. Yet the little blurbs about each garment and the funny drawings weren't anything that would suck her in and make her want to buy. But there was no sense arguing about it, especially in front of Jillian.

After two hours of her brazen flirting with TJ—she must've brushed up against him five times by Deb's count—they finally left.

As they walked to his truck, she couldn't help saying, "Jillian likes you."

"Of course she does. Garner Adventure is paying her shitloads of money."

Was the man that dense or was he delicately telling her to mind her own business? "Uh-uh. She wants to do you."

He stopped short. "Where the hell did you come up with that?"

"Seriously? Are you joking? '*Oh, TJ, I'm soooooo glad you liked the website.' 'Oh, TJ, can I have your babies?*'"

He laughed, shook his head, and resumed walking.

Any man with a pulse could've seen through Jillian's gushing and not-so-subtle touches. "You don't think she was flirting with you?"

"I think she was being nice and accommodating because she wants our business."

"Well, I think she was going to accommodate you right into the bedroom. You're not interested?"

"No, and if I was, I wouldn't share it with my employee." He shot her a pointed look and opened the passenger door.

Okay, her cue to stop. "Fine, TJ, we won't talk about it anymore. But she wants you."

"I'll keep that in mind." He opened her door and got in on his own side. "Did Jillian make you feel better about the online store?"

"You mean about the narrative?" She made finger-quote marks around *narrative*. Probably not smart to be sarcastic on her first day, yet she couldn't help herself. "I don't get it. but I'm probably not as sophisticated as the two of you."

He gave her a steely glare. "I saw your point."

Then why didn't you have her change it? she wanted to ask. But from his body language—he'd gone all alpha, don't-question-my-authority, which was oddly hot—she could tell he was done talking about the online store. Fine. He and Jillian had a lot more experience than she did. In fact, she'd felt like a fraud the entire time she was there.

"I want one of our freelance photographers to take you

and Darcy's pictures next week for the bio page," he said and started the engine.

"Really? You don't think it should just be family?"

He shook his head. "I want you in the picture."

She knew he meant literally, not figuratively, but something in the way he said it made her heart leap . . . and her head remind her she was a fool.

The whole drive back, TJ kept sneaking looks at Deb. She was beautiful. Not glamorous like Jillian or porcelain perfect like Mandy, but she did it for him. Always had.

"You eat at the diner?" he asked.

"No, why? You hungry?"

"Starved. You mind if we stop on the way?"

"Not at all. I could eat, too." She started digging through her purse.

"What are you doing?"

"Looking to see if I have any money. You cut up all my credit cards, remember?"

He tugged her purse away and put it on the floor by her feet. "It's on the company, Deb. I don't expect you to pay for your own food when you travel for GA."

"We went to Reno. I hardly call that traveling."

"Fine, pay for your own meal, then." *Jeez, it was a freaking dinner.*

"Okay, if GA wants to buy my dinner, far be it from me to stop you," she relented.

"Damned straight." TJ pulled into the parking lot of a steak house. "This okay with you?"

She scanned the front of the restaurant. It was old school, with double glass doors and a neon sign with a big cowboy boot that said, "The Golden Spur." "Looks great."

They went inside and were seated at a booth. He checked

his phone to make sure nothing had blown up at the office while he was gone.

"This place has a huge menu," she said, perusing the sandwich page.

The server came and she got a bacon cheeseburger, shoestring potatoes, and iced tea. He went with the bleu cheeseburger, steak fries, and a vanilla shake.

"Let me ask you something," she said when the waiter left. "Why wasn't there any video of you on GA's new website?"

He shrugged. "There probably wasn't any good footage of me for Jillian to choose from."

"Because Lord knows if there had been, she would've splattered it across the top of the page." Deb's lips curved up.

"We back to that?" He didn't understand what her obsession with Jillian was. If he didn't know better, he'd think she was jealous.

She put her elbows on the table, laced her hands together, and propped her chin on the top. "I think you should have some video shot of you extreme skiing and include it with the other clips."

"Why's that?" He took a drink of water.

"Because I've seen you shred a sheer line and it's a thing of poetry. It'll make excellent video."

He felt a surge of pride at the compliment. "Thanks, but it's not a vanity project. We've got footage of Win, and he's the king of the mountain."

"No, he's not." She shook her head. "Don't get me wrong; Win is good. One of the best. But you're better."

He wasn't; otherwise, he would've made it onto the U.S. Olympic team for freestyle skiing, not Win. It was a sore subject for him but nice of her to say just the same. "I think we're good without it."

"Just saying."

Their food and drinks came and he picked up his burger and took a big bite. "Big plans for the weekend?" It wasn't a particularly artful way to find out if she was seeing anyone besides waiting for Win to come around. By now, Boden could've asked her out.

"I'm working breakfast shifts at the Morning Glory Saturday and Sunday. Afterward, I'm going skiing. How about you?"

"I'll probably ski, too. It should be good with all the fresh powder." Usually, he spent his weekends working.

"You miss guiding tours?"

"Yep." More than anyone knew.

She pointed one of her fries at him and popped it in her mouth. "I thought you loved being Mr. CEO."

"Who said I didn't? I'm just feeling a little restless these days." She had a drop of ketchup at the corner of her mouth and he itched to wipe it off with his thumb. Or with his lips. Instead, he took another bite of his burger.

"How come?"

"Don't know. Midlife crisis, maybe." He hitched his shoulders, his lips curving up in the corners.

"You're a little young for that, don't you think?" She took a drink of her tea and stared at him over the rim of the glass. Big, bedroom-brown eyes. "Perhaps you need a Corvette and a girlfriend."

He laughed "A Porsche, maybe. How's a girlfriend gonna make me less restless?"

She lifted one dark brow.

"Are you telling me I need to get laid?"

"Do you?"

He took a long slug of his shake, then mixed the ice cream around and took another one. "You think this is appropriate conversation for the workplace?"

"You started it." Yeah, he had. Maybe he needed to brush

up on GA's employee handbook. "And it never stopped Felix and me."

"From talking about sex?" He didn't let her answer that. "You almost done?"

"We're not getting dessert?"

"If you want it." He held up his shake. "I already had mine." But he could do for some more, he thought, as he fixated on her mouth. Her pretty pink lips.

"You're paying, right? Then yeah, I want dessert."

He called over the waiter and asked for the menus again. She perused the offerings and decided on the apple pie à la mode. The server returned with a heaping portion and two forks.

"You gonna share?" he asked her.

She pushed the plate toward him. "Dig in."

He tried not to hog it, but it was damned good pie and it was fun fighting her for it. But mostly he liked watching her enjoy it, the way she licked the fork after each bite and closed her eyes. It made him imagine kissing her and the way she might lick . . . Nope. Not going there. And TJ forced the image out of his head.

"You going to Old Glory tonight?" she asked.

"I hadn't thought about it. Why, are you?"

She scraped a spoon across the plate, getting the last of the ice cream. "Probably, although it'll be packed with tourists."

They'd be up to take advantage of the snow, and on Fridays, Boden booked bands to play. A big draw.

He needed to stay away from her in the off-hours. Working together was hard enough. "Yeah, I'll go," he heard himself say anyway. God, he needed to start dating and swore to himself that he'd call Mandy. She was successful, driven, hot; just his type.

He paid the bill, and on their way home it started to snow

again. Sporadic flurries at first, but then it got heavy enough
for him to turn on his windshield wipers to full blast.

"I'm glad you're driving and not me," she said.

Her rattletrap was lucky to make it over a hill, let alone
through a few inches of snow. "You do anything about your
transmission yet?"

"I have to wait until I get paid. Then I'll hit you up for
your contact."

"All right. Just let me know."

Perhaps with her new salary she'd be able to buy a car.
Not his place to suggest it, though. Just like it wasn't his
place to dissuade her from Win. His brother was a great
many things. Excellent things. Fun, charming, and kind.
Win was and had always been a good person. Reliable,
though, he wasn't. But he was TJ's brother and the Garners
were fiercely loyal to one another.

It took them fifteen minutes longer to get back to town,
not that he minded. She looked good in the passenger side
of his truck. He parked in front of Garner Adventure and
started to get out.

Deb grabbed his arm. "I wanted to tell you something."

He shut his door and turned in his seat to face her.

"Thank you for including me in the trip to Jillian's and
asking for my opinion, even if you don't agree with it. FYI:
I still think the online store sucks."

He rolled his eyes. "Yeah, I got that." He paused, and
then for no reason at all said, "You may be right about it, but
Jillian has more experience than both of us when it comes
to retail, and the truth is, I don't always use my head where
you're concerned."

She jerked in surprise. "What's that supposed to mean?"

He let out a breath, tired of dancing around it. "You know
exactly what I mean. You also know that it's inappropriate

on so many levels I don't know where to start." Win. The
fact that TJ was her boss. The list went on and on.

When he attempted to get out of the cab, she tugged on
his arm.

"Deb." As warnings went, it was pretty weak. Downright
soft, but his resistance was wearing thin.

She gazed into his eyes and wouldn't look away. "Just
a little one." And then she came over the center console
and kissed him, barely brushing his lips. Yet he still felt a
tightening in his groin and a hot spark of pleasure spread
through him. Her hands clutched his shoulders and her soft
breasts grazed his chest and she smelled sweet, like talcum
powder. Everything about her was making it difficult for
him to breathe. If he didn't get out of the truck soon, he was
going to kiss her for real.

"Hey, Deb, you think we can get back to work now?" His
voice was hoarse and he couldn't seem to move.

"Absolutely, boss," she said in a whisper against his
mouth, and he felt his heart squeeze the same way it always
did when she graced him with a smile at the diner or waved
to him from across the room at Old Glory.

She scrambled back over to her side of the cab, hopped
out onto the street, and they walked together to the front
door, her hand on the sleeve of his jacket to keep from slipping on the icy sidewalk in her high heels. And that warm
feeling he'd experienced in the truck continued to wrap
itself around him like a down blanket.

They got inside and found Win leaning against the reception counter, and the air suddenly turned cold.

"Hey, hot stuff," he said, and Deb took her hand off TJ's
jacket and looked down at the floor.

Chapter Seven

"Earth to Deb." Hannah waved her hand in front of Deb's face. Deb was lost in her own thoughts, still reliving the not-quite-a kiss she and TJ had shared in the front of his truck. The way he'd felt so solid pressed against her and the sweet taste of his lips. And how she'd probably shocked the hell out of him. He certainly had shocked the hell out of her with his bit about losing his head where she was concerned.

"Are you listening to me? You need to insist that he change it." Hannah searched the bar for a server. Old Glory was filling up and Boden's staff had their hands full. "TJ's a great businessman, but his sense of aesthetics sucks."

Deb thought it was too soon to start throwing her weight around. Besides, what the hell did she know about an online store? If cute little drawings worked for J. Peterman, who was she to eighty-six it? No one, that's who.

"I don't know," she said. "This Jillian woman seems to know what she's doing. You should see her. She's like a movie star and wanted to do TJ on the desk."

Hannah laughed. "He has that effect on women."

Didn't she know it. He'd rocked her world and they hadn't even exchanged saliva. But she wasn't ready to think about it, let alone talk about it. Her friends had put up with years of her whining about Win. *Uh-uh, not going to do it again*. "Right? I never noticed it before, but he does, doesn't he?"

"Who does what?" Foster grabbed the chair next to Deb and tucked his messenger bag under the table.

"TJ," Deb said. "He's a chick magnet. Who knew?"

He stared at her like she'd just come out of a five-year coma. "Uh, like everyone. He's so Chris Hemsworth . . . and that body. To die for. Who's hot for him?"

"This web designer in Reno. We met with her about the GA site and she was all over him. '*Oh, TJ, you're so smart. Oh, TJ . . .*'" Deb did her best impression of Jillian, but it came out more like a bad Marilyn Monroe.

"Frankly, I'm surprised no one has snatched him up yet." Foster perused his menu and, like Hannah had done, gazed around the dining room, looking for a server. "Boden needs to hire better people. This is ridiculous."

"He's working on it," Deb said in Boden's defense.

"The only reason why TJ's still single is because he's too busy at GA to date." Hannah waved, trying to get Boden's attention. He saw her and sent a waitress over.

They ordered and Deb got something light because she'd already eaten with TJ. Boden sent over a complimentary basket of pub fries to hold them over until their meals came. The band was in the corner warming up. Pretty soon it would be too loud to talk.

"He said he was coming tonight." Deb scanned the crowd.

"Who? TJ?" Foster asked and emptied half a bottle of ketchup on his plate.

"Uh-huh." She kept searching. "I wonder if something came up."

Win was in the other room, playing darts with Josh. When they'd gotten back from Reno, he'd been more attentive than usual. Then, like always, he ran off to chase the next shiny dime. The man had the attention span of a gnat, except, of course, when he was focused on a new woman. Then she became the center of his world. Deb had been that center more than once. It was a little like crack, having Win worship at your altar. So much so that even when he cast you away, the withdrawal was intense enough that you'd sell your soul for a hit.

She'd lost a lot of time and expended a lot of energy feeding the Win addiction. Too much. And if Win was like crack, getting tangled up with TJ would be like Oreos. She'd read somewhere that eating the cookies activated more neurons in lab rats' pleasure centers than cocaine.

"Maybe he has a date," Hannah said. "Delaney wants to set him up with Karen, though Colt told her that TJ is interested in a woman who does event planning at the Four Seasons." She looked at Deb. "You hear anything about that?"

"Nope." Maybe the blonde from the other night. Deb would rather not think about it.

She sidelined the conversation about TJ's love life and they wound up discussing Deb's upcoming birthday party until the band started playing. Josh joined Hannah at their table. Win had disappeared, probably with a woman. Foster left because he had an early morning the next day and Delaney, who'd showed up solo, took his seat. Colt was on his way.

And suddenly Deb felt like odd person out, the only one without a significant other. She searched the crowd again, thinking that at least if TJ were here they could sit together. And talk the way they had at supper. But he was MIA. At the end of the first set, she decided to call it a night. She'd get a good night's rest and hit Winter Bowl right after her shift at the diner.

* * *

Saturday morning, TJ unlocked the door at GA to get his skis and nearly ran head-on into Win. He was drinking one of his disgusting green smoothies and eating a granola bar, which seemed like a weird combination to TJ.

"A little early for you, isn't it?" As far as TJ knew, Win didn't have anything on the schedule until ten.

Win scowled. "Couldn't sleep." TJ didn't want to delve too deep into the reason for that. "What are you doing here? I thought it was your day off."

"Came in early to audit the equipment before it all gets checked out for the weekend." Even when he was supposed to have the first real weekend off in three weeks, he couldn't help but come into the office. Someone should come up with a pill for that because they had one for everything else. "I'm grabbing my skies and heading out."

"Where you going?" Win followed him to his office, slurping on his drink.

"Winter Bowl."

"Winter Bowl? Your arthritis acting up? What's the matter with Royal Slope or the backcountry? You can't get Riley to take you up in the helicopter?"

TJ clenched his teeth. Win's swagger really got on his nerves sometimes. Maybe TJ didn't want to go balls-out. Maybe he just wanted to chill and spend a day outside. But that was his little brother, always swooping in, sucking the joy out of everything, and hogging the glory.

Hey, hot stuff. Give me a freaking break. But this wasn't about yesterday or about the moment he'd shared with Deb in his truck or Win's impeccable timing. This was just . . . ah, hell, he didn't know. He just felt agitated.

"Nothing wrong with Winter Bowl," he said, trying to quell his simmering anger by walking away.

"If you're a seventy-five-year-old grandmother," Win called to TJ's back.

He whipped around and glared at Win. "I guess not all of us can make the U.S. Olympic team. Oh, wait a minute, you did and then dropped out." He didn't usually throw that in Win's face, but his brother was asking for it.

"Fuck you." Win shoved him and stomped out of TJ's office.

"That was shitty." Colt appeared out of nowhere, filling up the doorway, wearing his self-righteous face.

Apparently, the whole family had decided to show up at seven thirty in the freaking morning. Most times, TJ couldn't get them to attend a meeting at nine.

"Get off your high horse, Colt." TJ grabbed his skis and pushed past his brother, who came after him.

"What the hell's the matter with you?"

"This place. That's what's the matter with me," he said, then shoved open the front door and walked out.

By the time TJ got to Winter Bowl, guilt gnawed at him. Win dropping out of the Olympics team was a sensitive issue for his little brother. TJ shouldn't have rubbed it in. It wasn't Win's fault that everything got handed to him, even things he didn't want. And it wasn't Win's fault that TJ worked hard for everything he got and even things he didn't.

After an hour of ripping down a black-diamond slope, he felt better. Two hours later, he sent Win a text: **Sorry.**

In response, he got a shaka-sign emoji. Hang loose. That was the thing about being a Garner. No grudges. As their dad liked to say, "There's no buddy like a brother."

Suddenly, he had an appetite again and went in pursuit of food, stowing his skis and poles on one of the racks outside the Four Seasons. In the lobby, guests sat around the huge stone fireplace on leather couches, having afternoon drinks. Not a bad way to spend a Saturday, TJ supposed, though

he'd rather be outside. He decided against the restaurant—
too formal—and waited in line at the café to get a sandwich.
Deb had said she was going skiing today and he wondered
if she'd gone to the Slope or Squaw.

When it was his turn at the counter, he ordered a ham
and cheese on sourdough, a bag of chips, two cookies, and
a cup of coffee. He took it to a table in the corner. For the
price, the sandwich should've been better, but he was
hungry and wolfed it down.

He unwrapped one of the cookies and ate it, stuffing the
other one in his pocket. After he cleaned up his mess, he
went outside to get his skis and boots. There at the rack
was Deb.

"You stalking me or are you actually skiing here today?"

As Win had so obnoxiously pointed out, Winter Bowl
wasn't really a place they went. Too filled with tourists. The
runs were nice enough but a little less challenging than
hard-core skiers were in to, including Deb. He'd come because it was good business for the resort's top management
to see a Garner here occasionally and he was the only one
willing to do it.

"Free lift tickets," she said. "One of my regulars at the
diner gave them to me. He's got a torn meniscus." She
bobbed her head at the hotel. "I was on my way in to get a
cup of coffee."

"I'll buy." And maybe they could talk about the thing that
happened in his truck. Hell, he didn't even know what to
call it.

"Nah-uh, I can afford it now that I have a real job." She
looked so happy that it made him feel outrageously good,
like he'd single-handedly put that smile on her face.

"Whatever you say, big spender." He trailed her into the
hotel, enjoying the view of her ass in ski pants. They went

to the snack bar and the girl working the cash register acted like they were old friends.

"I was just here," he told Deb when she raised her brows.

They took their drinks to a table with a view of the ski lifts going up and down the mountainside.

"You seem to capture hearts wherever you go." Her lips twitched with humor.

"It's a Garner gift," he said facetiously because the girl behind the counter was eighteen at the oldest.

"What happened to you last night? I thought you were coming to Old Glory."

He shrugged. "Got hung up at work. Was the band good?"

"I didn't wind up staying."

"No?" He waited to see if she'd say why.

She cupped her mug with both hands and took a sip. "I had an early morning at the Morning Glory."

"Yep. I know how that is. Were Colt and Delaney there?" He pulled his saved cookie from his pocket and pushed half of it toward her.

"Delaney came from work and Colt got there just before I left."

"You talk to her about your idea?"

"The jacket tent? Come on, be honest; you think it's silly."

"If I thought it was silly I'd tell you, Deb. You should've talked to her about it." He took a bite of his half of the cookie and gave her the rest.

She cocked her head to one side. "You really think I should tell her about it?"

"You're in charge of GA's merchandise. Hell yeah, you should tell her about it to see what she thinks."

She beamed, her whole face like sunshine, and the fact that he could light her up that way sort of sucked the air from his lungs. It was that heady. And dangerous to his constitution.

"Seriously, I can't believe I get to do this."

He leaned into the table and watched her closely. "So yesterday . . ."

"Uh-huh, what about it?" She moved forward until their shoulders were almost touching.

And that was when Deb's phone rang.

She grabbed it out of the pocket of her backpack. One look at the display and she quickly answered. It took TJ only a second or so to deduce that it was one of Deb's parents. A plumbing problem.

"I've gotta go," she said and stuck the phone back in her pack.

"What's going on?"

"My mom wants me to run over to the hardware store to get a P-trap. Their sink's leaking . . . water's everywhere."

"You've got someone to fix it?" TJ knew Sid had a bad back and Geri wasn't that handy.

She hitched her shoulders. "Yeah, me. Or a plumber, depending on how bad it is."

A good plumber in Glory Junction got sixty bucks an hour. "I'll give you a hand."

"No." She stood up. "It's your day off; you should get to enjoy it, not have to deal with a flooded kitchen."

That was the thing. He'd enjoy just about anything if it meant being with her. "No offense, Deb, but I'm guessing you wouldn't know a P-trap from a mousetrap." He shrugged on his jacket and followed her outside.

Chapter Eight

Win sat in his Jeep outside Britney's condo. She was supposed to have been home an hour ago, but as usual she was late and not returning any of his texts.

According to the airline, her flight from Palm Springs got into Reno six minutes early. He didn't know what the hell the holdup was, and frankly, he was tired of her bullshit. They needed to hash out a plan on where they stood and she couldn't be bothered. Apparently, discussions about bringing a child into this world weren't as important as Britney's social life. All weekend he'd stewed, and now he wanted to get the situation settled between them.

He checked his phone again. Nothing. The neighbors more than likely thought he was casing the complex, he'd been sitting there so long. Except Cami, who he got the feeling was working in cahoots with Britney to warn her off. He was just about to leave, fed up, when a Lincoln Town Car rolled up. Britney got out while the uniformed driver popped the trunk and proceeded to unload three large suitcases. It seemed like a lot of luggage for a three-day trip.

But that was Britney for you. She needed a trunk for her makeup alone.

This was the woman he was saddling himself with for the rest of his life. Good God. He watched her unlock her door while the driver lugged her suitcases inside and waited for him to leave. As soon as the Town Car pulled away, Win got out of the Jeep. Ambushing her was his best strategy. Otherwise, she'd continue to evade him.

She let out an inelegant snort when she found him at the door. "I just got home, Win. Now's not a good time."

Women were usually happy to see him.

"Too bad." He pushed past her. "We have to deal with this, Britney."

"No, I have to deal with it." She went in her bedroom and attempted to lift one of the bags onto the bed.

Win did it for her. "What's that supposed to mean?"

"It means it's my problem, not yours."

He didn't like calling a baby a problem, but he understood her fears. "Ultimately, it's your decision, Britney. But I'm here for you all the way."

"Yeah right." She started taking clothes out of the suitcase and refolding them.

He put his hand on the back of her neck and felt the tension there. "I won't bolt. You've got to trust me on that."

"Sure you won't." She sat on the edge of the bed. "I can't afford a baby."

He couldn't stop himself from doing a visual lap around the room. Pretty plush, right down to the 400-thread-count sheets. "I can."

She locked eyes with him. "They're expensive." What she meant was, she was expensive.

"We'll be fine, Britney."

"I have to think about it," she said, but he could see the wheels spinning in her head.

He sat next to her. "Take the time you need. Just don't push me away. I'm here and I'm not going anywhere."

"You're ready to be a father?" The way she said it reminded him of TJ. The subtext being, *everyone knows you're a fuckup*.

"I'm a Garner. We don't shirk our responsibilities." He clasped her chin in his hand and brushed a strand of hair away from her face. "I'll be a good father."

She pulled away. "I'm tired, Win." That was a first. For Britney, the party never ended, but maybe it was hormones. The websites he'd read said fatigue was to be expected in the first trimester.

"I'll stay the night." He'd do some household chores and help lessen her load.

"What for?" She sounded perturbed. "I'm going straight to sleep."

He jerked back. "I wasn't expecting you not to." Did she think he'd demand sex? "I just want to help, Britney. Is that so hard to believe?"

"I'm sorry," she said. "It's the mood swings; they make me bitchy."

He cleared her suitcase off the bed, took her shoes off, and swung her legs up. "You want me to make you something to eat?" Perhaps food would help.

She rested her back against the headboard. "No, thanks. Would you mind terribly if I spent the night alone?"

Here she was again, leaving him in limbo. He let out a breath. "I want to resolve this, Brit. The sooner, the better." Otherwise, it was more sleepless nights for him.

"I need time to think and you're crowding me. Frankly, that's why I went away." There was a long pause and then, "I might get an abortion."

"It's my baby, too," he said, knowing this was a touchy subject. "Shouldn't I be part of that decision . . . or at least involved in the conversation?" He put up his hands. "I'd never pressure you one way or the other; it's your decision. But I'd like to be included in making the choice."

She let her eyes close. "Fine, but I need some breathing room, some time to consider my options."

He knew when to stop pushing. "Okay, but promise me you won't run off again."

"I won't."

"No matter what you decide, we should see a doctor." He pulled the down comforter over her.

"All right. Just give me a few days."

Fair enough, he supposed. But it still irked him that they weren't getting anywhere. "Anything I can do before I leave?"

She shook her head. "Nothing I can think of."

"Then I'll take off." He kissed her on the cheek and started to walk away.

"Win, there is one thing," she called. "You think you could help me cover the rent this month? Harrah's has been slow and I rely on tips."

Not when he'd been there. He looked at her for a long time, then said, "How much do you need?"

"Knock, knock." TJ's door was open, but he seemed so immersed in what he was doing that Deb didn't want to startle him.

He glanced up, surprised to see her. "Didn't know you were here. You done at the diner?"

"Uh-huh, and I have tomorrow off, so I can put in a full day."

"Come in." He wheeled around in his chair and she noted

he'd ditched his Vasques for a pair of cowboy boots. Common enough in Glory Junction, but she'd never known TJ to don a pair. He wore them well. "You see those papers I left on your desk?"

"I did. But I'm not sure what I'm supposed to do with them." She sat on the couch.

"Pick out a few of the sweatshirt and T-shirt styles you think will sell best and decide which logo designs should go on which pieces. After that, we'll talk about numbers." He leaned forward. "Why are you looking at me that way?"

Because from the moment she'd walked in the room something in her chest had blossomed. Life suddenly seemed filled with possibilities. And even though she did her best to push down any hopes where TJ was concerned, she couldn't help but feel like he was one of those possibilities. "I can't believe I get to do this . . . shop with your money. It's like the best job ever."

His mouth curved up in a heart-stopping smile and damn. Foster was right. Chris Hemsworth. She was going to have to rewatch *Rush*.

"We'll see how you feel in two weeks when I work your ass off."

"Bring it on. Who do I talk to about getting some office supplies?"

"That would be Darcy. Anything else?" He was dismissing her and she wanted to loiter.

"Thank you for fixing my parents' leaky sink." She hated to admit it, but TJ was a better plumber than her. Over the years, living hand to mouth, she'd become a jack-of-all-trades and took great pride in it. But TJ had replaced the P-trap in half the time it would've taken her. "They loved seeing you."

"I should visit more often," he said and turned back to a stack of papers on his desk, his brows furrowed.

"Is everything okay? You seem distracted."

"Yep." He didn't look up and seemed to be reading and doing math on a calculator at the same time. "A group of clients trashed a couple of rooms at the Four Seasons and Stan the Man claims we caused him a hundred thou in damages. Just another Monday at GA," he trailed off.

Deb perched on the arm of TJ's sofa. "Who's Stan the Man?"

"The client who took a ride down Glory Mountain in a porta-potty."

"Oh yeah, I heard about that." She craned her neck to get a better look at what TJ was doing. "What kind of clients trash a hotel room?" GA's customers were typically families, corporate types, or well-to-do adventure seekers. Responsible people.

"A group of old college buddies who relive their glory days by breaking shit." He rolled his eyes.

"Don't you know that event planner at the Four Seasons?"

He lifted his head up. "How'd you hear about her?"

"Colt told Delaney you're interested in her. Delaney told Hannah and Hannah told me."

TJ shook his head. "Glad everyone's talking about my personal life."

"You could call her and ask her to help smooth things over with the Four Seasons' management. Or if you want, I could. What's her name?" Deb made the give-me sign with her hand.

"Mandy Forsyth." He fixed her with a look. "I'll take care of it."

Deb didn't recognize the name. Even though Glory Junction was a small town, the resorts were like countries onto themselves. A lot of the employees lived on the property or commuted from Reno.

"Well? You and Mandy Forsyth dating?" Her mind immediately jumped to whether he was sleeping with her, and then she wondered what TJ was like in bed. If he was as good as he was at extreme sports.

"Nope." He went back to what he was doing.

"So Mandy Forsyth isn't The One?"

"The one what?"

She reached over and poked him in the arm. "The One . . . your dream girl."

He looked up, shook his head, and went back to scribbling something on a piece of notepaper.

"Let's say for argument's sake you had one," she pressed, "what would she be like?"

"Hmm?" He wasn't even listening.

"Your dream girl," she said it loudly, like he was hearing impaired. "What would she be like?"

He stopped what he was doing, pulled his office chair closer, and acted as if he were considering her question. She knew he was pretending because he was doing an imitation of that famous sculpture of the naked guy, resting his chin on one hand.

"Brunette, five-seven, a hundred and forty pounds, brown eyes, fantastic athlete, nosy as hell, doesn't get any work done, has a shitty car."

"Ha, ha, very funny." She pushed his chair back and got to her feet. "And by the way, one hundred and forty pounds, really?" According to her scale this morning, 142 and change. But he didn't need to know that.

Deb went back to her office and, ten minutes into measuring the pros and cons of hoodies versus crew necks, she came to the staggering conclusion that TJ had just said she was his type. On Saturday, he'd watched her trudge through her parents' flooded kitchen in an old pair of waders and a Shop-Vac. And here they were today, engaging in sexy banter. While she tried desperately not to read too much into it, she experienced a zing of optimism all over again.

"What are you doing?" Hannah wandered in and checked

out the room. "Girl, you need some furniture." She plopped into one of the folding chairs that had been left in the room to die.

For the first time, Deb noted the white walls, the boring beige carpet, and the lack of any ornamentation at all. No one would ever believe that a fledgling retail goddess resided here. "I need the *Property Brothers*."

Hannah laughed. "Don't worry; I'll hook you up."

"Good, because I don't have time for decorating. You on a break from the store?"

"Uh-huh. I have one of my high-school kids today. What are you looking at?"

Deb turned the catalog so Hannah could see it. "TJ wants me to pick out sweatshirts. After I pick out the ones I want, I'm supposed to custom design them with these graphics." She pointed to various GA logos.

Hannah studied the offerings and noted the zip-up hoodie Deb had also admired. "These are wonderful but expensive. Pullover crew necks are going to be your best sellers because the price points are lower."

"That's good information." Deb jotted down the style number of the crew neck. "What else should I know?"

"You're buying for spring and summer, so don't get the ones with the fleece lining. Stick to lightweight. These are the most popular colors for women." She grabbed a pen and circled an assortment of pastels. "Men typically go navy, black, gray."

Deb continued to take notes. "Anything more?"

"Don't put Glory Junction on your stuff because if you do, you'll cut into my business."

"You don't have to worry about that. I have your back."

"You should do caps with the GA logo," Hannah continued. "Glory Junction and Sierra Nevada hats are my best sellers at the store."

"TJ didn't say anything about hats. Should I mention it to him?"

"Deb"—Hannah shot her an exasperated look—"this is your baby. Of course you should suggest hats and anything else you think of."

In this case, it was Hannah doing the thinking, but Deb wasn't above riding her friend's coattails. Glorious Gifts was hugely successful. Hannah's late aunt had founded the store, but it had been Hannah who had reinvented it and increased sales tenfold.

Deb found a pad of sticky notes and marked the sweatshirt pages with them. On her way out, she stopped at TJ's office. He was on the computer.

"Hey, can we meet tomorrow? I have the sweatshirts figured out and I think we should carry hats. Caps and maybe even some of those floppy ones, the kind military dudes wear, with the GA insignia."

He grabbed his phone and pulled up his calendar. "Ten a.m. work?"

Look at me having meetings. "Perfect. See you tomorrow."

He went back to what he was doing and she lingered because she liked looking at him. Watching him work . . . well, he was just so gorgeous. His sleeves rolled up just above his elbows, his hair tousled from repeatedly running his fingers through it, and his chin covered with dark stubble that hadn't been there this morning.

"You want something else?" he asked, giving her a slow once-over that made her tummy do funny things.

You. "Nope."

Chapter Nine

TJ was in a piss-poor mood Tuesday morning. He'd overslept, missed an important phone call, and hadn't had time for breakfast. And to keep things copacetic between GA and the Four Seasons, he'd agreed to pay two thousand dollars to cover the damage their clients had caused.

Stanley Royce was a whole other story. TJ was waiting to hear back from GA's lawyer before countering Stan's demands. He just wanted the guy to go away.

"I'm going to Tart Me Up," he told Darcy as he crossed the lobby. "Text me if you want anything."

Boden was unlocking the front door of Old Glory as TJ passed. "Morning."

"Morning." TJ stopped because in Glory Junction, if you didn't say hi to your neighbor, you were considered a douchebag. "How's it going?"

"Fair to middling. Haven't had these kinds of crowds in a while." Nope. Thanks to the snow, they were Disney on Parade, which was fine by TJ.

"Good times. Let's hope they last." TJ glanced at his watch. "I've gotta motor."

"Catch you later, then."

"Yep." TJ crossed the street to the river walk, where he'd

be less likely to run into one of the shop owners. He could really do without pleasantries this morning.

No such luck. Colt pulled up alongside him in his police cruiser and rolled down the window. "Where you going?"

"Tart Me Up."

"I'll meet you there."

Perfect. TJ rolled his eyes and walked the block to the bakery. Colt found a parking space and met him inside.

"Get me one of those ham and cheese croissant sandwiches and I'll grab us a table," Colt said.

"I've got to get back, Colt."

"You can spend ten minutes with your big brother." Colt was a bossy SOB.

It wasn't worth arguing with him, so TJ waited for his number to be called, ordered them both sandwiches and coffees, and joined Colt at the table.

"You and Win kiss and makeup?" Colt asked, snapping up TJ's sandwich and taking a bite before TJ could stop him. "Mmm, Swiss and bacon."

"You've got your own, jerk-off."

"I like yours better," Colt said around a mouthful. "You and Win?"

"We're good." TJ grabbed his sandwich back and accidentally on purpose kicked Colt's shin under the table. "Haven't seen him around much, though."

Colt took a slug of coffee. "He's been seeing a woman in Tahoe since summer. Who knows how serious it is, though? By now, he's probably hooked up with her sister."

Their youngest brother was certainly the playboy of the family. And the charmer. Josh, who was second youngest, was the war hero. As a kid, Josh had always been the determined one, the Eagle Scout, and the one voted most likely to be president. Colt had always been the one they'd all gone to to take care of their problems. Colt beat up the

school bullies, covered their asses from their parents' wrath
when they screwed up, and looked over them like a mother
hen. Somehow, TJ had earned the label of the studious one
and the go-getter. The one most likely to run GA while the
other brothers had all the fun.

Yep, he was living the dream.

"Don't give him crap about the Olympics anymore," Colt
said. "Not everyone is like you."

"Like me . . . what the hell is that supposed to mean?
Have you forgotten? I didn't make the team."

Colt didn't say anything for a while, just held TJ's gaze.
It was creepy how he did that. When they were kids they
used to play Made you Blink. Colt was always the last man
standing.

"So, what happened to keep you from qualifying, huh?
It's always been a mystery to me."

"I whiffed. Mystery solved."

"Bullshit," Colt said. "Of all of us, you're the one who
accomplishes whatever you set your mind to." He jabbed a
wooden stirrer in the air. "I have my theories about why you
washed out."

"Well, keep them to yourself. The whole thing is old
news." The truth was, he sort of had a chip on his shoulder
about it.

They turned their heads when a couple of women walked
into the bakery. Tourists, from what TJ could tell.

"What's going on with Mandy?" Colt asked, and TJ was
glad of the subject change.

"I took care of the Four Seasons thing without getting
her involved. I'm blacklisting those clients. They drink and
party too much and have become a liability. I don't care how
much business they give us."

"I'm with you wholeheartedly." Colt reached over and

tore off another piece of TJ's croissant. "But that's not what I was talking about. You should take Mandy out."

"Hey!" TJ swatted Colt's hand away from his food. The guy was a bottomless pit. "I'll get around to it." He wouldn't, but it was more prudent to agree than tell Colt he was hung up on a certain brunette who now worked for him.

"You don't sound very enthusiastic about it."

TJ shrugged. "Mandy's nice, but I'm not feeling it."

"Delaney wants to set you up with Karen, her manager," Colt said. "I told her not to meddle in your business. But I can tell her to go for it. What do you think?"

He'd met Karen a few times but couldn't remember much about her. He had a vague recollection of her at Delaney's big fashion show over the summer. Possibly a redhead, but he might've mistaken her for someone else. "Nah. I can find my own women."

"All right." Colt finished his coffee. "I'll tell her to set you up with her."

TJ shook his head. It was best to leave it alone. "You still doing the speed riding tour?" He ate the rest of his croissant before Colt got his fat hands on it again. Rachel made them from scratch.

"I told you I was." He got up and bussed his dishes. "How's Deb doing so far?"

"Good. We're meeting this morning on the sweatshirts and hats." These meetings would be the death of him. Every time they were alone together he felt an electric current in the air and then was reminded why the two of them were impossible. Still, he couldn't seem to help himself. The whole thing had disaster written all over it. "She's got vision."

Colt looked dubious. "I'm willing to give her a chance." TJ hadn't left him much choice.

"I'll try to stop by GA later," Colt said. "Let me know what our lawyers say about Stanley Royce."

After Colt left, TJ drained the rest of his coffee, got an apple turnover for Darcy, and walked back to the office. The sun had come out, but it was colder than it had been the day before. Forecasters predicted more snow sometime this evening. If it kept up, they'd have the best winter snowpack in years.

Darcy was fielding calls at the front desk, so he left the turnover with her and headed for the "executive wing." That was what he and his brothers jokingly called their parents' offices. His dad wasn't there; probably guiding a tour somewhere. And his mom wasn't in her office either. She'd been coming in less frequently, leaving all aspects of the business to her sons, i.e., him. After all these years, she deserved to slow down and spend more time with her friends and the various charity organizations that kept her busy.

Passing Win's office, TJ noted that his brother had made a rare appearance. Win was on the phone and TJ stood in the doorway, waiting for him to finish. The second Win spotted him, he started to wrap up the call. It was as if he didn't want TJ to know what he was talking about.

"Who was that?"

"No one." Win put his feet up on the desk. "Just a friend."

TJ sank into a beanbag chair. "Didn't these go out of style two decades ago?" Win didn't have a pithy comeback, a sure sign that something was wrong. "What's going on?"

"I've got nothing. You?"

"We just got a big family reunion. They booked for a week of activities in March. I'm gonna need you on that. We didn't really have the opening, but I couldn't pass up that kind of money." Especially after his two-thousand-dollar setback this morning and a looming lawsuit.

"Good," Win said, which surprised TJ. Usually, his

brother bitched and moaned whenever TJ took on extra clients. "I need a raise, TJ."

"Uh, okay, we can talk about that." They'd all forgone raises last year to help build the business. Win lived fairly frugally, so it was surprising that he was asking for one now. "Everything okay?"

"TJ, save the third degree, would you? I shouldn't have to grovel for a few extra bucks. It's not like I'm not earning it."

"Whoa." TJ held up his hands. "I thought I woke up on the wrong side of the bed. What the hell has you all revved up?"

"I just knew you'd turn it into a federal case, like you do everything."

TJ got to his feet and walked to the door. "Write up a request and put it on my desk and I'll get you a goddamn raise."

He crossed the hall, wondering what the hell had crawled up Win's ass. Josh passed him. "You know what's wrong with Win?"

"Nope. I'm meeting with a few lugers on the southside of Glory Mountain and I'm running late. Deal with it, okay?"

He always did. Instead of going to his office, TJ went to Deb's and popped his head inside. "You know what's eating Win?"

She lifted her head from the catalogs he'd given her on Monday. "No. I haven't seen him all day. Why, what's going on with him?"

"I have no idea, but he's acting like an asshole."

"Nothing new there," she said, and he noticed she was all dressed up. She'd done something different to her hair and had on makeup.

"What's with the new look?"

"This is the professional me, career woman extraordinaire." She stood up and did a little twirl. "You like it?"

Yeah, he did. Too much. The little knit dress showed off her legs and breasts. Deb had great breasts. And that hopeful look on her face, the way she wanted approval, stirred something in him. Then again, she always stirred something in him.

"We meeting?" she asked.

"Sure. Give me a second." He went back to his desk to get his iPad and stopped off in the lobby to check with Darcy—maybe she knew what was up with Win—but she'd gone on an errand.

"You ready?" He stepped into Deb's office.

"Uh-huh." She arranged the catalogs, which had Post-it notes stuck everywhere.

He grabbed a folding chair. "You need some furniture in here." A meeting table and some real chairs would be good. "I'll ask Darcy to order you some stuff."

She'd written out notes on a yellow legal pad. A little archaic, but he was glad to see she was prepared. "Do yourself a favor and get a tablet with your first paycheck."

"I have one. But it's broken. I'm gonna see if Duncan can fix it." Duncan was Glory Junction's official computer geek.

"Show me what you've got."

She laid out her plan, arguing the pros of crew necks over hoodies. "I think we should do both in multiple colors but definitely more crew necks."

"All right. How many do you want to do of each and what sizes?"

She froze. "I didn't think that far ahead. I thought you were going to help me with numbers. TJ, this is all new to me."

"I meant numbers as far as your budget. Don't worry, I'll help you." Even though the constant closeness was hell on his . . . everything. *You should've thought of that before you hired her, dumbass.* "We need to get things ordered and up on the website soon." Sales hadn't picked up since their initial trial. He hoped an attractive online store and new merchandise would spark renewed interest; otherwise a lot of people were going to be pissed off, namely his brothers. "Show me what you're thinking as far as which logo goes where."

She referred to her notes and Post-its. He had to laugh at her old-fashioned approach.

"I was thinking this one here." She pointed to the Garner Adventure graphic they used on their pamphlets.

"Yup. I like that."

"And this one here." She put the GA initials next to the picture of a hoodie and continued to go through her list, showing him which logo went where.

"It all works for me. Just come up with your numbers and get the stuff ordered. You also need to set up a meeting with Delaney and figure out what to stock in our inventory. We're done with beta. This is the real deal."

She wrote *call Delaney* on her pad. "Can you show me how to find customer orders? I couldn't figure out how I was supposed to log in to check that."

"Sorry. That should've been one of the first things I showed you. Go to the website."

She sat at her desktop and he pulled up a chair, giving her the information to log on as an administrator.

"Click there." He grabbed for the mouse and covered her hand, feeling instant heat.

Deb didn't move away, and for a minute, they scrolled through the orders together, his hand on hers.

Ah, jeez, they were at work and all he wanted to do was keep holding her hand. Like forever.

"Remember when you used to follow me around GA when your parents cleaned the offices?" The memory of her as an impish five-year-old with curly brown hair, big brown eyes, and boundless energy made his lips curve up.

"Uh-huh," she said softly. "I'd get into everything and you'd bail me out."

Grateful, she used to hold his face in her two tiny hands and stare up at him like he was the greatest thing since sliced bread. Those eyes, shining like the sun, never failed to make his chest kick.

"What made you remember?" she asked.

"No reason." Slowly, he slid his hand off hers, letting his fingers brush her soft skin before letting go, and resumed looking at the order page. He cleared his throat and tried for a normal tone. "We got one for Delaney's ski jacket and another for her bouldering shirt. Darcy can show you the shipping process. You have this under control?" He certainly didn't.

"I think so."

Good. Because if he didn't leave this room soon, he was going to make a move on her. "Bang on my door if you don't understand something." He stood up and headed out.

"Want to go to lunch later?" she asked. "I mean, if you aren't busy. You know, we could grab something together and I can pick your brain."

He should've said no, that he had plans. But *no* didn't seem to be in his vocabulary where she was concerned. "Come get me when you're ready."

When he got back to his office, he found Win's written request for a pay increase. TJ studied it and pulled up the budget on his computer. A few minutes later, he crossed the hallway to his brother's office.

"I'll put in for your raise this afternoon. You won't see the money until the check after next. If you need me to float you until then, I can do that." He made eye contact with Win and held it. "You into something I should know about?"

"I'm fine, just have expenses like everyone else."

TJ wanted to ask about these sudden expenses, but if Win wanted him to know, he'd tell him. "Okay."

"What are you doing for lunch?"

Since when did everyone want to go to lunch with him? "I'm taking Deb to lunch . . . for work stuff. You want to come?"

"Nah, not if it's a work thing." Win seemed preoccupied. "I've got stuff to do anyway."

How screwed up was it that TJ was relieved? How screwed up was it that he wanted Deb to himself, even if it was only for an hour?

"Let me know if you change your mind," TJ said.

He went back to his office and spent the next couple of hours working on schedules. They desperately needed more guides and he was always shuffling manpower to fill holes. As a result, GA was paying a shitload of overtime, which wasn't ideal.

A little after noon, Deb came in with her coat and hat on. "You ready? I'm starved."

He finished what he was doing and, out of guilt, stuck his head in Win's office to give him a second chance to join them, but his brother was gone.

"Where do you have in mind?" TJ asked Deb.

"We can go to the Morning Glory."

"All right, as long as you're not sick of the place." By his count, she still had a week left of working at the diner.

The Basque and Indian places were good, too, but the Morning Glory and Old Glory always seemed to be everybody's go-to restaurant, at least for lunch. Probably because it was close.

He stopped off at Darcy's desk to tell her they were out for lunch, then held the door open for Deb. Felix waved from the kitchen window when they walked in and told them to sit wherever they wanted.

"He lose another chef?" TJ asked.

"Not as of yesterday, but who knows? Let's get that back booth. Quieter." He followed and squeezed in across from her.

Ricki brought them menus. "You're keeping better company these days," she told Deb and ran her hands through TJ's hair. "You all need a few minutes?"

"I'm ready." He knew the menu by heart and Deb could probably recite it in her sleep. He motioned for her to order first.

"I'll have a CB with a side of fries," she said.

"What's a CB?"

"Cheeseburger," Deb and Ricki answered in unison.

"I'll have the same." TJ handed the menus to Ricki. "And coffee, please."

"Late night?" Deb quirked a brow and leaned over the table, giving him an excellent view down the top of her dress. Nice black bra.

"I was doing profit-and-loss statements." Boring as hell, but a necessity.

"You're no fun," she teased.

"What are you talking about? I'm lots of fun." He waggled his brows and she laughed, and the chemistry between them ratcheted up a hundred degrees. She had a way of making him forget about work . . . and that wasn't good.

"You come up with sweatshirt numbers for your order yet?" he asked to steer the conversation back to the job. This was supposed to be a business lunch, after all.

"I'm planning to talk to Hannah about it. See what she does a month."

"Smart." Ricki brought his coffee and he took a sip. "Keep in mind that we have a different clientele."

"I already thought of that, but at least I'll get an idea." She glanced at the door as a group of regulars came in. "You find out what the deal was with Win?"

"Not really." He didn't want to talk about Win's out-of-the-blue request for a raise. He didn't want to talk about Win, period.

More lunch goers came in and the noise level rose. "You gonna miss this place?" he asked.

"That would be a big no! I'll miss Felix, Ricki, and some of the other staff, though. The good news is, I'll still eat here." She leaned toward him again. "How come you're still single?"

The non sequitur threw him, and for a second, he considered telling her some version of the truth. But now that they were working together, that was completely unadvisable. Felony stupid, in fact. "Haven't had time to focus on that area of my life. Anyway, there's nothing wrong with being single. I'm only thirty-four."

"I'm not buying it," she said and rearranged the condiments in the basket on the table.

"Okay, don't buy it." He shrugged.

"The problem with you is that your standards are too high."

"Whatever you say." He looked at her, waiting. She clearly thought she was hugely perceptive.

"Colt's still my favorite Garner. But you're now running him a close second."

"That so?" He folded his arms over his chest. "What about Win?"

"Win's not even in the running anymore."

"Then what about Josh? Everyone loves Josh. You know, the whole war hero thing."

"Don't get me wrong, I'm crazy about Josh," she said. "But before him, I had Hannah all to myself. And I'm a petty person."

He chuckled at her honesty. But he'd never thought of her as petty.

Ricki returned with their food and rushed off to wait on the other tables.

"When did you come to the conclusion that I was second to Colt, which by the way, Colt? Seriously?" He took a bite of his burger. "Let me guess; it's because I gave you a job."

She cut her burger in half and stuck a couple of french fries under each bun. That was a new one on him.

"You're being cynical." She pointed her fork at him. "Not the job. You're the best-looking Garner, putting points strongly in your favor."

"Thanks . . . I think." He reached across the table and put his face an inch away from hers. "Are you flirting with me?"

"Oh, you know, I think I am."

He pulled back before he took their playfulness too far. "Well, don't, unless you mean it."

Chapter Ten

By Friday morning, Win still hadn't heard from Britney. Knowing what a big decision she was facing, he didn't want to come off pushy. But it had been three days and she'd promised to keep him in the loop.

If she decided to go ahead with the pregnancy, there were plans to make, like giving notice on his apartment, getting Britney on his insurance plan in case the casino didn't have one, and working out a flexible schedule so he could help out more. At least TJ had given him a raise. Between that and his savings, he'd be able to cover the cost of having a baby. He'd give Britney the weekend, but come Monday, he wanted answers.

"You cancel your bouldering tour?" TJ walked into Win's office.

"Yep." They both looked out the window at the snow-storm. Not quite a blizzard, but close. "It sucks, but I didn't think it was safe. Not for this group." They were novice rock climbers.

TJ didn't disagree. "What do you plan to do today?"

Win rolled his chair back and put his feet up on the desk. "It was a six-hour tour, so not much. You have any admin-istrative work you want to give me?"

"Not off the top of my head. I'll try to think of something. In the meantime, you could ask Darcy. She might have something."

"Where's Deb?"

"She has a breakfast shift at the Morning Glory," TJ said. "She should be in around noon. I don't think she needs any help, though."

"No?" Win sat upright and took a drink of his green smoothie. Today called for something hot and he wished he would've forgone his breakfast drink of champions and gotten coffee or cocoa. "I figured I could help her get more established."

TJ all but snorted. "It's not like you know anything about retail, but go for it, if you want."

"Getting some serious weather, huh?" Josh walked in and shook the snow off his jacket. "Is there anything to eat, or do I need to make a doughnut run?"

"Doughnut run!" Win and TJ said at the same time.

"All right. I'll get 'em as soon as I check my messages."

"I'll go," Win said. He was bored out of his skull just sitting in the office.

"This time don't skimp on the bear claws," Josh said. "Has Colt been in this morning? He'll want doughnuts."

"He's a cop." Win shrugged into his jacket and pulled a beanie over his head. "Don't they have unlimited access to their own doughnuts?"

"You're a moron." Josh shook his head. "I'll call him."

"All right," TJ said. "We'll make it an impromptu meeting. May as well do something productive."

"Anyone want anything else?" Win asked as he was leaving.

"Darcy made coffee," TJ said.

On his way out, he stopped off at the reception desk. "I'm getting doughnuts; you want anything?" he asked Darcy.

She shook her head and went back to her phone call.

He trampled through the snow—the city couldn't clean the sidewalks fast enough to keep up with the downfall—and by the time he got to the Morning Glory, his hands were numb from the cold. He should've worn gloves on the short walk.

Felix waved from the kitchen window and hollered for Deb to come behind the counter and help him.

"Hey," she said but didn't seem happy to see him. For a while now, she'd been giving him the cold shoulder.

"I come in search of doughnuts."

She looked down at the bakery case and called back to the kitchen. "How long for life preservers?"

"Ten minutes," Felix yelled back.

"I'll wait. Can I get a cup of coffee in the meantime?" He grabbed a stool at the counter. As a kid, he used to love sitting at the bar with a milk shake or a soda. All his brothers had.

She poured coffee into a white mug and put it in front of him with a cream dispenser. "Here you go."

"If you can break away from the diner, we're having a meeting at GA."

"Why? Is anything wrong?" She bussed the spot next to him and wiped down the counter.

"Nothing's wrong. We're a company; we have meetings. And it makes TJ feel important."

"Oh." She scanned the restaurant. "It's slow because of the weather. I'll probably be able to break away. We have a cook down, though."

That must've been why Felix was in the kitchen instead of working the cash register, like he always did.

"Whatever. If you can't come, no worries. It's not a big deal, just a way to kill time until the snow lets up."

"I'll see what I can do." She started to take a couple of menus to a booth in the back when he stopped her.

"Hey, you mad at me for something?"

"Nope." She turned to walk away and he took her arm. "Seriously, why are you pissed at me?"

"That's the thing, Win. I'm not." She turned her back on him and went off to seat Rita Tucker and a couple of council members.

He knew Deb had had it bad for him since high school, and he'd felt things for her he'd never felt for any other woman. He just wasn't sure what they were. Love? Hard to tell, though he'd never felt the things you were supposed to when you were in love with someone.

He'd never have a chance to find out now. As long as he was having a baby, he'd make it work with Britney.

When the doughnuts came out of the fryer, Felix put a couple dozen in a box and tied it with string. Win took them back to the office, where his brothers descended on the carton like vultures.

"Jeez, let me at least put them in the conference room."

TJ and Josh followed him, and Darcy brought a carafe of coffee and cups, which they set up in the middle of the meeting table.

"You save me a bear claw?" Colt came in and immediately started picking through the box. He got what he was looking for, put it on a paper plate, and took off his jacket. "It's bloody cold outside. I can't stay long; duty calls."

Darcy started to walk out and TJ said, "Stay for the meeting, okay?"

Win watched her face brighten. He didn't know what was so special about being asked to stay for a boring meeting and planned to ask TJ about it later. In any event, her enthusiasm buoyed him, and Lord knew he could use a little lift.

"What are we here for?" Colt asked while stuffing his

face. Clearly, he'd only come for the doughnuts. "Where's Mom and Dad?"

"We called it at the last minute, mostly because we don't have anything better to do," Win said.

"Speak for yourself." TJ grabbed a buttermilk bar. "I've got plenty to do."

"The meeting was your idea, dickwad." Josh filled a mug with coffee.

"All right." Colt, always the peacekeeper, held up his hands. "Give us a status report, TJ."

TJ pulled in his chair. "The website's being revamped and should be done sometime next week. Deb's working on ordering the sweatshirts and plans to meet with Delaney on the Colt and Delaney orders. Win got a raise and—"

"Whoa, what?" Josh glared at TJ. "Why didn't I get a raise?"

"Because I've been here longer than you," Win said.

"Well I'm older and have a wife to support." Which was bullshit because Hannah was killing it with Glorious Gifts and Win told him so.

Colt banged on the table to get everyone's attention. When the bickering stopped, he turned to TJ. "Is there money in the budget for Josh to get a raise, too?"

"No. Josh can have one next year, and maybe sometime this century, I can get one, too."

Colt took the coffee carafe from Josh, poured himself a cup, and asked him, "Can you live with next year?"

"I guess so, but why did Win get one?"

All eyes turned to him, and he sat there like the proverbial deer in the headlights.

"Because he asked," TJ finally said. "And he was due one."

Win made a note to himself to get TJ a better Christmas present than the rest of his brothers. Hell, maybe he'd make him the godfather of his baby. The thought made him check his phone for the hundredth time.

"You suck." Josh sailed a paper plate at his face.

Win got up and tried to give him a wedgie and they started wrestling.

"Let me know when you toddlers are done and we can get back to the meeting." TJ said.

Colt shot them both a look to behave, and because he was wearing a nine-millimeter on his belt, Win sat back down.

"Darcy wants a promotion," TJ announced, and this time all eyes fell on Darcy, who looked as if she wanted to hide under the table. Win was just glad the heat was off him.

"She's ready for something a little more challenging, right, Darce?"

Darcy started to choke on her cruller and Colt patted her on the back. She made this awful hacking noise in her throat, and Win wondered if one of them would have to give her the Heimlich maneuver.

"You okay?" TJ asked, and Darcy nodded as she continued to cough. "Don't die on us."

Jeez, way to make it worse, TJ. Couldn't he tell she was embarrassed?

"Come on, Darce, let's get you a drink of water." Win pulled her out of the chair and tugged her out of the conference room.

At the cooler, he filled a cup and handed it to her. "Drink."

She dutifully gulped, which made her cough even harder, her eyes filling with water. Uh-oh. At least they were all trained in first aid.

"Can you breathe?" he asked her and she nodded. A few seconds later, the coughing subsided and she took a few more swigs of water.

Colt came out to check on them. "Everything all right?"

"She's fine. We'll be right in." The last thing Darcy needed was an audience. As it was, her face was beet red and her eyes glassy, and Colt was damned intimidating, though chicks usually loved him. Lord knew why.

Colt got the message loud and clear and went back to the conference room. That was when Deb showed up in the lobby, wiping snow from her coat.

"Did I miss the meeting?" she asked, then paused to gawk at them. "Everything okay?"

"We're all good. Meeting's in the conference room." Win nudged his head at the door. "We'll be in in a second."

Deb cocked her head to one side. "Darcy?"

"I choked on a doughnut," she said and started to cough again.

"Let's go to the bathroom." She took Darcy's arm and wordlessly told Win to get lost.

He went back to the meeting. "Deb's with her."

"What the hell happened?" TJ asked. And the guy was supposed to be a genius.

"You embarrassed her and she choked on"—Win looked down at her plate—"an apple fritter. Good going, ace."

"Jesus, all I said was that she wanted a promotion."

"We've got to toughen her up." Josh grabbed another doughnut. "You can't be an honorary Garner and freak out at your own shadow. Even Win stopped wetting his bed two years ago."

Colt bit back a laugh and turned to TJ. "I'd hate to lose her. She's a hard worker and it's not easy finding good people in this town."

"I plan on promoting her as soon as I figure out a position. You have any ideas?" TJ gazed around the table.

Josh shook his head. "What does she want to do?"

"That's what I was hoping to talk about," TJ said. "Do she and Deb plan to join us anytime soon?"

How the hell was Win supposed to know?

Colt gazed at the clock on the wall and let out a breath. "I've gotta roll." He filched three doughnuts and wrapped them in a couple of napkins. When they looked at him like *seriously, dude*, he said, "For Jack and Carrie Jo, their reward for covering me back at the station house."

"Don't go yet." Josh had his laptop on the table and was reading something. "We've got trouble. Big trouble."

"What did we miss?" Deb asked as she and Darcy came through the door and grabbed a couple of chairs.

"This." Josh flipped the laptop around so it faced TJ. The rest of them got up to hover.

TJ scanned the page. "Son of a bitch."

"Hang on; I'm still reading." Colt crouched down to get a better look.

"I'll break it down for you," Josh said. "Colorado Adventure apparently had the same bright idea as TJ to sell sportswear and gear. The difference is, they got an entire feature article in *Outside* magazine about it. We're screwed."

"You didn't know about this?" Colt asked TJ.

"Yeah, I knew and plotted to keep it from you." TJ shot Colt a get-real look, then turned to Josh. "How'd you find this?"

"What do you mean, how'd I find it? I subscribe. Don't you?"

Everyone broke out talking at the same time, and Win let out a shrill whistle to shut them up. "People, it's not the end of the world."

Five pairs of eyes fell on him like he had shit for brains.

TJ plugged Colorado Adventure into the search engine on Josh's laptop. He navigated to the online store and angled the laptop so everyone could see it better.

Josh bent over to examine the page. "Except for the Colt and Delaney stuff and the merch with our company's logo, we carry pretty much the same gear. I don't know how much room there is in the market for two small outfits like GA and Colorado Adventure when you can get a lot of the same stuff at REI. You know what I mean?"

TJ continued to peruse the store, only half-listening. "I don't think their site holds a candle to our new one. When Jillian's done with it, it's gonna rock."

Deb snorted and TJ glared at her.

"What?" Win asked.

"Nothing." TJ waved him off.

Colt tapped the computer to return to the *Outside* article and shook his head. "You can't beat this kind of publicity. You and Deb better deal with it." He jabbed TJ in the arm to punctuate his point. "I've gotta get back to the station."

"Colt's right; Colorado Adventure has one hell of an advantage," Josh said.

"We'll come up with our own promotion," TJ said, but Win could tell he was worried.

"If you remember correctly, we were all against this store idea of yours." Josh took back his laptop and closed it. "See that we don't get crushed." He gazed out the window, where it was still snowing hard, and sighed. "No sense hanging around here. I'm taking the rest of the day off to catch up on chores around the house."

TJ got to his feet. Suddenly, he was in a rush to end the meeting.

Win rose and Josh shoulder-checked him on the way out. Deb continued to sit there, looking as worried as TJ had.

"Darce, come into my office for a sec," TJ said, motioning for Darcy to follow him down the hall.

"Uh-oh." Deb looked at Win, and together they started

clearing away the plates and napkins. "Darcy's not in trouble for nearly dying, is she?"

"Nah. TJ's not that much of a dick." His brother was going to apologize for embarrassing Darcy. Despite TJ's hard business persona, he was a softy where most people were concerned. Win might be one of the few people who actually knew that about him.

Deb threw the empties in the trash and was about to leave for her office when Win said, "What was that about the website? You and TJ have a difference over it?"

"Uh . . . we're just feeling our way around each other."

"Okay." Win was all for Deb working at GA but, like the others, was a little surprised TJ had given her the job. His brother's softness only extended so far when it came to GA's bottom line. Win saw Deb's potential—always had—but hadn't realized that TJ did. "Don't let my brother bully you. He can have that effect on people."

"He's not like that." Her voice was clipped, and if Win didn't know better, he'd think she was being defensive of TJ.

"He can be a hard-ass."

"No, he's fair. Expects everyone to live up to their potential. There's nothing wrong with that." She turned around and walked out.

Touchy much? Whatever. Win was too mired in his own freak show to argue. Let the two of them figure it out.

Halfway to his office, his phone pinged with a text. He fished it out of his cargo pocket. It was from Josh. A middle-finger emoji.

He rang his brother. "Seriously, dude? You're pissed that I got a raise?"

"Nope. You deserve the raise. I'm just pissed with you in general. Wanna have dinner at our place tonight? Hannah's making Sabine's pecan pie." No one could resist Hannah's late aunt's pie.

"I don't know yet. Can I tell you later?"

"Just show up if you're hungry. Colt, Delaney, and TJ are coming, so Hannah's making plenty."

As soon as he hung up, his phone rang. Britney. Finally.

Deb's piece-of-shit Honda was parked in front of his brother and sister-in-law's Victorian. TJ didn't know why he was surprised. Deb was Hannah's best friend and got invited to most family events. She shouldn't be driving on a bad transmission, though. With the weather as bad as it was, he understood why she hadn't wanted to walk. Still, she could've asked either him or Win for a ride.

He grabbed the bottle he'd bought at the fancy new wine shop near Starbucks. A few years ago, there wouldn't have been enough business to sustain an upscale liquor store in Glory Junction. But times had changed. The town wasn't called the St. Moritz of the West for nothing.

He let himself into a full house and found Foster fiddling with the music in the living room.

"Everyone's in the kitchen."

TJ made his way through the dining room and discovered his brothers huddled together at the kitchen island, dredging chips through a bowl of guacamole. Hannah, Delaney, Deb, and a gorgeous redhead were sitting in the breakfast nook, drinking wine.

TJ walked over and put his bottle in the center of the table. Hannah yanked him down for a quick hug and Delaney bussed his cheek.

"You've met Karen, right?"

"Yeah, of course." He turned to Karen, who was examining the wine he'd brought. "Nice to see you again."

"Nice to see you, too."

Deb seemed to be laughing at him, clearly aware that he

was being set up. She looked fantastic. A stretchy velvet top that emphasized her breasts and a pair of skintight jeans, tucked into riding boots.

Karen was the woman he remembered from Delaney's fashion show last summer. Curly auburn hair that fell to her back and green eyes that reminded TJ of a cat. She had on suede pants and a tight sweater that laced up in front and showed a good deal of cleavage. TJ assumed they were Delaney's designs.

Win came over, smelling like guacamole breath, and squeezed onto the chair with Deb. TJ's chest constricted and he joined Colt, Josh, and now Foster at the island.

"Talk her out of those boutonnieres," Colt told Foster. Christ, wedding talk; the last thing TJ wanted to hear.

"I picked out those boutonnieres," Foster argued. "You'll see, they'll be fabulous."

Josh socked Colt in the shoulder. "Suck it up, dude. You're outnumbered."

Colt glanced up at the ceiling, like he was praying for patience. "This wedding is gonna kill me." He cocked his head at the breakfast nook and poked TJ in the chest. "You say hello?" The man was about as subtle as a hand grenade.

"Yep."

"Why aren't you over there talking to her?" Josh asked. The whole family wanted to set him up and all TJ wanted was a home-cooked meal.

He reached for a chip and dipped it in the guac. "Because I'm hungry. You invite me for dinner and then you don't feed me." He eyed their full pilsner glasses. "Or offer me a beer, for that matter."

Josh walked over to the fridge and pulled out a micro-brew—presumably Colt's contribution—and got a glass down from the cupboard. "Here you go, Prince TJ. Supper should be ready soon, Your Majesty."

Someone in the nook let out a loud laugh and they all turned to see what was so funny.

"There goes Win, working the room," Josh said and shoved TJ. "Go over there before he starts working Karen."

Because everyone knew if he did, who she'd choose. The aptly named Win, that's who. TJ wasn't interested in Karen. And he certainly wasn't in the mood to lose.

"Something's not right with him," he said and watched Win check his phone, which seemed to have become his latest obsession.

"Something's never been right with him." Josh laughed and took a swig of his beer.

"No, seriously. He's not himself." The whole asking-for-a-raise thing had been a red flag to TJ. Win had never shown much interest in money before. Garner Adventure covered the cost of his addiction to extreme sports and his apartment was dirt cheap, just like most of his women.

"I've noticed it, too," Colt said. "He's going through the motions, phoning in the charm."

"Should we talk to him?" Josh asked.

Colt contemplated it. "Let's see if he can work it out on his own. Otherwise, he'll accuse us of big-brothering him to death. You agree, TJ?"

"For now." He continued to watch Win, who had his arm around Deb and was whispering something in her ear. TJ felt his heart fold in half.

There were many things you could say about the Garners. One of them was that they were loud and a little hyperactive. Okay, more than a little. Everyone talking at the same time and a lot of affectionate shoving. As an only child, Deb had never completely grown used to it.

Halfway through dinner, Josh let out a shrill whistle to

get everyone's attention. Colt's response was to bean him with a dinner roll. Because no one would shut up, Foster tapped his wineglass a few times with a spoon. And finally, the room quieted enough to actually carry on a conversation at normal decibel levels.

"I've got an idea for a snowboard that'll blow Colorado Adventure out of the water." Josh went on to describe his plan for the perfect freestyle board. The Garners were too daredevilish for a straight-up all-mountain board, like the one Deb used.

"Come up with a prototype," TJ urged and turned to Deb. "You test it and decide if it's something we can sell."

TJ winked at her, something Win did all the time. But with TJ it made her a little light-headed. She chalked that up to the fact that Hannah had the heat turned up to seventy degrees. Right; who was she kidding?

"I'll test it," Karen volunteered.

"The more, the merrier." TJ flashed her a courteous smile, then gazed across the table at Deb and Win, who had wound up sitting next to each other for no other reason than there were two empty seats available.

Undeterred, Karen put her hand on TJ's sleeve. "I hope we don't have to wait for Josh to finish the board before we ski together. Delaney says you're amazing on the slopes." She stretched out the word *amazing* because TJ wasn't just amazing; he was *amaaaaaaaaaaaazing*.

"Anytime," he said, as if he didn't work a hundred hours a week.

All night it had been: "*TJ, let me refill your glass,*" "*TJ, when it warms up we should go kayaking,*" "*TJ, you're so big and strong.*"

All right, Deb had made up that last one. But one more *TJ* . . . Just like Jillian, Karen was lapping him up like a feral cat with a bowl of cream. To TJ's credit, he didn't seem all that in to her, responding to her attempts at flirtation with polite smiles.

"Deb has an idea for something, too," TJ said. Everyone stopped talking and trained their attention on her. Ugh. She didn't want to describe her half-baked tent proposal in front of an audience.

"Uh, I'm not ready to talk about it yet." She shot TJ a dirty look.

"I showed you mine; you have to show us yours," Josh insisted.

She cleared her throat. "I'm still fleshing out the details."

"Come on, Little Debbie, tell us what you've got." Colt smirked. The nickname he'd given her when they were kids was wearing thin. And to think, he was her favorite.

"Fine," she said, knowing the futility of trying to hold out on this crowd. Garner men never took no for an answer. "It's a jacket that turns into a tent." She left out the part that it was Delaney's jacket. "For backpackers, extreme skiers, and rock climbers who want to go light." She scanned the room and, so far, no one was laughing. "I don't have a design or anything yet; it's just a loose idea I'm playing with."

"Anything like that already out on the market?" Josh seemed genuinely interested.

Deb grimaced because she hadn't researched it, just pulled it out of her butt where most of her good ideas came from. Knowing that innovators had already given the world Chia Pets, Squatty Pottys, and Snuggies, it seemed impossible that there wasn't a tent jacket out there already. "I haven't really explored it that deeply. It was just something I was brainstorming with your brother." She shot TJ another scathing look.

"I think it's definitely worth checking into," Colt said

around a mouthful of food. Most of the supper dishes had been cleared away, but he was still eating.

"We having pie?" Win asked.

All night he'd been distracted, like he was trying to work out a complicated puzzle in his head. Which was totally uncharacteristic for Win. He didn't do complicated. Deb got the impression he was champing at the bit to leave.

Foster leaned over and whispered in Deb's ear, "What's up with Win? He's acting weird."

"I don't know," she said. "But something's up." Ordinarily, he turned it on and off like a switchboard operator. But lately he'd seemed particularly detached. Not in a mean way. There wasn't a mean bone in Win's body. He was just absolutely oblivious sometimes.

Karen laughed again. Nails on a chalkboard, though no one seemed effected but Deb. Hannah got up to get the pie and Deb volunteered to help.

Alone in the kitchen, Hannah said, "I think TJ likes her, don't you?"

"She's a little aggressive, don't you think?"

"No." Hannah paused and studied Deb. "What's aggressive? She seems really nice to me. Delaney says nothing but good things about her."

"She just seems . . . I don't know."

Hannah got down plates and started slicing the pie. "There's ice cream in the freezer."

Deb got out a carton of French vanilla and found an ice cream scooper in the drawer.

"If I didn't know better, I'd think you were jealous," Hannah said and began plating.

"Of TJ and Karen?" She let out a laugh that sounded fake even to her own ears. "What have you been drinking?"

"He's better than Win. I love Win to death, but TJ's at

least got his act together." Hannah slid Deb a glance and Deb made a face. "What's wrong with TJ? He's smart, gorgeous, funny—available."

"He's my boss." Deb started a pot of coffee. She'd been in this kitchen so many times, she knew exactly where everything was.

"He's only been your boss for a few days. Before . . . how come you never considered dating TJ?"

If Hannah only knew how many times she'd lain awake at night considering what it would be like to date TJ Garner. "A little out of my league, don't you think?"

"Out of your league?" Hannah shook her head in disbelief. "Since when is any man out of your league?"

Ah, only a best friend would think she was equal to a man whose sole focus in life was getting ahead when all she'd ever done was stand still. "Win's more my level." And she hadn't even been able to hold him.

"So you're saying your type is a guy who changes women as often as he does his underwear." Hannah pierced her with a look. "What about Boden? He's made it clear he's interested."

"Um, not feeling the chemistry." Not like she did with TJ.

"Chip and I had a lot of chemistry and look how well that turned out." Chip had been a drunk.

"But it worked with Josh. No one has more chemistry than you and Josh."

Hannah had to concede that. They were so freaking in love it was sickening. The only couple equally sickening was Colt and Delaney.

"Garner men make the best partners when you pick the right one." To drive home the point, Hannah playfully bumped Deb's hip with her own on the way to the dining room.

Deb gathered up as many plates of pie as she could carry—her waitress training coming in handy—and followed. Delaney and Colt helped with the coffee. Karen continued to ply TJ with flattery and Win was somewhere else altogether.

After dessert, the guests started to call it a night. Foster helped with the dishes and was the first to leave. He had to be up before the sun came out for a flower delivery. Win took off a short time later and Deb started gathering up her stuff.

"We should go, too," Delaney said. "We'll walk you out."

Karen's face grew long. She'd come with Colt and Delaney and God forbid she should be pried away from TJ.

"Isn't Karen on your way?" Delaney said to TJ, angling to throw those two together come hell or high water.

TJ turned to Karen. "You live in the Aspens, right?" When she nodded, he said, "Sure, I'll give her a ride."

Disappointment punched Deb in the gut. As long as TJ was single, people were going to try to fix him up. And one of these days, he was going to fall in love. Who knew, Karen might be the one.

Everyone said good-bye and thanked Hannah and Josh for a lovely evening. They walked out into the cold night—at least it had stopped snowing. Colt, who'd parked in the driveway and was a cop down to his bones, waited for Deb to get safely in her car, even though this was Glory Junction. It turned out to be fortuitous because when she started her engine and shifted into reverse, her car wouldn't move. She put the Honda in drive and it made a high-pitched screeching noise. And still didn't budge.

Uh-oh; the transmission was officially dead.

There was a knock on her window and TJ motioned for her to roll it down.

"It won't go," she said.

"I can see that. Why did you drive when you knew you had a bad transmission?"

Because she was an idiot. "It was such a short distance, I thought I could make it."

He just stood there looking at her disapprovingly. *Screw you, TJ; not everyone can afford a brand-new Range Rover.* "Come on. I'll take you home."

"What about my car?"

"It'll be fine here until you can get a tow."

She didn't have money for a tow. He opened the door, held his hand out for her, and tugged her out of the car. Not knowing his own strength, she wound up hauled against his chest. He felt so warm and solid, she wanted to stay nestled there, his strong arms securely around her.

"What's wrong with your car?" Colt came up beside them and they quickly jerked apart.

"Bad transmission. I'll take her home."

Karen had gotten out of TJ's truck. "I'll go with Colt and Delaney because my place is out of the way," she said reluctantly, sounding as if she hoped TJ would argue with her. He didn't.

It appeared Deb had ruined Delaney's well-laid matchmaking plans. Call her a bitch, but she couldn't seem to work up any remorse over it.

Chapter Eleven

TJ had a breakfast meeting with Nate Breyer on Saturday. The hotelier owned and operated Gold Mountain, a cabin resort fifteen miles from Glory Junction. He also had a B&B in the neighboring town of Nugget and a fleet of high-end hotels in the Bay Area. He lived part time in Nugget and was up for the weekend. TJ thought they could do business together.

His phone got an incoming text. Nate was running ten minutes late, which worked out fine because TJ still wanted to drop by the office and get his tablet. He was moving slower than usual this morning.

The driveway was a slushy mess but easy enough to get out of without having to shovel. According to the weather, no more snow until next week. If he got a chance later today, he planned to do some skiing and take advantage of the champagne powder. He parked in front of GA and rushed inside to find Darcy bent over a calendar.

"Hey, Darce. What are you doing here on a Saturday?"

Startled, she jumped up and knocked her headphones off in the process. "You scared me." She turned off her iPod.

"Darce, the door's glass. Didn't you see me coming?"

"I wasn't paying attention."

He looked down at her desk to see what she was working on so intently.

"I'm trying to reschedule the canceled tours." She tugged her dress down and took her seat again.

"I told Win to do that." The asshole had dumped his work on her.

"He did do it. But some of the groups can't make the new dates work. I'm trying to rejuggle. But TJ, this is a screwed system." It was the most assertive he'd ever seen her. Of course, she had to go ruin it by saying, "I'm sorry. I shouldn't have said that."

"If it's true, you should tell me. Otherwise, I can't fix it. I still don't understand why you're doing this and not Win."

"I have time to kill before I pick up my grandmother."

Well, he didn't have time to argue about it. Nate was due to meet him at the diner in a few minutes.

"All right, but put in for overtime," TJ said. "And if you figure out a way to make the system better, let me know." There were always going to be cancellations due to weather, and reorganizing these trips had become a major pain in the ass.

He hurried to his office to get his tablet. On the way out, he called, "Don't work too hard."

She was so absorbed in what she was doing, she didn't hear him.

He walked to the Morning Glory, hoping to get a quiet table before Nate arrived. Deb saw him as soon as he came in, collected a menu from the box at the cash register, and started to show him to a booth.

"There are two of us." He nudged his head at the menus. "I need two."

Perhaps it was his imagination, but he thought he saw disappointment streak across her face. Deb grabbed another menu and led him to a seat.

"This okay?"

"Perfect." He took off his jacket and hung it on a hook on the wall, then slid into the banquette. "A cup of coffee would be great."

She ran off to get it and he checked his phone. Nothing more from Nate, so TJ presumed he'd be here any second. Deb came back with his coffee, a second cup, and a carafe.

"You want to order or wait for the rest of your party?"

"I'll wait," he said. She started to walk away and he grabbed her arm. "We need to figure out how to get a story in an adventure magazine like *Outside*." Colorado Adventure's head start was keeping him up at night.

"I don't have contacts like that."

Lauren would have. Then again, Lauren's smiles didn't wrap around his heart the way Deb's did. And that was an issue because where Deb was concerned he was all emotion, not business. "It would help if you could put more hours in next week, maybe assist with some of the administrative work so I can focus on getting some buzz on the retail end."

"I'll try, but I promised Felix two weeks." Someone at another table waved to get her attention and she had to run off.

Nate walked in the door and TJ stood up to shake his hand. "Good to see you."

Breyer was a few years older than TJ and a hell of a businessman, building the Breyer Hotel chain from the ground up. TJ could learn a lot from Nate. Even though they were in different industries, they were both selling luxury experiences.

They spent time exchanging pleasantries and talking about Gold Mountain. The summer resort had been run down when Nate and his sister bought it. But they'd completely renovated the place, including winterizing the cabins. Now it was as busy in winter as it was in spring and summer.

Deb came back to take their orders and hung around to eavesdrop.

"You know her?" Nate asked when she left to go to the kitchen.

"She's actually heading up our new retail operation at GA." He may as well have said, *We're amateur night here in Glory Junction*. Instead, he hastily added, "This is her last week at the diner."

"Watch out. Pretty woman like that and the next thing you know, you're marrying her." He grinned. "That's what happened with my wife. Luckiest day of my life when she walked into the Lumber Baron."

"Yeah. Not gonna happen."

Nate threw his head back and laughed. "That's what I said."

They talked business until their pancakes came, then talked some more. Nate had all kinds of ideas of how they could cross-promote. By the time TJ picked up the bill, his head was swimming with possibilities. After Nate left, TJ returned to GA to get his skis. Darcy was still there, her shoes off and a pencil through her hair.

"Still working it out, huh?"

She blew out a breath. "It's like dominoes. One tile falls and they all come crashing down. We have to come up with a better scheduling system. During the winter months, we have to set up two dates for every trip—an event day and an alternate day. Our clients need to agree to the substitute date up front. Otherwise, it becomes too complicated to reschedule and people wind up asking for their money back."

"I like it. Set up the new system." She stared up at him like she couldn't believe he was listening to her. "In the meantime, go home and have the rest of your weekend. Win shouldn't have dumped this on you."

"I don't mind." She started to say something but stopped herself.

"What, Darcy?"

She chewed the inside of her cheek and seemed to contemplate how to proceed. "He seems sad, that's all."

"Win?" He seemed distracted. TJ wouldn't necessarily describe him as sad. "What makes you think that?"

"It's not any of my business." She glanced at the clock. "I have to pick up my grandmother now." She gathered up the calendar and notes and stowed them in her big bag. "I'll come back."

"You don't have to, Darcy. It can wait until Monday."

She finished packing up and TJ heard the front door click closed as he went in search of his skis. He usually kept them in his office. But he'd recently cleaned and waxed them and had left them . . . somewhere. Maybe the equipment room, which resembled a war zone. Crap everywhere. He made a mental note to put Win on cleanup duty.

"What are you looking for?"

TJ jumped. "Dammit, Deb. Don't sneak up on someone like that."

"Sorry." She held up her hands, but a grin played on her pretty pink lips.

He had an overwhelming urge to put those pretty pink lips to work. On him. "What brings you in on a Saturday?"

"You said you needed help . . . I'm here." She looked at him like he was schizoid.

"I thought you had plans to ski." First Darcy, now Deb. Was he that much of a taskmaster?

"I talked to Hannah last night at dinner and got a better handle on the numbers of sweatshirts we should start with. She also told me how many hats to get. I thought I'd at least put the order in now; that way I can work with you on the Colorado Adventure thing next week in between my shifts at the diner."

"Get the order in and take the rest of the day off, Deb. We'll deal with Colorado Adventure on Monday." He was unlikely to find a magazine editor in the office on a Saturday.

"Then what are you doing here?" she asked.

"Getting my skis. I thought I'd get a little time in at either Squaw or Royal Slope."

"Ooh, can I come?"

He hadn't skied with her alone since high school and he wanted to. He wanted to badly. "Sure. How long will it take before you're ready?"

"Just long enough to get that order in and to change." She looked down at her diner clothes. Black pants and a white blouse. Not a uniform, but all the servers at the Morning Glory did black and white. Deb wore it better than anyone else there. Then again, she'd look good in a gunnysack.

He wanted to get an early start and if he helped her with the orders, they could hopefully get it done faster. "Go get started. Once I find my skis I'll help you."

"You don't have to. I could meet you at the lifts."

"Oh yeah, how you planning to get there?" He leaned against the doorjamb and folded his arms over his chest.

"Uh, good point."

"I called Roger to have him tow your car to that mechanic I told you about. The one who does the transmissions."

Deb got a panicked look in her eyes. "I can't afford that right now, TJ. You should've talked to me first."

"You can't leave the car there indefinitely. There's street cleaning. I'll take care of it for you. You'll pay me back when you can."

"That's very nice of you. But I don't know when that'll be. Besides, do you cover all your employees' car repairs?"

She knew damned well he didn't. "Deb, could you just take care of those orders? I want to get out of here."

"We're not finished talking about this."

Yeah, they were. "Come on. It's a rare day when I get to go skiing."

"You went just last weekend," she said and backed out of the equipment room.

Ten minutes later, he found his skis in the men's locker room. While he was there, he changed, got his boots, and carried them into Deb's office.

"How's it going?"

"Good." She remained fully focused on her computer monitor, looking ridiculously beautiful. Her dark hair spilling over her shoulders. He took a few moments to appreciate her. Last night, when he'd given her a ride home, they'd been all business. TJ was pretty sure she'd been upset about something, perhaps her car.

"This is kind of fun," she said, and he took his eyes off her long enough to collect himself. "So we don't have to pay until the stuff is delivered?"

"Normally," he said, his voice a little hoarse. "But because it's custom, we may have to pay in advance. Let me see." He pulled up a chair. She had on that perfume she always wore. Something light and sweet. "Yep, see here." He read her the fine print, pulled his wallet out, and flicked her a credit card. "Use that."

She punched in the numbers and printed an invoice. "I can't wait to see what they look like."

He wished he could get as enthusiastic over clothes as Deb, especially if they were going to sell them. He just wasn't that in to fashion—not that you could call hoodies fashion—never was. Josh's snowboard idea, now that was a different story.

"You ready?" he asked because sitting here so close to her was getting difficult.

"I have to go home first to change." She eyed him up and down, taking in his skiwear. "I can meet you back here."

"I'll go with you." It was a supremely bad idea. But apparently, he'd become the kind of guy who regularly showed poor judgment.

"I'm warning you, it's a mess."

He'd once had a girlfriend whose chow shed all over her apartment. Big clumps of red, dog hair everywhere. If that wasn't bad enough, she tossed her clothes on the floor. Dirty, clean, she didn't seem to care. The whole place was a laundry basket. It wasn't like TJ was a neat freak by any stretch. But the fact that she never scrubbed her bathroom— there was a film around the tub that gave it a third-world vibe—made him not want to stay over there. She was sensitive about it, accusing him of using it as an excuse to leave after they'd had sex because he wasn't that serious about her. He supposed there was some truth to it. After all, he could've just helped her clean the place.

He doubted Deb's apartment was that bad—or that he'd leave after sex.

"Let me just make sure the back door's locked." He checked it and turned on the alarm when they left. Glory Junction was a relatively crime-free town. But Garner Adventure housed hundreds of thousands of dollars' worth of equipment. No sense tempting fate.

They walked to the diner and climbed the stairs to Deb's apartment. She definitely wasn't going to win housekeeper of the year, but it wasn't that bad. A few dishes in the sink, some clutter on the kitchen table, and a bunch of magazines on the couch. It looked lived in, unlike his house, which was

neat as a pin. Not because he kept it that way but because
he was never there to mess it up.

"I'll be out in a second," Deb said and disappeared down
a narrow hallway to what TJ presumed was her bedroom.

He snooped around while she changed. There were lots
of pictures of her, Hannah, and Foster on a baker's rack in
the kitchen area. Mostly of them in various forms of drunk-
enness. He perused her bookcase and found a high-school
yearbook. He thumbed through the pages and a loose picture fell out. Deb and Win at their senior prom. Win had his
arm around her, a cheesy grin on his face, like the whole
thing was a big joke. But not to Deb. The camera, which
never lied, had caught her smiling up at him as if he'd hung
the moon—and her heart. TJ's slammed against his rib cage.
Carefully, he put the picture back between the pages and
closed the book.

He'd been in college when that picture was taken, sleeping and drinking his way across campus. Trying hard to
make the feelings he had for her go away. He'd come close
a time or two in grad school, met a few women who he
could fall for, but it'd never stuck. Then he'd come home
and there was Deb.

"What are you doing?" she called from her bedroom.

"Checking out all your stuff."

"Don't look too closely. I haven't dusted in two years."

She came out in a snug pair of ski pants and a zip-neck
top that clung to her every curve. For a second, TJ gawked
before catching himself. Deb didn't seem to notice—TJ got
the sense she had no idea how gorgeous she was—and just
went about her apartment, collecting her boots and skis.
On their way out, she tried to put on her jacket with her
hands full.

"Here." He took her skis and poles and helped her shrug
into the jacket.

"Can we go, Bennett?" She'd actually proven to be faster than most women. That was the thing about Deb; she was as much of an outdoor fanatic as the Garner brothers.

They walked back to TJ's truck and took off for the mountains.

"Squaw or Royal Slope?" he asked.

"The Slope."

He smiled to himself. For an official trail, Royal Slope was probably the most challenging run in the Sierra. Only very advanced skiers felt comfortable on the piste, though occasionally some jack-off new guy would try it and end up crashing.

"Unless you want to go backcountry?" she said.

"Nah, it'll take too long." Although the nonsanctioned trails were the best, daylight was burning. "Hey, let me ask you something. Does Win seem sad to you?" *Sad* had been Darcy's description. The only time TJ had known Win to be truly sad was when Josh had nearly lost his leg in the bombing. They'd all been devastated, not knowing if he'd ever walk again.

"No. Why do you ask?"

"He seems off."

"He's definitely been distracted," Deb said. "But isn't that just his attention deficit disorder talking?"

Is that what she called it? TJ supposed it was better than the alternative: treats-Deb-like-shit disorder. To be fair, Win didn't treat anyone like shit. He just went through life woefully unaware of how his indifference hurt others.

"If anyone would know, it would be you." TJ slid her a glance. He didn't know what was up with Win, but Deb's dismissal of it being anything serious was a relief.

"I doubt it. We haven't been close for a long time. Not even friends, really."

"Doesn't that change every couple of days with you two?" All part of Win's so-called attention deficit disorder.

"Not anymore," she said, an edge to her voice that TJ couldn't read.

"You moving on?" In so many words, she'd said she was, but TJ didn't necessarily believe her. The whole town assumed they would someday tie the knot. He wouldn't be surprised if Reno bookies were laying odds right now on whether they'd get back together. He shouldn't have asked. It was disloyal to Win.

"I told you I was," she said and sounded testy. TJ didn't know if she was trying to convince him or herself. "I don't even feel the chemistry anymore."

"A person can be great but just not right for you," he heard himself say and felt like a complete traitor.

"What about Mandy or Karen?"

He lifted his shoulders. "They meet the criteria on my list, but . . . not feeling it."

"You have a list?" Deb wiggled under her seat belt to turn sideways. She was laughing at him. "Of course you do."

"Anyone ever tell you you're nosy as hell?"

"What's on the list?" she asked, undeterred.

You. "We're not doing this again." Better to end the conversation now, before he told her the truth.

"Come on, tell me." She poked him in the shoulder. "Karen or Mandy?"

"Hey, I'm driving." He grabbed her finger and held on too long. "Neither."

"Give me a break; you wanted to sleep with Karen."

Maybe that's what she'd been pissed about last night. Or maybe he was delusional. Either way, he didn't want to sleep with Karen. He slid her another glance. "News flash: men want to sleep with women, period."

"I don't think you're like that," she said.

"Well, you're wrong." He pulled into the resort.

Unlike Winter Bowl, Royal Slope didn't have a hotel or a village with upscale shopping. It was fairly bare bones, with just a lodge that housed a snack bar, bathrooms, and a seating area with a fireplace. The no-frills atmosphere helped keep the price down and appealed mostly to locals and experienced skiers. Glory Junction residents got special deals on season lift tickets and, in the summer, cyclists used the gondolas to go to the top of the mountain and ride down. He and his brothers loved it. And it kept the resort alive after the snow was long gone.

TJ carried his and Deb's gear to the lodge, where they put on their boots and got in the chairlift line. Not much of a wait; the runs weren't too crowded despite the recent snow. TJ figured locals, fearing mobs of weekenders and tourists, had stayed home, opting to ski Monday through Friday. It was the kind of town where people took off in the middle of the day after a fresh dump to be the first on the mountain. Recreation was a way of life in Glory Junction, part of the reason his parents had moved here from the Bay Area and founded Garner Adventure.

They rode the lift up to one of the most difficult black diamond trails, got off the chair, and put on their skis. TJ let Deb go first so he could hang back and watch her. She was a fantastic skier, smooth, her body completely in tune with the terrain. Like a choreographed dance. He lagged behind her for a while, enjoying the view of her backside swishing across the trail. Eventually, he caught up and skied next to her. It was kind of scary how in sync they were together, intuitively knowing when the other wanted to speed up or slow down. For a time, they just traversed across the slope. But when they got to the bowl—the basin of the mountain—they picked up speed and made big, swooping turns. A few skiers stopped to watch.

Back at base, Deb asked if he wanted to go to the terrain park, a roped-off run that included jumps, assorted obstacles, and a half-pipe for freestyling and aerial tricks. A woman after his own heart.

They took the tram up and spent a good hour or two sliding across the fun box and up the rail and doing hucks off the jumps. When they got down they were exhausted. And cold.

He and Deb took a break in front of the fireplace in the lodge, removing their boots to warm their feet on the hearth.

"God, you're a good skier," she said and rested her back against his shoulder.

"You too." He draped his arm around her, then silently berated himself for doing it but kept it where it was.

"Why do you think you didn't make the Olympic team?" She moved her feet away from the flames and tucked them under her butt. He watched the move, a little awestruck at how limber she was.

"Not good enough," he said plainly.

"Yes, you were." She stuck her chin out, reminding him of her stubborn streak. "I used to watch you guys train. You were the best in the group."

But not as good as Win, who got a coveted spot and later decided he didn't want to go all the way, didn't want to put in the effort.

TJ shrugged because it was ancient history. "It probably worked out for the best." He'd gotten an MBA instead.

"Probably," she agreed. "An Olympic skier has a small window of prime time. Sponsors are always looking for the next pretty face. Not that you don't have a pretty face." She turned to look at him and snugged her head under his chin. Her hair smelled good, like some kind of fruity shampoo, and he felt himself instantly react.

Good thing for the long fleece. He inched away, even though he didn't want to.

"Did you always know you would run Garner Adventure?"

No, he'd wanted to be an international ski pro. Then he'd whiffed in those last few competitions and had lost his chance. That's where GA came in. He'd always been the logical brother to lead the next generation of the company. And the fact was, he loved being CEO of Garner Adventure. No regrets. None whatsoever.

But lately, pushing papers, juggling profit-and-loss statements, finagling deals to grow the company . . . well, it wasn't enough. He didn't know exactly what he needed to fill the void, only that he couldn't continue living the way he had these last ten years.

"For the most part," he replied. "Colt wanted to be a cop. Josh went off to school and then the army, and Win . . ." They both laughed. It was a long-standing joke that Win was the screw-up in the family, when the truth was, he'd turned out to be a rainmaker for Garner Adventure. With his wit and charm, he made friends wherever he went. And as good an athlete as he was, he was laid-back enough never to be intimidating. As a result, he attracted a good number of the company's clients, often big corporate accounts that wanted to team build. "Anyway, I was the one who showed the most interest in running GA."

"You're good at it," she said. "You could probably be working at a huge Silicon Valley firm, living large. But this is better."

He'd always thought so. "What about you? What did you want to be when you grew up?" He doubted she'd wanted to be a waitress.

"I don't remember ever really thinking about it. My family wasn't like yours. My parents worked hard just to scrape by. There wasn't a whole lot of encouragement to go to college or to have big goals. Not because they didn't want me to, but it just wasn't part of our world."

The Bennetts were good people. But yeah, she was right, at the end of the day, they didn't have enough energy left over to dream big for their only daughter.

"I know they've been having a hard time of it with your dad's back." He didn't want to say financially, even though he knew the truth. Deb could be touchy about it.

"Still scraping by."

"With the new job and salary, you'll be able to help more." He only hoped the retail venture was successful, especially now, with Colorado Adventure crawling up their ass.

"Because you believe in me." She was laughing at him, but there was something else there. Emotion in her eyes, like his words meant something to her, like they held weight, and like maybe no one had ever told her that before.

"I do." More than she ever knew. "You want to get going?"

"Probably." But she continued to sit with her feet tucked under her ass. "I'm hungry; are you?"

"I could eat, but not here." The food was crap. Prepackaged stuff that had been sitting around for God knew how long.

"I want french fries from Old Glory."

"Let's go, then."

They put on their shoes and he gathered up their hard goods and carried them to the truck. She tossed her boots in and he nosed down the mountain back to town. The wind was blowing hard and the day had gone from sunny to dreary. TJ dropped his skis off at GA, then continued to Deb's apartment before heading to the bar.

It was after lunchtime, but Old Glory was still pretty crowded. Boden came out from behind the bar to say hi.

He eyed their clothes and their sun- and cold-chapped faces. "You guys been skiing, huh? How about the two-top over there?" Boden pointed to a table in the back.

They took it and draped their jackets on the backs of their chairs. A server brought them menus, but they didn't need them. Deb asked for pub fries as a starter and they both ordered soup and sandwiches.

TJ got up and grabbed a basket of peanuts from one of the big oak barrels on the floor and set it in the center of the table. He cracked open one of the peanuts and flicked the shells at her.

She fired back and landed one smack in the middle of his forehead.

He pelted a whole peanut—shell and all—at her left breast. That had been totally unintentional. "Oops, sorry."

"You want to play hardball, I would cover the family jewels if I were you." She flipped one into his lap.

He held up his hands. "I surrender."

She brushed the shell she was about to aim at him on the floor. Their fries came and they temporarily forgot the peanuts. The server brought the rest of their order and they ate in companionable silence. Occasionally, he'd sneak a peek at her when he thought she wasn't looking and felt an ache of longing so deep that it hurt his insides.

"Quit staring at me."

"Don't flatter yourself, babe."

A text came in on his phone and he reached into his jacket pocket to check the display. They had a couple of tours today, including Colt's speed-riding trip. He wanted to make sure it wasn't an emergency.

But it wasn't Colt or any of his other staff. It was Karen.

Hope you don't mind that I got your phone number
from Delaney. Just wanted to say I had a great time
talking to you last night and if you're ever up for
coffee, drinks, or dinner, I'd be up for it too.

She'd signed it with a smiley face, which kind of bugged
him . . . and why did he freaking do that? Why did he always
try to sabotage any romantic prospect?

"Everything okay?" Deb asked.

"Yep." He went back to devouring his sandwich.

"It was Karen, wasn't it?"

Now, how the hell had she known that? "Yep."

"She's kind of pushy, isn't she?"

"You certainly seem to have a problem with her," he said.

She pushed her plate away and sighed. "I think I'm
jealous, to tell you the truth."

He assumed she meant she was jealous of Karen in
general. But he didn't ask her to clarify because . . . well,
hope sprang eternal.

Chapter Twelve

Britney had gone from radio silence to calling or texting Win every few hours or so. Friday night they'd played telephone ping-pong the whole time he'd been at Josh and Hannah's. And he was getting sick of it.

First, she'd asked if he could loan her enough money to take care of her power bill and the next thing he knew, she was asking for him to pay off her credit-card balance. He was willing to help any way he could, but her requests were growing ever bolder and he was starting to feel used. Or extorted. She'd keep him in the loop on the baby as long as he gave her cash. He wondered if he needed to get himself a lawyer, though he didn't know what that would do.

She had a right to take as long as she needed to make a decision, and if he was chump enough to foot the bill while she deliberated, so be it. But he had his limits, one of which was assuming the loan on her BMW Roadster. A) It wasn't practical for toting around a baby. B) She could get herself an economy vehicle, like everyone else.

For a card dealer, she lived mighty high on the hog.

Win parked his Jeep in one of the visitor spots. He was barely out of the cab when she texted him again.

Where are you?

Not bothering to respond, he opened the back and filled his arms with three bags of groceries and let himself into Britney's condo.

"Is that you?" she called.

"I come bearing food." He popped his head into the bedroom. Eleven thirty in the morning and she was still in bed. "Why don't you shower, dress, and I'll make you breakfast?"

"It's Saturday. Why don't you bring it to me in bed?"

"You feeling sick?"

"No." She stretched her long legs until her toes hit the footboard. Bright pink nails with sequins. He used to find them sexy.

"Then meet me in the kitchen." He walked out.

He put away the food he'd bought. Good thing, because as he suspected, there was nothing in her refrigerator except for a case of diet soda. In her pantry, he counted fourteen bottles of wine, six assorted bottles of liquor, four bottles of club soda, and little else.

In the other room, he heard the water go on. He cracked a few of the eggs he'd brought into a bowl. Not a gourmet cook, he managed to get by in the kitchen. Except for the occasional pastry—a Garner family tradition—he tried to eat healthy. He got the sense that Britney was a habitual dieter or ate out a lot. She drank like a fish, that's for sure. But with a baby coming, she'd have to lay off the booze. Which reminded him, as he filled the coffeepot with water, no caffeine. He put away the Starbucks beans he'd brought and hunted for a blender to make one of his green smoothies.

"What's that?" Britney came into the kitchen in her robe, her hair wrapped in a towel.

He looked where she was pointing. "Kale, cucumber, celery, apple, protein powder."

"I can see that," she said, her voice short. He chalked it up to hormones. "What's it for?"

"A smoothie."

She made gagging noises. "Not for me."

He looked at her for a long moment. "It's for me. But it wouldn't kill you to try it. It's good for you."

"Coffee." She made her way to the fancy brew and grinder on the counter. "I need coffee."

Win didn't want to tell her what to do. "You think that's a good idea?" His eyes went to her stomach.

"I think it would be a bad idea for everyone involved if I didn't get some. Soon!" She pushed him out of the way and scooped a bunch of beans from a canister into the grinder and flicked the switch.

They didn't talk over the whir. He started to fry up a package of turkey bacon while she stuck her head in the fridge, presumably to see what he'd brought. When the noise stopped, she said, "Did you get my note about the cable bill?"

"Britney, we're going to have to talk about that, but we'll do it after we eat."

She scowled, and then it was as if a switch went on in her head and her expression suddenly turned remorseful. "Am I asking too much? I don't mean to. It's just that I'm feeling overwhelmed and scared about the baby and about money. . . . Forget I even asked. It's humiliating."

Win knew she was intentionally guilt-tripping him, but it was working because he was a sap. He told himself it was for the kid she was carrying. "I'll do as much as I can, Britney. But I'm not wealthy and I've got my own expenses."

"I thought you owned a successful company." She sat on one of the barstools and watched him prepare her omelet.

"I own it with my family, five other people. And it's not Microsoft; it's a small adventure and extreme sports tour company." He'd told her that a million times before, but Britney only heard what she wanted to.

"Oh," was all she said and glanced at the kitchen clock. "You working today?"

"I have a cave tour tonight." Three families up for the weekend wanted to see the stalactites, stalagmites, and flowstones by lantern light.

Normally, retired park rangers did the tours for GA, but Win had offered to fill in. Mostly he conducted extreme sport expeditions with experienced athletes. Every now and then, though, he liked to see the look on the kids' faces when they got their initial glimpse of a cave or experienced the rush of a roaring rapid or learned how to paddleboard. He and his brothers had lived for that stuff when they were little and it was fun to be part of another tyke's first big adventure.

"I have friends coming over in two hours," she said and paused. "It's a girl thing . . ."

"You want me to leave?" He didn't know why he couldn't meet her girlfriends. Then again, if they were anything like Cami, he didn't want to. No sweat to leave. It wasn't like he wanted to hang out with her all day; he only came to be accommodating. And for the baby. "No problem. I've got things to do in Glory Junction."

He finished making her omelet, plated the bacon, and blended his smoothie. She ate half of what he'd fixed her and played with the rest until he took her plate away and rinsed it. The coffee she mainlined, making him shake his head. When he got home he was going to research the effects of caffeine on a fetus.

He cleaned up the rest of the kitchen while she got dressed. You would think she was going to a ball for how long it took her. When she finally came out she had on a micro dress, stiletto heels, curled hair, and a face full of makeup. It seemed a bit much for a group of female friends, but what did he know about stuff like that?

"I'm taking off," he said, a little relieved that he'd have the rest of the day to himself. It wasn't like he and Britney had that much in common. Sex was about it. And they weren't having too much of it these days.

"All right. And if you wouldn't mind leaving me that check . . ."

"I'd rather pay your bills directly," he said. "Why don't you give it to me and I'll take care of it?" Everything but the car. No amount of guilt would change his mind on that front. BMW, his ass.

"That's silly." She wrapped her arms around his neck and started rubbing on him. "I can just do it. Why make extra work for yourself?"

He extricated himself from her embrace and gave her a long, assessing look. "Don't push your luck, Britney. You want me to pay the bills, give them to me."

She let out a huff and went off to gather them up. The woman was a real piece of work. She came back a few minutes later with a stack of envelopes and stuck them in a bag.

"Here." She shoved it at him as if she were doing him a big favor.

"This is the thing, Britney: I'm not going to pay them next month unless you have an answer about the baby. I don't mean to rush you, but I don't want to drag this out either." He knew when he was being played, even by a pro. And he wasn't her goddamned sugar daddy.

She pouted, which he used to find alluring and now just irritating. "The outcome of my decision is lifelong, Win. Maybe not for you, but it will be for me. And for your information, I've made my decision."

He waited, angry that she'd saved this information until now. "Care to share this epiphany?" Though now that it was staring him in the face, he wasn't ready for the answer.

"I'm having it."

He gripped the counter to steady himself, not quite sure whether it was relief or terror he was feeling. Slowly, he made his way to where she was standing and planted a small kiss on her cheek. "We'll get married, then." He didn't wait for her response—his mind was made up—and walked out.

On his way home, he stopped at TJ's house, but his brother wasn't home. He really could've used someone to talk to. Colt was doing the speed-ride tour today, so that ruled him out. And Josh was helping Hannah at the store. Probably for the best. He still didn't know if he wanted to tell his family.

He had to go through downtown to get home and decided to stop off at GA for a while. It was better than hanging out in his empty apartment. There was no street parking due to the throngs of folks up for the weekend. He pulled around back to the rarely used lot designated only for GA employees. It was where they kept the minivans they used to shuttle clients. He slipped into a spot and used his key to go in the back door. There were lights on in the lobby and he walked up front to see who was there. Darcy.

She didn't hear him on account of the headphones she had over her ears. He didn't want to scare her, so he made a lot of noise until she stared directly at him and turned off her music.

"Why you working on the weekend, Darce?"

This time, she didn't turn her usual shade of deep red. "TJ asked me the same thing."

She was one of the few GA employees who weren't required to work Saturdays and Sundays.

"Is he here?" Win hadn't seen TJ's Range Rover parked outside.

"Earlier. He went skiing."

Win looked at his watch. "You've been here all day?"

"I was here in the morning, left, and came back."

Win grabbed a chair and sat next to her. "Why?"

"I'm trying to figure out a better way to schedule trips in the future. When we have to cancel because of weather, it screws everything up."

"What's up with the outfit?" She was all dressed up. Skirt, stockings, high heels. She looked nice. Even pretty.

"My grandmother and I had a tea this morning with her lady friends."

He pointed at the calendar he'd given her on Friday with his chicken-scratch notes. "No one is confirming the new dates?"

She blew out a breath, and he noticed she'd done her hair, too. Most of the time she wore it up or in a messy ponytail. "Yes, a lot of conflicts, so I'm trying to reschedule your reschedules." She laughed, the first one he'd ever heard from her. Usually, she sat quietly at her desk. Half the time they didn't even know she was here.

"Sorry." He eyed the calendar once more. "You want me to give it another shot?"

"That's okay. TJ said I should try to come up with a better system, so that's what I'm doing."

"For a promotion?" God, he hoped she didn't start choking again.

"Mm-hmm." Her eyes dropped to the desk and she started twirling her hair with her finger. "Why have you been sad lately?"

He cocked his head to one side. "Sad? What makes you think I'm sad?"

She sat up and actually maintained eye contact with him. "You just seem down in the dumps, extremely unfocused."

Wow, had it been that noticeable? He didn't know why he did it—they weren't even friends—but he told her the whole story.

"What are you planning to do?" she asked, no longer seeming all that bashful.

He got up and paced. It felt good to tell someone, though ten minutes ago, Darcy would've seemed like the most unlikely confidant. Not that he didn't like her, but they hardly knew each other.

"Be there every step of the way." It would mean being involved with Britney for the rest of his life, which he wasn't thrilled about. The more he got to know her, the more he didn't like her.

"Do you have a plan for how it would work?" She got up and dragged him to the big sectional on the other side of the room. "You're driving me crazy with all that pacing." She pushed him down, which was funny because she was half his size. And suddenly no longer afraid of her own shadow.

"You mean like whether to marry Britney? It makes the most sense, don't you think?"

"Only if you love her. It's the modern era, Win; men are no longer honor bound to marry a woman because of an unplanned pregnancy. Plus, you shouldn't bring a child into a loveless marriage. I was the product of one of those and I can tell you it sucked."

"You were?" She nodded. His parents still made out in the kitchen, they loved each other like crazy. "Between you and me, Britney's . . . difficult."

"How did you wind up with her in the first place?"

"Uh, the usual reasons." No way in hell was he telling Darcy the things Britney could do with her mouth. "It was casual, you know? We definitely weren't a thing. Now, though, I feel like I should be there and help take care of her." Prove to everyone that he was more reliable than everyone thought. Lately, that had become important to him.

She put her hand on his leg. "You're a good person."

Funny, no one had ever told him that before. The words most commonly associated with him were *womanizer*, *charmer*, *reckless*, and *fuckup*. *Irresponsible* got thrown around a lot, too. "I don't know about that. But it's important to me to do the right thing and be there for my child."

"You will be," she said with utter confidence. "And your family will help you. You guys are close and totally there for one another." Damned right, and the fact that she knew that put a smile on his face.

"Thanks for listening, Darce. But if you could keep it between us for now, I'd really appreciate it."

"I won't tell anyone."

He believed her. In fact, in all the seven months she'd worked there, she'd never talked as much as she had today. Maybe she was finally coming out of her shell.

"You should go home, Darcy. Salvage the rest of your weekend."

"I will. Just a few more minutes." She went back to her desk and began sorting through the calendars again.

The office phone rang.

Before Win could tell her to let it go to voice mail, she picked up. "Garner Adventure. This is Darcy, may I help you?"

There was a pause, then she said, "Oh no!" and started scribbling something on a pad of paper.

Win joined her, staring down at the pad, but couldn't make out what she'd written. He mouthed, *what?* but she shook her head, continuing to take notes.

She hung up and turned to him, her face now ashen. "The speed-riding tour . . . Colt . . . He's in the hospital."

"Which hospital?" It was like the time when they'd received the news about Josh and the explosion. Josh had been flown to a military hospital in Germany while the rest of them waited stateside for updates. The hours of not knowing, of praying, had been the worst of Win's life.

Win found it hard to catch his breath. All he could think of was getting to Colt.

"Sierra General. I wrote down the info—"

"Call TJ, Josh, and my parents!" he said and sprinted for his truck.

Chapter Thirteen

"What is it?" Deb shouted as TJ took off at a run.

"Colt." He didn't have time to explain. As it was, he'd only registered half of what Darcy had told him and didn't understand why the emergency responders had called her in the first place. Maybe they'd tried him and he hadn't heard his phone over the music in Old Glory. "He's in the hospital."

"My God. Wait for me." She caught up to him and hopped into the passenger side of his truck.

Good thing he'd parked close when they'd dropped off Deb's equipment. He started the engine, backed out, nearly colliding with a motor home, and sped to the interstate.

"Is it bad?"

"Not sure." All he knew was that Colt got caught in an avalanche. TJ assumed it happened during speed riding, but the details were murky. He just wanted to get to the hospital, to Colt. "Can you call Delaney? Wait a minute, don't. It'll freak her out."

"Someone has to tell her, TJ. She should be at the hospital."

"You're right. Call Hannah and tell her to do it. Someone needs to pick her up. She shouldn't drive herself." Damn, he wasn't handling this well, and he was in charge. The second oldest. He should have this; people were depending on him.

He heard Deb on the phone, giving instructions to Hannah. She sounded a lot calmer than TJ felt. Then again, Colt wasn't her brother.

After signing off, she said, "Hannah and Josh already thought of getting Delaney. They're on their way to her house now."

"Good." Josh was steady in a crisis—all that ranger training. "Did Hannah know anything about Colt's medical status?" He should've asked Darcy, but the urge to get to the hospital fast overrode it.

"Just that he's in the emergency room. Colt's tough; he'll be okay." Deb squeezed his leg and kept her hand there. Any other time it would've made him stiff as a rod.

It took them thirty minutes to get to Sierra General, the main hospital in Nevada County. Tourists, up from Sacramento and the Bay Area to see the snow, had clogged the roads, causing traffic to move at a snail's pace. At one point, TJ had considered ditching his truck and running the rest of the way.

He pulled up to the emergency entrance and jumped out, leaving Deb to park. Someone at the front desk told him where to go. He ran through the long hallway and took the elevator to the second floor. This wasn't his first trip to the emergency room. But on past visits he hadn't taken the time to memorize the layout of the place. His parents and Win were already there, having had a head start, and stood in the waiting room, talking to someone in scrubs. They looked grave but not hysterical, which in his mind was a good sign.

His mother wrapped TJ in her arms. "Thank goodness you're here."

"Is he okay?"

TJ's father stepped up. "He has a bad concussion, three broken ribs, and a possible fractured ankle. The good news is, he managed to keep the six members of his group safe. They all had avalanche beacons with them—thank God.

"What are they doing for his head?" Concussions were no joke.

"We're keeping him overnight," the man in scrubs—Dr. Jeffers, according to his name tag—said. "Tomorrow we'll evaluate whether to send him home. But he won't be skiing for a while, and Chief Garner will likely have to take a few days off work."

Footsteps echoed down the hallway. Josh, Hannah, and Delaney came racing toward them. Dr. Jeffers went over Colt's condition with them, repeating much of what Gray had already told TJ.

"I'd like to see him," Delaney said. She was losing it; TJ could tell.

The doctor nodded. "We're trying to limit visitors to one at a time until we get him a room. He also needs to rest. But I'll take you back for a few minutes."

Jeffers escorted Delaney down the corridor and they disappeared behind a set of double doors.

"Did you see Deb on your way up?" TJ asked Josh.

"Yeah. She's parking Hannah's car."

"What's Deb doing here?" Win asked.

"We were having lunch when Darcy called." TJ watched for Win's reaction, but he didn't give one. Either Win trusted TJ or he didn't give a shit.

He turned to his father. "Where are our clients?"

"Here." Gray let out a sigh. "They're being checked for mild hypothermia, cuts, and bruises."

"Do we need to call emergency contacts?"

"They don't want us to." Gray shrugged. "We're putting

them up at the Four Seasons. As soon as they're cleared to leave, we'll shuttle them to the hotel."

"What happened up there?" Josh asked.

Hannah got to her feet and turned off the TV. Until that moment, TJ hadn't noticed it was on.

"They were halfway down Sierra Peak when Colt heard thunder behind him," Gray said. "He knew immediately what was going on, managed to move the three skiers closest to him sideways to avoid the center of the avalanche. Another two were right under the slide and got buried. Colt shoveled them out. But when he went looking for the sixth member of their crew, there was another slide, or residual sluff, and he got hit with something and blacked out. Another party on the mountain came to his rescue."

"They found the sixth guy, right?" TJ assumed they must've or they'd all be out there now, looking for him.

"He'd already made it down to base. Colt thinks the two who got buried may have triggered it, but who knows."

Avalanches could be caused by something as simple as new snow dislodging the old, but more often, the trigger was the weight of a skier or group of skiers exceeding the strength of the snowpack. Everyone knew it was a risk in the backcountry. About thirty people a year died in the United States from snowslides.

Deb, accompanied by Jack and Carrie Jo, came into the waiting room.

"I was on duty and heard the news from the fire department," Jack said.

"How is he?" Carrie Jo asked.

"He'll be fine." Gray got up and slung his arm over Carrie Jo's shoulder. Besides being Colt's receptionist, she and Jack were his best friends.

Mary walked over to Deb and wrapped her in a hug. Win moved his jacket so Deb could sit next to him. And that old song, "Save the Last Dance for Me," popped into TJ's head and he pushed it away.

Delaney came back to the waiting room. Her face had regained some of its normal color and she was smiling. "He's doing well. Even argued with me over staying in the hospital tonight." She turned to TJ. "They're moving him to a room. As soon as he's situated, he wants to talk to you."

"Why him?" Josh punched TJ in the arm.

TJ socked him back. "Because you're adopted."

"Boys." Mary yanked TJ by the collar. "We're in a hospital."

"Sorry, Mom," they said in unison.

They all sat and made small talk, taking turns checking on their six clients. Colt had acted heroically and gotten himself hurt in the process. That was the reason he'd earned the trust of Glory Junction as police chief. Best chief the town ever had, even if TJ was biased. Win, he noticed, was unusually quiet. At least he wasn't screwing around on his phone every couple of minutes.

Deb, Jack, and Carrie Jo went off to scare up coffee for everyone. There was something going on with those two, but TJ didn't know what. He'd always liked Carrie Jo, who'd been in the same high-school graduating class as Colt, and hated her ex-husband, who'd been a pompous POS. And Jack was the man. Everyone loved Colt's assistant chief. It was good of them to come.

They returned twenty minutes later, laden with drinks. TJ noted that Deb had gotten herbal tea for his mom, who wasn't a caffeine drinker. All these years and she still remembered. A few times, Deb locked eyes with him. He flashed a wan smile and quickly looked away.

Darcy rushed in. She still had on her nice clothes from earlier but look frazzled.

"Hey, Darce." TJ rose to greet her.

"I drove the shuttle so I can take Colt's group to the hotel. How is he?"

A nurse came in and told TJ Colt was waiting to talk to him. Gray motioned for him to go and gave Darcy a status report. TJ took the elevator up two more floors and found Colt's room at the end of the east wing. For a rural area, it was a big hospital, serving a couple of counties. Colt lay in a hospital bed, covered in blankets. It was a single room with a few chairs scattered around the bed. A table with the usual hospital detritus had been pulled to his bedside, and Colt sucked water from a straw.

"Hey, asshole, thanks for not dying."

"You're welcome."

TJ walked closer and hung over him. "How many fingers am I holding up?"

Colt squinted a few times. "Fifteen, or is that little one your dick?"

TJ slugged him.

"Dude, broken ribs."

"Sorry, sorry." Sometimes they got carried away with the roughhousing. He sank into one of the chairs. "You feeling okay?"

"Never better." He shot TJ a look. "Our clients being treated?"

"Minor injuries. They're all going home . . . back to the hotel tonight. You've got half the town in the waiting room. Carrie Jo and Jack came."

"Jack'll have to run the show for a few days. My doc doesn't want me to go in, not even to do paperwork. Delaney will hold me to it."

TJ agreed with the orders. It was best to take a concussion seriously.

"I just wanted to make sure you're looking out for our clients," Colt continued. "They're all experienced skiers, but what happened up there had to have scared the hell out of them."

"Of course. As soon as they're released, Darcy will shuttle them to the Four Seasons." She was the best hire he'd ever made. She didn't know anything about extreme sports, but the woman got shit done. "I've got to give her a promotion before she goes somewhere else."

Colt nodded, but TJ could tell he was getting tired. "I should let you go, bro. Get some sleep."

"Wait a sec." He found the bed remote and lifted into a sitting position. "This . . . it got me thinking . . . I need a will."

"Ah, come on. Don't talk like that."

"It's no longer just me anymore, TJ." Colt had a way of modulating his voice so you didn't broach the conversation. TJ supposed it was a cop-authoritative thing. "If anything happens to me, I want to leave Delaney my share of GA. I want to make sure you, Josh, and Win are onboard with that. Will you talk to them about it?"

"Sure. But everyone will be fine with it. Just don't freaking die." He got to his feet. "Get some rest."

It was a dark discussion to have, TJ thought as he went back to the waiting room. None of them were even forty yet and despite their chosen professions, only Josh had come close to dying. But he supposed it was prudent when there was a significant other in the picture. Because TJ didn't have one, he didn't have to think about dying. As far as he was concerned, he hadn't started living yet. And for him that was a bigger problem than death.

Deb moved closer to Hannah and Delaney so they could drink their coffees together and talk. She'd texted Foster with the 4-1-1 on Colt's condition. By now, she knew the whole town was talking about the accident. Even though avalanches weren't that uncommon in the backcountry, it was big news in Glory Junction when emergency response was required. Thank goodness it hadn't been as bad as it could've been.

Jack and Carrie Jo had left, deciding Colt had enough family here to tire him out. Win seemed preoccupied, and Deb wondered if he was just upset about Colt, though his prognosis was excellent and even Delaney was in good spirits.

Gray and Josh went to help Darcy load their clients and their gear into the van and deliver them safely to the hotel.

To kill time, they talked about Delaney and Colts's wedding and Deb's upcoming birthday party. TJ finally came down and told everyone that Colt was doing fine but needed to sleep. Delaney went back up to sit with him for a while.

"He didn't want to see me?" Win asked.

"Nah," TJ said. "He doesn't like you much."

Win flipped him the bird and Mary shook her head. Her boys were a handful.

"Then I guess I'll go; no sense in sitting around here. You want a ride home, Deb?"

She contemplated it for a moment. But TJ looked as if he could use a friend. "I'll stick around a little longer and catch a ride with your brother."

Win didn't seem to care one way or the other and took off. TJ, Deb, and Hannah kept Mary company. Despite being a tough lady, the incident had shaken her, as Deb assumed it would any mother. When Gray and Josh returned, it was dark outside and it had begun to snow.

"You ready to take off?" TJ asked her.

They said their good-byes. Deb followed him to the elevator. When they got outside she showed him where she'd parked his truck and they walked to the far end of the lot. It was cold and she dug her gloves out of her pockets and slipped her hands inside them.

"I'll crank the heat up as soon as we get in the car."

She must've started shivering because he put his arm around her and pulled her tight into his side.

"You that cold?"

"I think it was coming out of the warm hospital." It had been seventy-five degrees in the building.

He continued to hold her, and she was strongly tempted to burrow closer; that was how good he felt. Not just warm but strong. And necessary. It was an odd way to describe someone, but in that moment, TJ felt inordinately necessary. Like he was part of her.

They got to his Range Rover all too quickly and he let go of her to open the passenger door. By the time she buckled up, he had the engine humming and the heat blasting.

"Better?"

It was better when I was snuggled next to you. "Mm-hmm."

He put his seat belt on and just sat there for a beat, the cab filled with their silence.

"Is anything wrong?"

"Nope." He pulled out and drove to the interstate, the sound of the windshield wipers filling the quiet. "How come you didn't want to go with Win?"

"I just didn't."

"You guys fighting?"

"No, nothing like that." She didn't want to talk about Win; there was nothing to say about him.

He dropped the inquiry and turned on the radio.

"Colt's good, right?" She wondered why he'd singled out TJ to go up to his room, though it probably had something to do with the clients.

"As good as he can be under the circumstances." He

paused, then said, "I wanted to guide that tour. Now I'm wondering if I would've reacted as quickly as Colt had."

"Without a doubt."

He glanced at her from the corner of his eye. "What makes you so sure?"

"I know your skills. They're every bit as good as Colt's and probably better."

He didn't say anything, just continued to drive. They made better time coming home than they had going to the hospital. Deb supposed all the weekend drivers were tucked in for the night. She wondered if TJ had had plans. It was Saturday, after all. As far as she knew, he hadn't returned Karen's text.

She wanted to ask but felt funny about it, especially because she didn't have any plans. Pretty pathetic.

"What are you thinking about over there?" he asked, and for a second Deb feared that he'd read her mind.

"Nothing. It just hit me that it's Saturday night."

"Big plans." His brows winged up.

"Shut up." She nudged his leg with the palm of her hand. "What about you? Hot date?"

"Hot date with my flat-screen and a beer."

It sounded wonderful to Deb. "You're coming to my birthday party next weekend, right?"

"So I've been ordered." He grinned. "It would be hard to miss, since it's at GA." Hannah and Delaney had gotten permission to use company headquarters for the party. It was that or someone's house, but the offices of Garner Adventure seemed more apropos, especially because it was Deb's new place of employment.

She almost blurted, *don't bring anyone*. The revelation that she was willing to take a chance on going for him was so scary that she needed time to examine it. And not while she was sitting close to him. Just his smell, a combination of citrusy aftershave, fresh laundry, and virility, intoxicated her enough to blur her judgment. He was the boy she could never have. *And her boss*, her mind screamed.

"How many people are coming to this shindig?" he asked.

"I don't know for sure," she said, happy for something to talk about. "Hannah, Foster, and Delaney are organizing it. The usual suspects, though."

"The big three-o, huh?" He turned down the heat because the cab of his truck had started to feel like a sauna.

"Yep. I know it's hard to believe." He must think she lived more like a starving college student. An apartment above a diner, a broken-down car, in debt up to her eyeballs. Karen had a fancy apartment, a glamorous job, and a cute little Miata she drove around town. She didn't know what Mandy drove, but it had to be better than Deb's Honda. And Jillian co-owned the design company doing GA's website and an espresso machine imported from Italy. All those women were about Deb's age.

"You still get carded?"

"Uh, sometimes."

TJ slowed to the speed limit as soon as they hit town. He turned onto Main Street and, despite the snow, a good crowd strolled in front of the restaurants and shops. They couldn't find a spot on the street, so TJ parked behind Garner Adventure in the small lot.

"You could've just dropped me," she said. "Unless you wanted to go inside." She tilted her head at the building.

"I'll walk you."

"Why?" It was safe and freezing outside.

"I could use the air."

She got that. It'd been a trying day, at least the last half of it. They walked together, but this time he didn't put his arm around her. Still, there was something there. A buildup of static electricity that caused an invisible crackling in the air and made her want to cling to him. She knew she wasn't imagining it and wondered what he was thinking.

They passed Old Glory and could hear dueling electric guitars coming through the walls. A small group stood near the door, cigarette smoke wafting in the air.

At the Morning Glory, TJ accompanied her up the stairs and waited while she fumbled through her purse to find her house keys. She thought about inviting him in for a drink but couldn't remember if she had any wine or beer. When she finally found the keys, he took them from her hand. He let out a breath as if he'd been contemplating something and a cloud of condensation formed in the air like smoke puffs.

Then he bent down and kissed her, gently pressing her back against the door. It was a bit of a shock, almost surreal. She was kissing TJ Garner.

He went slow at first, testing the waters. But as she arched into him, he took the kiss deeper, licking into her mouth, sliding his hands down her sides, and pulling her closer until she felt more than just his lips and tongue. She rocked into him and he grew harder against her as he continued to explore her mouth. The man was no novice. He made her want to lose her clothes—and her inhibitions.

Her arms wound around his neck and she rubbed against him, trying to feed the fire burning between her legs. He reached lower to her ass, pushing her firmly into his bulge, and groaned. His jacket was in the way, barring her from the hem of his shirt and his waistband. She wanted skin. She wanted him and the hot pull of his mouth all over her body.

His hands roamed over her chest, but the bulkiness of her ski jacket proved as much of a barrier as his did. They needed to get inside. He still held the key. She tried to guide his hand to the lock, but he wouldn't stop touching her.

Kissing her. Breathy sounds came from her mouth and she got up on her toes to take more of him.

"TJ?" she said against his lips.

He didn't answer, just kept on stroking the inside of her mouth with his tongue as his hands searched for her zipper.

"Please." Her body trembled.

He stopped and seemed to realize where they were. "Ah Jesus." He scrubbed his hand through his hair, his face so close she could feel his breath.

Shoving the key in the dead bolt, he unlocked the door and pushed it open for her to go in.

"Aren't you coming?" she asked when he just stood there, his hand extended with her ring of keys.

He pinched the bridge of his nose, and for a second, she saw indecision shining in his eyes. And then, just like that, he shook his head. "That shouldn't have happened."

But it had and she wanted to finish what they'd started. "Just come in and we'll talk about it."

"We both know that if I come in, there won't be any talking." He dropped the keys in her hand and jogged down the steps. "Good night."

"Good night," she whispered back and watched him disappear into the darkness.

Chapter Fourteen

On Sunday, TJ got up early to visit Colt at the hospital. His doctor wanted him to stay another night but Colt, being a stubborn ass, was fighting it. TJ hoped to talk some sense into his brother. Concussions were serious shit; people died from them.

His phone rang as he walked out to his driveway to determine whether he had to shovel snow to get out. It was Delaney.

"Hey. He didn't check himself out, did he?"

"Not yet. But if you don't get here soon and sit on his chest, he's going to. Believe me, I've tried everything else."

"Put him on," TJ said.

"Hang on a sec while I go back in his room."

TJ could hear someone on a loudspeaker in the background and figured Delaney must be in the cafeteria. A few minutes later, he heard the ding of an elevator and then rustling.

"Leave me alone," his brother's pissed-off voice came over the phone.

"You know that thing you want me to do?" TJ zipped his jacket and got in his Range Rover. His neighbor must've plowed his driveway because it was clear enough to get out with no trouble.

"Talk to Josh and Win about my will? Yeah, what about it?"

"If you don't stay another night, I'm not doing it." He turned on his Bluetooth and backed out.

"Fine. I'll do it myself."

"You suck, Colt. Why do you want to upset Delaney like that? Just man up and stay in the goddamn hospital."

There was quiet on the other end. TJ would've thought Colt had hung up on him except he heard his brother breathing. He took the turn to the on-ramp and hopped on the interstate. The roads had been cleared, but he was careful to avoid black ice. Although it had stopped snowing, it was still below freezing.

"You staying?" he asked, knowing Colt wasn't bluffing. His brother would pop that IV needle out faster than TJ could get there to stop him and limp out of the hospital because he was obstinate. They all were.

TJ took the Sierra Road exit and hung a left. "I'm pulling into the hospital now. You better be there."

"Hurry," Colt taunted. "Win just brought doughnuts and I'm not saving you any."

Win, huh? Shit.

The question was, should he tell him about Deb? The kiss. He tried to reason with himself that it wasn't as if he'd slept with her or even touched bare skin. So why rock the boat? Because unlike the first kiss, which had merely been loaded with suggestion, this one had been as intimate as sex. Leaving her apartment had been the toughest thing he'd ever done. And even though it would never happen again, the honorable thing to do was to tell his brother.

TJ found a spot in the overflow lot, banged his head on the dashboard, and counted to ten.

Confession time.

When he got to the fourth floor, the ladies at the nurses' station smiled at him and pointed to Colt's room.

"How'd you know who I was looking for?" It was a different shift of nurses than it had been the night before.

"Lucky guess," one of them said, and the others erupted in giggles.

TJ knocked on Colt's door, then let himself in to find Win sprawled comfortably in a chair and Josh standing against the wall, eating a doughnut.

"Did you save me a bear claw?"

"There's one in the box with your name on it," Win said. His eyes were bloodshot and he looked like he'd slept in his clothes. If TJ didn't know Win was a health nut, he'd think his brother had been on a bender. "Where's Mom and Dad, Delaney, and Hannah?"

"Hannah had to open the store. Mom and Dad are sleeping in after spending most of the night here," Josh said. "And Delaney went home to get Colt sweats."

TJ whipped the blanket off Colt. He had on one of those standard-issue hospital gowns. "Tired of your ass hanging out the back?"

Colt gave him a middle-finger salute and pulled the covers back up. "Give me one of those doughnuts."

"Surly, aren't you?" TJ grabbed him an apple fritter, got himself a bear claw, and looked at Win. "You didn't bring coffee?"

Win ignored him. TJ handed Colt his doughnut and pulled up one of the empty chairs to sit in.

"You talk to Jack?" TJ asked Colt.

"Yep. He'll be running the department until I come back. At least my ankle's only sprained. In fact, go ahead and elevate it for me."

"Do I look like Nurse Ratched to you?" TJ grabbed a

couple of pillows from the minuscule closet, piled them at the foot of the bed, and rested Colt's foot on top. "That good?"

Colt pressed the bed remote to elevate it some more. "Yup."

"You talk to them?" TJ cocked his head at Win and Josh.

"They're fine with it," Colt said. TJ knew they would be.

Josh rested against the windowsill. "I plan to leave my share to Hannah. I assume you're all good with that as well."

The three of them nodded. It was a somber conversation, but TJ supposed the hospital was a good place for it.

"What tours do you have going today?" Colt asked.

TJ ticked them off, including a snow kayaking group Josh was leading. And later in the day, Win was teaching three guys how to kiteboard.

"When is the new website going up?"

"Tomorrow." TJ was excited about the launch, especially the retail store, which he expected to bring in a lot more orders than they were getting with their current slapdash system.

Colt fidgeted with the bed remote again, lifting himself into a sitting position. "What are you planning to do about Colorado Adventure?"

"I'm gonna hire a hit man, what do you think?" Josh and Win laughed. Colt the cop just scowled. "I'll try to get a story about us in another adventure magazine. Given that we have Delaney Scott designing exclusively for us, it shouldn't be a problem."

"Damned straight," Colt said. "What's going on with you and Karen? It seemed like you two hit it off at Josh and Hannah's house."

TJ didn't know where Colt had gotten that from. Karen might be interested in pursuing something, but he wasn't.

"You planning to take her out or not?" Colt persisted.

Win and Josh perked up. For a bunch of guys, his brothers acted like grandmothers when it came to his love life.

"What are you, match.com?"

"How about Friday?" Colt was pushy.

Not gonna happen, even though he had nothing else to do on Friday night. Saturday was Deb's birthday party. He had to go to that, though he worried it would be awkward between them since they'd practically dry humped in public.

"What's wrong with you?" He turned everyone's attention to Win, hoping to change the subject.

"Nothing."

"You look like crap and smell like something died," Josh said, got up, and straddled one of the chairs backward.

Win straightened. "I've got some stuff I'm dealing with."

TJ and Colt exchanged glances, then Colt asked, "What kind of stuff?"

"Just stuff." Win wouldn't make eye contact.

"You dying?" Josh asked, which was sort of unlike him. Of all the Garners, he was the most serious. But the quip made Win's mouth quirk.

"Nope." He glared at Colt. "And it has nothing to do with the law either."

"I never said it did." Colt readjusted the pillow behind his head.

"Why not? You guys always think the worst of me."

"They do." TJ motioned to his brothers. "Not me, though."

"You most of all," Win said, and TJ felt a hot rush of guilt. Not just because there was some truth to it but because of Deb. He had to tell him. "It involves a woman."

It always did with Win, but TJ couldn't remember a time when a woman had his brother like this.

"What? Someone's husband after you?" Colt joked.

"That's exactly the crap I'm talking about." Win scowled and then blurted out, "She's pregnant."

The room went silent. Other than the low hum of the heater and the ticking of the wall clock, not a sound.

Colt eventually cleared his throat. "Who is she? And what are you planning to do?"

Win hung his head back and shut his eyes. "Britney, the blackjack dealer I've been seeing. We're getting married."

Stunned silence, and then Colt asked, "Do you love her?"

Win didn't respond, which was answer enough. No one would say he shouldn't marry her. As old-fashioned as it was, it was the way they'd been raised.

"Does she want to marry you?" Josh asked. Given the fact that they were talking about Win, TJ thought it was a foregone conclusion that she did.

"I don't think so," Win said, which drew looks of surprise from the rest of them. "I don't even think she likes me all that much. But I don't want her raising my kid alone."

TJ got up and leaned against the wall. "Nothing says you can't share custody."

"For the baby's sake, I think it would be better if we got married. She'll need support and I'm in a position to do that."

It explained the raise, TJ thought to himself.

"If she doesn't want to marry you, you can't make her," Colt said.

"I won't have to. She just will," Win said with his usual amount of confidence.

Josh got to his feet and joined TJ on the wall. "Why not do what TJ said and share custody?"

Win sidetracked. "I'm bringing her to Deb's party."

Despite her story that she was over Win, TJ knew this would crush her. "It's Deb's big day. Don't bring her."

"Britney's part of my life now," Win said, looking down

at his boots. "Deb and I are buds, that's all. Last I heard, Boden was in to her."

Glad you're so well informed, TJ wanted to say.

"We'd like to meet her." Colt was always the pragmatist. "You need to loop Mom and Dad in on this. Soon."

"I know." Win scrubbed his hand down his face. He was going through hell.

"We're here for you," TJ said. "Whatever you need."

"I know. If you could not tell anyone right now that would be good. And I need to talk more with Britney . . . figure out a date."

"Of course," Colt said. "For now, this is just between us. But Win, don't wait on telling Mom and Dad."

"I won't." He got to his feet. "I've got my kiteboard group and then I'll go over to their house and talk to them. See you guys tomorrow."

He left and they all stood around staring at each other. It wouldn't be so terrible bringing a baby into the family— they all liked kids—but not like this. Not in a loveless relationship where Win was trying desperately to do the right thing, even though it so obviously made him miserable.

"Well, shit," Josh finally said. "Our little brother is all grown up."

"Our little brother apparently doesn't know how to use a condom." Colt let out a breath of frustration.

"You don't know that." This wasn't the time to rag on Win. What was done was done. TJ turned to Josh. "I know we said we wouldn't tell anyone, but maybe Hannah could give Deb a head's-up."

"I try to stay out of that, but I'll tell her. Otherwise, she'll kill me." Josh pushed off the wall. "I better go, too." He walked over to Colt's side and leaned over the bed. "Take care of yourself, old man."

When it was just the two of them, TJ said, "This has got disaster written all over it, doesn't it?"

"I don't know, Win'll be a good dad. He's a screwup, to be sure, but a good-hearted screwup."

That was the truth. "You okay if I go?"

"I'll probably slash my wrists from loneliness." Colt snorted. "Just leave the doughnuts."

TJ met Delaney on his way out of the hospital. She had a bouquet of get-well balloons in one hand and Colt's duffel in the other.

"How's our patient?" she asked.

"As ornery as ever." He kissed her cheek. They talked for a little while in the lobby, but Delaney was anxious to get to Colt's room. TJ told her, "He's all yours."

He went outside to find that the temperature had warmed to a balmy thirty degrees. It would've been a nice day for skiing, but he didn't feel like it, a rarity because he always felt like skiing. But the night's kiss still had him tied in knots. He didn't want to complicate Win's situation by telling him.

He got in his truck, drove back to Glory Junction, and exited on Main Street, cruising slowly past the Morning Glory. Deb was working today. He considered going in and getting a cup of coffee but went to GA instead. His default safety net.

Chapter Fifteen

After her shift at the diner, Deb stopped off at Sweet Stems. Foster was cleaning the shop.

"No events today?" Usually on Sundays, he juggled weddings, parties, and banquets.

"Nope. I'm using the opportunity to catch up." He swept plant debris into a big pile, straightened up, and gave her a thorough once-over. "What's wrong?"

"Nothing." She didn't know why she bothered to lie; the man was clairvoyant.

"Hold the dustpan for me." She crouched down and he made quick work of shoveling up the mess. "Is Win being his usual jerk-off self?"

"No." Lately, he'd been more attentive than usual, which wasn't saying much. "What if I told you I was sort of crushing on someone else and he's turning out to be a lot like his brother?"

Foster stopped what he was doing while her words registered. "You're freaking kidding me. TJ?" He was the only Garner brother besides Win who was still single. "Holy crap. When the hell did this happen and why have you been holding out? Does Hannah know?"

"No one knows, and I may be temporarily insane, so

don't get too excited." The last thing she needed was to make the same mistake on a second Garner man.

He grabbed a chair and shoved it at her. "Sit and tell me everything." He hopped up on his worktable to listen.

"There's not much." No way was she telling him that she'd harbored feelings for TJ since . . . well, forever. "Ever since he hired me, we've been hanging out, mostly doing work stuff, though we went skiing together." She told him about the kiss.

"Get out. I can't believe you kissed TJ Garner."

"You think it's bizarre?"

"Because of Win?" He shook his head. "Don't get me wrong, honey, Win is adorable. But he's definitely Liam Hemsworth to TJ's Chris Hemsworth. Thor, sweetie. It's no contest."

She blew out a breath. *I'm so not doing this again.*

"Will it be uncomfortable at work?"

"Maybe. A little. You think he likes me?"

"He kissed you like he meant it, right?"

"It could be that he's a really spectacular kisser." *Spectacular* was way underselling it. But why had he kissed her in the first place? It wasn't like he was hot to get in her pants. She'd practically begged him to come inside and he hadn't. "We'd be weird, right?"

Foster thought about it. "Let's just say it would be unexpected, given your feelings for Win."

Win wasn't the problem. "I mean, do you think we're mismatched? You know, supersuccessful alpha guy with lives-above-a-diner gamma girl."

Foster laughed. "Cut yourself a break. You're in management now. I don't think you're mismatched at all. In fact, now that you mention it, I don't know why you two never dated in the first place."

She let out a breath. "Fear of the Garner man curse: heartbreak."

"There's always Felix."

She and Felix fought constantly and he had ten years on her. "Ack. I need to forget men and focus on work. I might actually be good at this retail thing if I knew what the hell I was doing. Tomorrow, GA's launching its new website. TJ thinks sales will go crazy with the online store."

"You sound doubtful."

"It's not the merchandise," she said. "We have great stuff. But I'm not thrilled with the retail part of the website. It reminds me of Banana Republic catalogs before the Gap bought it. Before I was born."

"Did you tell TJ?" Foster picked up a loose spool of ribbon on the table and wound it tight.

"Yep. He sided with the web designer, because she actually has experience in this area." She shrugged her shoulders. "For all I know, the site will be a runaway hit. It better be because one of GA's largest competitors is also selling merch and they got a huge spread in *Outside* magazine."

"Ouch. That's not good."

"Nope." Deb took the spool from Foster and hung it on the pegboard behind her. "TJ wants me to help get GA a story. I don't have any contacts in the magazine world."

"Is there anything else you can do to bring attention to the online store? What does Nike do?"

She chortled. "Nike is Nike. It doesn't have to do anything."

He hopped off the table to find cleaning solution. "Nike had to have done something to become as big as it is."

"I suppose it helps that the company sponsors high-profile athletes," she said. "GA's an adventure company, not a manufacturer. But something like that might work . . . a spokesperson for the gear we sell."

"You have anyone in mind?"

"Nope. But it's definitely something to think about. It would be great to promote the merchandise on a bigger stage than just our website."

"Listen to you." Foster laughed. "You sound like a marketing executive."

"I sort of do, don't I?" *Color me proud.*

"In the meantime, what about TJ?"

She wanted to put him out of her mind but couldn't stop reliving the kiss. Over and over again. "I'm not going to think about it and try to make it to thirty drama free."

"What are you wearing to your party?" Foster got down a square glass vase, some floral foam, and started making a gorgeous arrangement with white roses, lilies, snapdragons, and spiral eucalyptus.

"Who ordered that?" It was so pretty.

"It's for you." He continued to work his magic, deftly positioning the assortment of flowers. "They're past their prime but still have a couple of days of life in them."

"Sort of like me." She laughed.

"You haven't even hit your prime yet." He glanced her way. "Well, what're you wearing?"

She hadn't thought about it. Maybe she'd borrow something from Hannah, whose wardrobe was more robust than her own. Of all of them, Delaney had the best clothes, but Deb would worry about spilling shrimp cocktail sauce or strawberry margarita on one of her pieces. Her designs cost more than Deb spent on groceries in a year.

"I don't know yet. Maybe I'll wear the dress I got at Hannah's store the Christmas Josh came home."

"The really fitted one?"

"Uh-huh." Hopefully, she could still squeeze into it.

"That one's good," Foster said, and put the finishing

touches on the arrangement. Jeez, he was fast. That would've taken her all day and it still would've looked like a five-year-old had made it.

The phone rang and Foster answered it. "She's here," he told whoever was on the other end of the line. Probably Hannah. They talked for a few minutes, but Deb couldn't make out what they were saying.

After hanging up, he said, "Hannah wants you to go over to the store."

"Okay." She'd pick up coffee on the way because Hannah couldn't leave Glorious Gifts unless she had one of her high-school kids there.

He handed her the vase with the flowers. "Call me afterward."

"Why?" Not that they didn't talk to each other constantly, but the way he said it seemed . . . dire.

"Hannah will tell you."

"You're freaking me out, Foster. Is Hannah okay? Does it have something to do with Colt's accident?"

"Everyone's fine. Just go over there."

Deb took her flowers and walked the block and a half to the gift shop, ditching the coffee idea. She could go later. Hannah waved from the back of the store, where she was helping a couple of customers. Deb put her arrangement on the counter and sat in a big upholstered chair Hannah was selling. Recently, she'd branched out into more home furnishings, which went over well with the influx of new part-time residents.

The women Hannah had been helping paid for their items at the cash register. One of them was purchasing the angora scarf Deb had been eyeing but couldn't afford. Everything seemed normal. Hannah would've locked up the shop if there'd been an emergency. It was probably some small issue about the party and Foster, being Mr. Perfect, had overreacted.

The ladies finished their transaction and went on their way.

"These are lovely." Hannah held up the arrangement. "Did Foster make it for you?"

"He said the flowers were close to their expiration date. They look fresh to me." She got up and joined Hannah by the cash register. "How's Colt today?"

"Good. They're having him stay one more night in the hospital as a precaution. But Josh said he's doing well. Delaney brought wedding stuff to the room to drive him crazy."

"Was TJ over there?" Deb tried to sound nonchalant.

"I think so. Why?"

"Just curious."

Hannah put down the arrangement. "He get you home okay last night?"

"Mm-hmm," Deb said and thought, *if Hannah only knew.* Foster would eventually tell her. Those two couldn't keep anything secret.

"I wanted to talk to you about something, but you have to promise you won't let on that you know."

"Oh my God, you're pregnant!" Deb knew Hannah and Josh had been trying since his last leg surgery. No wonder Foster wanted her to call him. They had to plan a shower.

"Come sit down." Hannah motioned for Deb to take the big upholstered chair again and she sat in one of the pine gliders she got from a furniture maker in Nugget. They'd become one of her most popular items.

Hannah was a fabulous merchandiser and had accessorized the swing with red plaid pillows with white-eyelet ruffles for Valentine's Day. She had a knack for making every day in the store look festive. And now there'd be a nursery to decorate.

"I'm not pregnant, Deb. That's not what I wanted to talk to you about." Hannah's brows furrowed. "It's Win."

Deb gripped the rolled arms of the chair. "He's okay, right?"

"He's been seeing that card dealer in Tahoe, the one from last summer. She's pregnant and they're getting married."

At first, Deb thought she'd misunderstood. They? Who were they? And then it hit her like a Mack truck; Win was getting married to a stranger. She sat there, silent, waiting for it to sink in and for her to feel something. Disappointment, anger, an enduring sadness. After all, for fifteen years she'd told herself that he was the one. The man she was destined to be with. She'd waited, consoling herself every time he was with someone new that he was sowing oats, raising hell, playing the field, all those clichés. And when he was done, he'd come back to her. Everyone in Glory Junction expected it, even his mom and dad. She'd fantasized about that day like little girls planned their weddings. He would rush into her arms, maybe cry a little bit, and tell her he'd wasted all that time when she'd always been The One. The only one. The one he wanted to spend the rest of his life with.

That's the way it was supposed to be, except it wasn't. Win was marrying a blackjack dealer from Tahoe.

And while she should've been devastated, she wasn't. In fact, the most emotion she could summon was nostalgia for her lost youth and melancholy for wasting so much time and energy on something that would never be. And, oddly, relief, like she'd shed a dress that never really fit right, even though she'd forced herself to believe it was the best one in her wardrobe.

"I have to go." She needed to be alone, to think about this development and reevaluate her closet, so to speak.

"Deb, don't leave. Let's talk about it."

The last thing Hannah called before Deb walked out the door was "Win needs your support."

Win had always had her support. That was the problem.

The next morning, Deb went into GA bright and early. She had a dinner shift at the diner, but her time there was winding down. Felix had found someone to replace her and she'd be spending her remaining time at the Morning Glory training the newbie.

The day was turning out to be mild, a welcome break from the cold, snowy days they'd been experiencing. Despite Glory Junction thriving financially from snow, no one was complaining about the slightly warmer weather.

Deb wore her best outfit and knee-high boots, last year's splurge and one of the reasons her credit cards were maxed out.

She found the whole crew, even Gray and Mary, gathered around Darcy's computer. Win was conspicuously missing, probably picking out a tuxedo somewhere.

"Come see the website," Josh called to her.

TJ glanced up from the monitor, gave her a once-over, but didn't say anything. She joined the huddle and watched over Darcy's shoulder as she clicked through the various pages. The staff section was gorgeous, even better than it had been in Jillian's office. The pictures of the Garners danced off the page. Even the ones of her and Darcy were great. And the little bios were fun without taking themselves too seriously.

The videos on the homepage were enough to make anyone sign up for a tour. Deb was exhilarated just watching, and she regularly did most of the sports portrayed in the short clips. She still thought they should've included one of TJ doing moguls or aerials. He really was beautiful to watch and it seemed a shame that they'd missed out on an opportunity to further wow prospective clients.

The services page did just what it ought to do, in her opinion. No mysteries about price or what was offered. Jillian had made it simple to read. But when they came to the retail store, her heart dropped. It was even worse than Deb had remembered. Completely devoid of the same dynamism as the rest of the site. She suspected Jillian thought it was stylized, but to Deb it was just boring. Nothing that sold the clothes.

"Great job, you two." Gray draped his arms over her and TJ's shoulders. Crazy to give her credit; she'd had nothing to do with the site other than to drink really good espresso. But the Garners were great that way.

"You guys like it?" TJ said to Colt and Josh, and Deb hoped one of them would say something about the retail store.

"Blew me away, dude." Josh pounded TJ on the back.

"Killer." Colt leaned against the desk to keep from putting weight on his bad ankle. "I've gotta get home before Delaney goes to the hospital and finds out I checked myself out."

"Darcy, Mom?" TJ turned to the two women.

"It's gorgeous," Mary said.

Darcy nodded her head, and Deb watched her to see if she was thinking the same thing about the store. Poker face. Obviously, no help in that corner. She'd wait and see. Perhaps it would be fine and sales would come pouring in.

TJ was beaming, clearly thrilled with the end product— and the praise. A warmth furled through her. It was nice to see someone so passionate about what he did. And even though he was really good at it and a badass, he still needed a pat on the back every now and again. Which was sweet. And utterly human. Until recently, she'd never seen TJ that way. His self-assuredness had intimidated the hell out of her. And his attitude toward anything outside of work had seemed robotic.

But the guy who had kissed her Saturday night had been all man.

The cluster broke up. Mary left for an appointment and Darcy had to answer the phones. Josh had a group of tobogganers, Gray needed to make a bank deposit, and TJ headed to his office. She stood there for a second before remembering that she had her own office and made her way to it.

Inside, she didn't recognize it. The walls had been painted a soft beige and the big upholstered chair in Hannah's store now sat in her corner, next to a floor lamp. A matching love seat faced it and a glass coffee table had been placed in the middle, forming a cozy seating area. There was even a jute rug. The other side of the room, where it used to be empty, was now occupied by a round conference table and four chairs. In the center was Foster's floral arrangement, the one she'd left at Glorious Gifts when she'd found out the news about Win. Framed pictures of her skiing, rock climbing, and kayaking lined the wall behind the table. She had no idea where they'd come from. Next to her desk was a rolling rack with a few carefully hung samples of the clothes they were selling on the site. Over her computer hung a corkboard. Across the top, someone had artfully painted, "Time to get shit done." It looked like Foster's writing.

There was a big bow tied around her chair with an envelope. She pulled it off the ribbon, sat down, and read the card.

"Happy birthday from all of us." It was signed Hannah, Foster, and Delaney.

She gazed around the room and a tear slid down her cheek. It was the nicest thing anyone had ever done for her. Too bad she felt like a total fraud. The only reason she had the job was because TJ felt sorry for her. She had no delusions otherwise. She had no experience, no education, and what she knew about retail could fit on a price tag.

This was an office for an executive. Someone who knew what they were doing, not her. She grabbed a wad of tissue from the box on her desk and blotted her eyes. It sure was fabulous, though. Better even than Jillian's.

"Hey." TJ stood in her doorway, his hands stretched over his head, gripping the top of the casing. The muscles in his arms flexed.

"Hey," she said back.

If he noticed she'd been crying, he didn't say anything, just glanced around the room. "You like it?"

"I love it."

"They were here all night. The walls are probably still wet." He came in and sat in her big chair, his long, denim-encased legs sprawled out in front of him. "FYI, I contributed the conference table."

"Thanks. It's awesome." She wiped her nose.

"I thought we should probably talk after . . . you know."

She tried to act casual. "We were both coming down from the adrenaline rush of Colt's accident and kissed. No big deal." She didn't know how she managed to pull that one out of her ass. It sounded patently absurd, but she didn't want him to think she was reading too much into it. Clearly it hadn't been all that for him; otherwise he would've come inside.

At first, he didn't say anything, just let the words hang between them. "Good. Obviously, it'll never happen again."

"Obviously," she repeated, and hoped it didn't sound as sarcastic as she'd meant it.

"I guess by now you've heard about Win." His face softened. "I'm sorry, Deb."

"Don't be. I've been an idiot." She turned away out of embarrassment. "I wanted to talk to you about the online store." *That's right, keep things professional.*

"What about it?"

."I was thinking that besides trying to get a feature article in an adventure magazine, we should try to do something high-profile, like maybe sponsor something where we have athletes wear Delaney's stuff and let the world know that it's exclusive to Garner Adventure."

"Okay," he said, surprisingly open to the idea. "Find the athletes and the event. As long as it's not too expensive, I'm good with it."

"Really?" She'd expected him to shoot it down as he had her recommendation to give the online store more wow factor.

"Sure. Why not? Just remember, we're still dealing with Stanley Royce and I don't know how much that'll cost us in the end, so we've got to watch our spending."

Deciding to press her luck, she said, "Now that the stakes are higher, you sure you don't want to change the look of the online store?"

TJ's response was to glare at her. He got to his feet. "Your car's done. I can take you to pick it up later if you want."

"That's all right; Hannah or Foster can take me. How much do I owe you?"

"Consider it a birthday gift," he said.

"I'll pay you as soon as Felix gives me my last check."

"I said it was a gift, Deb." He glowered and walked out.

Chapter Sixteen

TJ returned to his office, called up the new Garner Adventure website, and stared at the retail page. Though he hated to admit it, Deb might be right. Jillian's online store was creative, appealing, clear, concise, and easy to use, but it lacked Garner Adventure's kick-assness.

Or did it? TJ was finding it difficult to be objective where Deb was concerned. All he could think about was the kiss she'd called *no big deal*. Hell yes, it was a big deal. But if she wanted to pretend it wasn't, fine by him. What did she know about his kisses anyway? Or about websites, for that matter. Jillian had built a successful business creating company's online stores. She presumably knew what she was doing.

He continued to scroll through the site, trying to remain neutral while examining it closely. Delaney's adventure wear—many of the pieces named after the Garner brothers, like the Win Windbreaker, the Colt Cargo pants, the Josh Jams, and the TJ Gives Me a Rash Guard (Colt's idea)—was displayed in pencil sketches. They also had a couple of pages dedicated to their guides' favorite accessories, including a headlamp for cave tours, a water bottle with holder, and a snake bite survival kit. Each had a quirky anecdote about why the item was useful. They had hats and mountain-climbing socks and bouldering gear. Each described with a bit of humor.

So what if it was more refined than GA's rough-and-tumble image? Everyone, except Deb, had thought it was great.

He clicked off the page, threw on his jacket, and left the building in pursuit of fresh air and coffee. The day had gone from sweet to sour thanks to a certain brunette siren.

"We were both coming down from the adrenaline rush of Colt's accident and kissed. No big deal." Her words stung. Deep down inside, that kiss had given him a scintilla of hope that perhaps she could feel something for him.

She'd dashed that dream with two sentences.

It was for the best. They could be normal at work without any messy complications.

On his way to Tart Me Up, he stopped off at Glorious Gifts. Hannah was stocking one of the shelves with Valentine's Day cards. He assumed they were for the last-minute rush, because Valentine's Day was on Wednesday.

"You missed the unveiling of the new website," he said.

She straightened from trying to lift a box and he got it for her. "Where do you want it?"

"Over there." She pointed to the counter. "Thanks. I wanted to come over, but I'm the only one in the store today."

She continued to take cards out of the carton and line them neatly next to each other on the rack. He thumbed through a few, reading the inscriptions inside. Stupid holiday but good for Hannah's profits, he supposed.

"Did everyone love it?" Hannah asked.

Everyone but Deb. "It was a big hit. Check it out when you get a chance."

He walked around the store, browsing. In recent years, his sister-in-law had slowly changed the inventory from kitschy tourist items to upscale home furnishings, clothes, and accessories. Her aunt had founded Glorious Gifts when downtown Glory Junction was just beginning to see the spill off from the ski resorts. Then the real estate market boomed and the store took off. Unfortunately, Sabine got cancer and died, leaving everything to Hannah.

"Deb called. She's crazy about what we did in her office," Hannah said. "I'm so glad we got it done in time. Even though her birthday isn't until Thursday, I wanted her to start the week off with it decorated."

"Good timing." TJ took a smartphone cover with a cartoon map of Glory Junction off a display table and placed it on the counter. "You got any idea of what I should get her?"

"A birthday present? Ah, that's thoughtful of you, TJ. She had her eye on an angora scarf that I sold on Sunday. I think I can get another one in time. You want that?"

What did he know about angora scarfs? "She really likes it?"

"She was crazy about it. But I'll warn you, it's pricey, even with the friends-and-family discount."

"Go ahead and put it on my card. I'm taking the phone case, too."

She went to the back of the store, grabbed some wooly thing, and scanned the price. "This isn't it, but it cost the same."

"Will you wrap it for me when it comes in?"

"Of course." She rang up the phone case. "I'll put a card in there from you and bring it to the party, unless you want to give it to her before, instead of with everyone else."

"The party's fine." He needed to keep things normal between them, not single her out for special attention.

"You planning to bring Karen?"

What was this fixation everyone had with his love life? "Nope, riding solo. Who's going?"

Hannah ticked off a bunch of names. In Glory Junction, you couldn't invite one person and leave another out for fear of offending someone. In a small town, word of a party spread.

"Is Karen invited?" He'd never gotten around to returning her text, so seeing her at the party could be awkward. "What about Mandy Forsyth?"

"Karen is; not Mandy, though." Her lips tipped up as she gave him a look. "You've become sort of slutty, haven't you?"

He laughed. "Nope, that's Win's bag. I'm the boring, corporate guy, remember?"

"No Garner has ever been accused of being boring." She leaned over the counter and kissed his cheek.

Deb had. His kisses . . . no big deal . . . *give me a break.*

"I guess we'll be meeting this Britney woman at Deb's party on Saturday," she continued.

"Yep." He started for the door with his package. "Thanks for taking care of the gift for me."

"Hey," Hannah called. "This is going to sound crazy, but what about you and Deb?"

When he didn't say anything, she waved her hand in the air. "I know, nuts. Never mind."

Outside, he crossed the road to the sunny side of the street and walked to the bakery. Rita Tucker passed him in her beat-up Chevrolet pickup, slammed on her brakes, and backed up.

"Want a ride?"

"Nah; it's a nice day to walk," TJ said.

"I wanted to talk to you about next year's calendar."

The last thing he wanted to do right now was talk to Rita about her cheesy calendar. Everyone put up with it because it raised a lot of cash for the volunteer fire department, but it was pervy as hell. Last year, she'd wanted him to pose as Mr. July, oiled up in a Speedo. But he drew the line at anything that showed the outline of his balls.

"Uh, I'm pressed for time, Rita. Let's do it another day."

"All right." She had a smoker's voice that sounded like truck tires on a gravel road. "Let's put our heads together and come up with a date. I have a bunch of new locations I want to try out."

She took the pictures and did the "styling" herself. The photos were always slightly out of focus and epically inappropriate. They'd all hoped that once she became mayor, she'd turn the calendar over to someone else, someone with taste. But no such luck.

"Sure." An Audi pulled up behind her and the driver tooted his horn. Five to ten years ago, honking your horn at another motorist in Glory Junction would've been a hanging offense. But with all the new part-time residents up from the city, the town had thrown civility to the wind. "See you later."

She drove off in the direction of city hall and TJ continued to the bakery. The breakfast rush was over and he didn't have to wait long for his number to be called. He got a large coffee and a box of Danish to bring back to the office. Rachel came up front from the kitchen to say hello.

"How's Colt? Heard he got caught in a sluff."

"He got out of the hospital this morning and is doing well. A few days of home rest and he'll be right as rain."

"Good to hear," she said and took the pastry box from the kid working behind the counter, opened it, and threw in a few more pastries. "Tell everyone hi for me at GA."

"Will do and thanks, Rachel." TJ had always thought she and her business were great additions to Glory Junction.

He took the Danish back to the office and everyone

descended on the box like scavengers. A few guides had come in to collect their paychecks and stood around the lobby, chowing and telling stories about their recent expeditions. TJ listened for a while before getting back to work. He grabbed an apple turnover and brought it back to Deb.

"Knock, knock."

"Come in."

He found her sitting in front of the computer, tapping keys.

"Food." He set the napkin with the turnover down next to her. "What are you doing?"

"Filling orders."

"Yeah?" He stepped closer to look over her shoulder. It took all his willpower not to spout off about Jillian being right. "How many we get?"

"Three: one for a Colt and Delaney bouldering shirt, another for a fleece, and a third for a pair of Garner Adventure hiking sticks. They came in over the weekend."

Before the new site launched, which took the wind out of his sails.

"How many did we get today?" They'd announced the new online store in GA's monthly newsletter, offering everything from free shipping to deep discounts. A number of adventure blogs had plugged them as well. Business should be thriving.

"Let me check." She refreshed the page, but there was nothing.

TJ pulled up a chair. "Huh; maybe it's not working." He called up the website on his phone, went straight to the retail store, and ordered a pair of cargo shorts. "Refresh it again."

She clicked her mouse on the reload icon and there was his order. He checked his watch. "It's still early. By the end of the day, we should be getting plenty of action."

"I hope so."

"You feeling okay?" Her eyes were puffy.

"About Win? There hasn't been anything between us for a long time, and frankly, what we had was more like puppy love than the real thing." She turned to face him, her eyes holding his. "I'm looking for the real thing."

"Aren't we all?" he said and leaned in.

She smiled. Just a small one, but it filled him to brimming, making his heart hammer in his chest. She put the pastry down and briefly touched his hand. And without thinking, he wiped away a smudge of pastry with his free thumb and ever so lightly touched her lips. If she didn't realize then what he felt for her, she either had cataracts or was comatose.

There were footsteps in the hallway and he quickly turned his head. Darcy stood in the open doorway, blushing. She must've assumed she'd be walking in on an intimate moment between him and Deb. Karen brushed by her.

"Hey," she said in a singsong voice that sounded overly cheery. "I didn't expect to see you here."

He was CEO of the company; why wouldn't he be here? "What brings you to GA?" He rose and shook her hand.

She laughed off his awkward reception and pecked him on the cheek. "I'm here to meet with Deb. Delaney is home, taking care of your brother. What about you?"

"We launched our new website today, including the retail store," Deb said. "TJ and I were going over the orders."

"How's that going?" She tilted her head to get a look at Deb's monitor.

"Not too—"

"Great," TJ cut Deb off. "We've got some friendly competition with an adventure company out of Colorado, but it's all good. I'll leave you two to your meeting."

Deb nodded and he watched her for a few heartbeats,

wondering if something significant had happened between them before they were interrupted.

"Cute space," Karen said, taking quick stock of the room.

TJ went back to his office, irritated by Karen's timing, and pulled a Win by lying longways on his couch. There were a dozen reports on his desk that needed attention, but the thought of burying himself in paperwork made him want to run for the hills. In all the time he'd been running GA, that had never happened.

He heard a scraping noise and spied Darcy loitering by his door. *What now?* "You need to talk to me, Darcy?"

She shuffled in. "Sorry for interrupting you and Deb."

"You weren't interrupting anything." He wished she would stop apologizing all the time.

"Uh, you were obviously having a moment."

He swung up into a sitting position and leaned over to close the door. "We were not having a moment."

She took the spot next to him on the couch. "If you say so." Shy Darcy had become too bold for her own good. "Anyone with half a brain can see there's something between you two."

And she'd become too perceptive. "There's nothing between us."

"Except that you're crazy about each other. I noticed it at the meeting the other day, the way you kept following each other with your eyes across the room."

"She's crazy about someone else," TJ said and blew out a breath.

"She might think she is, but she's not. In any event, we have a bit of an emergency."

He straightened, trying to put Deb out of his mind. "What is it now?"

"Roger Cooley canceled on us."

That wasn't good. "He was leading the ice surfing group, right?"

"Uh-huh. It's supposed to start in"—she glanced at the clock on his wall—"thirty-six minutes."

TJ would certainly call that an emergency and racked his brain for someone they could get on short notice. "What about Win?"

"He's AWOL," she said.

"I just remembered I gave him the day off."

He thought about who else might be available. Not Colt, obviously, and Josh already had a tour. Most of their part-timers weren't up to it. Ice surfing was for pure adrenaline junkies, allowing for speeds of up to seventy miles per hour. It was for extreme thrill seekers . . . like him.

"I'll do it," he said and jumped up from the sofa.

"You never leave the office in the middle of the day."

No, he didn't. He also didn't leave piles of paperwork that needed tending on his desk, unfinished. "Times are changing."

"But who'll run the place while you're gone?"

"Go for it," he said, and went in search of his board.

Chapter Seventeen

It was Valentine's Day and Win wanted to do something nice for Britney. Being pregnant couldn't be easy, so he wanted to give her the whole nine yards. A card, flowers, candy.

He sorted through Hannah's racks, hunting for Valentines that weren't too lovey-dovey but held an appropriate sentiment. *I tolerate you* or *There is no one else I'd rather lie in bed and look at my phone next to* wasn't going to cut it. But something in that general vein would do the trick.

Monday, he'd spent the day with her and they'd had a heart-to-heart. She'd agreed that their best course of action was to get married.

Now, faced with the reality of being a husband and father, he was scared shitless. This wasn't the life he'd mapped out for himself, at least not at thirty and not with Britney. But as the adage went, he'd made his bed and he had to lie in it. Thankfully, he had a supportive family. While his parents weren't thrilled about how this had gone down, his mom was already knitting a baby blanket and his dad had offered to help him buy a house in Glory Junction that would fit a family.

He kept telling himself it would be okay.

"Here's the last of the chocolates." Hannah came from the back, holding a box of Godiva. "I talked to Foster and he said he'll squeeze in your arrangement. Don't expect anything too fancy. He's slammed. That's what you get for waiting until the last minute."

Win picked up the green smoothie he'd placed on the counter and took a swig. "I've had other things on my mind."

"I know." Hannah's expression turned sympathetic.

His secret was out. It had taken his brothers less than a day to tell their significant others. Win supposed it was better that way. Now he didn't have to explain it to everyone.

She nudged her head at the shelves of cards. "You want me to help?"

"Nah; this one will work." It said, "HBO and chill?" with a heart at the bottom. It was a step up from the one that said, "You suck less than most people," which he wasn't even sure was true. He put it on the counter, tossed his empty smoothie cup in the trash, and tugged his wallet out of his cargo pants.

As usual, Hannah gave him the friends-and-family discount. "Josh says you're bringing Britney to the party Saturday."

"Yep. Time for her to meet the fam."

"We're looking forward to it." She reached over and took his hand. "You okay with all this?"

He lifted his shoulders. "I'm good with it. Really good." He forced a smile.

"Congratulations."

He paid, took his card and candy, and walked to Sweet Stems. There were three people ahead of him in line. Foster took a huge arrangement out of the refrigerator for the first guy, who turned out to be Chip.

"For Val?" Win asked.

"Yeah." Chip got this goofy grin on his face. Honest to

goodness, Win had never seen him so happy, not that he would ever tell his sister-in-law that. Hannah was head over heels for Josh anyway. The two of them had always been meant to be together. Win was glad that both Hannah and Chip had found their soul mates. "You getting flowers for someone?"

"My fiancée," Win said.

Chip did a double take. "You're getting married?" He paused, and Win could see him working something out in his head. "Ah, makes sense now why you hired Deb. When you two tying the knot?"

"We're not. You don't know her; she lives in Tahoe. And if I don't get these flowers to her soon, I'll be sleeping on the couch." Win shouldered his way past Chip to the counter.

Foster finished up with his last customer. "Give me a second," he told Win and went into the back room. He returned a short time later with a bouquet that looked a hell of a lot better than a last-minute job, at least to Win.

"Nice, dude."

Foster snorted. "You're lucky I fit you in. You owe me, so I hope this woman is worth it."

Everyone knew Foster was fiercely loyal to Deb. Despite the fact that there was nothing going on between them and hadn't been for a long time, there were still people in Glory Junction who assumed they'd wind up together. It was the quirk of a small town.

"I appreciate it, Foster. Anything you need, man, I'll make it happen."

Another snort. "Six-foot-two, financially independent, and not a lot of baggage."

"That's sort of a tall order, don't you think? But let me see what I can do." Win slid his credit card toward the cash register. "I'm bringing Britney to the party Saturday. Deb'll be cool with it, won't she?"

Foster glowered at him. "She's over you."

But on Win's way out of the store, Foster whistled the tune of "It's My Party."

Foster just wanted to bust his chops.

The police station was next to Sweet Stems and Win decided to pop in on Colt, who, against his doctor's orders, had gone back to work. Anyone without an appointment had to get by Carrie Jo, who was harder to breach than a razor-wire fence.

"Did you bring those for me?" She reached for his bouquet and he yanked it away.

"Nope, but maybe I should've." He eyed her up and down. "You're looking good, Carrie Jo."

"And you're a flirty tramp. Your brother's in his office. Go ahead in."

Win walked in to find Colt fumbling with a roll of wire ribbon. "What're you doing?"

"What does it look like I'm doing? Put your finger here," he told Win and attempted to tie a bow on a poorly wrapped package covered with hearts.

Win did as Colt asked. "Ow, that hurts. What, did you forget to get Delaney something for Valentine's Day?"

"What, did you forget I had a near miss with death?"

"Exaggeration much?" Win grabbed the ribbon away from Colt, tied the bow, and plopped down on the couch.

Colt assessed his flowers. "You should give me those."

"Not happening, dude. They're for Britney."

"Mom says you've got your first doctor's appointment in a few weeks. How you doing with all this?"

"Fine." Win hoped if he said it enough times it would be true.

Colt studied him for a while, then nodded. "You don't have a tour today?"

"I did this morning at the ass crack of five in the backcountry. I'm done for the day and am heading to Tahoe. You and Delaney have big plans?"

"Dinner at home. She's worried I'll faint from too much exertion." He made a mocking face. "What about you?"

"No plans in particular." As usual, Britney was being cagey. First she had to work, then she didn't. He figured he'd pick up a pizza and a quart of ice cream.

Colt kicked his feet up on the desk and leaned back in his chair. "TJ have any plans?"

"Not that I know of. Is he seeing that Karen chick?" Lately, he and TJ had been like two strangers passing in the night. Win supposed they both had a lot on their mind. TJ had been immersed in the new website and launching the online store and Win had a baby on the way.

"Dunno. He's not a sharer like the rest of us."

Win laughed, got up, walked over to Colt, and gave him a noogie. "Just came to see if you were still kicking. Looks like my work here is done."

"Have fun in Tahoe, asshole."

Win flipped him the bird and went on his way. His Jeep was parked on the street in front of GA. He loaded it with his Glorious Gifts bag and the flowers and made the thirty-minute drive to Tahoe. Cami was outside her condo, getting her mail, when he got there. She did a finger-wave thing and tried to flirt with him.

"Those for Britney?" she asked, cocking her head at his Valentine's Day gifts.

No, they were for Steph Curry. "Nothing gets past you, Cami." He tried to sound teasing and made a straight line for Britney's door.

"She's not home."

He rang the bell.

Cami came over to the little fence that separated the two condos and hung her head over.

"She left about thirty minutes ago."

"She's probably getting us dinner," he lied, feeling like a goddamn idiot. Not two hours ago they'd made plans for him to come over.

"It looked like she was going out for the evening to me." Cami gave a small shrug and walked away.

He waited for her to go inside her place, went back to his Jeep, and called Britney. "Where are you?" he asked when she finally answered.

"Out with a few friends, having drinks."

"We had plans." He gritted his teeth. *And why the hell are you drinking?*

"Jeez, I'll be home in twenty minutes. You're so uptight." There was music blaring in the background.

He pulled the phone away from his ear and counted to ten. Uptight? Most people would say he was the polar opposite. "I went to a lot of trouble and I don't like getting stood up."

"Fine, I'll come home, then." She was walking because he suddenly heard the dinging of slot machines.

"Are you okay to drive?"

"Oh, for God's sake, Win. There's a key under the mat; make yourself at home." She hung up, and for a second he thought about motoring right back to Glory Junction. But he had to make this work. For the kid's sake.

He returned to her unit, hoping like hell to avoid Cami, and found the key. Inside, he put the flowers in water, scared up a number for a pizza delivery joint, and put in an order. The kid said to expect an hour or more wait. What did he expect? He got a beer out of her fridge and turned on the TV. She had a sixty-five-inch flat-screen in the great room and another one in her bedroom. He flipped through the channels and found a show on bull riding. Now, that was something he'd like to try.

Thirty, forty minutes later, she walked in the door. "Are you over your snit?"

She took off her stilettos and dropped them on the floor. He couldn't believe this was the woman he was winding up with. The girls he'd always dated wore hiking boots. He preferred it that way.

"Why did you tell me to meet you here if you were planning to go out with your friends?" It was inconsiderate, not to mention flakey.

"It was a last-minute thing," she said and sat on the couch with him, cuddling under his arm. "What did you get me for Valentine's Day?"

"It's on the counter." He nudged his head at the kitchen.

She rocketed up and went to have a look. "The flowers are pretty." She dug through the Glorious Gifts bag, took out the card, read it, and put it to the side. Her hand reached into the bag again and pulled out the box of chocolates, her expression doing an instant cliff dive.

"You don't like candy?" Win asked.

She pushed the box next to the card, her disappointment evident. "I do, but given that I'm pregnant with your child, I was expecting something glittery."

"I told you I'd get you an engagement ring." Lord knew, she'd insist on the biggest one she could get her hands on. Another thing he missed about the women he used to date. They were down to earth, not all about the bling.

"That shouldn't count." She pouted. "This should've been something for just me. Something special." *And something expensive*, Win added to himself.

Jesus Christ, she was demanding. And materialistic. "I'm not made of money, Britney, and whatever I have we should use for a house."

She waved her hand around the condo. "I have a house."

It was a one-bedroom without a backyard. Not exactly a place to raise a kid. But it wasn't worth fighting about right now, not while she simmered over the fact that he hadn't bought her the Hope Diamond.

She was starting to bust on his last nerve. And with each and every day, it was becoming abundantly clear that he was embarking on a freakin' nightmare.

Chapter Eighteen

The moment TJ met Britney Sheldon, he had a visceral dislike for her. It wasn't just the way she'd asked Darcy to get her a drink as if she was part of the waitstaff or her ostentatious habit of shoving the rock Win had given her under everyone's nose. Everything about her felt like a user.

She'd walked into the party and sized up Garner Adventure like she was calculating its worth, tabulating the net value of every piece of furniture and person in the place. She seemed to turn her nose up at the casualness of the event, especially the food. Boden had catered all Deb's favorites. Pub fries, chicken wings, sliders, and onion rings. Win had brought Britney a plate and she'd whined that she didn't want grease to get on her clothes. But most of all, he didn't like how she'd given their mom the cold shoulder.

Mary had opened her arms to give Britney a hug and Win's fiancée had pushed right past her for a glass of champagne. TJ wasn't even sure if she was supposed to be drinking. But as the future mother of TJ's niece or nephew, he didn't want to judge Britney too harshly and fervently hoped she just made a lousy first impression.

"I hate her." Darcy sidled up next to him. Their little

mouse of a receptionist was learning how to roar. Tonight, he liked it. "She's mean to Win."

"Win can take care of himself. Walk with me." He wanted a beer and there was a keg out back. When they were away from everyone, he asked, "Any other impressions?" Clearly, Darcy was one of those still-waters-run-deep people. She'd certainly called him on Deb.

She rubbed her hands together. It was chilly. "I'm pretty sure she's a gold digger."

TJ was pretty sure she was right. He let out a breath. "Then she's gonna be disappointed." Garner Adventure was a prosperous business, but it was far from a Fortune 500 company, and from the looks of Britney's fur jacket and designer clothes, she had some expensive habits. But Delaney would know better about that kind of stuff. Maybe it was all knockoffs. In any event, if Britney thought she was marrying into the likes of the Walton family, she was sadly mistaking.

Especially now. Stanley Royce wasn't going away and the retail experiment hadn't gotten nearly the amount of orders he'd projected. Over the last week, he'd been in freak-out mode.

"She doesn't even act like she likes Win," Darcy said.

TJ laughed because under normal circumstances it would've been poetic justice. Women had always slavered over his love-'em-and-leave-'em brother. "It's out of our control, Darcy. What about Deb; you think she's having a good time?"

"Uh-huh." She gave him a long appraisal, started to say something, and stopped herself. Then settled for, "It's a nice party. Hannah, Foster, and Delaney must be really good friends for all the effort they put in."

"They did a great job." He filled both their cups and got Darcy in before she froze.

As she drifted off to talk to someone, he thought about how he wanted to give her that promotion. But if Stanley got his way, that probably wasn't going to happen. Hell, at the rate they were going, he wouldn't be able to justify Deb's position much longer. Tonight, though, wasn't the time to think about it. He didn't want to ruin the party.

He scanned the room, searching for Deb, and spotted her talking to Foster, her head back, laughing. Her dark hair cascaded over her shoulders and her eyes sparkled and he felt his pulse quicken. Looking at her now, she reminded him of high school. At the time, she'd been a freshman frantically trying to remember her locker combination as she fumbled with the dial. With four years under his belt, he knew how to crack a locker without knowing the number sequence. Much to the consternation of the faculty, he and his friends did it all the time.

"You need help, Little Debbie?"

"Don't call me that. But yeah." She'd looked up at the clock on the wall with those big, brown eyes of hers, scared of being late, and then back at him. "Please."

One well-placed punch with the side of his fist and the locker door popped right open.

"Thank you." And for one fleeting second, he'd been her hero.

Colt slapped him on the back, pulling him from his memories. "What are you staring at? You're looking over there like you're love sick for Fost—" His mouth went slack. "Holy shit, no way. Deb?"

"Everyone's waiting for the band." TJ tried to walk away, but Colt jerked him by the arm.

"No, you don't." Colt pulled him into a quiet corner. "This explains why you gave her the job at GA."

"I gave her the job because I thought she'd be good at it

and Lauren didn't want it. Don't read shit into stuff that isn't there."

"You're lying," Colt said. "I don't know how I missed it, I don't know how any of us missed it, but it all makes sense. Ah, Jesus, this has been going on for a while, like maybe forever, hasn't it?"

"There's nothing going on. She's always been Win's."

Colt looked at him for a long time. Too long. "So you admit you've got a thing for her?"

"What does it matter?" TJ tried to walk away, but Colt wouldn't let him.

"Does she know?"

How could she not? "I don't think so."

"You should tell her, TJ."

"She wanted Win, not me."

"Win's out of the picture." Colt gazed over at Britney, who was standing against the rock wall, looking terminally bored while she texted on her phone.

"I don't want to be Win's sloppy seconds." This time he did walk away.

"Or are you just afraid to take a risk?" Colt jogged after him. "We all know that's why you didn't make the Olympics team. You were a better skier than Win—hell, you're a better skier than me—you were more dedicated, and you have more fire in your belly than anyone I know."

Hannah and Delaney were headed toward them. TJ glared at Colt. "You really want to do this now?"

"Ready to get the music started?" Hannah exchanged a glance with Delaney. "Something wrong?"

If Colt opened his fat mouth, TJ was going to deck him.

Colt shoved his hand through his hair. "Nope. Let me get the rest of the band." As he walked away, he whispered to TJ, "Tell her."

Hannah and Delaney followed after Colt and TJ went

over to the food table to grab a slider. He hadn't eaten all night. Rachel stood there, perusing the offerings.

"Why didn't they have me do the food and not just the cake?"

Ah, was this going to be a war between Old Glory and Tart Me Up? *Somebody spare me, please.* "I wasn't in charge, Rach, otherwise I would've chosen you for sure." He hoped Boden hadn't heard that. The truth was, he liked both places equally.

"Thanks, TJ." She plucked a ministeak sandwich from one of the platters and took a bite. "A little overdone, but not bad."

"What are you talking about?" Boden came up from behind them and pointed at her sandwich. "That right there is a perfectly cooked medium-rare piece of meat."

Time to exit. On his way to get a beer refill, he could still hear the two of them bickering. Colt and his band were warming up on the makeshift stage. Hannah, Foster, and Delaney had rented a dance floor and within the hour, the place would be loud and sweaty. That was when TJ planned to make a discreet getaway.

He'd come for Deb but wasn't in the mood to party. Outside, he found the birthday girl alone, pumping the keg.

"I'll do that," he said and took her place. "You look great, by the way."

She had on a little black velvet number, black stockings, and high heels. The outfit should've been outlawed in all fifty states.

"Thank you. You too. I like the bolo tie." She handed him her cup. "What's up with Darcy? She seems more flustered around me than usual."

"She thought we were fooling around the other day when she and Karen walked in on us."

"We weren't, at least not that time."

"Nope, not that time." He held her gaze until she looked away.

"What do you think of Britney?" she asked. Nice change of subject.

"Too soon to tell." He wanted to be loyal to Win. "You?"

"She seems nice."

"Liar." He grinned and filled both their glasses.

"God, she's awful." She pretended to shudder. "Are you going to dance with me?"

"Nope. I'm gonna go home."

"You can't." She tugged on his arm, making him slosh beer on his boots. "Let's go inside. It's freezing out here."

He wasn't in a rush because the cold was doing nice things to Deb's breasts. But he followed her inside anyway. The band had started and they were just in time to catch the tail end of a Rolling Stones' song.

"It's my birthday and you have to dance with me. It's the rule."

He wasn't aware of any such rule. "Where does it say that?"

"In the Bible. Come on," she cajoled. "It won't kill you. We can make it a slow one if you're worried about your moves."

He wasn't much of a dancer, but slow sounded nice.

"Okay, one dance. But that's it."

Colt played another fast song. The Beatles' "Birthday," and TJ shook his head. He wanted a slow one. Hannah and Delaney got Deb, and the three of them danced together. Deb swayed, moving her hips from side to side. He liked watching her, and a couple of X-rated images flashed in his head, which he tried to block without much success.

Midway through the tune, Deb grabbed Darcy. Who

knew their diminutive, shy receptionist could dance? But she strutted her stuff across the dance floor. It was the first time TJ had seen Win smile all evening. No Garner man was immune to four ultrahot women wiggling around in short dresses.

He gazed across the room and spied Britney snagging another glass of champagne and wondered if she had a drinking problem. Maybe two well-spaced drinks over the course of the night were okay for a pregnant woman; TJ didn't know. But she was slamming them one right after the other. And that couldn't be good.

He glanced over at Win, who got up, walked over to the bar, and whispered something in her ear. Britney put the glass down, but TJ saw deep resentment in her body language. She was fuming.

"Looks like Win's got his hands full." Josh joined him over by the rock wall. They'd moved the rest of the equipment from the gym to their private offices to make more space for the party. Every year they threw a Christmas open house, so they had the drill down.

"I'm hoping it's nerves. Under the circumstances, it can't be easy to meet the entire Garner clan at once."

"Except she's not even making an effort. Mom and Dad have tried to engage her in conversation several times. She was too busy searching for her next drink or texting on her phone to talk to them. They're about to become her in-laws, for heaven's sake."

"What about Win? He seem okay to you?"

Josh sighed. "It's hard to tell. You know how he is."

Win rolled with the punches and wasn't one to complain. Although until now, his life had been a cake walk. Doors always opened for Win and opportunities always knocked.

He seemed to have been born under a lucky star. TJ guessed not so much anymore.

"He'll have to figure it out as he goes," TJ said. "And we need to give her a chance."

"You're right." Josh turned when Hannah called from the dance floor. She crooked her finger for him to join her. His lips curved up and he shook his head.

"Go on." TJ pushed him "Let's see ya make a fool of yourself."

"Bad leg, remember?"

"Your leg is fine. Get out there."

The song ended, temporarily saving Josh. Colt launched into a ballad and the women came off the floor. A few couples replaced them, including Boden and Karen. Josh went off to dance with Hannah and Deb grabbed his arm.

"You promised," she said and tugged on him.

"Okay, okay." He let her lead him to the center of the floor.

The song was the Bonnie Raitt classic "I Can't Make You Love Me," and TJ wondered if Colt had played it on purpose. Nah; Colt wouldn't be that cruel. Just a painful coincidence.

Deb put her arms around his neck and pressed tightly against him. His heart raced and he palmed her waist, remembering their kiss. A release of adrenaline from Colt's accident. *Yeah right.*

They swayed to the music, and she fit so well in his arms and felt so perfect with her head nestled under his chin that he didn't want the song to end. She ran her hands up and down his back and molded herself even closer against him.

Gazing up at him with light in her eyes she said, "Don't go, okay?"

He chuckled. "From you, like this, or the party?"

"None of it," she whispered, and he felt his heart stop.

They continued to dance—if you could call it that—rocking in small circles, his hands at her back, his mouth hovering over her hair. She smelled like sunshine and strawberries. Her fingers played at the nape of his neck, arousing him. She pressed into his groin and he thought he might go off right there in the corner of the dance floor.

"Not here." If they didn't stop, the entire town would start to notice. He glanced around the room. Deb's parents were in the corner with his own, engaged in conversation. Colt, the asshole, held a hint of a smile as he extended the song with a melodic solo on his Martin guitar.

She played with his hair and he was about to reach his breaking point. "Deb?"

"Hmm?" She stared up at him.

"Let's go to my office."

With the music so loud, he wasn't sure she heard him.

"Your office," she murmured and started to dance him in that direction.

Jesus Christ . . . he couldn't believe he was doing this. But that was the thing about Deb. She made him let go.

"Let's try to be discreet, okay?" He reached for her hand and silently led her down the hallway.

The band had shifted into something fast-paced. TJ didn't recognize the song, but he could barely hear it over the pounding of his pulse. He wanted to make this so good for her.

He had to push the door hard so it would open with the weight bench in the way. They heard someone coming out of the bathroom and he put his finger to his lips. He smothered her giggle with his mouth, managed to kick away the bench, and shut the door before anyone saw them.

She wrapped herself around him. "You feel so good; like

you did the other night, but even better." Her hand moved to his belt buckle. "And you smell good, too."

"Are you drunk?" He nuzzled close to her ear.

"A little buzzed, but not drunk. Why?"

Because he yearned to do this so badly that his body was on fire for her. That was the thing; he was jumping into the flames, knowing full well he'd get burned. If she was drunk, though, he'd walk away. It would take every ounce of willpower he had, but he'd do it.

She put the flat of her hands against his chest, went up on her toes, and kissed him. "You taste good."

She dragged the bolo tie over his head and started to unbutton his shirt. With every scrape of her hand, he sucked in a breath. He pushed her down onto the sofa. It was too small for them to both get horizontal on. But he had other plans.

He kneeled in front of her and pushed up her dress. Her stockings were the kind that only went to her thighs. He had no idea what was holding them up, but just looking at them made him harder. She watched him, her eyes heating, her mouth forming a small *oh*. He slid her black-lace panties down her legs and slipped them over her shoes until they fell to the floor. Deb reached out and tried to pull him on top of her.

"Not yet," he whispered and ran his index finger down the inside of her silky leg.

She shivered and he followed the trail with his lips. The stockings smelled like her and he liked the sensation of them against his skin. He wanted to see her breasts and reached up and unzipped the back of her dress, pulling the neckline down. She had on a black lace bra that matched the panties. He'd never cared much about underwear, only what was under it. But on her . . . The bra plunged low, giving him a good view of her plump, firm breasts. He rimmed the edge of the lace with his index finger, dragged the straps over her arms, and pulled down the cups until she spilled out. He circled her nipples with his tongue, which drove her crazy. She leaned her head against the back of the couch while her whole body vibrated. She was unbelievably responsive.

"TJ, please." She went for his belt again.

He moved her hands away, spread her legs, and tested her with his mouth.

"Oh my God." She levitated off the couch.

"Good?" As if he needed to ask. He delved his tongue in and out of her and heard the sharp intake of her breath. The woman was a hair trigger away from an orgasm.

"Do you have a condom?"

"Shush," he told her and continued to kiss the insides of her legs, feeling her slickness with his finger. "You're so wet." For him. The realization of that made his chest expand.

She pulled at his shirt and he lifted it over his head. Her hands moved up and down his arms and over his chest. She couldn't seem to get enough of him. He continued to work her with his mouth, licking and laving and touching her everywhere. Reaching for her breasts, he weighed each one in his hands.

"TJ? Please. I need you."

"Soon," he said, wanting her to come like this first, wanting it to be the best climax she'd ever had.

This time he tried two fingers, feeling her stretch to accommodate him. He came up over her and kissed her lips while stroking her with his hand.

"I can't take anymore." Her eyes were closed and she was shaking.

"Let go then." He trailed kisses down her throat and sucked her breasts.

"I want you, TJ," she said, and he moved lower until he

covered her with his mouth, working her some more with his tongue. "Oh yes, yes."

He watched her come apart, her body shuddering as she called out to him over and over again. Nothing made him more aroused than hearing his name on her lips. He continued to fondle and kiss her until she went limp, breathing like she'd been in a downhill ski race.

There was noise in the hallway, two or three people talking. Deb, still sporting the afterglow of her orgasm, jerked her dress up. Coming in here during the party had been risky. TJ found his shirt on the floor and quickly pulled it on.

Deb clutched his arms and in a low voice said, "But we're not done yet."

His mouth quirked. "You look done to me."

"What about you, though? And I wanted . . ." She trailed off, her face turning red. "Don't you?"

Hell yeah, he did. "You're the guest of honor. People are probably looking for you." He kissed her and she wrapped her arms around him. In another minute, he'd have her dress completely off and Deb on her back.

The voices grew louder. Damn. He swept the floor, found her panties, and handed them to her. "We've gotta get back out there."

"What about after the party?" she asked shyly.

"You want to come home with me?" His lips tipped up and he felt his lower half spring back to life.

She pulled her bra straps up and turned to finish righting the top half of her dress. She tried to put her underwear back on without him seeing—ridiculous, because he'd seen all of her. He turned away to give her some privacy and did up his buttons.

"I do," she said.

* * *

Deb went back to the party feeling warm all over. What he'd just done . . . well, it had been sublime. Best present ever.

The band was on break and Colt came up to give her a hug. "Where've you been, birthday girl?" He sounded like he was teasing, and she suspected he might've seen her and TJ slip away. Mortifying if he had. She didn't want the reputation of being a Garner groupie.

"TJ wanted to show me something." She prayed Colt didn't ask what, because she didn't have a good lie at the ready.

He hitched his brows. "Yeah?"

Her eyes dropped to her shoes and she hoped her stockings weren't bagging around her knees. Should've checked that before leaving TJ's office.

Colt put his finger under her chin and lifted her face. "Of all of us, he's the best, you know? Smarter, deeper, better-looking, greater athlete, and the most loyal."

She'd known all those things were true. But why was Colt telling her this? She held contact with him, looking for answers. All she saw in his deep brown eyes was merriment. He was playing with her.

"All you Garners are highly overrated."

Colt leaned his head back and laughed. "I don't think so, Little Debbie."

She punched him in the arm and he put her in a headlock. Josh told him to quit roughhousing and to play more music. TJ came over and slipped a beer in her hand. It felt like something a boyfriend would do.

The band started up again. "This is an oldie but a goodie," Colt told the partygoers. "And it's dedicated to the birthday girl."

"Brown Eyed Girl."

Boden grabbed her around the waist and swung her onto the dance floor. Everyone cheered except TJ, who scowled.

She stowed that information away for later and danced. After Boden came Foster, then Jack—who held his police scanner while attempting the Texas two-step. There was Josh, who turned out to be completely devoid of rhythm. Hannah stood to the side, laughing her ass off. Unlike Josh, Felix could boogie, surprising for a guy who'd busted practically every bone in his body snowboarding.

Rita Tucker did some kind of Stevie Nicks crackhead dance that was bizarre, to say the least. But hey, it was great to have a mayor who let her freak flag fly. Morris Finkelstein, Deb's favorite senior-citizen diner at the Morning Glory, tried to teach her to waltz. Deb would never make it on *Dancing with the Stars,* but she was having a hell of a good time.

TJ leaned against the wall, his hands shoved in his pockets, watching her make a fool of herself. Occasionally, she'd sneak a glance at him, and her entire body would tingle, remembering what they'd done on his love seat. The man had surpassed his boardroom skills in the bedroom. Or at least his office.

He could also rock a pair of Levi's. Just seeing him, one broad shoulder cocked against the wall, his booted toe tapping to the music, made her want to find out what going all the way with TJ Garner was like. He'd proven to be the king of foreplay, giving her one hell of a memory to kick off the year of being thirty.

He saw her looking and flashed a cocky grin, perfect white teeth gleaming in the dim light. She promised herself it was his move; no more begging. She was done with that. Part of her new life as a grown-up.

Hannah suddenly came over Colt's PA system. He pulled the mic back from her mouth when feedback filled the room, and she said, "Time for Deb to blow out her candles."

Rachel wheeled in a table with the most gorgeous birthday cake Deb had ever seen. It had been decorated to look like a ski resort with chairlifts, runs, mini pine trees, and itty-bitty skiers. Deb hated to cut into it, it was so beautiful. She took a few photos with her phone to save it for posterity.

Everyone sang "Happy Birthday to You." Deb made a silent wish to spend the night with TJ and blew out the candles. All thirty of them. Rachel cut the cake, served slices onto plates, and Deb helped her pass them out, nearly catching TJ in the gut with her elbow in the process.

"I didn't see you there. Chocolate or vanilla?"

"What if I want both?" He made it sound sexual.

Two could play that game. "All you have to do is ask and you shall receive." She handed him two plates, one of each, and a fork.

After the guests got theirs, she found a quiet corner to eat her piece before someone came over to talk. She loved Rachel's cakes and wanted to savor every last drop.

"Care if I join you?" TJ pulled up two chairs. Her feet wanted to kiss him.

"Mmm. Good cake, huh?"

He checked her plate. "Don't like chocolate?"

"I like it. I'll probably go back for a second piece."

He cut a piece and offered it to her. "Take a taste."

She scraped it off the fork with her mouth. "Wow, that may even be better than the vanilla."

Colt and the other band members had started tearing down the stage. Foster waved from across the room and blew her a kiss, signaling he was leaving. He had a mother-daughter tea at a local bed-and-breakfast that he was doing the flowers for on Sunday. She made a telephone sign with her fingers—*I'll call you.* Delaney glided around the room in one of her bazillion-dollar outfits, picking up trash. Hannah, Josh, and Darcy were stacking chairs. Deb looked up at the wall clock. Whoa; it was past midnight.

"You have to work at the diner tomorrow?" TJ asked her.

"Nope. Felix gave me the day off. I'm going over to my parents' for dinner." Her mom was making pot roast, her favorite.

"Want to take off?"

She looked at him, trying to make sure he meant to-gether. The whole night . . . well, she'd felt like Cinderella at the ball. "Don't you think I should help clean up?"

"No." He got up, took their plates, and dumped them in the garbage. "Let's go."

"I should at least say good-bye and thank everyone for the party."

"All right, then come back to the parking lot. Hurry."

Uh, impatient much? Deb didn't plan to question it. She wanted this. Bad.

Deb made the rounds, thanking and kissing everyone.

"We'll take your gifts home and you can come over to-morrow and open them." Colt virtually pushed her out the door while Delaney stood with her mouth agape, perplexed at his boorish behavior.

As Deb left, she heard Delaney say to Colt, "What's gotten into you?"

He knew, that's what. Just the thought of facing him Sunday made her flush with embarrassment. Yet it didn't stop her from following the driveway to the back lot, where she found TJ revving his engine.

She hopped in the passenger seat and waited for him to tell her what they were doing. He didn't say a word, just drove. It soon became clear that they were going to his place, not hers, which would've been closer but less dis-creet. Come to think of it, she'd never been to his house before. She knew it was at the lake, close to his parents', and that he'd done a lot of work on it.

"What are you thinking?" she asked when she couldn't take his silence any longer.

"For once in my life, I'm trying not to think and just do."

"I'm looking forward to seeing your house," she said lamely because what she was really looking forward to was more of what they'd done in TJ's office. "You've never had me over before."

He didn't say anything, just headed for the lake. It was too dark to see much, but Deb knew the homes were huge on this side of town. A lot of city transplants had supersized the old, modest houses.

TJ took the road that wound around the shore. She'd spent many summers here on the beach, swimming, canoeing, waterskiing, or just lying on the sand. Even with the crowds, it was one of her favorite places in Glory Junction.

He reached over and put his hand on her leg. His palm felt good. Warm and reassuring and like it fit there. Like they fit.

He pulled into a driveway, and a motion light flicked on, illuminating the house. It was a rustic, mountain-style home with brown shingles and chocolate-brown trim. Great curb appeal, but then, she hadn't expected anything less from TJ.

He got out and came around to her side, offered her a hand out, and held it as he unlocked the front door. They walked into a small foyer and he guided her into the living room. Huge windows overlooked the lake. The kitchen was open to the rest of the front room, and that, too, had amazing views of the water and the Sierra mountains. All his furnishings and built-ins had clean lines. It was three times the size of her apartment and crazy neat.

"It's beautiful, TJ." She walked around, examining everything. "It's a grown-up's house."

"That's me," he said wryly, standing off to the side, letting her snoop. "A grown-up."

She turned to face him. "Nothing wrong with that." In fact, compared to what she was used to, it was an absolute turn-on. "Do you have beach access?"

He led the way to the staircase and took her down. She hadn't realized it was a three-story. From the front, you couldn't tell, but the house was built on a slope with a full above-ground basement, which he'd turned into a man cave. Pool table, foosball, and an enormous flat-screen. He opened a pair of glass doors and flipped on a switch, lighting a large wooden deck and a walkway to the beach and a dock.

"Seriously? Is that yours?" She stared at the towboat moored there.

"Yep. When I got the place, the dock was rotted and falling apart. Once I fixed it, I figured I needed the Moomba Outback."

A speedboat like that cost a pretty penny, and to be right on the water . . . wow. If it weren't so cold, she would've slipped off her shoes. Instead, she tottered on her high heels through the sand and onto the dock. "This place is truly amazing. I can't believe I've never been here before."

He came up behind her and put his hand on her back as if he was afraid she'd tumble into the lake. "You were always welcome."

"In the summer, I want to go waterskiing." She pointed to the boat.

He grinned. "I can make that happen."

She continued to take everything in. There was a hot tub on the deck she'd missed, a table and chairs, and two chaises. The sight of the lounges next to each other made her wonder who had been out here with him and what they had done together. It was a silly reaction, but the thought sparked a flash of jealousy.

"You ever have parties?"

He laughed. "Yeah, with all my extra time."

"You do work a lot."

"I think Colt and I are tied." Besides running the police department, Colt spent his after-hours guiding tours for GA. But now that Delaney was in the picture, he'd been taking more time off. TJ, on the other hand, never stopped. Win always said he was a workaholic.

"Can we go in that?" She nudged her head at the hot tub. "I didn't bring a suit, but I could borrow a T-shirt from you."

"It's your birthday. Birthday suit." He thought that was hilarious, but his gaze heated and she saw desire swirl in his blue eyes. And then he kissed her. Under the moonlight, as the water lapped against the pier.

It was wildly romantic. She pressed up against him, letting the warmth of his arms and mouth travel through her. His body felt hard, especially the ridge in his pants that throbbed against her belly. She moved her hands down his back, grabbed his bottom, and pulled him tighter, trying to quell the pulsing between her legs.

He still tasted faintly of chocolate from the birthday cake and a hint of beer. And he smelled like heaven. She felt her stomach dip and her heart pound and realized this thing between them, whether it was extraordinary chemistry or insatiable lust, was different from anything she'd ever experienced.

He continued to kiss her, his tongue dancing with hers, his hands caressing her arms, back, and butt. She let out a moan of pleasure and he lifted her like a bride and carried her in the house, up two flights of stairs. In the dark, he found the nightstand lamp and switched it on, then dropped her in the center of the bed, falling on top of her. They kissed some more, the warm pull of his mouth making her flesh turn to goose bumps.

He came up on both elbows, gazed down at her, and

swallowed hard, his face filled with a combination of longing and wonder. She'd never had a partner look at her that way. Like she mattered more than life itself. It made sex different. Meaningful, but scary.

Gently, he lifted her and unzipped the back of her dress, tugging it off so she lay there in nothing but her bra, panties, and stockings. His lips moved down her body, over lace, satin, and skin, his hands reverently fondling her breasts and the curves of her hips. One by one, he rolled her stockings down, the sensation driving her crazy with need.

She grasped his shoulders and tried to pull him down, but he was too strong and determined to get the rest of her underthings off. Deb pushed up his shirt, letting her hands graze his firm abs and felt him shudder. One-handed, he nimbly undid his top few buttons and yanked the shirt with the bolo tie over his head. She rose on her hands to see him. The man was breathtaking, with a smattering of dark hair trailing down his chest, disappearing underneath the waistband of his jeans. Those needed to go, too. She was dying to see the rest of him. She lay back down and began working on his belt buckle as he continued to kiss and touch her.

He was thorough. Most of Deb's liaisons had been a lot of *wham bam, thank you, ma'am*. She got his belt undone and his fly open. Impatient, he did the rest, shucking both his pants and boxers.

Deb gulped. TJ was as beautiful below the waist as he was on top.

He unhooked her bra, slid down the straps, and tossed it somewhere on the floor with the rest of their clothes. Next came her panties. He dipped a finger inside her while his other hand played with her breasts.

"You're very good at this," she said, even though she was finding it difficult to string two coherent words together.

"I want to make it perfect for you," he whispered.

"Why?" No one had ever been that conscientious before.

"Because I . . . Stop asking questions and let me make you scream." He took her nipple between his lips and sucked.

She laughed uncontrollably because what he was doing tickled. "Oh, oh, TJ."

He tilted his head to look at her, then moved his mouth to her neck, murmuring, "I want you, Deb. I've wanted you all night."

"Do you have protection?"

She heard the scrape of a drawer and saw him grab a handful of condoms from the nightstand. He ripped one of the packets open and rolled the condom down his length. With his knee, he spread her legs and penetrated her with one powerful thrust. She gasped and he froze.

"Too much?"

"No, it's good. So good."

He moved slowly, pushing in and out of her, his face taut with concentration. As Deb grew more accustomed to him, she followed his rhythm until they were in perfect sync. It was so primal and intense that she couldn't talk or think or even hear anything other than their moans and heavy breathing. All she did was feel and be in the moment.

TJ kissed her long and hard, whispering sweet words against her mouth. "God, you're beautiful." His fingers combed through her hair, finding the back of her head, cupping it so his tongue could delve deeper.

She could've drowned in his kisses, they were that good. She could've drowned in the circle of his strong arms.

He upped the pace until he was pounding into her. She wrapped her legs around his waist, matching him stroke for stroke. Deb loved watching the muscles in his back bunch, watching his body bow and his hips piston back and forth.

"You close?" he asked, his neck straining. She could tell he was teetering on the edge.

"So close, but I want to make it last." Forever. She arched against him.

"I can't hold on much longer."

His words—the fact that she could make TJ Garner lose control—in and of itself was an enormous turn-on. But the things he was doing to her . . .

She tilted her head back on the pillow, closed her eyes, and shouted out his name. Her body quaked, the orgasm rolling through her like seismic waves. It seemed to last forever as he pumped harder. Stronger. Then she heard him grunt and felt him tremor. Even after it was over, they kept moving together, milking every last drop.

Afterward, he flipped over to his side and kissed her forehead and then her eyes and her nose and finally her lips. The sweetness of it sort of undid her and she turned her head, hoping he wouldn't see her get emotional.

Too late, because he asked if she was okay.

She rolled to face him. "I'm good," she said, luxuriating in the afterglow. "How 'bout you?"

"Good." But his expression was inscrutable, like it always was.

"Do you want to take me home now?"

"No."

"Good." She smiled because she didn't want this night to ever end.

Chapter Nineteen

TJ got up before Deb and brewed a pot of coffee. From what he could tell, it was shaping up to be a nice day. Sunny, and if the thermometer on his deck was correct, not too cold. He'd woken up with Deb curled up next to him, her head on his chest, and had felt a shot of warmth spread through him that continued to linger.

His phone dinged with a text. It was from Colt: an emoji of a big question mark. The guy was worse than a teenager. Next thing, he'd be passing TJ notes at recess. TJ didn't bother to respond. It was none of Colt's business. He did wonder where Win and Britney had disappeared to last night, and if anyone would know, it would be Colt. For now, TJ was letting the mystery remain.

He dug through his refrigerator to see if he had any eggs. Some bacon would be nice, too.

"What are you doing?"

TJ jumped and hit his head on the top shelf.

"Sorry." She had one of his Cal Berkeley sweatshirts on. It came to her knees and she'd had to roll the sleeves up. But no skimpy lace lingerie could compete. She looked unbelievably sexy in the sweatshirt with her hair a wild, tangled mess and her lips red and puffy from all their kissing.

He had a mind to throw her over his shoulder and go back to bed. But last night had been a one-off. Smart to remember that.

"Do you have an extra toothbrush by chance?" she asked.

"Under the sink in the guest room."

"Wow, you have a guest room?"

"You want eggs?" He'd found a dozen the housekeeper must've brought from her chickens.

"Uh, sure. You need help?"

"Nope. Go ahead and brush your teeth or whatever you need to do."

She crossed the living room and he indulged in a little ass staring as she jogged up the staircase. Then he got out the bacon and put it in a pan. He wasn't much of a cook, but bacon and eggs he could handle.

By the time she returned, he had their two plates on the kitchen island and was pouring their coffee.

"Smells good." She grabbed the stool next to his and plucked at the sweatshirt. "I forgot to ask if I could borrow this."

"No problem." He tried not to gape at her breasts.

"You have a pair of sweatpants I can borrow?"

"Yeah, but they won't fit you."

She picked up her fork and tried the eggs. "I'll make them work. Better than doing the walk of shame in my party dress."

"Are you ashamed?" He took a sip of coffee and watched her over the rim of his cup.

"It's just an expression, TJ." She ate a strip of bacon, licking her fingers. He wondered if she was intentionally trying to drive him crazy.

"You didn't answer my question."

"Of course I'm not ashamed. Are you?"

He shook his head. "Nope."

She leaned into him. "Don't let what I'm about to tell you go to your head, but it was the best night of my life." She quickly amended, "That is, sexually."

The best night of her life, huh? TJ felt his chest fill with pride.

"What about for you?" Deb asked. "No, don't tell me, not unless I was the best night of your life."

"It was up there." He nodded and stole a piece of bacon off her plate. There was no way in hell he was telling her that the night had exceeded every one of his late-night dreams about her. "Definitely up there." He grinned, and she pummeled his back.

"Want to go out on the boat?" he asked, making a split-second decision to ditch the piles of work waiting on his desk. It was Sunday, after all, and first thing Monday he had a meeting with GA's lawyers, which wasn't going to be any fun.

"Hell yes." Her eyes danced with excitement. That was the thing he loved about her; she was always up for an adventure. "You're not going to GA?"

"Don't sound so shocked. I'm trying to get a life." His knee brushed against her bare legs. And, God, did she have killer legs. "I'll try to dig up something for you to wear. It's too cold to go out like that."

They finished eating and he poured them more coffee so they could linger. Besides appreciating her in his bed, he liked having her in his kitchen. "It was a good party last night."

"Are you kidding? It was a great party." She turned sideways in her seat. "Thank you for providing the venue."

"Wasn't me. I hear Hannah and Delaney have an in with some of the owners."

She gave him a salacious once-over and he felt his groin

tighten. "Some might say I do, too." She paused. "Is it going to be awkward at work, TJ?"

"Probably." Their eyes met and locked. "Let's not think about it now and enjoy the day." It was unlike him to shirk responsibility, especially when he had the floundering retail venture hanging over his head. But for once in his life, he planned to enjoy his day off and the woman he'd wanted for a lifetime.

His cell rang and he looked at the caller ID. Colt. Either he was being a relentless meddler or something was up. Against his better judgment, he picked up.

"What?"

"Nice greeting. You alone?"

"Nope."

A moment of silence, and then Colt said, "Congratulations. Don't hurt that girl or I'll personally kick your ass."

Hurt her? Now that was ironic. "What do you want, Colt?"

"I just wondered if you'd heard from Win. None of us knows where he and Britney disappeared to last night. Probably her place in Tahoe, but he's not answering his phone. Is he on the schedule today?"

TJ hadn't looked at the tour plan. "Don't know, but Darcy would. Want me to call her?"

"Nah, I'm sure he's fine. You know Win; never charges his damn phone."

"All right, but if you hear from him, you'll let me know?"

"Yep. Sorry for the interruption. Go back to whatever you were doing." Colt chuckled and hung up.

"What's wrong?" Deb got up and collected their dirty dishes.

"You don't have to do that." She wasn't working at the diner. "No one's heard from Win since last night."

"You worried?"

"He's fine." The last thing he wanted to do was talk about Win. "I'll find you something to wear." He dumped the rest of his coffee down the drain and went upstairs to rummage through his clothes. Perhaps he still had something in his closet left over from the seventh grade or one of his overnight female guests had left her pants behind.

The best he could do was a pair of sweats with a drawstring waist. They would still be huge but better than nothing. He jogged down and handed them to her.

"There are assorted shoes in the mudroom." Over the summer, his mom, Hannah, and various other women had left their Top-Siders and flip-flops on his boat. He'd amassed a fairly large collection.

She took the sweats and returned twenty minutes later, dressed and ready to go. "I found a scrunchie in your guest room; hope you don't mind that I used it."

He didn't know what the hell a scrunchie was. "Help yourself. You find shoes?"

She modeled her feet in a worn pair of Sperrys. They went downstairs and he got two jackets out of the closet and handed her one. It would be chilly on the water.

Deb ran her hand over the felt on the pool table. "Let's play when we get back."

He wanted to play, just not pool. "Sure."

When they got outside, he peered across the lake. There were hardly any boats out. Too cold to waterski or wakeboard. It was still a nice day to cruise. They walked down the dock and she helped him untie the boat. He gave her an arm to get in and took the wheel, slowly idling past the no-wake zone. When they got farther out, he'd show Deb some speed. He glanced over at her sitting on the bench across from him—and damn. She looked good in his boat. The wind whipping through her hair, a smile lighting her face like the sun.

Once they got away from shore, he let the throttle out and watched as her expression turned animated.

"My God, I love this," she shouted over the roar of the engine.

"Check this out." He turned on the surf system and pointed off the stern at the waves he'd created with the flick of a switch.

"You better take me wakeboarding in summer, TJ. I can't believe you've been keeping this from me."

He grinned. TJ's industry was filled with show-offs, tools who bragged about their equipment, their toys, and their athletic prowess. He'd always steered clear of boasting. If you're the best or have the best, you don't need to talk about it. That had always been his philosophy. But just this once he wanted to impress a girl. Not just any girl, but Deb Bennett.

"You want to take the wheel?"

"Seriously?"

He slowed down so they could switch places and crooked his finger at her.

"Don't leave," she said. "The last thing I want to do is crack up your boat."

He laughed because there was little chance of that on the open lake. TJ maneuvered her so she was basically sitting on his lap. "Go ahead." He moved his hands away and let her take over.

She drove, opening the boat up on the straightaways for maximum speed. Exhilarated, she threw her head back, letting the sunlight dance on her face, and laughed. He wrapped his arms around her waist, feeling the excitement of the ride thrum through her.

"This is amazing."

"Even better when you're shredding."

She turned to face him, her eyes sparkling. He swore she

was the female version of a Garner. No mountain too big to climb, no ski run too wild to tame, and no wave too unruly to ride. Man, did he love her spirit.

"I can't wait for summer." And to prove it, her teeth chattered.

"Cold?" He used it as an excuse to hold her a little closer.

"A little."

A little, his ass. Her lips had turned blue. "We should go in."

"You steer." She relinquished the wheel to him but made no move to leave his lap. "I don't want to crash this beautiful boat into the dock."

He took them in slowly, reluctant to give up any time with her alone or otherwise. Tomorrow would come soon enough, when he'd go back to being her boss and dealing with their struggling retail venture.

She hung over the side of the boat. "It doesn't have a name."

"Not yet. Got any ideas?"

She thought about it for a while. "How about *Boys and Toys*?"

"Nope. How about *Catch Me If You Can*?"

"Ick, sounds like that Leonardo DiCaprio movie." She leaned back against him and let her head drop onto his shoulder.

"*Blood, Sweat, and Beers*?" His lips brushed her hair.

"Better, but still not loving it."

"*Livin' Large*?"

"Cliché," she said.

He maneuvered the boat in one-handed, keeping the other one around her. She nestled closer, fitting perfectly tucked in against his chest.

"*Whatever Floats your Boat*?" she offered, and they both laughed.

He came in parallel a few feet away from the dock, swung the wheel to port, and kicked the engine into reverse. As the stern moved closer, he put the boat in neutral, letting it side-slip right up to the wooden pier. Easy. The tough part was breaking away from Deb to tie up his dock lines.

"Where you going?" She clung to him like a monkey with her arms around his neck, and he carried her to the port side of the boat.

"Gotta secure her. Wanna toss me the line?"

He hopped onto the dock and she threw him the rope, which he tied to a cleat, then repeated the action with the fenders. TJ reached inside of the boat, grabbed Deb around the waist, and hoisted her onto the dock.

"How 'bout *Foolin' Around*?"

"Huh?"

"For the boat's name. *The Foolin' Around*."

"Not bad." He played with the zipper on her jacket. She raised her face to his, her lips, chapped from the cold, calling to be kissed. He leaned in and touched them with his mouth. Feather soft at first because he told himself that he only wanted a small taste. But when she opened to him, twining her arms around his neck, he was a goner. He deepened the kiss, using his tongue and even his teeth.

"Let's test out the name," he said against her mouth. And they spent the rest of the afternoon in his bed, fooling around.

Win leaned against Garner Adventure's front counter while Darcy searched her computer for first trimester symptoms on her computer monitor. He watched the door. Soon his parents and brothers would start arriving for work and he didn't need them in his business, especially after the bad impression Britney had made at the party Saturday night.

"Well, what does it say?" he asked, impatient.

"That pregnant women have mood swings." She flipped him a look over her shoulder as if to say, *duh*.

"I know that, Darce, but how pronounced are they?"

"It depends. Was she a bitch before she was pregnant?"

What happened to sweet, little Darcy? Win wanted to know. It was as if mad scientists had replaced her with an evil clone.

"Can't say." They didn't exactly do a lot of talking before he'd put a bun in her oven. "I guess she was never real warm and fuzzy. You didn't like her, did you?"

"She just didn't seem to make much of an effort to meet your family or friends." The silent question hung in the air. *You sure you want to marry this chick?*

He'd felt it from his father, his brothers, and possibly his mother. And now Darcy, the most objective person watching his train wreck. The rest of them wanted him to marry someone like Deb. How could he blame them? For all intents and purposes, Deb was perfect for him.

"She was having a bad night." Though he'd gotten her the damned ring she'd wanted. He'd be paying it off until the cows came home, and the cost had cut a fair amount into his house budget.

"Ya think?" There she went with the sarcasm again. "I hope you told her that she embarrassed you."

"She didn't embarrass me," he said, and even to his own ears, he sounded defensive.

She fixed him with a get-real look. "She should've."

"Jeez, Darcy, don't hold back."

"You wanted to know." She leaned back in her chair, and for the first time, he noticed she was pretty well endowed in the chest area.

You're an asshole, he told himself. "I'm gonna go flip tires. I'm available on cell."

"Flip tires? Is that some kind of code for something?" She folded her arms over her rack as if she knew he'd been checking it out and made *flip tires* sound like a euphemism for jacking off.

He wanted the old Darcy back. "It's an exercise thing . . . at the gym."

She shrugged and went back to her computer. He picked up his duffel and headed out just in time to pass TJ, who was on his way in.

"Where you going?" TJ had more pep in his step than usual. The idiot was downright glowing, if a dude could even do that.

"The gym. What, you make some sort of a million-dollar acquisition this morning?"

"No. Where'd you come up with that?"

"You look happier than usual," Win said.

TJ moved off the sidewalk so a woman with a stroller could get by. Win knew exactly what TJ was thinking: *That'll be you soon.*

"Where'd you go Saturday night?" TJ asked. "One minute you were at the party. The next, you and Britney were gone."

"She wasn't feeling well," if you counted having a giant meltdown as sick. She'd been furious that he'd told her to stop drinking and had ordered him to take her home. Win hadn't heard from her since.

"Colt couldn't reach you Sunday," TJ said and studied him.

"My phone must've been off. Plus, I had that rock-climbing group."

TJ continued to do that spooky, I-know-you're-lying thing with his face. Someday, he'd make a gnarly parent. "Everything okay?"

You mean besides the fact that my life's blowing up?
"Everything's great. How 'bout you?"

"We've got some issues I want to talk to everyone about. You available for an emergency meeting later today?"

"Sure. I'm doing a snowboarding exhibition at Winter Bowl, but it shouldn't take more than a couple of hours. Does two sound good?"

"Let me check with Deb, Josh, and Colt and get back to you."

"Roger that," Win said and walked to the street where he'd parked his Jeep. TJ and his freaking meetings.

He made it to the gym in record time. The weekenders must've all gone home, leaving the roads wide open. Inside, he spotted Deb doing reps with a 250-pound tire. Not too shabby. She was hella fit and he took a moment or two to watch her. Great form. Her squats were unequaled.

She saw him and nodded her head in greeting, her hands too occupied with the tire to wave. He gave her a thumbs-up and made his way into the locker room to change. By the time he came out, she was done with the routine and stood by the watercooler, wiping sweat from her face with a towel.

He went over to apologize for leaving her party so early. "Good workout?"

She was out of breath but managed a "Yep."

"Sorry I ducked out of the party early. Something came up with Britney and we had to leave." He went in to give her a belated birthday hug, but she stopped him.

"Kinda rank right now."

"Got it." He grinned. "Anyway, happy birthday, Bennett. Hope it was a good one."

She started to speak, stopped, and finally said, "It was a beautiful party and I had a wonderful time. I hope Britney's okay."

"She's fine," he said. "You headed to work?"

"My last shift at the diner. Yay! If I get off early enough, I'll put in a few hours at GA."

"TJ get in touch with you about the emergency meeting?"

"No. What emergency meeting?" She folded her arms over her chest.

Oops. He'd gone and stepped in it.

"Don't get your panties in a bunch. TJ isn't keeping anything from you." He maneuvered her away from the cooler so someone could get a drink. "I just saw him twenty minutes ago and he brought it up. Probably hasn't even had his morning coffee yet. He'll call you."

"He better." She started for the women's locker room.

"I'll see you in the office later." He went to get a lane before they were all gone.

Not even halfway down the aisle, his phone chimed with a text. He should've left the damn thing in the locker room but was technically on the clock. He glanced at the message, expecting it to be a calendar invite from TJ. Nope. Britney had apparently returned to the world of the living.

I'm out of decaf. Can you bring me some?

He rolled his eyes. At least she was staying away from caffeine. And, hopefully, vodka.

Deb showered, wrapped herself in a towel, and grabbed her phone from her gym bag. There was a little bench in the shower and she perched on the edge of it with the curtain closed and called TJ.

"Why didn't you tell me about the meeting?" she asked, her voice terse. They'd been together most of Sunday and not once had he mentioned a meeting. "Are you unhappy with my work?" She knew sales weren't good, but that wasn't her fault.

"Where'd you come up with that?"

"Win. He said you'd called a meeting," she said.

"Win? When did you see Win?"

Who cared? The point was the meeting and the fact that they'd slept together and now he was keeping secrets about her job from her. "At the gym."

"You two went to the gym together?"

"For Christ's sake, forget about Win. Are you going to fire me because we had sex?"

"What?" There was a long pause.

The water went on in the stall next to hers and she wondered if whoever was in there had heard her. If so, the news that she and TJ had gotten horizontal would be all over town by the time she got to the Morning Glory.

"Deb, look at your goddamned messages."

She took her phone away from her ear and scrolled through her emails. Uh-oh. Ten minutes earlier, he'd sent her a calendar invitation. She banged her head against the curtain. *Who me, paranoid*?

"Uh, sorry, I hadn't seen it." She cringed. "I've got to go to make my shift. I'll see you at the meeting." She hoped Felix would let her off in time, especially after the stink she'd made.

He clicked off. Not even nine in the morning and they'd already had their first awkward postcoital encounter. Still, she'd spend another night with him in a heartbeat. The whole experience had been magical. Not just the sex, which alone was unrivaled, but everything. Sleeping curled up next to him, breakfast in the morning, the boat ride, pool, foosball, dinner, then *The Big Lewbowski*. Who knew it was his favorite movie, too?

The scary part was how deep she was getting in. If she didn't watch it, she'd drown.

She hurriedly got dressed, thanking the good Lord Jesus that this would be the last she'd ever don her diner clothes again. For the first time in a long while, she got in her car with confidence that it would actually start—another wonderful thing TJ had done for her.

A big bouquet of balloons greeted her at the host stand at the Morning Glory. It wasn't until she read the inscription—"Fine, go"—that she realized the balloons were for her.

"An Adam and Eve on a raft and wreck 'em," Ricki called into the kitchen, then came over to give Deb a hug. "We'll miss you, girl."

Ah hell; she wiped a tear at the corner of her eye. "Don't tell Felix."

"Now that you're a big executive, you still planning to eat here?"

"I'm hardly an executive, but of course I'll still eat here. Best tuna melts in town." They were the only tuna melts in town. Boden and Rachel wouldn't compete with Felix's signature dish.

"Enough chitchat," Felix hollered from the back. "Get to work, ladies."

Deb exchanged looks with Ricki and they erupted in laughter. The restaurant was unusually slow. Weekends in Glory Junction typically bled into Monday, but not today. Deb spent the first hour of her shift refilling the salt and pepper shakers and cleaning up the condiment caddies. Here and there she waited on a few tables, mostly locals who congratulated her on the new gig at GA. Jack came in to get his daily fried egg sandwich, which he brought back to the police station and presumably ate at his desk.

She'd never realized how buff he was, and come to think

of it, he was doing something different with his hair. "You look good, Jack."

He puffed up at the compliment. "Thanks. I've been doing CrossFit with Carrie Jo and sometimes Foster."

Foster had mentioned something about it, though with Sweet Stems doing a bang-up business, he barely had time to breathe, let alone go to the gym.

"Good for you," she said.

Felix bagged Jack's breakfast sandwich, poured him a to-go coffee, and off he went. Rita Tucker came in an hour later and sat at the counter, where she ordered her regular: cottage cheese with fresh pineapple and a slice of dry wheat toast. No wonder the mayor was thin as a string bean. Late morning, they got a second round of breakfast diners, but for the most part the service was noneventful. Deb's replacement came in around noon to relieve Ricki, but Ricki stayed anyway.

After the lunch rush, Felix called the waitstaff into the kitchen. The cook brought out a cake and everyone gathered around to wish Deb well. She choked up a wee bit because as far as she knew, Felix had never made this big a fuss for anyone else.

"We're slow today, so anytime you want to take off, Bennett, you're free to go."

She'd make the meeting at GA. Her pulse quickened at the thought of seeing TJ. A combination of nerves and anticipation filled her. She was fully prepared for him to treat their liaison as a onetime fling. It didn't mean she wouldn't be disappointed.

After cake, she went into the back room, cleaned out her locker, and tossed her apron in the hamper. She had just enough time to run upstairs and change. On her way out of the diner, she found TJ standing at the counter, talking to Felix. He gave her the dude head nod, which meant they were back to being whatever they'd been before they'd slept together. Why was it that she always wound up in the friend zone?

"Getting doughnuts for the meeting?" she asked, trying to sound casual. Professional.

"Yeah. You have any preferences?"

"I just had good-bye cake, so I'm sugared out for the day, but thanks." She grabbed her balloon bouquet. "See you in a few."

Deb wrestled the balloons out the door and jogged up the stairs to her apartment. She wasn't there more than five minutes when someone knocked. TJ. He stood at the threshold, holding a white pastry box, staring back at her through the peephole.

She swung open the door. "What's up?"

He shouldered his way in, placed the doughnuts on the kitchen table, grabbed her around the waist, and kissed her into next Sunday. "If this isn't okay, tell me now and I'll stop."

She didn't say anything, just kissed him back with everything she had. Next thing she knew, he was pulling her shirt over her head, his hands roaming over her tummy, rib cage, and breasts. When he went for the front clasp on her bra, she waltzed him toward the bedroom.

"We don't really have time for this," he said.

"Haven't you heard of a quickie?"

His mouth curved up in a sexy grin and he dropped her bra somewhere on the floor as they kept moving. "It'll have to be very quick. I need to talk to you."

She put her finger over his lips and pushed him onto the bed. "No talking." She wanted him so badly her entire body burned with it.

He got her pants off and then his own. Next came their underwear. His hands covered her breasts and with his thumbs, he drew circles around her nipples. She straddled him, rubbing against his erection until it made her wild. He still had a thermal shirt on. Too worked up to pull it over his head, she inched her hands under the hem and flattened her palms on top of his chest and began to slip him inside her.

"Condom, baby." He rolled out from under her and hung over the bed, scrounging through his jeans' pockets until he found his wallet. Within seconds, he grasped a foil packet, tore it open, and suited up.

He tried to mount her, but she wanted to be on top. Happy to accommodate, TJ pulled her over him into a sitting position and entered her in one powerful thrust. She rode him like that while he touched her everywhere, his eyes filled with desire as he watched her sway over him.

"Jesus, it's good like this," he said, clutching her hips and moving her faster. "I like looking at you . . . so beautiful."

"Oh, TJ." She adjusted herself to take more of him and he moaned his approval.

One-handed, he tugged off his shirt and she felt the muscles in his arm constrict. She could look at him this way—any way—for hours. A big, dark-haired Adonis. And those blue, blue eyes, so gorgeous. And the way he looked at her, like she was the most precious thing in the world, got her right in the gut.

Not going to love you, TJ Garner. Uh-uh.

But it was already happening. In a big way. And she suspected there wasn't a damn thing she could do about it.

She leaned her head back and closed her eyes, ready to come crashing down. "So close."

He touched her, releasing the last of her reserves, and she shattered. He followed her with a long, loud grunt and she fell flat on top of him. They lay there, breathing hard, as he caressed her back.

His hands sifted through her hair and he kissed her so

passionately that she felt a pool of warmth collect in the bottom of her stomach.

"You okay?" He cupped the sides of her face.

"Yes. You?"

"Never been better. But I should probably get rid of the condom." He pulled out of her, but she hung on.

"Just a second more."

He rolled her to her side and ran his finger across her lips, his eyes a deeper blue than she had ever seen them. "We do need to talk."

Ah, here it came. Pretty soon, in the nicest way possible, he was going to tell her that they would always be best buddies, but that he wasn't ready to get serious with anyone. Then the inevitable, *But if you want to keep having sex, I'm totally down with that. Of course, we wouldn't be exclusive. But you're cool with that, right?*

She swung her legs off the side of the bed, grabbed her robe off the back of the door, and shrugged it on. He collected his clothes from the floor and disappeared inside the bathroom. She used the opportunity to slip into a fresh pair of panties and bra, then dug through her closet for a dress.

She had it halfway on when she felt his solid form behind her. His hand moved to her zipper and he closed the back of the dress. For some reason, she found the gesture even more intimate than sex, and it took every ounce of fortitude she had not to cry.

His hand moved to her neck and kissed her throat. "Let's sit in the living room for a minute."

She found her boots and followed him to the other room, where they both sat on the couch.

"What do you need to tell me?" She wanted him to get it over with. Then she could make up an errand she had to run so she could lick her wounds in private. Why did she always do this?

"I didn't want to catch you off guard at the meeting, but our lawyer says we should settle with Stan the Asshole Royce. Ordinarily, we'd let our insurance company battle it out with him. But in this case, it's just better to make him go away. Fast, before he can do any damage to GA's reputation, because he's threatening all kinds of crap." He paused and tilted his head to see if she was grasping the situation. "It puts us in a precarious position money wise. And our retail sales . . . well, we're an adventure tour company, not REI."

She gasped. "TJ, we just started." This wasn't at all what she'd expected him to say. Relieved he wasn't calling off whatever this thing was that they had going, she didn't want him to shut down the store. She was just learning how to do this, and Deb hoped she could be good at it soon. "With a little time, I think we can turn a profit. Please tell me you're not giving up."

"Not yet," he said, and she could see the strain in his face. "But GA is a relatively small company; we can't wait years to see a return. We just don't have that kind of capital."

To pay her salary and the cost of the merchandise. She knew that was what he meant and didn't blame him a bit. He was running a business, not a charity. But it seemed so soon to throw in the towel.

"What about Delaney? She designed a whole line for GA," she said.

He let out a humorless laugh. "Delaney hardly needs GA. She was doing us a favor, not the other way around. There isn't a retailer in the country that wouldn't pick up her adventure wear. Department stores were clamoring for it before she told them we had the exclusive. Don't worry about Delaney."

"What about a magazine story?"

"I'll talk about that at the meeting, but I don't think it's gonna happen, Deb." He looked so sad that it tore at her.

"What if I can turn things around with my idea of sponsoring someone . . . a big athlete?" It was reaching for the stars because she didn't have those kinds of contacts.

He blew out a breath. "Yeah, sure, give it a try. But no one will blame you if it doesn't work. You're . . . we're . . . in a little over our heads here."

"I thought you believed in me." *Or did you just want to get me into your bed?*

He tilted his head and looked at her. Really looked. "I do believe in you, Deb. Always have. But you're not a miracle worker. No one saw this thing with Royce coming. It wasn't even our fault, but sometimes you just have to suck it up. It's the cost of doing business."

"Let's be frank here," she said. "Is my job on the line?"

"I can't continue losing money indefinitely, Deb. I can't put my family and their business at risk. But I'm not ready to call it quits this minute. So if in the next couple of weeks you can bring up our sales, we'll reassess. If not . . . I'll find another position for you."

There were no other positions. She shouldn't even have the one he'd given her, and the last thing she wanted to do was put him in a bad spot by making him feel like he had to keep her. "All right; deal on." At least she wouldn't have to go crawling back to the Morning Glory right away. She supposed there was always bartending at Old Glory.

She wanted to ask him about their relationship. What were they? But decided she'd had enough bad news for one day. Better to enjoy whatever it was they were doing while it lasted. Otherwise, his answer was bound to disappoint her.

He glanced at his watch. "We better get."

She grabbed the box of doughnuts and they walked down the stairs together and down the block to Garner Adventure.

Darcy lifted her head from her computer as they came in the door.

"Coffee is on and the meeting room is set up," she said.

"You're in on this, too, Darce. Send calls to voice mail for the next hour."

Darcy visibly brightened, and it occurred to Deb that TJ was a really good boss. And a really good man.

Chapter Twenty

TJ took the pastry box from Deb and delivered it to the conference room while she made a pit stop at her office. Win came in and didn't waste any time picking through the doughnuts. Darcy trailed in, checked the percolator, and sat next to Win. Deb appeared, and the vision of her on top of him, naked, immediately popped in his head. He tried desperately to think about scheduling and payroll, anything that would distract him from revisiting their nooner.

"How was your last day?" Win asked her.

"Good. Felix got me balloons and the staff got me a cake."

And TJ had given her an orgasm. He was going to need to have a conversation with Win soon. Not about the orgasm, but about him and Deb.

Colt and Josh came in together and pulled up chairs to the table. Although TJ and the lawyers had already briefed his parents, his dad came for the meeting and sat across from TJ. Gray gave him the nod to start.

"I'll cut right to the chase so as not to waste time," he told everyone. "Our lawyers want us to settle with Stanley Royce."

"Why?" Win stood up. "We didn't do anything wrong."

"Because in the digital age, Royce can drag GA's name through the mud, which he's threatening to do. It's just not worth it."

"So basically, it's extortion," Josh said, looking pissed.

"Pretty much," TJ agreed.

"Just so we don't get a bad Yelp review." Josh wouldn't let it go. He'd always stood firm when it came to principle. TJ was more of a realist.

"How much is it going to cost us?" Colt wanted to know because he was all about the bottom line.

"He wants six figures. Our lawyers think he'll walk away for between fifty and sixty-five thousand."

Win let out a low whistle. "That's a lot of money for a guy who ignored the danger tape on that porta-potty."

"What about insurance?" Colt crossed his arms across his chest.

"They want to fight it, we want it to go away. Not to mention that if we go through them, it'll likely cost us more in premiums over the long haul."

"Your brother's right; settling is our best option," Gray broke in.

"Where do we take the money from?" Josh asked, and everyone looked at TJ.

"Our reserves, which means we'll have to be careful about not robbing Peter to pay Paul."

"Put that in English," Colt said, frowning.

"So far, the retail operation isn't paying off the way I'd hoped. It's still early, but we're only getting a few orders a day. We did better when we beta tested. Either our clients were initially psyched about buying swag and quickly got over it, or Colorado Adventure is taking all our business. Right now, we're financing the store with our reserves, which was always the plan until it became profitable. But now . . ."

"What about a magazine article?" Josh asked.

"I called Dan Reed at *Outdoors*, Stephanie Row at *Adventure,* and Wendy Miller at *Action*. None of them are interested because *Outside* already did the story on Colorado Adventure. It would be too similar. And even if they were interested, their lead time is three months, so a story wouldn't even run until June."

"And by then we'd be out of business," Josh said.

TJ nodded, because at this rate it was true.

Colt clenched his jaw, typical Garner body language that signified he was pissed. Colt didn't say anything, but TJ was sure he'd get an earful after the meeting, in private.

Deb cleared her throat. "I have a few ideas."

"Like what?" Win got up and poured himself a cup of coffee.

She sheepishly turned to TJ, then said, "Some tweaks I want to make to the online store and a few other . . . uh, assorted things."

"In other words, we're winging it." Instead of directing his words at Deb, Colt glared at TJ.

"This is new to all of us, Colt. And no one could've predicted Stanley Royce rolling down the mountain in a porta-potty."

Colt nodded. "That's the truth. Hopefully, you can bring up sales or I'm telling Delaney to cancel her exclusive deal with us." With that, he got up and walked out.

"Someone woke up on the dick side of the bed this morning." Win took a sip of his coffee.

Josh leaned his chair back on two legs. "Hannah might have some ideas."

Selling gift items and home furnishings in a tourist town wasn't the same as selling adventure gear, but TJ would be grateful for any insight.

"I'll talk to her," Deb said.

"What other ideas do you have?" Win asked Deb, and she told them about sponsoring athletes.

"I think that's a great idea, kiddo." Gray squeezed the back of Deb's neck, looked at his watch, and stood up. "I'm going to leave the rest of the meeting to you guys. I have a tour in twenty minutes."

After Gray left, Deb asked, "Do any of you know anyone who'd be willing to represent Garner Adventure in competitions?"

Win thought about it for a few seconds. "The problem is, anyone with a big-enough name already has sponsorship." He looked at Josh. "Can you think of anyone?"

"Not off the top of my head. I love Delaney, her stuff is killer, but her reputation is in fashion. The big leaguers wear Spyder, Burton, North Face, you know the names."

Deb nodded. "I'll do some asking around." No one had to tell her it would be an uphill battle. She knew how pro sports worked.

"We all will," Josh said. "I've got a cave tour in two hours and need to get the equipment ready."

TJ bobbed his head at Darcy. "You have anything you want to add?"

She shook her head. "I'll help Deb with whatever she needs."

"Thanks," TJ said. "Then I guess we're adjourned."

Josh grabbed another doughnut on his way out and Darcy got busy on the cleanup. Win and Deb helped and TJ went back to his office, feeling discouraged. Ten minutes later, Win came through his door.

"You that worried?" he asked.

"We'll lose our initial investment, but it won't be the end of the world." Though TJ knew he couldn't justify Deb's position without the retail division.

"You can't let her go, bro." Win had obviously read TJ's mind. "Everyone already thinks you gave her the job because of me. Then to lay her off . . . People can be cruel, TJ."

"I didn't realize you gave a shit about her."

Win jerked back. "Whoa. Where's that coming from?"

TJ tried to rein himself in. None of this was Win's fault. "We're getting ahead of ourselves. Hopefully, things will pick up."

Win stretched out on TJ's couch. "I'm confident it will."

That was Win, always an optimist. It drove the rest of them crazy.

"How was the exhibition?"

"I barely made it in time. Britney needed me to come over."

"Everything okay?" TJ closed his door.

Win sighed. "Not the greatest, to tell you the truth." He rubbed his hand down his face, and for the first time, TJ saw the toll this was taking on his brother. "I thought maybe I could grow to love her, you know? But TJ, I don't even like her."

For a long time, TJ didn't say anything. He just let Win's words sink in. Garners didn't walk away from their responsibilities, but shotgun weddings seemed arcane nowadays. "What would happen if you didn't marry her?"

Win pinched the bridge of his nose. "Don't tell anyone this, but I don't trust her with my kid."

"The drinking?" Britney had downed more glasses of champagne at the party than TJ could count and he hadn't been keeping constant track.

"Not just the drinking." Win paused. "This is a hell of a thing to say, but I get the feeling she's using the baby as collateral."

"What do you mean?"

"Like it's her ticket to financial security." Win sat up. "Like it's extortion."

TJ didn't know her, but he trusted Win's instincts. And from the minute he'd met her, he'd gotten a gold-digger vibe. "What are you going to do?"

"What can I do? It's my kid."

TJ wished there was something he could say. It was a screwed-up mess, and if he could save his brother from going through this, he would.

Win pushed off the sofa. "I've got to motor. See you tomorrow."

"I'll walk you out." TJ needed to smooth things over with Colt. He swiped his jacket off the hook and followed Win outside, where they parted ways.

TJ continued to the police station, where he found Carrie Jo in a heated argument with Jack. Colt came out of his office, yelled for the two of them to shut up, and motioned for TJ to come inside.

"What was that about?"

"Who knows? They're like two randy high schoolers. I wish they'd just sleep with each other and get it over with." Colt sat behind his metal desk. "So, we've really gotta pay off Royce, huh?"

"It seems like our best option." TJ took a seat on the couch. "We'll survive it."

Colt gave him a hard look. "I'm gonna reiterate how much I love Deb. You know I love her. But TJ, we're running a business here." He took a breath. "What's going on with you two?"

"Nothing," unless you counted over-the-top great sex.

"Nothing?" Colt shook his head. "If you don't want me to know, then tell me it's none of my goddamn business, but don't give me this nothing shit."

"It's complicated." Not just because for the last fifteen years everyone had had the expectation that she would wind up with Win, but he might have to fire her now. And that was a straight-up deal breaker. You couldn't give someone a whole new shot at life and then rip it away without it blowing up a relationship.

Colt got up and joined TJ on the sofa. "If you care enough about her, you'll make it happen, despite the complications."

Easy for Colt to say. He wasn't responsible for the family business; TJ was. And Deb wasn't what he'd come here to talk about.

"I want to make this right with Delaney," TJ said, changing gears. "If she wanted to branch out to other retailers, I would understand. She should strike while her line of adventure wear is hot."

"My fiancée's stuff is always hot. You'll have to talk to her, TJ. I'm staying out of it."

"I will. In the meantime, you need to talk to Win." TJ wouldn't divulge any of their baby brother's confidences, but Colt was good at fixing problems.

"What's he done now?"

"I don't think he should marry Britney." He rose and paced the room. "You met her."

"Too soon to judge." Colt went back to his desk and checked something on his computer. "Mom and Dad want to have her for dinner so we can get to know her better. But I'll talk to Win."

"Maybe Josh could talk to him, too." Win needed all their support right now.

"Sure. But Win's a grown man. At some point, we have to let him handle his own problems."

"Just talk to him. That's all I ask."

* * *

Deb took the long country road to Delaney's head-quarters. The former John Deere warehouse was a funny place for one of the world's premiere fashion designers to house her business, but somehow it worked. Of course, Delaney had done all kinds of renovations before occupying the building. Now it was a showplace.

Deb thought if anyone would know how to increase sales it would be Delaney. She might not be a sports enthusiast, but she ran a retail empire.

A guard at the entrance recognized Deb and let her through the gate. Colt had insisted that Delaney put in security. The warehouse sat in the middle of nowhere and stored millions of dollars' worth of samples and equipment.

Deb parked and went inside.

"Can I help you?" the receptionist asked. It was Candace Kelly, who Deb had gone to high school with.

She wanted to say, *Really, Candace?*

Just then, Karen happened to come out to the lobby. As usual, she was perfectly put together. Cute suede skirt and a sweater to die for. Not the kind of stuff you saw around Glory Junction. Deb thought about her with TJ and felt a familiar stab of envy. TJ could have any woman he wanted.

"Hey, Deb. You here to see Delaney?"

"If she's not busy." She probably should've called first.

"Come on back." Karen led the way, and Deb flashed Candace a snarky grin.

"She's in the design studio. Hang tight." She dropped Deb in Delaney's office and went in search of her.

Delaney floated into the room in amazing wide-legged trousers and a matching blazer, looking runway gorgeous. Jeez, Deb could get a complex hanging out around here.

"You designed that, didn't you?"

"I most certainly did." Delaney kissed Deb on both cheeks. "Great party the other night."

"Thank you, Delaney. It was the best birthday I ever had." Of course, the after-party had been even better.

"It was mostly Hannah and Foster. Those two know how to throw an event." Delaney slipped off her shoes and sat next to Deb in one of the overstuffed chairs, tucking her legs under her. "You here just to say hi or to talk about the adventure wear line?"

Deb let out a breath. "I came to pick your brain. You're going to hear this from Colt, but so far our sales aren't doing as well as we had hoped."

Delaney shifted in her seat. "The online store has only been up a week. That's way too early to gauge your progress."

She told Delaney about Stanley Royce and how a settlement with him would bite into the company's budget.

"TJ's pretty worried about it and it's my job to make the retail end a success." TJ believed in her and she didn't want to disappoint him, or herself. "The sad truth is, I don't know what I'm doing. I'm here to ask for any guidance you can give me."

Delaney went to her desk and picked up the phone. "Candace, can you please bring us some soft drinks. Thanks."

She sat back down. "First, you have to spill about what's going on with you and TJ."

"Huh. What are you talking about?" Deb played dumb. And honestly, other than sleeping together, she had no idea.

"Come on." Delaney all but rolled her eyes. "I saw you two at the party, I saw you disappear together, and Colt's convinced you met afterward."

Ah, crap. "Do people think it's pathetic, like I'm a Garner groupie?"

Delaney laughed. "Honey, we're all Garner groupies. But I know what you're asking and no, of course not."

"It just sort of happened. I don't even know what it is yet. There've been no discussions." Just a lot of sex.

"What do you want it to be?" Delaney asked.

"I don't know yet. I'm still digesting it and I don't know where TJ stands. He's not exactly forthcoming."

"Have you thought about asking him?"

Candace knocked, then walked in with their drinks. Deb hoped she hadn't heard anything. In high school, Candace had been a gossipmonger.

"Thank you," Delaney said and took the tray from her.

Deb waited for her to leave while Delaney poured them both flavored, fizzy water. "I don't want to yet." She leaned her head back on the couch. "I just want to enjoy it."

"I think you should talk to him, Deb. TJ strikes me as a fairly deliberate person, not the kind to mess around with a longtime family friend without having emotions invested in it. I'd hate to see either of you get hurt." Delaney handed her a glass. "Okay, enough talk about your love life. Let's get down to business. First off, sales and marketing aren't my areas of expertise. I'm a designer and my ex always ran that part of the company. If you wouldn't mind, I'd like to ask Karen to sit in on this. This is more her forte."

Deb didn't know how TJ would feel about someone outside the Garner family knowing GA information. But she wasn't too proud to pass up help from an expert. "That's fine."

Delaney left the office and returned a few minutes later with Karen in tow. Deb explained her thoughts on the online store and they gathered around Delaney's laptop to look. Karen made groaning noises.

"Then I'm not off-base thinking this isn't helping us?"

"Noooo," Karen said. "It's all wrong for your brand, don't you think, Delaney?"

Delaney grimaced. "I wish I would've paid more attention to this. It was a cute idea in the eighties, not so much anymore. And especially not for a company that's promoting hands-on performance wear."

"I'd present the clothing and gear in regular photographs and illustrate performance with pictures and videos of guides actually wearing the stuff while skiing, bouldering, mountain biking, whatever." Karen pointed to the text. "Forget these cute little sayings. Show me, don't tell me."

That was exactly what Deb had thought and felt vindicated hearing Karen confirm it. She'd have to convince TJ, though.

"Change all this," Karen continued. "Your biggest challenge is getting the word out, and we can certainly help with that." She looked at Delaney. "We can add Garner Adventure to that big ad we're doing in *Women's Wear Daily*."

"Absolutely." Delaney poured more fizzy water in her glass. "Though I don't know how much that will touch on the adventure-sports market. But we can come up with a list of possible advertising vehicles for GA."

Deb cleared her voice. "About our market: I was thinking that we should sponsor athletes. A skier, a big-time kayaker, a rock climber, like that. The problem is, the high-profile ones all have big sponsors already. It's not like we can compete with Reebok or Under Armour, uh, no offense."

"None taken." Delaney's lips curved up. "I'm known for couture and ready-to-wear, not adventure clothes, so I see your dilemma. Though I think it's a great idea if you can make it work."

"I don't think you necessarily need someone high profile," Karen said. "What you need is a high-profile event. A big amateur ski competition or toboggan race, something like that. It would be great if it was televised or had a social media component. Your clientele is the weekend warrior, not a pro. That's who you want to appeal to, so you need someone who does this stuff for fun but is very proficient at it."

"Someone who can win," Deb said, loving the idea.

"Ideally," Karen agreed. "And Deb, you have to promote the heck out of it. Are you on Facebook, Twitter, Instagram, and Pinterest?"

She winced. "No. I guess I should be, huh?"

"Yep. Garner Adventure's online store needs to be all over the place," Karen said.

"What about the tent jacket?" Delaney asked.

Deb wondered if Delaney was joking. "Is that something you'd be interested in designing?"

Delaney paused. "Uh, it's not my brand nor do I know anything about tents, but I think it's a great idea. Let me ask around to see if there's a designer better suited for it. It's something that could be exclusive to GA and bring traffic to the site."

"Absolutely," Karen said, and for the next hour they outlined a strategy.

By the time Deb pulled up in front of GA, it was dark and her head was swimming with ideas. When she got inside, everyone had gone home for the night. Everyone but TJ.

"Hey. I thought you'd left early."

"Nope." She shook her head. "And I'm glad you're still here because I've got a ton of thoughts on how we can increase sales."

"Yeah?" His lips tipped up in a heart-stopping smile and her stomach did pirouettes. "Whaddya got?"

"I met with Delaney and Karen and they gave me a whole approach."

"They're high-fashion, Deb. Not our market."

She poked him in the chest with her finger. "Instead of being a know-it-all, why don't you listen to what I have to say?"

"Can we eat first? I'm starved."

"Sure." Was it a date or a work dinner? "Where do you want to go?"

"Indian place." The restaurant's name was Zaika, but everyone regularly referred to it simply as the Indian place.

"Let's go." She swung her tote bag over her shoulder. It had all the notes she'd taken at Delaney's.

They walked the few short blocks to the restaurant. Deb felt a chill nipping at her legs. She should've worn tights or leggings under her dress.

TJ gazed up at the sky. "More snow's on the way." He casually draped his arm over her shoulder and she had an overwhelming urge to snuggle closer.

She thought about what Delaney had said, about how TJ likely cared or he wouldn't be fooling around with her. She dared to hope but didn't know how to open the conversation.

"What are you thinking?" he asked.

"Nothing . . . Is Colt mad that you hired me and not someone with crazy marketing skills?"

"No," he said, but she knew he was lying.

Deb understood that Colt was only looking out for his fiancée's best interests, which any good boyfriend or husband should do. And sweetly, TJ didn't want to hurt her feelings, so in a way he was looking out for her. The knowledge of that warmed her even more than the gas fireplace at Zaika.

One of the owners showed them to a table, and TJ asked for an order of naan while they perused the menu. He kept sneaking peeks at her, and she wondered if he was thinking about earlier, about their spontaneous sex.

"You want wine or beer?" he asked.

"Just water. I want to go over the stuff I learned."

His eyes were on her lips, but she didn't think he was listening to a word she was saying. "Do you want to wait until we're done eating to talk shop?"

"We can talk about it," he said, but he didn't seem that into it.

"Then quit staring at me."

"Why?" he asked, and she couldn't tell whether he was teasing.

"Because it's hard to concentrate and I'm trying to prove myself, TJ."

He pulled his chair in closer to the table. "Okay, tell me what you got."

"Don't get mad, but both Delaney and Karen agree with me that the online store isn't the flavor we want. Karen had some ideas that I totally agree with. Can I talk to Jillian and make the changes?"

Their waters and naan came. Deb ordered her usual chicken tikka. TJ got the tandoori and a bunch of sides for the table.

"We'll have to pay her," TJ said. "I hope it isn't throwing good money after bad."

She couldn't guarantee it wouldn't be or that it would even increase sales. But she didn't think it could get any worse. "How much money are we talking about?"

"If we can keep it under a thousand bucks, go ahead. Anything over that and I'd be inclined to say no."

"But if it's under a thousand, I can do what I want?"

He slowly nodded, but she could tell he was already regretting his decision.

"You sure?" She was giving him a chance to back out, even though her gut told her the online store was all wrong and it would be well worth the money to make the fixes.

"Yeah, go ahead."

She tilted her head, skeptical. "Are you just trying to get me in the sack again? Because, TJ, you don't have to work that hard."

He tossed his head back and laughed. "I want to continue sleeping with you, but that's not why I'm letting you spend the money. Why can't you believe that I have faith in you? You never struck me as someone with low self-esteem."

"Are you angry that I went to Delaney and Karen?" It probably wasn't a good business practice to tell your star designer that her clothes weren't moving. But Delaney was part of TJ's family.

He let out a huff. "Drastic times call for drastic measures."

"Delaney didn't think it was drastic. She thought we haven't given it enough time."

"I wish we would've gotten the spread Colorado Adventure got in *Outside* magazine."

Their food came and the server took his time removing the domes from all the platters. After the waiter left, TJ put a scoop of everything on her plate.

"The retail store was my idea." He shoveled in a bite. "I sold everyone on it, even though they argued that we didn't have the resources. So every day it doesn't make a profit and every day it takes our focus away from the adventure tours is on me."

"That's a lot of pressure to put on yourself. There's no way you could've known about Royce." He shrugged and she continued. "You came up with an idea you thought would make money. If it winds up you were wrong, no one is going to blame you."

"I'll blame myself."

"Jeez, TJ, you'll get an ulcer like that."

"Successful people have ulcers, Deb."

She pointed her fork at him. "You're already successful."

He waited to stop chewing his tandoori chicken and said, "Not in everything. I haven't done a good job of finding balance in my life."

"Explain," she demanded.

"I don't want to be just a paper pusher. And I don't want the buck to stop only at me."

"You don't want to be in charge anymore?"

I don't want to be the only one in charge." He served himself more helpings of the side dishes. "I'd also like to guide an occasional tour."

"Easy enough. You need more minions. Give me and Darcy more responsibility."

He laughed. "You've been here less than a month and you already want a promotion. Let's see if we can save the retail division first."

She wasn't looking for a promotion; she only wanted to help. "Sure, but would divvying up the responsibility give you more balance?"

He stopped eating and looked at her for a long time. "I want someone to come home to."

The statement threw her. Men, at least the ones she knew, didn't say things like that. "Who do you want to come home to?"

Maybe he hadn't found that person yet and was still looking. Or maybe he already knew. She held her breath waiting for the answer, her heart racing.

His blue gaze held hers. "It's complex."

It wasn't her, then. Disappointment cut through her like a blade. By now, she would've thought the muscle tissue of her heart was callused enough that nothing could hurt her. But she was wrong.

When "Oh" was all she said, he pointed to the last piece of naan. "You going to eat that?"

"Go for it." She suddenly wasn't very hungry anymore.

"It's settled, then. I can talk to Jillian about changing the online store?"

"Yep. What else you have?"

She spent the next thirty minutes absently going through the ideas Delaney and Karen had mapped out.

After dinner, TJ paid the bill, helped Deb on with her jacket, and walked her home. He'd wanted to tell her the truth when she'd asked who he wanted to come home to. A crowded restaurant, where anyone could overhear their conversation, didn't feel like the right place. And the timing couldn't be worse.

They were immersed in trying to save a shaky retail venture. He wanted her to succeed so badly that he was taking stupid risks with his family's money. For instance, throwing cash at a website that was only a week old. But he didn't think straight when it came to her.

That was why it seemed like a bad time to profess his feelings for her.

Without thinking, he slipped his hand into hers. If it wasn't so cold, he would've liked to have strolled up and down Main Street with her. During the holidays, there were horse and carriage rides. The company was considering extending the service into spring, but so far, that hadn't happened.

"You want to get dessert at Tart Me Up?" he asked. It was getting late. They should probably just call it a night.

She took his wrist and looked at his watch. "I think they're closed by now."

They'd made it as far as the Morning Glory, which, unfortunately, was the end of the line.

Upstairs, she motioned for him to come inside. He promised it was just for a minute, just long enough for her to turn on the lights. He was tempted to see if she wanted to go for a second round of what they'd done earlier, but it didn't seem right to continue like that. Friends with benefits. It wasn't enough for him.

Standing in her tiny front room, with the streetlights shining in, she gazed into his eyes, expectantly. *Ah hell, go ahead; tell her.*

"You," he said in a soft voice, not quite a whisper. "I want to come home to you."

Chapter Twenty-One

Deb woke up to find TJ wrapped around her. Wedged between his arms, her back tucked against his chest, she felt dizzy with joy.

They'd spent the night doing all kinds of things. Naughty things that made her hot just thinking about them.

I want to come home to you, he'd said.

Though it wasn't a declaration of love, it was as close as one came. At least for Deb. She was willing to bet he'd eventually say those three magical words. But under no circumstances would she say them first. Not ever again.

"What time is it?" TJ asked in a groggy voice.

She rolled over so she could face him and stared into a pair of arresting blue eyes. "Almost nine."

"I'm officially late and don't give a damn." His mouth tugged at the corners.

"I do. I need to get in and call Jillian." She started to move toward the edge of the bed, but he held her down and tickled her, making her giggle uncontrollably. "Seriously, TJ. I've got a company to save."

"The company's fine." His mouth covered hers and he kissed her. "But I'll let you save the retail division."

"And I'll let you take a shower with me." She broke free

and raced to the bathroom, shouting, "You better hurry before I use all the hot water."

She should've known better than to challenge a Garner that way. He hopped off the bed and practically beat her to the bathroom. Of course, he had an unfair advantage—nakedness. His broad shoulders and washboard abs, bronzed from working in the sun, even in winter, were a hell of a distraction.

She turned on the shower faucet, waiting for the old pipes to finish belching and the water to turn hot before getting in. It was a standard-size tub, but with TJ it suddenly felt small. He grabbed the soap off the ledge and washed her, slipping his hands everywhere while she whimpered with pleasure.

Deb tilted her head back to look up at him. His eyes lighted with tenderness, and something moved in her chest. He kissed her, the pull of his mouth warm and sweet and tantalizing. She clutched his shoulders, pushing her body against his, reveling in his solidness.

"I don't have a condom." He started to get out of the tub and she pulled him back.

"By the time you get back, it'll be ice cold . . . crappy water heater. Stay and hold me."

He took her in his arms and covered her lips with his. Like before, the kiss was slow and hot. But this time it was more intimate. Full of unspoken meaning . . . and promise. Different than anything she'd ever felt before. They stood there, locked together, until the hot water turned freezing.

TJ got out first, found a towel, and wrapped her in it.

"I'm gonna run home for some clean clothes," he said, and returned to Deb's bedroom to put on the ones he'd worn the day before.

Deb searched through her closet for something presentable to wear in case Jillian had time to meet with her today.

Considering what a good client Garner Adventure was, Jillian should make them a priority. *Don't I sound like a corporate type?*

"This one or that one?" Deb held up a sweater dress in one hand and herringbone slacks and a blazer in the other.

TJ nudged his head at the sweater dress. "That one for sure."

She smiled to herself because the little scenario felt domestic and she liked it. But something had been nagging at her. "TJ?" she asked, feeling a bit reluctant to broach the subject because this thing between them felt perfect right now and she didn't want to screw it up. "Er . . . how are we supposed to handle us at work?" Or in public, for that matter?

He didn't respond at first, which she saw as a red flag. Then he finally said, "Uh, I need to talk to Win, so I'd appreciate it if we could keep you and me on the down low for a while."

The idea of being a secret couple rubbed her wrong, but she understood how it could be awkward, given her past with Win.

He lifted her hair and kissed the back of her neck, and any trepidations she had melted away. Someone's cell rang, and it took Deb a second to determine that it was TJ's. He reached for it on the nightstand, checked the caller ID, and put his finger to his lips before answering. From the sound of the conversation, it was one of his brothers. She finished getting dressed, and by the time she was done, TJ had signed off on his call.

"Josh." He rolled his eyes. "I'm an hour late and everyone freaks out." He grabbed his wallet and car keys. "I'll see you in the office."

She zipped up her boots. "If I get an appointment with Jillian, I'm going to Reno."

"Okay." He kissed her good-bye. "Drive carefully."

It had snowed overnight. She chose a wool coat instead of her ski jacket, gave TJ a head start to his truck, and headed out. At GA, Darcy had brewed a fresh pot of coffee and Deb helped herself to a cup.

"Hey." Win reached around her waist and pulled her in for a peck on the cheek. "What up?"

"Just working. How 'bout you?"

"I'm taking a few guys up for some freestyle skiing in the backcountry in about an hour." Win glanced toward the hallway. "Have you seen TJ? He's usually here by now, but it doesn't look like his computer is even on."

"Nope." She felt yucky lying. "I've gotta get to work, make a few calls."

"Sure, go do your thing."

She went to her office and booted up her computer. There were only two orders from the online store. One for a sweatshirt, the other a hat. Oh boy, not exactly taking the world by storm. She looked up the number for Jillian's company and reached her directly. Forty minutes later, she was on the road with a plan to turn sales around. And to prove—mostly to herself—that TJ had made the right decision hiring her.

By the time TJ got to the office, he was two hours late and he didn't care. Let someone else worry about the day-to-day problems for a change.

Today, he wanted nothing more than to ride a wave of happiness. Because if they couldn't save the store, it wouldn't last for long.

"You have ten messages," Darcy said as he passed through the lobby.

He stopped at her desk and scooped up the stack of call-back slips. "Anything important?"

She did a double take. "I thought you said everything's important."

He might've said it once upon a time.

"I got all the rescheduled tours on the calendar," Darcy continued. "Everyone is onboard. Want me to give you a copy?"

"Nope," he said. "I trust you."

He started to walk away when she called, "Are you sick or something?"

"Never felt better." He tried to sound casual when he asked, "Is Deb in yet?"

"She went to Reno to meet with our webmaster."

That hadn't taken long. He liked her initiative but was disappointed. He'd been looking forward to seeing her. After all, it had been a full hour since he'd seen her last.

In his office, he booted up his computer and sorted through the pink slips. Nothing that couldn't wait. Most of them were vendors trying to sell GA something. He sneaked a look at their daily sales, and despite his good mood, his heart dropped.

"You're here." Colt came in without knocking. Typical.

"You off today?" He was in plain clothes instead of his uniform.

"Wedding stuff." Colt pulled a face. "You sick or something?"

"No." Why was everyone asking that?

"Win said you haven't been here all morning."

"All morning. It's only ten thirty. I slept in. What's the big deal?"

Colt sank into the couch. "You never sleep in and you're always here at seven, like clockwork. Everything okay?"

TJ got up, shut the door, and sat back down. "I was with Deb last night."

"Yeah?" Colt sat straight up and smiled. "How's that going?"

"Good." That was an understatement, but he wasn't sharing the details with his brother. "I need to talk to Win about it."

"Probably a good idea just to prevent any weirdness. I'm betting he'll give you his blessing."

TJ let out a breath. "You talk to him about Britney?"

Colt nodded. "He's determined to marry her and we need to support him in his decision."

Perhaps Win knew what he was doing. He typically steered clear of the hard stuff. Hell, he'd had the chance to be an Olympic star and quit just because the strict regimen wasn't his jam.

And then there was the fact that if Win married Britney, he'd leave the road wide open for TJ and Deb. The self-serving thought sort of horrified him. But it was there nonetheless.

"Is Mom still having that dinner?"

"Saturday night. Didn't you get the memo?" Colt grinned because their sweet little mother became a drill sergeant when she threw one of her supper parties. All Garner men were expected to drop their plans and show up.

"Guess I know where I'll be." He could bring Deb to his parents' house, make them official there. "How do you think I should tell Win?" This wasn't email material. *Hey, I'm with the woman everyone thought you'd marry.*

"Win's got bigger fish to fry right now, so just be straight with him. Take him for a beer or something." Colt glanced at his watch. "I've gotta roll. Delaney and I are meeting with Foster about flowers." He made a gun with his finger and put it to his head.

TJ chuckled. "I still don't know why you don't go to Vegas and get it done before she changes her mind. You aren't exactly a prize."

Colt gave him the finger and took off, leaving TJ to wonder what to do with the rest of his day. He had a pile of work on his desk, calls to return, and a retail venture to revive. But there was fresh snow on the ground.

Screw it.

He went in search of his skis and on his way out called to Darcy, "You're in charge while I'm gone. Don't take crap from anyone."

Chapter Twenty-Two

"Come on, Teddy. Can't you help a girl out?" If Deb could finagle this, she'd be golden.

"You know what you're asking? TJ Garner hasn't competed in more than ten years. I love the guy, but, Deb, this is the big time."

She got up and shut her office door. "Give me a break, Teddy. It's not the FIS Alpine Ski World Cup or even the X Games."

"We draw some of the most famous freeskiers in the world. Even though I want to help you out, it's a by-invitation-only event. Just twenty-three people made the cut this year."

"Get us an invitation, Teddy." She wasn't backing down. The White Crush Invitational was the perfect contest to promote Garner Adventure. Hosted at Sierra Resort, just twenty miles down the road, the event included everything from big-mountain skiing to backcountry slopestyle. Camera crews from as far away as Switzerland trekked in to film the competition. "You owe me."

She'd set him up with his wife, one of her best friends from high school, while volunteering at a World Cup event at Squaw many moons ago. Teddy had been one of the organizers, and Bonnie, a competitor. Now he ran White

Crush and wielded enough power to get anyone an invite to compete in the all-day event. But Ted was right; White Crush wasn't your basic slalom race. It was extreme skiing at its finest. The kind with so much razzle-dazzle that it made people want to buy stuff, at least to Deb's thinking.

"You're planning to wear me down, aren't you?" Ted laughed.

"I don't think it's much of a stretch, Teddy. It's not like TJ can't hold his own. He was winning all the major junior freestyle competitions in high school and was on the World Cup circuit by the time he was nineteen."

"He's been out of the game a long time." Teddy let out an audible sigh.

"What would be the harm? Worse comes to worst, he wipes out. End of story."

There was a long silence. "I suppose I could get him in as an honorary local." A lot of invitational-only events let in a few community contestants as a goodwill gesture. "Just know, he's the first to get cut if we go over time or the weather turns bad."

"I can live with that." She wanted to jump up and down with excitement. While it wasn't the Olympics, it was a significant contest, with plenty of publicity behind it. It was grander in scheme than what Karen had suggested. But Deb's philosophy was, go big or go home. This kind of event would put Garner Adventure and its gear on a world stage. Especially because Deb planned to dress TJ from head to toe in the exclusive skiwear GA sold. "Thank you, Ted."

"Remember," Ted said, "he's mostly there as a ceremonial nod to the Sierra Nevada. A native son, so to speak. I'm emailing you the entrance form now. Make sure you get it back to me by the end of the day."

"I will." She knew how last minute this was. But the timing couldn't be more perfect.

After Ted, she called Jillian to see how the changes for the online store were coming. The last few days had been a whirlwind. Sales were practically nonexistent and TJ was growing more frustrated. Sometimes she wondered if he kept her on because of their newfound relationship, which was going a hell of a lot better than their retail endeavor. Still, she could see the toll their lousy sales were taking on him. TJ took everything personally when it came to the business, and she could tell he felt like he'd let his family down.

She wanted so much to fix it for him—and to be good at something meaningful. Something she could be proud to call a career.

"What's going on?" TJ knocked and poked his head inside.

"Something big." She pumped her fist in the air. "You need to call a meeting. We need all hands on deck for this one."

"What is it?" He sat in the big upholstered chair and stretched his legs out in front of him, and her girl parts lurched.

For a second, she considered crawling into his lap, but they were trying to maintain professionalism at work. Plus, he still hadn't told Win, who'd been making himself scarce these days. He had Britney and a baby to deal with.

"I want to tell everyone at the same time. But I think this might make the difference in sales."

"Does it have to do with the website?" He leaned forward, and Deb could tell she'd piqued his curiosity.

"Nope. Sponsorship."

He tilted his head. "You found someone big?"

"I sure did," she said. "When can we have a meeting?"

He tugged his phone out of his pocket and checked his calendar. "If we can get everyone here, I can schedule it for this afternoon. That work?"

"Yep." She bobbed her head at his phone. "See if everyone can make it."

He crooked his finger at her. "Come here."

She crossed the floor and he pulled her down on his lap and kissed her. His hands shimmied under her blouse, turning her insides to liquid heat.

"The door's open, you know," she said. If they kept this up, no telling what Darcy or one of the others might walk into.

He let out a frustrated grunt. "Let's run up to your place for a quickie."

In the last couple of days, they'd been doing a lot of that. TJ Garner had become downright irresponsible. They'd been together every night and had even managed to sneak in an hour here and there of skiing. Sometimes she'd wake up with TJ lying next to her and reach out to touch his skin or his hair just to make sure he was real. She'd always been of the theory that if it seemed too good to be true, it probably was. But everything with TJ kept getting better.

"Text everyone to see if they can come to the meeting first."

He grinned and scooted her off his lap. "You sure you don't want to tell me first?"

"I'm positive." She wanted to surprise him. And she wanted everyone to know that she'd finagled a spot in White Crush on her own, with no help from TJ. And that she could do the job and wasn't just a Bennett living off the kindness of a Garner.

He studied her face. "Deb, I'm really impressed with how invested you are. But there's a chance that no matter how much we try, we won't be able to save it. It'll kill me to concede defeat, but at some point, you have to cut your losses. It's good, sound business."

The subtext was, he'd have to cut her. She got it. GA couldn't continue to keep her on the payroll if her division bled money faster than a knife wound. But she worried that it would change the dynamic of their relationship. How do you fire your girlfriend—she was pretty sure she was his girlfriend—without causing a deep rift in the balance of things? That was why she had to turn sales around.

"I know. But I think I've come up with a plan that'll at least give us a fighting chance."

"I can't wait to hear it." He got up. "Let me call in the troops."

Three hours later, she sat at the head of the table in GA's conference room. Everyone, except Win, had come. She cleared her throat and made her big announcement to a round of loud applause and cheers.

Gray squeezed her arm affectionately. "Way to go, kiddo. That'll be tremendous PR for Garner Adventure."

"I can't believe Ted Jordan went for it," Colt said. "It's BIO. I think Win got an invitation to compete five or six years ago, but it's mostly for guys on the circuit."

"I guess it helps that they're holding it here this year," Josh chimed in. "Dad's right; you can't buy better marketing."

Deb beamed. "I've got big plans to promote the brand the day of the competition, right down to what TJ's going to wear." *Listen to me; I sound like I actually know what I'm doing.* "Then we'll prominently display everything TJ wears in the contest on the website."

"I love it!" Mary clapped.

"I wish I had my snowboard ready."

"Because it's all about you, Josh." Colt smacked his brother upside the head.

"Boys." Mary glared at them sternly.

"Delaney's looking for a designer who can do a proto-type of the tent jacket," she said. "Who knows, it might be ready in time to promote on the website, too."

"I'll help with whatever you need," Darcy volunteered.

"I'll take you up on it, Darce. And by the way, the competition comes this year with a thirty-six-thousand-dollar purse. I mean, if we win it." The contest would be tough, with some of the top extreme skiers in the country, but even after all these years Deb thought TJ was a force to be reckoned with. He was the most consistent freeskier she'd ever seen. Even though he didn't compete anymore, TJ could still huck a ninety-foot backflip and shred the backcountry like a snow god.

Everyone looked across the table at TJ, who'd been conspicuously quiet. Caught up in everyone's excitement, Deb hadn't noticed until now. But he was glowering and looking angrier than Deb had ever seen him.

"TJ?" She forgot herself and reached for his hand.

He jerked it away. "It probably would've been a good idea to check with me first, don't you think? I don't compete anymore," he said and walked out, slamming the door behind him.

TJ took his bike to Misty Summit and spent a couple of hours careening down the mountainside in the snow. It was his answer to therapy. Speed and nature. And it was better than biting Deb's head off, which he supposed he'd already done. He knew she was just trying to help, but she shouldn't have made the commitment for him without asking first.

The last thing he wanted to do was relive one of the worst experiences of his life. It might've been more than a decade ago, but on that day, he'd not only lost a slot on the

U.S. Olympic team but he'd lost a dream. One missed jump had ruined his chance to qualify. His overall score was one point shy of making the team. And Win got the spot that otherwise would've been TJ's.

He was done competing.

His phone vibrated in his pocket. More than likely one of his buttinsky brothers, but when he checked caller ID it was Deb. He didn't have anything to say to her, so he let it go to voice mail. How could she know him so little as to think he'd want to make a fool of himself in front of his family, friends, and the best freeskiers in the world? When he was fortunate to have time to ski, it was purely recreational. These competitors had been training for years.

He rode for another hour and went home. Let someone else worry about Garner Adventure for a change. Around eight, there was a knock on his door, and when he peered through the peephole it was Colt, holding a six-pack of beer.

Great.

He opened the door and swung his arm across the threshold, ushering Colt in. In the kitchen, he got down two pilsner glasses and pulled out one of the beers. "You here to lecture me?"

"I'm here to see what the hell that was at GA. Deb's trying to do something to help the business and you were an ungrateful child."

"She should've talked to me about it before submitting my name."

"What's the big deal?" Colt grabbed one of the beers, twisted off the top, and shunned the glass, drinking it straight out of the bottle. "You spend a day big-mountain skiing. I can think of a lot of worse things to do."

"I don't compete anymore."

Colt stared him down. "You don't compete or you're afraid to compete?"

"I don't have time to compete. I run a business, Colt. I run it because no one else in this family can be bothered with the day-to-day crap that makes the trains run on time. Why does everything always have to fall to me? Why don't you compete, or better yet, Win?"

"Because you have the best chance of winning." Colt put his beer down on the counter and gave TJ a long, assessing look. "Why is it that everyone knows that except you?"

"Bullshit!" TJ said. "You and I both know that if anyone of us can even place in the White Crush, it would be Win."

Colt laughed. "Seriously, what is it with you and our youngest brother? Win's good, maybe even great. But you're the fucking maestro of the mountain. Sometimes I think you sabotage yourself just so you can put on this loser act of yours.

"Do what you want," he continued. "No one is forcing you to compete. But know this: We're not going to keep financing a losing venture. If you and Deb can't save the online store in the next couple of weeks, we're voting to close it down. And TJ, as much as I love Deb, we can't keep her on just because she's your girlfriend. You've already promised Darcy a promotion. There isn't room in the company—or on the payroll—for two if there's no store. This is a business; we have to run it like one."

TJ had always run it like a business. He'd been the one to dedicate his life to growing their profits, not Colt or anyone else. For that reason, he resented Colt's self-righteous speech. Colt wasn't the boss; TJ was. But he couldn't deny the truth. Without the store, Deb held a position the company simply couldn't afford.

He'd fix things some other way. But not by skiing in the White Crush. He'd given his blood, sweat, and tears to GA; no way was he giving his soul.

Chapter Twenty-Three

In usual Britney psychotic fashion, she'd changed her mind about going to Win's parents' for dinner.

"Not an option," he'd yelled at her over the phone. "My mom's hosting this for you and me. Be ready when I get there, Brit."

He was pretty sure his demand would go unheeded. Britney did whatever the hell she wanted, regardless of hurting or embarrassing others. The only trump card was Win cutting her off financially. And if she reneged on going tonight, he'd do it. He'd stop paying her rent, her utilities, and all the other bills she'd saddled him with.

He nosed into a guest parking space as close to her condo as he could find. As it was, they were running late. His mother had gone to a lot of trouble; he didn't want to spoil her party.

As it was, he'd been avoiding his family the last few days, not wanting to answer a lot of questions about Britney and their so-called plans. One day they were getting married, the next they weren't, depending on Brit's moods.

But it wasn't just about Britney.

On Tuesday, he'd overheard TJ and Colt talking at Garner Adventure. Thin walls and doors. His brother and Deb, huh? It certainly explained why TJ had hired her. The truth was, Win didn't know how to feel about it. In a lot of ways, Deb had always been his best friend. Maybe he'd led her on to think there was more between them, and maybe he'd always figured someday there would be.

But with all the crazy changes in his life, he needed at least one constant and Deb had always been that. Until now. He didn't know if she'd be at dinner tonight with TJ. Every time he'd seen his brother this week, Win had taken a detour. If TJ was bringing her, the sad and simple truth was, seeing them together was going to hurt.

He got out of his Jeep, slammed the door, and marched up Britney's front steps. She opened before he could knock.

"Good, I'm glad you're here." The woman was psychotic.

"Forty minutes ago, you threatened to cut off my balls. What is it with you, Brit?"

She grabbed his arm and pulled him inside. "You want the neighbors to hear?" Britney clearly meant Cami, who had ears the size of rabbits.

He followed her into the living room. "Nice flowers." There had to be three dozen red roses in the arrangement. He fervently hoped he hadn't paid for them.

She was at least dressed appropriately. A long, flowy top and nice pants, instead of one of her sequined numbers or something else over the top for a casual country dinner.

"Let's go," he said.

"We need to talk." She pulled him toward one of the sofas.

He was through talking. "We're late, Britney. My mother went to a lot of trouble to do this. The least you can do is be polite and show up on time."

"I'm not marrying you, Win."

He sat down and rubbed his hand down his face. She was

pushing him past furious and it took a lot to make Win mad. "Are we doing this again? Make up your goddamned mind, Britney. But know this: I'm raising my baby."

"It's not yours," she said and sat next to him. "I'm marrying the baby's real father."

For a second, he wondered if he'd heard her right. "What are you talking about?" Was this another one of her stunts? That was par for the course with Britney; she was always working her next con, always upping the ante for the big score.

"Win, did it ever occur to you that we always used condoms?"

Yeah, and she'd said she was on birth control. But shit happened. He didn't need a sex-ed class to know that. "Cut to the chase, Brit. Have you been lying to me this entire month?"

She at least had the decency to look guilty. "You don't know what it's like, Win. You come from money, a supportive family, and brothers who would do anything for you. I'm on my own, without any support system."

He stared her down, his jaw clenched. "Did. You. Lie?!"

"Yes." A tear slid down her cheek, which instantly filled him with guilt. He didn't like making women cry, but this was unacceptable. She'd sent him to hell and back these last few weeks.

"How am I supposed to believe you? What did you do, Brit, hook a bigger fish?"

"I can have a paternity test done at the end of the first trimester to prove it to you, but I know without a shadow of a doubt that it isn't yours. I've always known, Win. Cortland is giving me an allowance until we get married and I'll pay you back for every cent you gave me."

Cortland? What the hell kind of name was that? Whoever he was, let Britney be his problem from now on.

"Why didn't you just tell me the baby was someone else's in the first place? I would've helped you if he wasn't willing to step up, Brit."

"I was scared," she said, and another tear made a slow pass down the side of her face. "But it's all good now. Cortland's decided to do the right thing and you won't be stuck with me." Britney flashed a weak smile. "Or a baby."

And Win was willing to bet Cortland made three times as much money as he did. Britney had probably choreographed everything just right. "How'd you work that, Brit?"

Her expression turned sheepish for an instant, and then it went hard as granite, the face of a scrapper. "I threatened to go to his family as soon as it was safe to do the paternity test."

"And what makes you so positive it's not mine?"

Her eyes dropped to her feet. "The timing. I'm a little more pregnant than I led you to believe."

"I was there when you took the test, Brit."

"Uh . . . it wasn't my first test. You and I had a break in fall, when I met Cortland. That's when it happened."

He tilted his head against the back of the couch and let out a breath. "So, if Cortland hadn't come through, you would've married me under false pretenses." He should've been angrier, but all he felt was tired. Bone-tired.

She didn't say anything, which answered his question. He reached across the table and removed the small card from the stick in the floral arrangement. It was signed *Cortland*. At least Win hadn't paid for it.

"How far along are you, then?" He got to his feet.

Again, guilt flitted across her face. "Ten weeks."

"I want that paternity test, Britney." He actually believed her, but he wouldn't put anything past the scheming witch.

She nodded and rose, too.

"I'll call you in a few weeks," he said and walked to the door.

She followed him and took his arm as he started to leave. "I'm sorry, Win. You're a good guy. But look at the good side of it; you're free."

He shook her hand off his biceps and walked out. Free? He was happy to be rid of her, that was for sure. But he still felt like he'd lost something. Something he hadn't even known he wanted.

Win got in his Jeep and made the drive to his parents' house. It took him forty minutes in traffic. People who didn't know how to drive in the snow. When he got there, everyone was already around the table. Everyone except Deb. Win assumed TJ was waiting for the right moment to break the news that they were seeing each other to him.

A room full of eyes stared at him as he stood there, probably looking like road kill. He certainly felt like it.

"Is Britney not coming?" his mother asked hesitantly.

"Nope. The wedding's off and the baby's not mine. Let's eat."

Deb got to work bright and early Sunday. She planned to spend the day fine-tuning the online store. Jillian had showed her a few tricks to make the site come up in searches more often. Although they still weren't getting many orders, she was satisfied that they were doing all they could, including notifying their thousands of newsletter subscribers of another blowout sale.

She planned to talk to some of the local ski resorts and the kayak and bike rental places about carrying flyers and needed to update all GA's printed materials with the store's link. Jillian had also helped her create a new Garner

Adventure signature for all the employees to use in their emails that was clickable to the webpage.

If TJ would give her the budget, she wanted to run a few ads in adventure magazines and websites. The rest was word of mouth, which meant they needed their guides to wear the gear and push the merch. Next week, she'd schedule a meeting to discuss it, including giving everyone a fun pitch they could use at the end of every tour to send clients to the site. Hannah had helped her with it.

But frankly, she was putting all her hopes in White Crush; that was, if TJ even planned to show up. She hadn't talked to him since the meeting at GA on Friday. Not for lack of trying, that's for sure. Two days and he hadn't returned her calls. Colt had told her to give him space, that it wasn't her, that it was the idea of competing again. She had no idea that it was such an issue. He'd always sloughed off missing his shot at the Olympics. If she had known how much angst it caused him, she never would've signed him up in the first place.

She checked the time. Before everything had gone south between them, TJ had promised to come in today and work with her on a PowerPoint presentation for the meeting with the guides. Deb hadn't the foggiest idea how to make one. He'd confirmed this morning with a short text: I'll be there. But he was late, probably lagging after a late night at his family's for dinner. Given all the turmoil, she hadn't gone. The fact was, TJ hadn't been able to get Win alone long enough to tell him about them. Deb thought it was unnecessary to be so formal about it, but TJ thought it was important.

Noise in the lobby pulled her out of her chair. She went up front to see what the ruckus was, hoping TJ had finally arrived. But it was Win, and he was dragging an antique wooden canoe through the reception area.

"What are you doing with that?"

He jumped, surprised to see her. "You scared the crap out of me."

She grinned because it was fun sneaking up on Win.

"Give me a hand with this. I want to take it to the back and patch the hole."

Baffled, Deb asked, "Why didn't you park in the rear so you didn't have to lug it across the building?"

"Because the front door was closer. I carried it from home and it's twenty degrees out and this weighs a hundred pounds." He said it to her like she had a comprehension problem.

"What are you doing with this old thing anyway?" They made much lighter ones nowadays. And why in God's name had he carried it across town?

"My brothers and I built it when we were kids. It's great, when it holds water."

Patching an old boat that couldn't be used until spring seemed like an odd way to spend the weekend. But she didn't argue and grabbed an end. They tried to get it around a tight corner between the reception counter and the wall, but the ridiculous thing was cumbersome.

"Do-si-do it," Win instructed.

Wasn't that a square dancing move? She ignored him because she didn't know what the hell he was talking about and tried to flip the boat on its side, hoping it would buy them more space that way.

"Not like that; like this." He hefted up his side, causing her to lose her grip.

"Win, you're going to drop it."

"For Christ's sake." He lifted the whole thing himself over the counter while she scurried around to pick up her end again.

In the process, she collided with him and their legs got tangled up. Next thing Deb knew, they were both sprawled on top of each other on the floor. Win had somehow managed to wrangle the canoe out of the way so neither of them hurt themselves. Deb felt like she was in an *I Love Lucy* episode.

"Get off me, you big lug." She pushed on his chest, but he lay on top of her, laughing his head off. She started laughing, too. "Seriously, you're crushing me."

He lifted up on both elbows and hung his face over hers, "Not until you say 'Uncle.'"

She never got to say it because at that very moment TJ chose to walk in.

He stood there, frozen, an imperceptible twitch in his left cheek. "That certainly didn't take long." And just like that, he turned around and walked out.

"Shit, get off me." Win rolled to the side and she scrambled to her feet as fast as she could and went after him.

But Garners were fast and he was gone, the exhaust from his Range Rover tailpipe leaving cloudy puffs in the air. Win found her a couple of minutes later on the sidewalk, bent over with her hands on her knees.

"You better get inside without a jacket."

She didn't feel cold, only numb. "I need to go find him. You think he'll go home?"

"Maybe or to Royal Slope."

She shook her head. "His skis are here."

Deb started to walk home to get her car keys, but Win grabbed her arm. "Let him cool down."

"You don't understand; he thought we were . . . because he and I . . . oh, Jesus." Then it dawned on her that Win already knew because why else would he say to let TJ cool down? "Did he tell you last night?"

"No. Let's go inside before you get hypothermia."

She followed him. He went in search of her jacket because she'd begun to shiver. When he came back, she put it on and he motioned for her to sit on the couch.

"What do you mean, no?"

"He didn't talk to me about it." He sank down next to her, and for the first time, she noticed the brackets around his mouth and the bags under his eyes. "I overheard him telling Colt on Tuesday. Things blew up last night, and I suspect he didn't think it was the right time."

"What happened? Did you two fight?"

"Britney broke the news that I wasn't the father of her kid. She's marrying the real father. . . . I'm off the hook."

Deb jerked in surprise. "Oh, Win, are you okay?"

"About Brit? Hell yeah. The baby? It's strange, but I miss not having him . . . or her. Does that sound crazy?"

"Not at all." For all his faults, Win could be sensitive— and good as gold. She'd always loved that about him. "It'll happen for you. But next time, it'll be under better circumstances."

"I know." He slapped her leg, an attempt at reassuring her that he was okay.

"I need to go, Win. I need to talk to him."

"Does he love you?" Win asked, his voice soft.

"I don't know." *You. I want to come home to you.* "But I love him."

"You do?" He studied her, because they both knew what he was really asking.

"With all my heart."

"Then you better get moving," he said and got up to tug her off the sofa.

"Are you really okay, Win?" His eyes were slightly glassy.

"Just a lot of changes." He pulled her in for a hug. "I'll talk to TJ, too. We'll get this straightened out."

"I don't want to put a wedge between you two."

"Never." He shook his head. "We're Garners, Bennett; we stick together. And TJ's the best of the bunch. You chose wisely, Grasshopper."

She grinned because Win was loyal and amazingly self-deprecating when the time called for it. But most of all, he was a true friend.

She ran home, got her car keys, and drove to TJ's place. His truck was parked in the driveway. Deb rang the bell, and when that didn't rouse him, she banged on the door a few times. Finally, she whipped out her cell and called him.

"I'm at your door and I know you're home. It's freezing out here, so please let me in."

She waited and waited and nothing. Undeterred, she went around back. Sure enough, she found him working on his boat. What was it about Garners and their boats in winter?

"Hey," she called as she walked down the dock. "I've been pounding on your door."

He didn't say anything, just gave her a cursory once-over.

"Can we go inside and talk? I don't know what you think you saw, but nothing was going on, TJ."

"Maybe not this time." He went back to hosing down the sides of the Outback. Fruitless, because it was just going to snow again.

"Please." She stood there feeling helpless, especially with him ignoring her.

He glanced up from what he was doing and gave her a long perusal, then shut off the hose. It took him time to wind it up and hang it on the hook. Without a word, he went inside the house. She assumed he meant for her to follow.

They both removed their boots just inside the door. He didn't bother to wait for her to finish, climbing the stairs to the main floor.

She found him in the kitchen with his head in the refrigerator. "Didn't you have breakfast?" It was an inane question, but under the circumstances she needed a neutral topic.

"No. I was planning to take you to the Four Seasons for brunch." And then he'd walked in on her and Win's fall and had assumed the worst. Deb didn't know how to straighten this out.

"I was helping Win carry the canoe to the back of the building and we tripped over each other, TJ. That's all it was. When you walked in we were laughing about it, nothing more."

"Did he tell you about Britney?" He grabbed a carton of juice and poured a glass. "He's free now. You two can go back to whatever you were before."

"Now you're being an asshole. You know damned well there hasn't been a Win and me for ages."

Just looking at him standing there, still bundled up in his ski jacket, even though it was seventy degrees inside, he was so handsome, so good, so beyond anything she could describe. Compared to her feelings for TJ, Win had been a schoolgirl's crush, and her heart folded in half because she was about to lose him.

He pulled out a stool for her at the bar, sat in the one next to it, and let out a long sigh.

"Win and I grew up together," she said. "We're always going to have a special bond. But I love you . . . I'm in love with you . . . not Win."

The declaration seemed to startle him and he jerked back.

"I love you, TJ," she said it again, so he'd get it through

that thick, analytical skull of his. It wasn't Win she wanted; she wanted him. "You've made me happier than I ever knew I could be. When you walk into a room, my whole body feels like liquid fire. Don't you get it, TJ? It's you, only you."

He took some time to digest her words. She could see his mind working, the trepidation in his eyes. "I've got to talk to Win."

"He knows. He overheard you and Colt talking."

"Ah, Jesus." He pinched the bridge of his nose, then abruptly got to his feet. "I've gotta talk to him."

"What about us?"

"I don't know, Deb. I just don't know." He palmed his keys and was out of there like a shot.

So much for telling him she loved him.

Chapter Twenty-Four

TJ yanked Win's earbuds out. He didn't know how his brother could concentrate with the music blaring in his head like that.

"Oh, hey." Win turned off his iPod and the electric sander. He had their old canoe up on a pair of sawhorses and was doing something to the bottom.

"Why didn't you tell me you knew?"

Win flipped his goggles to the top of his head. "I was a little busy watching my life blow up. And by the way, we weren't making out. We fell while Deb was helping me with this." He pointed to the canoe.

"You could've said something, Win."

"You could've not gone behind my back. If you were interested in her, you should've said so."

Win was right. The guilt was eating TJ alive. "I should've. But you're an asshole, Win. How many years did you take her for granted? How many years did you lead her on with your hot-and-cold act?"

"How many years have you been secretly wanting her? Huh, TJ?" Win waved his arms in the air. "A long time, wasn't it? After hearing you with Colt, I started to put things together. The way you always came around when you knew she'd be at Old Glory, your doughnut runs to the Morning Glory, even back in high school. There you were, opening her locker, helping her make the varsity ski team, giving her rides before she could drive."

It was all true, and there was nothing TJ could say in his own defense, except that he loved her. He always had. But he loved his brother, too.

"I'll back off," he said. "You can have her as your number one fan again. I know how you like that."

"You're a dick, TJ." Win shoved him against the wall. "She wants you, not me."

"She'll get over me now that you're back in the picture." He shoved Win back. "You can resume your on-and-off-again bullshit."

Win raised his fist and TJ blocked it. "Grow the fuck up, Win."

"You grow up. She loves you. She told me she loves you." That took the wind out of TJ's sails. How many people had he hurt?

"She loved you first." He gave his brother a small push and started to go.

"Don't walk away. Don't you fucking walk away," Win yelled, but TJ kept going. He wanted out of this building, where the walls were closing in on him. "I should've known you'd give up without a fight. You're weak and you're a quitter. Colt told me about White Crush. That's what this is really about. You can pretend that Deb and I did you wrong, but we all know that it gives you the perfect excuse to walk away from the competition."

TJ whipped around and got in Win's face. "What did you say?"

"You heard me. You're so damn afraid of losing that you're willing to walk away . . . from Deb, from the retail division you started, even from a stupid contest. You think

I'm a quitter, but I at least made the team. You sabotaged yourself. I know it, Colt knows it, Josh knows it, Mom and Dad know it, and you know it."

How had they gone from Deb to the U.S. Olympic ski team? He let out a rusty laugh. "You're the quitter, Win. You were that close"—TJ made an inch with his fingers—"to competing for the gold and you walked away. So don't tell me that I'm weak."

"You're a wuss is what you are, always afraid I'll beat you. Here's a news flash for you, TJ: you're the easiest son of a bitch I've ever competed against because you don't even try. You don't even try, TJ."

"Screw you, Win." TJ slugged him in the face. Hard. "What would you know about anything when everything is handed to you? The best woman in town . . . in the whole goddamn freaking world . . . loves you and you throw her away."

Win sat on the floor, holding his face. "Who's throwing her away now, TJ?"

He didn't need this crap, he didn't need Win, and he sure as hell didn't need to be at Garner Adventure on a Sunday. On his way out, he grabbed his skis and drove to Royal Slope, where he spent the rest of the afternoon beating the crap out of the snow.

When he got home, his answering machine was lit up like a Christmas tree.

The first message was from Colt. "I think you might've broken Win's nose. He was too damn pretty anyway. Call me."

Josh. "Damn, that's a mean right hook you got. Call me."

The last one was from Win. "You nearly ruined my modeling career. Lucky for you, my nose isn't broken. Call me."

Nothing from Deb, which served him right. She'd told him she loved him and he'd said nothing. Not a damn thing.

It was all for the best. A couple weeks from now, he'd have to do the hardest thing he'd ever done in his life. He'd have to pull the plug on GA's failing retail undertaking and put Deb out on the street.

"No word from TJ yet?" Deb didn't know why she kept asking. All week he'd been a no-show at work. He hadn't called or even emailed her, just leaving her to twist in the wind.

"He's still camping." Darcy glanced up from her computer monitor and frowned. "How many orders did we get today?"

"Three." It was better than the day before, but not enough to keep the lights on. "I don't know what to do about White Crush. I'm assuming we need to scratch him."

"Can Win do it in TJ's stead?"

"Not sure." The entrance form had been for TJ. Deb didn't know if Ted would let her change contestants at the last minute, especially when she'd had to beg to get TJ the coveted invitation to begin with. "I'll ask."

Lord knew they needed a miracle to reboot the store. If sales continued to lag, she didn't know what they would do. The money they'd invested in T-shirts, sweatshirts, and hats alone . . . well, Deb didn't want to think about it.

"At least the weather's been perfect," Darcy said. It had been snowing nonstop. In the past, organizers had had to cancel the competition when the weather hadn't cooperated.

"Where's TJ camping?" Deb couldn't help asking. It was crazy cold for sleeping in a tent.

"Somewhere near the ocean is all I know." Darcy's eyes dropped to her desk, clearly uncomfortable that she knew where TJ was and Deb didn't. It was obvious the whole office was aware that she and TJ had been seeing each other before he'd gone off the grid.

And, once again, the Garner family had a front-row seat to Deb's humiliation.

"Hey." Josh came in and shook the snow off. "Anyone hear from TJ?"

"He's out of cell range," Darcy said. "He only calls when he goes into town; Gualala, I think he called it."

Josh took off his hat and gloves and shoved them in his parka pockets. "Next time he does, tell him to get his ass home. I can't do his job and mine."

Josh was nothing but bluster. Everyone was just worried about TJ. It wasn't like him to take off like this without notice. It wasn't like TJ to do anything unpredictable. And Deb only had herself to blame.

"I'm going to lunch," she told Darcy and Josh, needing fresh air. These last few days, she'd been in the office for eight- to nine-hour stretches, trying to do everything humanly possible to turn things around. She'd taken over GA's rarely used Twitter account, directed the company's Facebook fans to the online store, and posted tons of merchandise pictures on Pinterest and Instagram.

Hannah, Delaney, and Foster were already at Old Glory, holding a table. Someone had ordered pub fries, but Deb couldn't work up an appetite. Boden waved from the bar and she waved back.

"I gather from the long face you still haven't heard from him." Foster pulled out the chair next to him for Deb.

"Nope. He's camping somewhere in Mendocino County."

"The guys go there a lot," Hannah said and passed her hand over Deb's. "This isn't like TJ."

Deb shrugged. "I'm over him." The expressions around the table screamed, *Liar, liar, pants on fire.* "He should've at least had the decency to break up with me before he ran away from home."

She supposed he sort of had at his house Sunday, but she'd been in denial.

"Colt says he's sorting his life out." Delaney grabbed a fry and popped it in her mouth. "I think things may have been building for a while."

Hannah nodded in agreement. "Just give him time."

"Like I gave Win?" She was never doing that again. "I'm putting all my energy into my job now."

Unfortunately, there was a good chance she was going to lose it. At least working at GA had showed her what she was capable of. Even if she got canned, she'd find something else. In her short time at GA, she'd discovered that she liked marketing and maybe even had a knack for it. There was also school. Nothing seemed impossible anymore. And although he'd broken her heart in a million pieces, she had TJ to thank for that.

"How's the store doing?" Foster asked.

"Not so good. Colorado Adventure's head start really put a crimp in our sales."

"I've been seeing your tweets." Delaney tried for a reassuring smile. "You're doing a great job. You could always come work for me . . . be my social media person."

It was so sweet of Delaney to make the offer, but Deb wouldn't mix business with friendship again. This time she'd do it on her own. "Thanks, Delaney. I haven't given up on GA yet. White Crush could go a long way to putting us on the map. I'm planning to talk to the organizer about substituting Win for TJ."

"There's an idea, though Colt says TJ's a better skier."

What difference did it make if TJ was a no-show?

"How's Win doing?" Hannah asked.

"I think he's okay. I really haven't talked to him much." She'd been too twisted up over TJ.

The server came and took everyone's orders. Deb used the opportunity to check her phone. Nothing from TJ and nothing from the office. She slipped the cell back into her bag and rejoined the conversation.

When she got back to GA, Win was on his way out.

"Want to come?" He motioned to the snowboard he had under his arm. "Josh wants me to try it out."

"It's his prototype?" That had been fast. She reached out and ran her hand down the sleek board. "Nice."

"But how does she handle? That's the question."

"You heading to the Slope?"

"I thought I'd test it at the terrain park at Winter Bowl," he said. "Come with me. You can try it, too."

"Not this time. I've got too much to do." She started to ask if he'd heard anything from TJ but stopped herself. "Hey, would you be willing to take TJ's spot at White Crush?"

"You haven't heard from him, huh?" He reached out and squeezed her shoulder.

"No." She dropped her head so he wouldn't see her eyes fill up. "It would be good to have an alternate, you know, in case he doesn't show up."

He didn't say anything at first; then, "All right. Put me down." But he seemed hesitant.

"Delaney and her crew are working on ski pants and a top with a big GA logo. Could you swing by Colt and Delaney so she can get your measurements?"

"Okay," he said, but again, she got the sense that he wasn't too enthusiastic about it. Deb couldn't tell whether it was the bother of getting his measurements taken or if he didn't want to compete. The latter would surprise her. Win may not have liked the strict regimen of training, but he was a showboater and loved the attention of a crowd.

She let out a puff of air. "It isn't like TJ to leave us in the lurch like this."

"You probably should've asked him first." Win rubbed his chin. "Since his FIS Alpine World Cup flub, he doesn't compete anymore."

"Colt told me. TJ always played down not qualifying. I had no idea it was this big of a deal. If I had, I never would've entered him."

"You were just trying to help." He gave her another squeeze and looked up at the sky. "Count me in, but I'm burning daylight."

"Have fun." She watched him jog off, clutching the new snowboard.

In her office, she checked the website again for sales. An order had come in while she was at lunch for one of Delaney's bouldering shirts, and she chalked the sale up to revamping the online store. Why not take credit? She'd had Jillian incorporate short videos of their guides demonstrating the functionality of the clothes. According to the handful of reviews they'd gotten, the videos seemed to be working. Just not fast enough.

Delaney had found someone willing to do a prototype of a tent jacket. If everyone liked it, Deb was thinking of doing a GoFundMe campaign to raise capital to put the jackets into production. That way GA wouldn't have to foot the cost. Naturally, that was if she was still with the company then.

She worked a few hours, took a break, and used it as an excuse to pass by TJ's office. He wasn't there, of course. But perhaps if she walked past the room enough, he'd magically appear. A man could only live so long out in the wilderness. Though, for all she knew, TJ was shacking up at a five-star hotel with room service and cable.

By her third or fourth pass that afternoon, it was becoming abundantly clear she was more than a little OCD.

"The guy needed a vacation. I don't think he's had one in six years," Josh said as he brushed by her in the hall. "He'll be back . . . eventually."

Hopefully to compete in White Crush on Saturday. That was only four days away. "Yep," she said and went back to her office.

Chapter Twenty-Five

Deb ducked under the rope and found Colt and Josh. "It's good to know people, huh?"

They got to stand in the section cordoned off for friends and family of the contestants, getting the best view of the competition right next to the judges, who watched live feeds of each skier on a big screen.

There'd been no word from TJ. He apparently didn't care whether the online store lived or died. Or about her, for that matter. To not even call or email . . . whatever. She was so over him.

Right; that's why I cry myself to sleep every night.

By now Win was probably waiting his turn at the helipad. He was last on the roster, which meant they'd be here a good long time. And if the event went overtime, GA could get bumped. Ted had already worked miracles by getting them an invite.

Colt shielded his eyes and searched the crowd. "Delaney and Hannah should be here any second."

"Where's your mom and dad?"

"They're sitting in the lounge, watching it on TV. They'll join us closer to when Win's up."

It was clear and sunny but colder than usual for late

February. Deb couldn't blame them for wanting to stay near a heater.

Josh surveyed the scene with a pair of binoculars. "They're getting ready to start."

"How do you think Win will do?" she asked.

Josh let the field glasses dangle around his neck. "Not as good as TJ would've done, but our little brother's got some moves. This is the big leagues, though. Most of these guys are ten years younger and full-time competitors."

"Even if we don't place, it's good exposure." Colt squeezed her shoulder. "You did good, Little Debbie; the best you could've under the circumstances."

She knew that was Colt's way of saying, *no hard feelings when we let you go*. It was purely business. She got that and had no unrealistic expectations. It just would've been nice if TJ had given it his all. Even if he couldn't bring himself to compete, he should've been here to cheer GA on and promote the brand.

Foster pressed against the rope. Without the proper credentials, he couldn't get in the VIP section. "I brought you these." He passed them coffees.

Deb cupped hers and held it to her nose, enjoying the steamy warmth. "You're a king among men."

A voice came over the PA system, announcing the first skier, a name Deb vaguely recognized. The truth was, she hadn't kept up with the sport for a while. Not since TJ and Win had left the circuit. Josh raised his binoculars, while Deb watched on the judge's screen. The skier had an impressive ride until midway down the mountain, when he accelerated off a cliff and wiped out in the snow.

"That's gonna leave a mark," Colt said. Deb didn't think he'd score.

The second competitor had a better run, performing a 360 off a sharp peak that had the crowd roaring.

"Whoa, that's some nice freestyling." Josh handed her the binoculars.

Matt Adache was up next. Deb had known him for ages and, unlike the young guns, he was in his thirties.

"Holy hell, you see that?" Colt watched the screen as Matt hucked a crazy backflip, then ate it, losing one of his skis in the process. "Ouch. That's gotta hurt."

Hannah and Delaney joined them just as Angel Gonzalez—another old friend of Deb's—executed a perfect no-fall cliff drop that left everyone's mouth hanging open.

"She's the one to beat so far." Colt helped Delaney under the rope.

"Anyone hear from TJ?" Hannah reached around Josh and stuck her hands in his jacket pockets. Watching it made Deb's heart ache. She shook her head, and Hannah pursed her lips in disappointment.

"There's plenty of media here," Delaney said, trying to be optimistic. "CNN scheduled an interview with me. I'll be plugging the adventure line. Hopefully, that'll help."

Deb crossed her fingers. A big fashion icon like Delaney . . . well, it certainly couldn't hurt. But the audience they were trying to reach were more outdoorsy and sporty than couture. While Delaney appealed to the trend conscious, Deb didn't know how seriously she was taken as an adventure wear designer. She was still unproven to this crowd, who were hard-core about their gear and equipment.

They continued to watch as each participant performed two minutes of heart-stopping tricks down the mountain, including midair spins, massive 360s, and big cliff drops.

"Bam!" Josh cringed as one of the competitors kneed himself in the face, dripping blood from his nose and mouth.

As they neared the end of the list, Deb got antsy. In her opinion, Angel had had by far the best run to this point. Colt and Josh, on the other hand, liked a guy Deb had never heard of. Kel Jarvis. But the judges would wait until the end, when they could compare video side by side.

Gray Garner ducked under the rope and held it up for Mary "There's some tough competition." They both joined the huddle. "I'm liking that Kel fellow."

"Angel was wonderful," Mary said.

"Don't count Win out." Gray draped his arm around Mary, and Deb's chest squeezed. Two generations of Garner couples in her face.

The MC announced TJ's name and Deb held her breath. "Teddy must've forgotten to scratch him and add Win." She'd rectify the mistake as soon as Win made it to base.

They all focused on the top of the mountain, but it was hard to see from the rotor wash of the helicopter. Then boom, Win emerged from the fog, bombing down a death-defying line, including crushing three cliff drops in a row, then hucking a mind-blowing backflip.

Whoa; not Win's usual style. He was definitely showy but typically a little sloppy. But today, pure precision on a grand scale. They watched him do a few more aerials, including a full twist on the first flip of a double somersault that boggled the mind it was so beautiful.

"He's in rare form," Josh said while the others shielded their eyes to block out the glare of the sun.

Gray kept his gaze pinned on the big screen as Win performed a Randy—a flip with two and a half twists.

Colt squinted. "Let me see those binoculars." Josh handed him the glasses, and Colt peered up at the slope. "Holy crap, that's TJ."

"No way," Josh said and examined the judges' video screen. "You're right. When the hell did he get here?"

Deb practically strangled Colt, trying to get the straps of the field glasses off his neck and watched TJ shred the rest of the line. He faltered two-thirds of the way, taking a jump wrong, but quickly recovered. It would definitely cost him some points but . . . *Oh my God*!

"I always knew he was the man." Josh pounded Colt on the back. "We're gonna win this mother!"

"*We're*?" Colt hitched a brow. "From where I'm standing, it looks like TJ's doing all the work."

Mary gripped Gray's arm and watched the live video feed intently. Every time TJ performed a trick, Gray pumped his fist in the air.

Hannah scanned the crowd. "Where's Win, then?"

Deb couldn't take her eyes off TJ. He was amazing to watch, pure litheness. No matter where he placed, he'd made her so proud. But why hadn't he told her that he planned to compete?

As he made it to the bottom of the mountain, the crowd roared with approval. Colt and Josh ducked under the rope and shouldered their way through the horde to get to TJ. Deb started to follow, but self-doubt stopped her. If he'd wanted to see her, he would've called. In all the excitement, Hannah and Delaney gathered her up in a hug.

"You did it," Delaney said. "I predict you'll be slammed with orders on Monday."

"We don't know if he won yet," though Deb didn't think it would matter. His performance alone might be enough to put their little store on the map.

"Go congratulate him." Hannah gave her a gentle shove.

"I will. I'm waiting for the spectators to thin out," she lied. What she wanted to do was get the heck out of Dodge before the entire Garner family witnessed her humiliation. It seemed pretty clear—to her, at least—that she and TJ were over. He'd all but said it after she'd declared her love for him.

What about us?

I don't know, Deb. I just don't know.

He may as well have said that he didn't love her. That she wasn't worth fighting for.

"TJ freaking crushed it." Win jogged up, a big grin splitting his face.

"At first, we thought it was you," Hannah said, and Win went on to tell them how TJ had shown up in the eleventh hour, and how'd they'd switched clothes under the bleachers.

In all the excitement, Deb snuck away and went home. Her work here was done.

TJ found a parking space in front of the diner, climbed out of his truck, and took the stairs to Deb's apartment two at a time. She opened the door before he could knock, her ski boots slung over her shoulder.

"Congratulations," she said. "You killed it today. What you did on that mountain was awe-inspiring. But if you're here to officially dump me, consider it done. I'll have my resignation on your desk by Monday. Now, I'm going skiing; kindly move out of my way."

He took the boots from her, dropped them on the floor, and pulled her hard against his chest. "I'm here to tell you that I've loved you since you were a kid. That I never stopped loving you, not the entire time I was away at college, not when I came home to run GA, not ever. And I'll never stop. You're in my blood, Deb Bennett."

She pushed off his chest, looked up at him, her heart in her eyes. "I guess we better go inside."

"Inside would be good." He followed her, kicked the door closed, and kissed her with the same intensity and passion he'd felt up on the mountain. All in.

His hands were in her hair, tilting her head back, and his mouth covered hers. . . . God, she tasted good. Like coming-home good. She was hugging him for all she was

worth, and for the first time in a week, he felt right with
the world.

"Do you love me?" he asked against her lips, and she
broke away and slugged him.

"I already told you I did, but you didn't believe me."

"Tell me again," TJ said and hauled her against him, his
arms circling around her. He needed to have her close . . . to
hear her say it.

"I love you, TJ. I've loved you forever. Long before Win,
when we were just kids."

And with those words, he felt himself relax. He felt the
vice squeezing his chest loosen and he let out a breath.

"You were the one I wanted, but I never thought I could
have you." Her eyes filled. "And TJ, I'm really, really mad
at you."

He forced himself not to smile. "What can I do to make
it up to you?"

She grabbed his jacket in both her fists and yanked him
down for another kiss.

Bang, bang, bang.

"What the—" Someone was pounding on the door.

"Let us in, asshole."

"Shush," TJ whispered. "If we're quiet, they'll go away."

The banging continued. It sounded like a herd of ele-
phants running across Deb's entryway.

"Oh for God's sake." She let go of TJ and opened the
door. Win, Josh, and Colt stood there, their faces pink from
the cold.

"It's about time," Josh said, rubbing his hands together.
And the three of them muscled their way in. "The judges
gave you third place."

"Third?" Deb grabbed her cell phone off the couch.
"That's bullshit. I'm calling Ted."

Colt pulled the phone out of her hand and looked them both over. "What were you doing in here?"

TJ grabbed Colt's arm and started to walk him to the door. "Time for the three of you to leave."

Win sprawled out on the couch and grabbed the remote control.

"What the hell are you doing?" TJ threw his hands up in the air.

"I want to see if you made the evening news." Win turned on the TV and channel surfed.

TJ grabbed the remote out of his hand and flicked off the power. "TiVo it at your own house."

"Don't you want to know what happened after you left?" Josh asked.

"Not particularly. But you know what would be really great? You leaving."

"Wait a minute." Deb looked at Colt, then back at Win and Josh. "What happened?"

The three of them rushed TJ, tackled him to the floor, and in unison shouted, "You won the People's Choice for first place." They all began pounding his back at the same time.

"Would you get the hell off me?" TJ shoved at Colt because he was the biggest. "Deb and I have stuff to talk about."

"Dude, did you hear us?" Win shouted. "The people loved you."

Every year, White Crush let spectators choose their favorite performance with voting on the event's website. It wasn't the Olympics, but, yeah, it was something. TJ got up and Deb threw her arms around him.

"You won, then," she said and started kissing his face over and over again.

Colt looked at them, then kicked Josh in the butt. "Let's go. We've outworn our welcome."

"You think?" TJ said and lifted Win off the floor by the collar of his jacket.

Win grabbed TJ around the waist. "You did it, man! Group hug."

The next thing TJ knew, he and Deb were sandwiched between his crazy-ass brothers.

"Let's not get carried away," TJ said. "I came in third."

"No," Colt said. "You came in first! The people are always right." He grabbed Win and Josh. "We're out of here. Carry on with whatever you were doing." And the three of them walked out the door, leaving them to celebrate in private.

"Where were we?" TJ backed Deb against the wall.

"Here." Deb molded herself against him, and they made out for a good long time before she dragged him to the couch, where they made out some more.

"Why didn't you tell me you were going to compete?" she asked.

TJ rubbed his chin. "It was sort of a last-minute decision. The truth: I was scared shitless, but I didn't want to disappoint you."

"I'm sorry, TJ. I never meant to put you in an uncomfortable situation. I had no idea that—"

"Shush." He kissed her. "Back to you loving me."

"Forever." She brushed his still-warm lips with her finger. "But I'm serious about leaving Garner Adventure. I don't want you to lose money because you were trying to help me. You don't need the pressure, TJ. I want you to be happy."

He looked into her brown eyes and saw so much love

there that it slayed him. "Deb, I was never going to let you go, not from the company . . . not from my life. Ever."

"TJ—"

"Shush." He rested his forehead against hers. "The job's yours, Bennett. And you're mine. Let's start the next adventure together."

Epilogue

One year later

Nature had accommodated them with freshly fallen snow, giving Deb the wedding she'd always dreamed of. She wore a white Colt and Delaney ski outfit and TJ wore black. A hundred of their best friends and family were gathered at the bottom of Royal Slope, where Rita Tucker was set up to officiate.

"You ready?" TJ gave her a quick kiss, then flipped his goggles over his eyes. "Let's do it, baby."

"Wait a sec." She grabbed his arm. "Before we say our vows in front of everyone, I want to tell you something in private."

"What's that?" He grinned like a loon.

"That I love you and that you make me so happy I don't know what to do with myself. Thank you for being my dream man."

He winked. "Right back at you." This time he kissed her long and slow. "I love you, Deb. Always have, always will."

If they didn't have everyone waiting, she would've liked to have stayed in his arms for a while longer. She never tired of their marathon make-out sessions. "We have to go, don't we?"

"Yep. But tomorrow, honeymoon."

Mmm. Honeymoon. They were going to Aspen for a week of R&R and skiing. The last year, they'd both worked hard. TJ to find more balance in his life and she'd turned herself into a hard-core businesswoman.

The online store was now responsible for 30 percent of GA's profits. No one, not even TJ, had projected that kind of volume. She'd used a combination of social media, word of mouth, and targeted marketing to grow the venture. And, of course, it helped that their merchandise was phenomenal and that they had Delaney's star power pushing it. But in the end, it had been TJ's People's Choice award in White Crush and her tent jacket that had fueled the turn-around.

Not only had she made a success of GA's retail division, but she'd helped pick up the slack so TJ could conduct more tours and have more leisure time to do the things he loved, including her.

"Ready?" TJ nudged her ahead.

Unlike normal, when they would've torn down the run at breakneck speed, she and TJ took their time, traversing the trail and commemorating this perfect moment. This had been the wedding she used to joke about with Foster. Funny, how just when you thought life had ripped you off, it threw you the greatest gift of all.

When they finally reached the bottom to a crowd of cheers, Win moved into the best man slot and Hannah took her place as maid of honor. Rita shushed the attendees as she prepared to lead the ceremony. With the mountains covered in snow, it truly was a white wedding day. Even the sun cooperated, peeking through the clouds and shining its blessing on the ceremony. Colt, Josh, and Foster ushered everyone to their seats. Unlike TJ, they'd worn suits. The bridesmaids—Darcy and Delaney—shimmered like icicles in their silver dresses. Later, for the party at the Four Seasons, Deb planned to change into the wedding gown Delaney had specially designed for her.

Before reciting their vows, Deb took a minute to peer at the guests. Mary Garner and Deb's mom were already dabbing their eyes with tissue. Boden was flanked by a stunning blonde Deb had never seen before. Rachel, who'd been put in charge of the hot toddy and hot cocoa bar, was rushing to grab a seat. Carrie Jo and Jack waved from the second row, while Morris Finkelstein tried to untangle himself from a bright plaid blanket. From the corner of her eye, she spotted Felix, who, in a rare moment, smiled.

Rita stumbled through her prepared remarks. A public speaker she was not. But Deb wouldn't have anyone else. Here in these mountains she called home, surrounded by the most important people in her life, she loved and felt loved.

When it came time for the *Do you take* . . . exchange, Deb slipped her hand into TJ's, gently squeezed, and mouthed the words, *I want you*.

His blue eyes swam with amusement—and pure adoration. He leaned closer and whispered in her ear, "I want you, right back."

Connect with U s

Visit us online at
KensingtonBooks.com
to read more from your favorite authors, see books
by series, view reading group guides, and more.

for sneak peeks, chances to win books and prize packs,
and to share your thoughts with other readers.

facebook.com/kensingtonpublishing
twitter.com/kensingtonbooks

Tell us what you think!

To share your thoughts, submit a review,
or sign up for our eNewsletters, please visit:
KensingtonBooks.com/TellUs.